BROKEN
Trust

PACIFIC PREP BOOK ONE

R.A. SMYTH

Broken Trust

ISBN: 9798526869829

Cover & Interior Design by Nikki Epperson. All Rights Reserved.

Editing by Heart Full of Reads Editing Services.

Formatting by Rachel Smyth.

My name is Hadley Parker, and today I take control of my life.

Today I start school at Pacific Prep. This is my new lease on life, and I won't be wasting it.

I need this, now, more than ever. I need the education, the promise of a future that I wouldn't get anywhere else.

These rich kids don't like me though.

When Hawk Davenport decides he doesn't want me here, his friends back him.

Along with Hawk, Westley Warren, Cam Rutherford, and Mason Hayes rule this school and nobody dares go against them.

They don't know the real me. I won't back down.

Pacific Prep Playlist

Popular Monster – Falling in Reverse

Fuck Away the Pain – Divide The Day

I Scare Myself – Beth Crowley

Letdown – Letdown

Let it Burn – Citizen Soldier

My Monsters – New Year's Day

Cruel World – Tommee Profitt, Sam Tinnesz

Last One Standing – Icon For Hire

Dancing with the Devil – Demi Lovato

Silent Scream – Damien Dawn

We Fall Apart – We As Human

Hard To Kill – Beth Crowley

Hatefuck – Cruel Youth

Warrior – Beth Crowley

Maniac – Conan Gray

Middle Finger – Bohnes

All Eyes on You – Smash Into Pieces

...And many more

Check out my Facebook Group for the list

– Rachel's Rebel Rehab

Prologue

He's back. I knew he was coming—he always does—same day every month. Not once in all the years I've been here has he missed a visit. When I was younger, I used to enjoy it. He'd bring me a toy and I'd get to play with it all day. We never got toys here.

Things have been changing over the last few years. Now, instead of toys, he brings jewelry and dresses. He likes me to get all dolled up for him, even though we don't go anywhere or do anything. The way he looks at me when I do as he says? It's not how you should look at someone over half your age. It's dark and possessive.

It's not just the gifts and the looks. It's the way he drags his seat right over beside me, the slow trail of his fingers down my arm, the casual graze on the side of my breast.

It's the way he talks about the future, like it's a given I'll be in it with him. He says I'm going to go live with him some day. He'll buy me whatever I want and we'll visit places all around the world. I've never gone anywhere before. I've never left this place. The thought of seeing *the world* sounds unbelievable. This place is not somewhere any kid should grow up, where any human should live. His promise could be my ticket out of here. I'd finally be free.

Yet, I don't miss the domineering way he fixes the necklace around my neck, making sure it sits perfectly. I don't miss the low timber of his voice as he whispers, "Mine," and rests his heavy hand possessively on my thigh.

He might be my escape out of this place, but he would only cage me in a different type of prison. I wouldn't be any more free than I am right now. If anything, the things he says he wants to do to me would only ruin me faster.

Hadley

Chapter 1

I readjust my duffel bag on my shoulder while I take in the towering wrought iron gates in front of me. Who knew a set of gates could hold such significance? Most of the students here probably don't bat an eye as they pass through them, the cold iron representing nothing more than the start of a new school year. To someone like me, it symbolizes so much more. The opportunity for a private education. The chance at a new life, a future. Freedom.

Taking in the school crest branded on the gates, my eyes hover over the three words the school has chosen to embody everything they stand for.

Felicitatem. Patientiam Operatur. Dignitate.

Prosperity. Perseverance. Prestige.

No, I sure as hell do not speak Latin, but I do know how to do a google search. Only one of those words resonates with me. Perseverance. I've endured my fair share of shit so far in this reasonably short life. As for prosperity and prestige? Well, only the wealthy can afford that shit, and I'm sure as fuck not that.

Ignoring the judgmental eyes from the passing chauffeur-driven cars as they make their way through the gates and up the tree-lined drive, I trail after them, taking in the campus as I walk.

The campus is vast and fancy as hell, with its grandeur buildings, perfectly manicured lawns and trimmed hedges. I can just about make out a football field and tennis courts, as well as some sort of sports center in the distance.

I walk past a large building that is somehow even more prestigious looking than the others. It's got more steps leading up to it than any normal building needs, meaning it towers above me, with its large glass windows and dramatic floor-to-ceiling columns.

Above the large wooden doors, a plaque reads 'Davenport Hall'. Well, whoever the Davenports are, they have more money than they clearly know what to do with. What school needs a hall like that? I bet it's only used a few times a year. *What a waste!*

Strolling on, I watch as cars stop in front of another building up ahead of me. Students climb out, most of them with their parents, looking around warily before following their parents up the steps—freshmen kids, I bet. As they disappear through the front entrance, uniformed men rush over to the cars and start lifting luggage out of their trunk, placing them on carts and, I'm assuming, taking them off to the students' accommodations.

Older students who have their own car—which appears to be everyone over the age of sixteen—climb out of their vehicles in the parking lot opposite the main building, greeting their friends, laughing and joking with one another as they slowly make their way toward the school. They all look perfectly presented in their school uniforms, not a crease to be seen or a hair out of place. With their white teeth, flawless makeup, and expensive haircuts, they look like models or celebrities, all of them oozing the sort of confidence that only comes with having money.

I cast a quick glance down the front of my white shirt. The school had it delivered to me for today, but, despite it being exactly the same as everyone else's, it doesn't hug my slim frame or accentuate my boobs like it does on other girls.

I run my hand over the shirt, smoothing it out, pulling on the ends of my green, gray, and black tartan mini-skirt so it sits a little lower. I'm not used to wearing short skirts and it feels like a light breeze would give everyone a firsthand view of my basic white underwear.

Approaching the main school building, I follow behind a group of girls, only half listening to them as they catch up, ranting and raving about their summer vacations spent in far off exotic countries, while my eyes roam over the building.

It goes without saying that this is yet another fancy as fuck, ostentatious structure that resembles what I imagine a 17th century manor house would look like. I have to crane my neck back to see all the way up to the roof, the three stories looming over me. It's built in the same fashion as the hall I just walked past, composed of dark stone and large windows.

Walking between two large columns, I ascend the stairs, making my way through the large entryway into the open foyer beyond. The atrium is the depth of the building, with large glass doors, providing an unobstructed view of an enormous courtyard beyond, lined with shrubs. There's a massive marble fountain in the center, with picnic tables and benches placed around the open space.

Glancing around, I notice there are corridors branching to the left and right, and a staircase leading up to the second floor, with a balcony overlooking the atrium. Students and their parents are dispersed around the room, saying their final goodbyes, while others move out to the courtyard where I can see others milling around.

"Finally," a tall girl with perfectly curled white-blonde hair, way too much makeup, and sky-high heels snaps, striding toward me, her hips swaying seductively, her tartan skirt swishing against her thighs with every step she takes. "It's about time you showed up."

"Me?" I ask, looking behind me in case she's talking to someone else.

"Yes. You. Who else would I be talking to?"

She casts her eyes over my appearance, her lips pursing in disapproval as she takes in my curly blonde hair that's impossible to tame and face clear of makeup. Self-consciously, I run my hand through the mass of curls in a vain attempt to flatten them a bit. I don't get a chance to say anything, not that I have any idea what to say to this weirdo who's snapping at me, when her eyes fall on my worn duffel bag.

"What is that?" Her nose scrunches up in disgust as she waves her hand toward my bag, her dislike of my non-designer, tattered duffel written all over her face.

"Uh, my bag?"

"Why do you have it here? You're supposed to leave all of your belongings with your driver for the bellboys to collect."

Drivers? Bellboys? What fresh hell have I subjected myself to?!

Seeing my look of utter confusion, she rolls her eyes, sighing in exasperation before glancing around the hall.

"You," she calls out, waving over some guy in a uniform as he passes by us, heading out toward the parked cars. He looks like he should be working in a high-end hotel, not a high school.

Barely sparing him a glance, she gestures toward my duffle bag, "Take this...thing," she sneers, "to, uh"—she glances down at a page in her hand—"Hadley's room."

The guy goes to grab my bag and my hand instinctively tightens around the strap, preventing him from taking it from me. We remain in a standoff for a few seconds, him giving me a weird-ass look before I relax enough to let go, letting him walk away with every single thing I own in this world.

Turning back to the annoying girl in front of me, eyeing her up with a critical gaze, I ask, "Eh, who are you? How do you know my name?"

Her lips pinch together in disapproval as she looks down at me. At five-foot-six, I wouldn't call myself short, but between her height and the six inches her heels give her, she's a good head taller than me.

"I'm Bianca," she responds snootily, with all the arrogance of a rich brat as she tosses her hair over her shoulder. She acts like I should already know who she is. Placing her hands on her hips, she sighs. "I'm supposed to show you around today."

Well, that statement was overflowing with enthusiasm. I'm guessing she wasn't given much of a choice in the matter, and I can't help wondering how she ended up stuck with the job. I have to bite my tongue to stop myself from letting her know I'm just as thrilled to have her as a guide as she is. "I take it you got a welcome pack? With a map?" she snarks, not really sounding like she cares one way or the other.

"Yeah, I did."

"Good, then I'm sure you can work it out for yourself." She raises an eyebrow at me. "You are here on an academic scholarship after all."

Barely holding back my retort, I roll my eyes at her as soon as she turns her back to me, taking off across the foyer, not bothering to check if I'm following her. I am, of course—I don't see I have a choice. She forced me to hand over my bag, with my map and everything in it, to that guy. And I have no clue where the accommodation building is, or what I'm even supposed to be doing this morning.

"This is the main building, where most of your classes will be. There's an east and a west wing," Bianca explains, pointing to her right to indicate the East wing before pointing out the West wing on our left. I'm honestly surprised she's bothering to tell me anything, but I guess she feels like she needs to at least explain the basics. "The east wing is where all the science, math, and computer classes take place; while the art classes, English, history, languages, all that sort of stuff, is in the west wing. The music department has its own building, and anything drama related is held in the auditorium."

She pulls open the door into the courtyard, the buzz of other students chatting and calling out to one another reverberating around us, drowning out the noise of water trickling from the fountain. By now, the quad is filled with students from all years. A few of them hang back, lazing on picnic tables and laughing with friends, but most of them have joined the throng of students slowly making their way into what I'm guessing is the auditorium—a large stone building on the far side of the quad.

Bianca and I join the back of the crowd, slowly inching our way onward. I can feel the press of bodies around me, people jostling me as they join the crowd behind us. The more they push and shove, my heart rate starts to spike and my chest feels tight. *Why the fuck can people not respect personal boundaries. The quad is fucking huge, you don't need to be shoving against me.* I scowl at the girl behind me as her shoulder knocks into me for the third time, my dark glare succeeding in getting her to back up a step as Bianca scans the crowd, oblivious to the students around us as she looks for someone in particular, most likely her friends. She doesn't spare me a glance when she says, "Stay in your lane, and you'll get through the year without any problems."

"My lane?" I question, confused about what she means.

She sighs, and I don't miss the snooty bitch rolling her eyes at me before penetrating me with a deadpan stare. "There's a you, an us, and a them," she explains, as though it's obvious and she shouldn't have to clarify any of this for me.

"A what?" I shake my head slightly, not understanding her at all.

"You," she sneers derisively, her voice making it clear she thinks she's so much fucking better than I am. She roams her eyes over my less-than-perfect uniform, scowling, before dropping her gaze to my combat boots, her nose wrinkling in disgust. *Yeah, okay, the boots aren't exactly school attire, but they're sturdy, and I could do some damage to her with them if she doesn't stop looking at me like I'm shit on the bottom of her designer pumps.* "The scholarship students."

Ah, yes. Us common muck scholarship students that are unfortunate enough not to be born into a life of luxury, and have to actually work for everything in life.

"Us refers to every other student. The ones that actually pay to attend this school," she says pointedly, once again emphasizing—in case it wasn't already obvious—that we're lesser because we don't have buckets of cash to spend on an education. I doubt she would be open to seeing my point of view if I tried to explain that hard work and dedication make me just as entitled to be here as her precious money does.

"And them?" I ask curiously, wondering who she could possibly be referring to. She's just lumped the entire school into the 'you' and 'us' categories...so who is left?

Her eyes flash up to something behind me. "Them," she repeats absently, her tone breathy, her eyes glazing over at whatever has caught her attention.

Spinning around, I see exactly what has her so distracted. Or more specifically, *who*. Striding through the crowd, who part for them like they are gods, are four of the most striking guys I've ever seen. I'm not sure if the whole courtyard hushes, or if I just become so focused on them that everything around me fades into the background, but all I can hear is the blood pounding in my ears as I soak up the mouthwatering sight in front of me.

All four of them confidently strut through the crowd, looking like one of those sexy-as-hell TikTok videos. All they need to do is remove their tops and flex their muscles, except I'm pretty sure more than a few girls around me will faint. I can't even be sure I wouldn't be one of them.

I focus on the guy to the far left, who's tall and lean, perfectly put together in his gray slacks, white shirt, and forest green blazer as he strides across the courtyard. Every step is filled with arrogant confidence. My eyes roam over his face, noting his short, blond haircut, narrowed eyes, and pinched lips. Everything about him screams 'stay the fuck out of my way'.

My gaze sweeps to the guy beside him. He's built like a fucking tank. At over six and a half feet tall and built like an MMA fighter, he's easily double the size of every other student around us. Similarly to the first guy, everything about him screams unapproachable. His features look like stone, with his sharp, angular jaw, high cheekbones, and icy glare. A few loose strands of his dark brown hair fall forward into his eye, somehow only adding to the fierce image he's working. I can feel my mouth going dry as I drink him in, before I quickly glance away.

The third guy is the complete opposite of the first two. His black tie hangs loosely around his neck, the top button of his shirt undone. His blazer is nowhere to be seen, and where the first two guys don't bother to pay attention to anyone around them, he constantly nods his head at guys as they call out 'hellos', sending flirty looks to the girls. He's got a tall, lean, swimmer's body, built for speed and agility, and short yet stylish blond hair.

He catches me staring at him as he lifts his hand, running his fingers through his short strands. His eyes drop down my body, a salacious grin spreading across his face as he lifts his eyes back up to my face, giving me a dirty wink that I'd love to say doesn't affect me, but damn, I'm as much of a sucker for that wink as every other girl around here seems to be.

Embarrassed by the sudden racing of my heart and the heat in my cheeks, I quickly move on to the final guy in the group. Again, he's completely different from the first three. I can immediately tell he's the shy, quiet, studious one. He's got dark floppy hair that's hiding his face from my view, but as he flicks it out of the way, I can see that he's got a broad jaw and sharp features. He's wearing thick black-rimmed glasses, giving him, combined with his meticulous uniform, the overall appearance of a nerd. But on his lean, slightly muscular frame, it looks super hot, like Superman before he puts on his cape.

His hand flattens over his shirt, ironing out invisible creases before his head snaps up, his intense gaze meeting mine, having apparently sensed me watching him. Unlike the flirty look the last guy gave me, his is filled with uninterest, his lips pinching together in what looks like disapproval. *What an ass. We can't all have perfectly ironed uniforms and look like gods.*

The noise filters back in around me as the four of them disappear into the auditorium. With them no longer occupying my every thought, I realize I've been standing in the middle of the courtyard gaping at them. *Talk about embarrassing.*

Glancing out of the corner of my eye to see if Bianca, or anyone else, noticed my moment of distraction, I find her still drooling after the guys. At least I wasn't the only one who lost some common sense in their presence.

"Who are they?"

Damn girl, get your inner slut under control, I mentally berate myself when my voice comes out all husky.

Bianca must pick up on it too as she spins toward me, her eyes narrowing. "Out of your league," she snaps before storming off, following them into the auditorium.

I cast a quick glance around me and see that most of the students have also disappeared. Not knowing what else to do, I quickly scramble after Bianca, trying not to lose her in the sea of students.

Passing through the large double doors into the hall, it takes a second for my eyes to adjust after the brightness of the California sun outside, but after a few quick blinks, the room comes into focus. There's a large, empty stage at the front of the room, with a podium off to one side. The rest of the space is taken up with wooden pews that are slowly filling with students. *You'd think such a fancy school could afford something comfier than wooden seats.*

Spotting Bianca making her way toward a crowd of rich girls, I follow her. I don't particularly want to sit with her and her friends, but it's not like I know anyone else. I'm just about to slide inconspicuously into the last seat in the pew when Bianca glances up, noticing me.

"No. You don't sit with us," she snarks, her outburst garnering the attention of her friends, who all sneer at me. *They don't even fucking know me.* "Scholarship students sit at the front," she snootily states, pointing to the front of the hall.

Whatever. Like I said, I didn't want to sit with them anyway. I guess our 'tour' is officially over.

"Oh, and Henry," she calls after me, deliberately butchering my name. I turn around to glare at her, my teeth gritted. She's wearing a sickly-sweet smile, which morphs into a superior smirk when she sees she has my attention. "Welcome to Pac Prep."

Rolling my eyes at her cattiness, I ignore the other students whispering around me as I storm down the aisle, slipping into an empty seat in the first pew as the headmaster steps up to the podium.

He casts his eyes over the room, taking his time to survey us, before leaning into the microphone. "Quiet down, students." His booming voice echoes out across the large space, everyone quickly settling into a hush, focused on the front of the room. "For all of our new students, I am Mr. Phister, your headmaster."

Mr. Phister? For real? Glancing around me, I notice a few other students holding back a laugh.

"Welcome to the start of a new school year! I'm sure all of our returning students will make our new pupils feel welcome and help them adjust to life here at Pacific Preparatory."

Hmm, I somehow doubt that based on the less than stellar welcome I got this morning.

"You must be a new scholarship student," the girl beside me leans over and whispers, pulling my attention from the drivel coming out of the headmaster's mouth.

"That obvious?" I ask rhetorically, taking in the girl beside me. She's got short, black hair pulled back in a functional ponytail, and an innocent-looking face—or maybe it just looks that way because she doesn't have layer upon layer of makeup caking her face, like every other teenage girl around here.

It suddenly makes sense how Bianca knew I was a scholarship student. We just don't look like the other kids at Pacific Prep. Our hair doesn't have that same glow, and our skin doesn't look like it's been moisturized to within an inch of its life.

I guess that's what happens when you don't have unlimited money to spend on haircare and beauty products.

The girl smiles back at me, showing me her slightly crooked teeth. It's a real, genuine smile, nothing like the fake, cosmetically enhanced ones Bianca's friends wore.

"Are you a senior?" she whispers.

"Yeah."

"I'm Emilia. Stick with me, girl. I'll show you the ropes."

Hadley

Chapter 2

After what felt like a never-ending assembly, the headmaster reiterating the rules and reminding us of what he expects from us this year, he finally let us go.

"Ugh, thank god that's over!" Emilia groans as we get to our feet, the auditorium erupting into a cacophony of noise as conversations start up again and students make their way toward the exit. "Come on, I'll show you around."

"Thanks." I give her a grateful smile as we make our way back out of the auditorium, relieved I'm rid of Bianca and to have an actual guide to give me the lay of the land.

Once we step out into the blinding sun, Emilia turns around to the other students that were in the pew. There's six of them in total—four boys and two other girls. "We'll catch up with you guys in a bit," she calls out.

Two of them mumble a goodbye while eyeing me warily as Emilia turns back to me with an excited grin on her face.

"Okay, so this is the main school building, obviously," she explains, waving toward the large building I met Bianca in. "The music department is over there, and the admin building is behind it," she points at a large rectangular building off to my left before tugging on my arm and taking off in the opposite direction. "Who was supposed to be your guide?"

"Bianca," I deadpan, giving her a look that says everything about how great an introduction to Pac Prep that was.

"Ha," the caustic bark erupts from her, "I bet that went well."

The main building is behind us as we head down one of the various paths. Off to my left is a dense-looking forest, with grass lawns to my right all the way down to an extensive-looking sports complex at the far end of the campus.

Pointing to a large structure up ahead, Emilia explains, "That's the library. It's open pretty much twenty-four seven. There's also a computer suite in the main building where you can go to do work or print stuff off, although no-one ever really needs to print anything here. You'll have a tablet in your room where the teachers upload their worksheets for each lesson and you just fill them in on that."

A tablet? Damn, that's fancy! Although I've never used one before, so I'm sure that's going to be a fun learning curve. What the hell was wrong with good old-fashioned pen and paper?

Strolling past the library, it's just as old and grandiose looking as everything else here, but there's something more inviting about it than the other buildings. Maybe it's knowing it's a place of solitude, of losing yourself in work or a good book, that makes it more endearing.

"So, what's your deal?"

"My deal?" I question, turning to look at Emilia. Her lips are puckered as she runs her eyes over me, trying to figure me out.

"What's your story?"

"What's yours?" I retort, not comfortable telling a complete stranger who I am or where I come from. I know she's more like me than the pretentious rich kids, but there's still a difference between coming from a poor family, and having no family at all.

Instead of being put off by my prickly behavior, her smile grows wider, like my response has surprised her and she is more than prepared to rise to the challenge. Internally snorting, I can't help but think she's got a pretty huge hill to climb if she wants to be my friend. I don't exactly do friendships; or relationships of any shape or form. I'm just not wired for that. As soon as that line is crossed, there's a requirement, a sense of responsibility. You're expected to be there, to show up, to give a damn.

From what I've seen, someone always lets the other person down, and it either blows up in your face, or resentment slowly builds up, rotting everything good you once had from the inside out. Yeah, no thanks. I don't need anyone but myself.

Emilia shrugs her shoulders, not having the same reservations about divulging her life story to a virtual stranger. "It's just me and my mom; she's a nurse. We do okay—not anything like this." She chuckles, waving at our surroundings. "But we get by. Growing up, she was always telling me to strive for more, to want a better life. She works her ass off for everything we have." Her gaze turns distant as she falls into memories. "I'm here as much for her as for myself. I want both of us to have a better future."

"That's really admirable." I've never been close enough with anyone to take care of them like that. Everything I do is for me—to make *me* a better person, to improve *my* life. There's never been anyone else. Well...there *was* someone. But I don't let myself think about her now.

She once again turns that blinding smile my way.

"Okay, your turn."

Butterflies take flight in my stomach, my palms sweating as I bite down on my lower lip. "I'm a foster kid." There, I said it. "I turned eighteen last month, so apparently that makes me an adult now and responsible for myself."

"You can't be doing too bad if you're here," Emilia reasons, giving me a soft smile.

"Yeah, I guess," I acquiesce, not wanting to disagree with her and get into a whole conversation about it, as we stroll through the grounds, the other students around us enjoying their last day of freedom before classes begin tomorrow. Some of them are crowded around benches on the various paths crisscrossing through the lawns, and a group of guys are tossing a ball back and forth.

"The dorms," Emilia points out, indicating two long, rectangular structures, "and that's the dining hall." Another large hall is situated between the two of them, all three buildings have the same gorgeous aesthetic as the rest of the campus. "Boys are on the right, girls on the left."

She directs me toward the girls' dorms, and we step into a bright foyer with a small seating area and a coffee bar off to one side, and a set of stairs leading to the upper floors. With the white painted walls and black fabric sofas, everything is sleek and modern looking, in complete contrast to the old style of the building.

"Scholarship students, regardless of what year they are, are all on the ground floor, then freshmen on the first floor, sophomores on the second floor, yada yada. At least, that's how it is in the girls' dorms."

"What do you mean by that?"

"The boys' dorms are different. The Princes have had the whole top floor to themselves since first year and everyone else squishes into the lower floors." Emilia explains all this while she opens a door at the back of the foyer that leads down a wide, white-walled hallway with doors leading off it in both directions. Just like the foyer, everything looks freshly painted and sterile looking. Each door we pass has a girl's name on it along with various stickers and posters personalizing it, distracting me for a second until her words register with me.

"The Princes?"

"Yup," she says, popping the 'p.' "They rule the school. If you think the teachers are in charge here, you're wrong. *They* are. Their great-great-whatever grandfathers founded the school or something. From what I've heard, everyone in their family has gone here, and ruled the school when they did. It's a tradition thing." With a casual shrug of her shoulder, she waves it off.

"Right." I don't really understand what she means. How can teenage boys rule the school? All I've ever known is that adults are the supreme figures and threatening their place of authority only ever ends badly.

"You probably saw them this morning, they're impossible to miss."

My mind immediately skips back to the four guys I saw earlier. With their superior presence and the way they caught everyone's attention, they must be who Emilia is talking about.

"Yeah, I think I did."

She nods knowingly, expecting that answer.

"This is me." She raps her knuckles on a door as we walk past, stopping outside the last room, at the end of the hall. "And I'm guessing this one is yours since it's the only empty one."

She pushes the door open and I step into a moderately sized room, my mouth hanging open as I'm met with more white walls and dark wood furniture, the room containing all the basic furniture one could need—a bed, desk, wardrobe, bookcase, and a chest of drawers. Walking over to the window and glancing out, all I can see is the surrounding forest. From this viewpoint, I'm unable to see the paths, meaning no-one can peek into my room, providing me with some modicum of privacy.

"Most of us stick posters and stuff over the walls, or if you have your own bed covers or whatever. As long as we don't leave any permanent damage, they don't mind what way we decorate." At Emilia's words, I turn back around to take in the room again. There isn't a huge amount of space to move about, but it's more than I'm used to. Glancing at the bed, I let out a sigh of relief when I find my duffle already there, the stress lifting off my shoulders at seeing it again. It maybe sounds stupid, but when your entire life is in a bag, it's not easy to let it out of your sight.

"Your key will be in the door and your tablet is on the desk. The showers are across the hall. Everyone on the floor shares them, but it's not too bad of a rush in the morning."

I don't know what to say. It might not look like much, but a whole room to myself? Not having to share with other people? And, looking at the door, I see there's a lock. I also noticed a lock on the window. This room could literally be my haven away from the world. I don't have posters or anything to decorate the place with, but regardless, I can picture myself living here, doing my homework or reading a book. No one could come in and bother me or catch me unaware; I could be happy here.

Thankfully, Emilia doesn't pick up on my sudden muteness, and after a few more minutes, asks, "Do you wanna check out the rest of the campus?"

I absently nod my head, my eyes still roaming over the room. "Sure, that sounds good."

We spend the rest of the afternoon wandering around. Emilia showed me the rec center where they have several small cinema rooms for people to chill, a game room, coffee shop; and even a small shop selling stationery, snacks, and anything else you could possibly need, before taking me over to the sports complex. I've never seen anything like it; you could more or less do any sporting activity you want. It even came complete with a sauna and spa. The entire campus is insane, resembling more of a self-contained village than a school. You literally don't have to leave the grounds for anything.

It's late in the day when we enter the dining hall for dinner. Apparently, breakfast is the only meal of the day with a set time for each year. For the rest of the day, the dining hall is open and you can come and go as you please.

A few of the tables are occupied when we enter, making our way toward the buffet tables. Instead of grabbing a tray, though, Emilia stops beside a kiosk with a computer screen, tapping away on it. I peer over her shoulder as she chooses what meal she wants from the online menu, selecting her table number before stepping to the side, so I can enter what I want.

"Hot meals are selected here, or you can use the app on your tablet. You can also order anything to go, or grab something from the buffet," she explains as we make our way to an empty table at the far side of the room. She explains it all so casually, but this cannot be the norm at most high schools. It's definitely a far cry from what I'm used to.

She must see it written on my face, as she releases a small chuckle. "I know, I know. It's crazy, right? It takes a bit of getting used to. I swear, I walked around here with my mouth hanging open for most of freshman year."

"Yeah, I bet. I'm struggling to wrap my head around it all. Everything just seems so...over the top."

"Ha, yeah. That's putting it mildly. Wait 'til you get to know the other students. Some of them..." She shakes her head, like she's struggling to find the right word. "Let's just say they can be pompous, entitled assholes."

"From what Bianca said, I gather the scholarship students and the rest of the school don't get along?" I ask, keen to get more information on how everything around here works. I definitely don't need to go pissing off the wrong people right off the bat.

"Ahh, she gave you the whole 'you, us, and them' spiel?" Emilia shakes her head, rolling her eyes. "She's the worst, thinking she's so much better than everyone else. Just 'cause her daddy owns an oil emporium doesn't mean she doesn't eat, sleep, and shit like the rest of us. She's kind of right, though. We tend to stick to ourselves. It's not necessarily because the other students want nothing to do with us, but we just don't have anything in common. Bianca and her friends are the only ones that seem to openly dislike us."

Absorbing all the information she's sharing, I enquire, "What about the Princes?"

"They don't really have anything to do with us." She shrugs. "Or anyone, for that matter. They're a tight-knit group, mostly keeping to themselves and rarely interacting with anyone outside of the four of them, unless they're looking to get laid or someone pisses them off. Cam would be the most social out of all of them." My ears perk up at the name, remembering the guy that winked at me. He was definitely the outgoing one of the group.

The door into the hall opens before I can ask anything else, a reverent hush settling over the few students here as the guys themselves enter, not sparing a single glance around the room as they make their way toward the buffet table. My attention is immediately drawn to Cam, taking in his cocky swagger as he talks away to the guy beside him, seeming oblivious to everyone's eyes on him.

"Who are the other three?" I ask Emilia, unable to tear my gaze away from Cam.

"The guy Cam is talking to is West Warren." West is the hot nerd from this morning. Unlike Cam, his eyes roam over the room in a studious fashion before he turns back to respond to whatever Cam said. "The angry-faced one is Hawk Davenport, and beside him is Mason Hayes."

The four of them have such a beguiling presence, making it impossible to not watch their every move. They appear relaxed, talking to one another while they wait for their food; but Mason's tense posture, and the way West flicks his gaze around the room, gives away the fact they know everyone is watching them, and they aren't as comfortable with all the attention as they pretend to be.

"Earth to Hadley." Emilia laughs, my cheeks pinking at having been caught out practically drooling over them as I turn back to look at her. "I know, they're sex on legs," she continues to laugh, "but trust me, they aren't worth it."

My eyebrows jump up in surprise. "You've slept with one of them?"

"I fucking wish!" She chuckles. "Sadly, no, but every girl in this place wants in on that. The girls here are like sharks, especially when it comes to bagging themselves rich boyfriends. And *everyone* wants their very own Prince. If they smell blood in the water, they will tear you to shreds."

I'd like to see those rich bitches fucking try, but yeah, I don't need that drama. As tempting as they might look, I'm sure there's less problematic dick floating around this place that will do the job when my horny side surfaces.

"What's Cam's surname?" I ask before said horny side can make an unwanted appearance. Sadly, those gorgeous boys will only be featured on my nightly bean screen.

"Rutherford, why?"

I shrug my shoulders. "Just curious."

It's only once the Princes leave the hall, that everything returns to normal, students going back to eating their meals and gossiping. It's crazy the effect four teenage boys can have on an entire room of people, but I can't deny their magnetism doesn't affect me.

"We do a movie night on the first day of term, if you wanna come and meet the other scholarship students?"

"Yeah," I nod my head, "that sounds like fun."

***

At eight o'clock, Emilia knocks on my door and we make our way across campus to the rec center, stopping at the shop on our way to meet the others. Using some of the allowance we're given as part of our scholarship, we buy snacks for the movie before heading to the cinema room that's been booked for the night.

The room comprises several rows of comfortable seats and a large screen taking up the whole wall, with speakers embedded on either side. Two boys are standing at the side of the screen, presumably getting everything set up, while the others are spread out across the front row, talking and laughing with one another, barely looking up when we enter.

"Hey guys." Emilia smiles, walking down the aisle to the front row. "This is Hadley. She's a new scholarship student," she explains. "Hadley, this is Mary and Abigail." Emilia gestures toward the two girls, one of whom is stuffing her face with popcorn, giving me a quick wave when I glance in her direction, while the other is cuddling up to a dark, shaggy haired boy. "That's Todd, Abigail's boyfriend, and Michael; and the two setting up the movie are Andrew and Samuel." The two tinkering with the screen glance over, waving hellos before focusing back on what they were doing.

Todd gives me a small nod as Abigail smiles from his lap. "Hey Hadley, nice to meet you." She giggles as Todd buries his face in her hair, distracting her.

"Nice to have a new face around." Michael smiles as Emilia directs me toward a spare seat beside him, sitting down on my other side. "I hope you like Blade. It's Samuel's turn to pick the movie tonight, and he seems to think we can watch all three in one night." He chuckles, leaning in closer to me so his arm brushes against mine on the armrest.

"I've never seen it," I admit.

His eyebrows rise with surprise. "Well, you're in for a treat then—as long as you like movies with blood, guts, and gore."

"I can definitely handle a little blood." I grin as the lights are dimmed and Andrew and Samuel take their seats, the beginning credits of the movie rolling on the oversized screen.

We make it through two of the movies before it hits midnight and everyone agrees it's time to call it a night. I actually had more fun than I expected, listening to the others talk and bicker about the movie. I didn't have much to contribute, but it was interesting watching them all laughing and getting along. It was all so normal.

We say goodbye to the boys outside their dormitory, before walking over to our own. "You have fun tonight?" Emilia asks once Mary and Abigail have gone into their rooms.

"Yeah, I did. Everyone seems really nice." I smile wearily. It's been a long, chaotic day, and bed is definitely calling my name.

"They are. Anyway, I'll see you in the morning. You can get your first experience of the real Pac Prep." She laughs, opening her door.

Oh great, just when I was beginning to think maybe this place wouldn't be so bad.

"Night," she says, giving a final wave as she closes the door.

"Night."

Hadley

Chapter 3

"What is your schedule like?" Emilia asks me at breakfast the next morning. I'm sitting at the same table as yesterday, pressed between her and Mary, listening to the others chat around me while I devour the delicious breakfast in front of me. I've always been a food lover, but I've *never* had food like this before. I'd swear I'd died and gone to heaven if it wasn't for the uncomfortable uniform I'm wearing and the sounds of other students echoing around us.

"Uh," I hesitate, trying to remember what classes I have today. It took over an hour, after I got back to my room last night—of me trying to figure out how to use the damn tablet—before I finally managed to pull up my schedule. *What the hell is wrong with a printed timetable?*

"Gimme your tablet," she says, holding out her hand, quickly realizing she would be quicker to look it up for herself. Grabbing it out of my bag and handing it over, I get back to my breakfast as she taps away on it, pulling up the schedule much quicker than I could have.

"Oh, we have English together this morning, and a few other classes during the week. That's awesome, I can show you the way once we're finished eating."

Downing half my glass of orange juice, relishing the fresh, tangy taste, I nod at her, letting her know that sounds good. There was a paper version of the map in my welcome pack that I was able to look at last night, and I've shoved it in my bag for today when I inevitably get lost. The campus is just so widespread, it's impossible to remember where everything is, so I definitely won't be turning down her offer of assistance.

"What did you think of the movie last night?" Michael asks from across the table.

"I loved it." I barely get the words out between forkfuls of the fluffiest pancakes I've ever tasted. How do they make them so light? Doused in fruit and syrup, it's the best meal I've ever had.

A grin lights up his face. "We could—"

He doesn't get any further as the noise in the hall dies down to a deathly hush. The Princes rise to their feet, and everyone forgets their food and conversations drop immediately to give the rulers their full attention. It was the same when they entered the hall half an hour ago too, everyone silently watching them as they headed to a table at the far end of the room.

The hall is designed so the kiosks, buffet, and collection point are all to one side of the room, with large tables interspersed around the rest of the space. The best one in the room is by the large windows, overlooking the grassy lawn and boys' dormitory. Of course, that's the Princes' table, and no one is allowed to sit there, unless invited or so Emilia informed me.

"Today is the first day of senior year," Hawk shouts out. "So I'm sure you all know what that means." A round of excited whispers sound through the room before he speaks up again. "We each pick one girl who is ours for the month. That girl will be our date to parties, will sit with us at breakfast, and, basically, belong to us for the month."

"What is he talking about?" I whisper to Emilia.

She rolls her eyes. "It's a stupid-ass senior year tradition that was started by their forefathers, where they basically pick a girl to fuck and flaunt for a month, then the next month they pick someone new and do it all over again."

"What the fuck?!" I whisper in shock, gaping at her. "Are you for real?"

"Yup," she confirms, nodding her head.

"What if the girls they choose don't want to be picked?"

Emilia snorts. "Girl, there isn't a person in this room that would turn down their offer."

I cast a quick glance around the room, taking in the excited looks in girls' eyes as they whisper frantically to their friends, pulling their cameras up on their phones and tablets so they can check their makeup, glancing furtively toward the Princes. She's right. Every single one of them wants to be claimed by one of those idiots. *Talk about feeding their arrogance.*

"You mean you'd say yes if one of them asked you?"

"Hell yeah, I would! Have you *seen* them? They're real life porn! My vagina would have to be a shriveled bean sack to turn down the fine-ass dick those boys have." I can't help snorting at her antics, despite the craziness of what she's saying. "Not that it matters, scholarship students don't get picked."

Why doesn't that surprise me?

My attention focuses back on the Princes as Hawk moves around from behind his table, his eyes scanning the room as he stalks across it, like a lion on the prowl. He moves between a few tables before pointing at some girl I don't know. After a round of ear-piercing squeals from the nominated girl and her crowd of friends, they eventually settle down as Mason steps forward. The whole thing is ridiculous. I can literally hear the voiceover of some 'Animals in the Wild' documentary.

'Here we have the male Homo sapien prowling through the assembled females in search of his intended mate. Where the female primate gravitates toward males that ooze money and arrogance; the males are drawn to purely superficial matters like physical attraction, or whether or not she has a gag reflex.'

"So what, the girls are like their girlfriends for the month or something?" I ask as Mason chooses his girl, another round of squeals erupting in the otherwise quiet room. With his bulky size and bland expression, he's really not someone I'd want to spend much time alone with. Sure, he's hot and clearly popular, but he doesn't look like the type you'd have a titillating conversation with. He gives off that whole 'I could kill you and not even blink an eye' vibe. Not exactly alluring.

"I wouldn't necessarily say that, more like their fuck buddies. The girls get that elevation in status and the attention they crave, and the Princes get a sure thing booty call when they want it."

"Romance at its finest," I swoon, my voice thick with sarcasm.

"Ha." Emilia laughs. "Right?"

Cam steps forward next. Unlike the first two, he makes a complete show out of the thing, lifting his hand to run it through his short blond hair in a sexy 'I know I'm hot shit' kind of way, getting the crowd riled up and flirting with the girls before finally choosing some blonde chick. She jumps out of her chair in excitement, flinging her arms around his neck, clinging to him like a spider monkey. As he gently, yet firmly, extracts himself from her embrace, I get a look at her face, actually recognizing this girl.

Bianca.

Of course it is. They're the perfect prom king and queen pair, with their same colored hair and incredible looks.

When he's finally managed to shake her off, Cam heads back to his table. I expect West to move forward next, doing the same as the other guys, but he barely spares the room a glance, pointing absently at the closest girl to him before dropping into his seat, ignoring the final round of exciting murmurings as he stares pointedly at his tablet, working away at something.

"Pfft, what a farce." Samuel shakes his head, annoyed at the whole show. "They can get any girl they want, why do they need to make a spectacle of picking girls?"

"It's just another way for them to exert their dominance and control over the year," Todd responds dismissively. "Forget about it. It's not like it will make any difference to us."

The Princes settle back into their seats, indicating the end to this morning's events, as the rest of the hall buzzes with this morning's excitement. The tables with chosen girls are a hive of energy, the girls who were selected grinning and flaunting their new status, while the others throw them jealous glares.

"I can't believe I just witnessed that," I mumble, mostly to myself.

Mary responds anyway, "I know, right? It's insane."

"Completely antiquated," I agree. "I just don't understand how every girl falls at their feet like that."

"They're the Princes." Emilia shrugs nonchalantly, as though that's justification for this whole insane thing.

"More like the Pricks," I grumble, rolling my eyes, getting a laugh from the rest of the table.

"The Pricks of Pacific Prep." Emilia snorts. "Fitting."

The rest of breakfast goes by quietly, everyone chatting away and catching up after the summer. Michael tries to draw me into the conversation several times, by asking about my summer and childhood, but I evade the topics with vague responses, and Emilia quickly comes to my rescue.

"Come on, we better get to English if we want good seats," she says, grabbing her backpack and getting to her feet. I quickly follow her, giving Michael and the others a brief smile and wave goodbye as we head out.

Making our way over to the main building, Emilia navigates us through the west wing. Both wings have three floors to accommodate classes for each subject, with the top floor of the west wing comprising computer suites for classes and personal use.

We push our way through the throng of other students, finding their first class of the day, until I spot Mr. Greer's name on a plaque on the classroom door, recognizing it as the name of our English teacher. Stepping into the classroom, I notice a few other students are already there, chatting to one another while they wait for class to begin. Mr. Greer glances up as we enter, giving us a nod before returning his attention to the papers on his desk.

The tables are all set out in groups of two, and Emilia grabs my hand, dragging me over to an empty table on the far side of the room, where we can sit together. Dropping my bag, I pull out my tablet and a notebook, already knowing I don't have a hope in hell of taking notes on that thing. The screen is too tiny, and even if I could navigate to the virtual notebook, any time I attempt to use the stylus, it ends up zooming all over the place and making a mess.

It's not long until the room fills with people, only a few empty seats left when the bell rings. I'm bent over my desk, writing, so I don't see them arrive, but I feel the room go still around me, signifying their presence. I don't even have to look up to hazard a guess at who just entered, but they draw my eyes to them like they are a hypnotic force, pulling me in.

Cam and Mason stroll into the room like they own it. Well, if the names on some of the buildings are any indication, they do own it. I spotted all four of their surnames on various buildings around campus yesterday, making it more than obvious who owns this school.

Bianca has once again wrapped herself around Cam, fawning all over him while he's too busy making an entrance, putting on a show for the rest of the class, just like at breakfast this morning.

A pretty brunette is standing awkwardly beside Mason, casting unsure looks his way. I vaguely recognize her as the girl he chose this morning. Unlike Bianca, she's making a conscious effort to not touch him. I can't blame her. As if his size isn't intimidating enough, the whole stony expression he's got going on is a sufficient warning to stay the fuck out of his way.

He and Cam head toward the back of the room, claiming a table together, and the girls follow, taking the seats directly in front of them, whispering quietly to each other and casting coquettish looks back toward the guys.

The final few students stumble in and, when the class is full, the teacher gets to his feet, rounding the desk.

"Alright, class," Mr. Greer begins, casting his eyes over each of us before a huge shit-eating grin crosses his face. "Now that you've gotten comfortable in your new seats beside your buddies, you're all going to get up so I can put you in alphabetical order."

A resounding groan echoes around the room, and Emilia pouts, the expression making me chuckle as everyone clambers to their feet.

"Stand along the back wall," Mr. Greer calls out, happily, deriving far too much pleasure from his students' grumblings, as we all do as he asked. "When I call your name, come and take your seat."

Starting at the beginning of the alphabet, he calls out, "Dustin Aberman," and a short, stocky kid quickly scurries toward the front of the class. This continues on for several more minutes until Bianca's name is called. With her hips swaying like she's striding down a runway and *not* simply walking across a classroom, she makes a whole parade of claiming her seat.

Emilia's name is called next and, with one final sulky look, her eyes silently begging me for help, she moves to sit next to Bianca. Neither girl looks happy to be sitting beside the other.

"Hadley Parker," Mr. Greer calls out several names later, pointing to a table against the wall at the back of the room. I hurry over to it, dropping into the chair as he calls out the next person's name. "Cameron Rutherford."

I have to physically restrain my eye roll as he strides toward me, his warm brown eyes alight with mischief and a confident smirk playing at the corner of his lips.

"New girl," he purrs, sliding into the seat beside me, leaning in as he drops his arm over the back of my chair. He flicks his tongue out, running it along his bottom lip in a deliberately seductive way. My eyes trail the movement like it's the most fascinating thing I've seen in a long time. *Hell, it's definitely the hottest.* How can he be such an arrogant ass and sexy as fuck all at the same time?

Unable to hold back that eye roll any longer, I let it loose, focusing on my workbook and deliberately trying to ignore the sex lollipop eyeing me up.

"Harley, right?"

What the hell is with these people and names?! How difficult is it to get someone's name right? Mr. Greer literally just mentioned it.

"No," I respond, still refusing to look at him. It's bad enough having him this close to me, where I can breathe in his stupidly expensive aftershave that smells like bad decisions. "Close, though."

I cave and glance subtly in his direction out of the corner of my eye. His eyes are narrowed in concentration as he tries to recall what the teacher said.

"Ahh," he exclaims, banging his hand on the table, having apparently figured it out. "Hadley." He looks triumphant, a proud grin spreading across his face.

Raising my eyebrows and pursing my lips in a sarcastic gesture, I bob my head, still not looking at him as I doodle in the corner of my notebook.

"Right, class," Mr. Greer calls out, having finished with the last few students. "We're going to start the term off with a project. Each pair is to pick a book off this year's reading list and write a ten-thousand-word report on it." Groans and murmurs erupt around the classroom, which the teacher promptly ignores, raising his voice. "Everyone should contribute *equally*."

Great, now I'm stuck doing an assignment with Mr. Flirtypants. I highly doubt the Princes do their own homework either, so I'm probably going to be stuck doing the whole thing by myself. *Super fun.*

"You can spend the rest of the class discussing it in your pairs," Mr. Greer tacks on, solidifying the craptastic day this is turning out to be.

"Guess we're assignment buddies," Cam purrs, sounding way too pleased about it.

"Yeah, I guess so."

"You know what that means? A lot of late nights, alone in the library."

Why does his voice have me imagining all the dirty things we could get up to in the dark stacks? And the way he bites his lower lip has me wanting to replace his teeth with my own.

Snapping myself out of it, I focus on the project, instead asking, "What book do you want to do?" in an attempt to bring the topic back to safer territory.

"The first party of the year is this weekend," he states, completely ignoring my question. I may as well have said nothing. "You should come."

"I'll think about it." My reply is blunt as I once again attempt to shut down the conversation and get back to the assignment. Besides, I've never been invited to a party before and I don't know if parties are something the other scholarship students go to. I'm also not sure I want to subject myself to the company of these kids any more than I have to.

"If you give me your room number, I can pick you up."

How sweet that would be, if he wasn't full of dirty intentions.

"I don't think your new girlfriend would be too happy about that," I respond, gesturing to Bianca who is glaring daggers at me from across the room. I don't know what she thinks is going on over here, but I have no doubt I'm the one she's going to have issues with.

Cam snorts, shaking his head. "That's just for show. It doesn't mean anything, it's just some stupid tradition."

"Then why do it?" I'm genuinely curious. If he and the others don't give a shit, why subject themselves to that? Wouldn't they rather be free to date and screw whoever they want, instead of saddling themselves with a girl they couldn't care less about each month?

"Because it's expected of us."

There's something in the tone of his voice that makes me lift my head to look at him. *Really* look at him. I'm not sure what it was I heard, but his face gives nothing away. "It means *something* to the girls you chose."

He gives me an indulgent smile, leaning in even closer. "It would, to someone like you," he begins. I'm about to call him out on what exactly he means by 'someone like you' when he continues on, "But for them, it's got absolutely nothing to do with us. They want to be seen with us because of *who* we are and what we can offer them. If we fell to the bottom of the totem pole tomorrow, someone else would take our place and none of those girls would give a shit about us. All they want is status, money, and power."

"And you get absolutely nothing out of it?" I argue, letting him know I'm not buying his whole 'woe is me' act. I wouldn't be surprised if what he's saying is true, but it's by no means a purely selfish gesture on the guys' part. He simply shrugs his shoulders. "Tit for tat. Everyone knows what they're signing on for."

I lean in so our lips are a hair's breadth apart. I'm playing with fire, I know it, but it doesn't stop me. "The look on Bianca's face says otherwise."

A cheeky grin lights up his face, excitement brimming in his eyes. "Don't tell me you're going to let something like that scare you off?"

"Please." I snort. "She's a kitty cat. I could destroy her in my sleep."

I mean it, but I'm not about to start drama just for Cam's amusement. There are enough idiots around here feeding his arrogance, he sure as hell doesn't need me adding to it.

"Mmm, I'd love to see that."

"Yeah, I'm sure you would. Too bad I don't go for rich dudes with fake girlfriends."

Hadley

Chapter 4

"Girl, you're sitting beside *Cam Rutherford*!" Emilia squeals as we leave English.

"It's really not as great as you're making it out to be. All he wants to do is flirt with me," I groan as she tucks her arm into my side, directing me to my next class. For real. We got nothing done the whole lesson. Any time I brought up the project, he would divert the topic to something dirty. "And did you see the looks Bianca was sending me? I've barely been here a day and I already have an enemy."

She cackles at my dramatics, but seriously, it's not the best start. I didn't want to make waves here. The goal was to fly under the radar and focus on my work before getting the hell out of here and moving on with my future.

"I think I'd happily flunk English if it meant Cam flirted with me." She sighs dreamily. "Any of them, really. Although Hawk and Mason are intimidating as fuck...but imagine all that aggression being released in the bedroom." I fear I've lost her to her daydreams as she full-body shivers at whatever she's thinking about—I'm pretty sure I don't want to know...unless one of them is doing it to my body.

***

Thankfully, the rest of the day was uneventful. No other Princes were in my classes, and I didn't see them when I went to grab lunch with Emilia and the others. I don't know what it is about them. I can't deny their pull over me. Whenever they're around, I find myself watching their every move, wanting to learn more about them.

Unfortunately, my lucky streak comes to an end on Tuesday afternoon, when, sitting in my business class, all four of them stroll in. The teacher literally takes one look at them and his eyes bug out of his head as he swallows around a lump in his throat, his voice becoming high pitched. *Is he for real? He's a fucking teacher and they're just students.* Maybe it's the fact all four of them are in his class. They do have the air of an indomitable force.

The four of them move toward the back row, a couple of students already sitting there quickly scurrying out of their chairs to sit elsewhere. Cam winks as he walks past my table, deliberately brushing the back of his hand against my shoulder, sending an involuntary shiver through me. *Goddammit, how can he elicit that response from me so easily?*

"Alright," the teacher begins, starting the lesson. As he drones on about some cost-benefit analysis theory, my eyes roam over the class, taking in the other students. Except for Mary sitting in the row beside me, there are literally no other females in the class. *Weird.*

Feeling eyes on me, I subtly glance out of the corner of my eye until I find Mason in the far back corner of the room, his intense gaze drilling into the side of my head. *What the hell?* His forehead is furrowed, and he's got a frown on his face as he leans over to Cam beside him, his hair falling forward to cover his eyes as the two of them whisper before Cam looks in my direction.

The teacher telling us to get started on a worksheet on our tablets pulls my attention back to the lesson, but I swear, for the next hour I feel Mason's eyes on me, and, when the class finishes and the room empties, there's a crackle in the air as he walks past. Not knowing what to make of it, I shake it off and move on to the next class of the day.

As the week drags on, I'm constantly aware of their presence, subtly stalking them with my eyes when we're in the same room. There's just something about them. I can't put my finger on it, but it has me obsessing over them for no good reason.

As much as I've tried, I haven't been able to forget about the strange shock I got the other day with Mason, and it would be impossible to ignore the wetness in my panties every time Cam throws me a dirty wink—which is far too often. For the sake of my laundry, he needs to stop.

Every morning, my eyes inadvertently drift their way as they each sit with a girl draped all over them. Even the mousy girl, Vivian, who Mason chose, has come out of her shell. I can only imagine what went down between them to have her suddenly being more self-assured around him. The show we're all forced to witness every morning though, is vomit inducing. West is the only one who seems to have any sort of morning etiquette, blatantly ignoring the girl—Brittany—he chose. She certainly gives it her best try to garner his attention, though. It's almost painful to watch as she tries to get him to eat food from her fork and runs her hand suggestively down his arm until he shakes her off.

Hawk and Mason don't seem to have the same issue with their girls. Both of them spend the better part of breakfast attempting to see what base they can get to before someone in the hall stops them—newsflash, no one is ever going to stop them. I'm pretty sure one day, soon, we're going to walk in and find one of them full-on fucking a girl over the table. I'm going to have to start storing cereal bars in my room. Seriously, who wants to see that shit when they're trying to eat? Or, you know, *ever*? They have forever ruined pancakes for me, and I'm not fucking happy about it.

Cam is the most baffling. One day he seems to lap up Bianca's attention, flirting and getting on with her, and the next he's shoving her away, wanting nothing to do with her. Yet every day, he winks in my direction, always making a point of brushing up against me when we pass in the halls. Every time he does, my pussy fucking weeps for more. I like to think I'm a resilient woman, but damn, he's doing a good job of wearing me down. He doesn't even need to say anything to me. A dirty look and casual touch is all it takes, apparently. I'm not used to having to deny my sexual urges, and Cam is really testing my resolve.

When it comes to all four of them, I can't wrap my head around any of it. What confuses me the most is the way the guys get on. When they're around everyone else, it's like they wear these shields, hiding their true thoughts and feelings, but I've caught glimpses of them alone, in the library or sometimes late at night in the dining hall when they seem so much more relaxed, more open, joking and laughing with one another. It makes no sense. This is supposed to be their domain, their territory to rule over, but most of the time, they look fucking miserable.

It's become a bit of an obsession, the way I watch them. I'd believe it was just my innate senses identifying a possible threat and reacting, but the way my stomach took flight and my every sense was attuned to Cam's closeness in English tells me it's so much more than that. I don't know what to make of it, or what the hell to do about it. Ignoring it seems like the best option for now. I probably just have a stupid crush on him and it will pass. If only we didn't have to do this project together, then I could actively avoid them all, until whatever the fuck has gotten into me, goes away.

"What do you think you're doing with Cam?" Bianca's annoying voice calls out, stopping me in my tracks. I should have known this was coming after my attempt to wind her up in English earlier in the week.

Slowly turning around, I narrow my eyes at her. "Excuse me?"

"He's mine. Don't think I haven't seen you panting all over him, hogging all of his attention."

I chuckle in disbelief. "Are you for real?"

"I saw you in English, flirting with him."

"You mean *talking* to him?"

Ignoring me, she continues on her rant, going on about how it's her turn and he's hers. I don't know, I'm not really listening to her.

"Look," I snap, cutting across whatever she was rambling on about, "I'm not interested in him." *Liar. Liar. Liar,* my inner slut insists, but I shut her down quickly. *We're living in denial, remember?*

"I'm serious," I assert when she continues to look dubious. "He asked if I could go to some party with him, but I told him no."

That was apparently the wrong thing to say, as her face turns red, steam practically pouring out of her. "He what?!" she screeches, her fists clenching in anger.

My eyes widen as I stand frozen, unable to do anything but stand and watch the volcano that's about to erupt in front of me. *What the actual fuck?*

"Stay away from him," she snarls. "I'll make your life here miserable if I catch you sniffing around him again."

She storms off down the hall and I watch her go, completely baffled as to what the fuck just happened. Choosing to forget about our little run-in, I saunter off in the opposite direction, continuing on my journey back to the dorms.

Rounding the corner, I crash into a solid chest. "Ouch," I cry as I bounce backward, rubbing at my nose. Who the fuck has a chest that hard? There's no way that can be normal.

"Watch where the fuck you're going," a deep voice snarls, his shitty tone immediately getting my back up.

"Excuse me?" I bark back, glaring up into Hawk's dark, stormy gray eyes. There's something familiar about them, but I can't place it. Maybe it's the sea of anger I can see raging within them. Who knows!

"You heard me," he growls, shoving past me.

For fuck's sake, it was a bloody accident on both our parts. Is a simple 'sorry' too much to ask for? Apparently so.

"Fucking asshole," I grumble, shaking my head as I take a step forward. Getting back to my room before I run into any more rich shitheads is the best idea I've had all day.

"What the fuck did you just call me?" His voice is a low rumble, threaded with dark promises of violence, halting me mid-step as I slowly turn around to face him, taking in his menacing expression. The hairs at the back of my neck stand at attention, a warning if ever there was one that this brute in front of me is a real and serious threat.

He's not the first man who thought he could intimidate me, just because he was bigger and scarier looking, and he sure as fuck won't be the last. At this point, his shit slides right off me.

I raise my chin, unflinchingly staring him down. "You heard me."

A snarl rips out of his chest, like he truly is part beast, but I continue to stand my ground, refusing to be cowered.

"Hawk, man, there you are," Cam calls out as Hawk takes a threatening step toward me. I have no idea what he was going to do, but it's probably for the best that Cam has shown up. "What's going on here?" he asks, his gaze bouncing between us, likely seeing the furious expressions on both of our faces and sensing the tension rippling in the air around us.

"Nothing," I spit out between gritted teeth. "Your buddy was about to make a horrible decision he'd later regret."

Another growl is the only response Hawk appears to be capable of right now as Cam, picking up on the pure rage seeping out of Hawk, angles his body between us...in some attempt to protect me? Either way, I've no intention of sticking around to find out.

I take a step back, then another, refusing to turn my back on either of them.

"Come on, man," Cam encourages, clapping his hand on Hawk's shoulder. "We've got shit to do."

It takes him another minute, but finally, Hawk seems to relent, giving a sharp nod and letting Cam steer him backward. His eyes never leave mine though, until the two of them round the corner, disappearing out of sight.

Jesus, fuck. Can I not just get to my room in peace?

That night, I'm working in my room when there's a knock at the door. Expecting it to be Emilia, I answer in nothing more than an old pair of gym shorts and a ratty t-shirt.

"Michael," I gasp in surprise.

"Sorry." He looks embarrassed as he rubs awkwardly at the back of his neck. "I know it's late. I was craving some ice cream, and I thought I'd see if you wanted to grab some? I noticed your light was on, so I figured you'd still be up."

"Eh, yeah. Sure. Just give me a sec," I rush, caught off-guard and feeling flustered. Grabbing a baggy hoodie, I quickly throw it on over my top, grabbing my key and locking the door on my way out.

"How's your first week going?" he asks as we head outside into the cool night air. It's nearly midnight and there aren't many students around as we walk over to the dining hall.

"Yeah, it's going good. The workload is intense, but I'm slowly settling in."

"Good, I'm glad. It's been fun having you around this week."

His words take me by surprise, as I wrack my brain to think of even one moment that he could maybe classify as me being 'fun', but I come up empty. I've hardly spoken to any of the other scholarship students all week, too busy with classes; and four assholes have been consuming my every spare thought.

Reaching the dining hall, he holds the door open, gesturing for me to go on ahead of him. Giving him an unsure smile, I step in, just as a hurricane of white-blonde hair barges past, knocking me against the wall.

"Out of my way, bitch," Bianca snaps as she storms past me, rushing out the door.

Turning to watch her, she power walks as fast as she can in her heels, racing back towards the girls' dorms.

"I wonder what that was about," Michael says, looking as bewildered as I do.

"No idea." I shrug, casting my eyes around the room. The hall is empty, except for the four assholes themselves at the back of the room. Cam is stomping across the room toward them, his brows furrowed and a scowl etched across his face as he runs his hand frustratingly through his blond hair. Hawk's storm-induced eyes zone in on me as soon as I step into the hall, like he has some sort of sixth sense that I'm here.

“Ice cream?” Michael prompts when I make no attempt to move from the doorway.

“Right, yeah.” Shaking myself out of the distraction, I try to ignore their magnetizing presence pulsing from the back of the room, screaming at me to look their way. Instead I follow Michael over to the freezer. I’m quickly pulled out of my thoughts by the vast range of flavors facing me. In front of me are tubs containing every flavor of ice cream imaginable. I couldn’t even tell you the last time I had ice cream. I remember eating it once as a child—some sort of fruity, berry flavor, I think. It was the sweetest thing I’d ever had.

Scanning the labels, I hum and ha for a good minute before deciding on a peanut butter one, grabbing the tub and sitting down at what I’ve come to discover is the designated table for scholarship students.

My eyes once again flick up, seeing all four boys huddled at the back of the room at their usual table, deep in conversation. Forcing my attention back to Michael, I pop the lid off my ice cream and, scooping out a spoonful, I bring it to my lips.

A soft moan escapes as my eyes drift shut, savoring the sweet nutty flavor. *Oh my God, that is fucking delicious.*

“Good?” Michael chuckles quietly, digging into his own tub.

“So good,” I agree, laughing too. “I, uh, don’t get to eat much sweet stuff,” I tell him, feeling like I need to explain myself.

“How come?”

“I, eh, grew up in foster care. You don’t exactly get offered many niceties.” Refusing to look at him, not knowing what sort of response I’ll get to that, I focus on making designs in my ice cream with the spoon, the lighter tone from a moment ago now gone, along with my desire for anything sweet.

His voice tells me nothing about what he thinks of my childhood. "That must have sucked."

"Yeah." I give a sad sort of chuckle. "You could say that."

We lapse into silence. *Great, I've managed to make it awkward already.* How can I be so shit in social situations?

"I'm sorry," I blurt when the silence becomes too much, "I didn't mean to put a downer on things. It was nice of you to invite me out."

"It's all good. I asked you out 'cause I wanted to get to know you..." His words drift into the background as movement at the back of the room pulls my focus, and I glance over his shoulder to see the Princes getting to their feet.

Cam still looks annoyed as he turns to face me, his eyes meeting mine and he freezes in place, obviously not realizing I was here. Something passes between us. I don't know what it is; I don't even know how to describe it, but I can feel it throughout my entire body. This visceral reaction to him, kind of like an electric shock, lighting up my every nerve, snapping me to attention. It's more intense than anything I've ever experienced before. *What the hell is this?*

Someone knocks into him, breaking whatever weird spell that was between us, and I flick my eyes to find Mason glancing between the two of us, looking confused. He says something to Cam who shakes his head before the two of them take off, moving to trail behind Hawk and West as they leave the hall.

"—would you want to go? Hadley?"

"Huh?" I focus back on Michael, realizing I haven't heard a word he's said. "Sorry, what were you saying?"

He glances quickly at the door before looking back at me. "I was saying there's a party tomorrow night, down by the beach."

"Oh, yeah, Emilia mentioned it to me."

"Yeah, all the scholarship students go, kinda like one final blow out before the workload piles up. I, uh, was wondering if you wanted to go."

"Sure," I agree, nodding my head. "Can't miss the first party of senior year, right?"

He's got a huge grin on his face. "Great. I can pick you up."

"I thought everyone went as a group?" I ask, confused.

"Well, I mean, yeah," he stumbles, his cheeks pinking. I don't know why he's suddenly looking so nervous, though.

"It probably makes more sense to walk down as a group," I reason, trying to ease whatever awkwardness he's feeling.

"Right, of course," he mumbles.

The conversation between us sort of dries up after that. I don't know what happened or what I missed, but neither of us seem to know what to say to rectify things, and we soon call it a night and go our separate ways.

West

Chapter 5

“What was that all about?” Hawk asks, tipping his head toward where a pissed off Bianca just stormed out.

“Nothing.” The scowl on Cam’s face says otherwise as he storms across the canteen toward us.

“Things have been weird between you two all week,” I point out. He's been all over the place with her, like he can’t make up his mind if he wants her or not. Something that is never usually an issue for Cam. If she’s half-way good-looking with a decent set of tits, he’ll stick his dick in her.

“It's nothing,” he growls more vehemently, collapsing into the seat beside me, spreading his legs wide and slouching as he leans against the backrest.

Hawk gives him a once-over before glancing around at the rest of us, a serious expression on his face. "Who's the new girl?" he asks. "What's her deal?"

"Hadley?" Cam's head snaps up, his ire from a moment ago forgotten. Hasn't Hawk been listening to Cam all week? I swear she's the only thing he's been able to talk about. I'd bet my left nut she's the reason he's all over the place with Bianca. He's the only one of us who's been looking forward to the senior year tradition of picking a girl each month—although Hawk and Mason seem to be enjoying themselves alright—and now it's here he couldn't care less. He thinks he likes the variability, the idea of always having a new girl, but really, he loves the challenge of chasing after a girl. Now he's set his sights on someone unattainable. He knows scholarship girls are never chosen. Besides, it's not like our parents would ever be okay with us dating someone so far beneath us—their words, not mine. Personally, I have nothing against the scholarship students. If anything, I probably have more in common with them than the rest of the wealthy, vapid kids we go to school with. Certainly, they are my primary competition for the highest rank in the year.

"Yeah. Who is she? Why is she here?"

"Dunno." Cam shrugs. "She's a scholarship student, why?"

"Why are we even talking about her?" Mason interjects before Hawk can answer, his pinched, closed-off expression taking me by surprise. What's gotten up his ass? "We've more important things to discuss. West, have you found anything new?"

All eyes turn to me as I purse my lips, shaking my head in defeat. "Nothing," I growl, frustrated with myself. I've spent hours upon hours trying to dig deeper, but every time I've come up empty. "The two organizations are being treated like separate entities. The only thing I could find in common was the logo."

"That's it?" Cam gawks, staring at me in disbelief, but what did he expect me to find? "No employee logs or property reports, or second bank accounts or anything?"

"No, Cam. Nothing." He narrows his eyes, not appreciating my pissy attitude, but tough shit, I am pissed. I'm pissed at our parents for hiding all of this from us—hell, I'm fucking furious they're even involved in any of this. I'm angry with myself for not finding out sooner and for not being able to get all the information we need now. I don't even know how I feel about the fact the futures we were expecting to have are all lies.

Rubbing his hands down his face, Hawk sighs, staring at me intently. "Keep trying. You might come across something. In the meantime, we need to come up with another way of getting what we need."

We all nod in agreement, all of us on the same page. We can't do anything without more information, so for now we just have to sit back and pretend life as a Prince is nothing but easy lays and keg parties.

The next day, I'm sitting at the computer desk waiting for the rest of the class to filter in. It's the last class of the week, and I can hear the excited hums of the students around me as they gossip about tonight's party. It's the first party of the year and it's always a blowout.

I'm honestly too tired to give a shit. Between Cam's argument with Bianca last night and all the other shit we're already dealing with right now, we're barely keeping our heads above water. Not to mention I'm already regretting the decision to go along with this whole stupid girl of the month thing. Next month, I have to pay more attention, instead of picking whatever random girl is closest to me. It hasn't even been a week yet, and Brittany is driving me mad, hanging all over me at meals and seeking me out between classes. It's completely insane. She's become a clingy, psycho, stalker girlfriend overnight.

What's even worse is that it's not because she's crazy in love with me or some shit like that. She sees me as a stepping stone to get to the others. All she ever does is ask me about them, and I've seen the way she ogles Mason. I get it. I'm not as buff or as in your face as they are. I don't have the angry, smoldering look that Hawk has, nor Cam's flirty charm. The girls even seem to like the whole silent, mysterious thing Mason has going on.

I'm the quiet, reserved one of the group, the nerd. I'm the guy the girls try to get close to, hoping to gain some insight into the others. At least, that's how it used to be. They quickly realized I'm a vault.

Don't get me wrong, I still get girls willing to settle for me. After all, any Prince is better than no Prince. Apparently. But there's something about knowing someone is only with you because of what you are and who you're friends with that makes it pretty damn difficult to find anything appealing about them. It sure as hell doesn't entice me to stick my dick in them.

So instead, while the others have been off getting their dicks wet on the regular, I've spent the last few years learning code and fine-tuning my programming skills. That's how I was able to dig up dirt on our parents' company. Dirt that changed our whole perspective on things. There's so much about our lives, our families, we've been completely clueless about, until now. We've been running around being the entitled rich assholes everyone expects us to be, not giving a shit about our futures, while all this underhanded crap has been happening right under our noses. We've been too focused on getting girls and going to parties, but not any longer. This year is different. Shit has gotten fucking real.

The problem is, now that we're aware of exactly what our parents are up to, we have no idea what the fuck to do about it. It's been a point of contention between us, only made worse by all the petty shit we've had to put up with in school for appearance's sake, and to keep our parents off our backs.

I'm barely paying attention to the room around me, too lost in the minefield that is our new reality, so I'm taken completely by surprise when someone sits down beside me. Everyone knows not to sit with us unless invited.

Turning my head, I guess I shouldn't be surprised to see the new girl sitting there. Like I said, everyone else knows better. I watch her out of the corner of my eye as she checks out the whole setup; the computer screen, keyboard, and mouse, before hesitantly moving the cursor around the screen, clicking on the username and frowning at the screen in confusion.

She glances around the room, her frown only deepening when she notices everyone else is already logged in and getting on with their work. There is a teacher—if you can call him that—who oversees the lesson, but since it's a computer science class, we're pretty much left to our own devices. Each lesson plan is already uploaded for us to work through, and Mr. Hughes usually pops his head in once or twice during the hour to make sure we're all behaving, but that's it. Mostly, the students fly through whatever we're supposed to be doing, then spend the rest of their time mucking around.

"Your login details will be on your tablet," I tell her absently, not removing my focus from my screen. I normally wouldn't get involved in other people's problems, but I tell myself I'm only helping her out because her mindless clicking of the mouse is already driving me bats.

"Oh," she replies, darting a quick glance my way. "Thanks."

She pulls her tablet out of her satchel and fumbles around on it. I try to tune her out, ignoring her sighs of frustration—*I did my part, I helped her, I am under no obligation to do more*—as I struggle to focus on my own work, something that usually isn't an issue. Ordinarily, it's the other way around, and I forget the rest of the world exists until the bell goes, or one of the guys pulls me out of my zone.

When it's apparent I won't be able to concentrate with her constant grumblings, I swivel around in my chair, turning to face her and snatching the tablet off the table.

"Hey," she gives off, scowling at me as she tries to yank it back. Ignoring her, I tap away until I open up the document that has all her login details, handing it back to her without another word. She looks at me quizzically, hesitating before reaching out and taking it from me. I don't know why she's giving me that look. Sure, people give us a wide berth, but it's not like I've done anything to her to make her so untrusting of me.

Glancing down at the screen, she gives me a final look before turning back to her computer and typing in the details. Watching her, it's the most painstaking thing I've seen in a long time. She uses only her index fingers, taking forever to find the next letter on the keyboard. I swear it takes her five full minutes to enter her username and password—it's like she's never used a computer before.

Once again, I try to ignore her presence, concentrating on my own work. I've already completed the advanced computer science course, but I had been planning on using this class to learn a new programming language, hoping it might help me find out the information I need.

"Um, do you know where I can find the lesson plan?" she asks, cutting through my thin veil of concentration. *Ah, who am I kidding? I have no idea what I had planned for today.*

This time, when I look her way, she's gnawing on her bottom lip, looking at me with an unsure gaze. The gesture captures my attention, drawing my eyes to her plump pink lips, the way the skin disappears between her teeth. I have this sudden urge to replace her teeth with mine. *I wonder what she tastes like.*

With her combat boots, and the way she keeps adjusting her uniform like it's a strait jacket, restricting her movements, she's a far cry from anyone else at Pac. Her mess of curly hair and sharp looks scream defiance and rebellion. I bet she tastes like trouble and every dirty thought I've ever had.

"Never mind," she blurts out, her cheeks pinking as she waves me away, mistaking my silence for a refusal. "I can work it out."

"It'll be on your personal drive," I rush out, shaking my head in an attempt to dislodge the dirty thoughts I was heading toward. *What the fuck is wrong with me?* It's been quite a while since a girl has gotten that reaction from me. And a scholarship student? She's probably only here to bag herself a rich husband. Definitely not the sort of drama I need to saddle myself with.

When she continues to look at me like I've spoken Klingon, I decide I may as well forget about my own lesson plan, and help her out. It has absolutely nothing to do with the fact she's uniquely attractive or intriguing, but because it's the polite thing to do.

Sliding my chair over beside hers, I'm enveloped by the vanilla and honey scent of her shower gel, losing myself for a moment in her eyes. I can't quite place the color—blue, but with a hint of something else. They're captivating, like looking at the sky just before it's about to rain.

She watches me with a mixture of wariness and curiosity as I adjust my glasses, grabbing ahold of her mouse. I show her how to access her drive, and it becomes clear pretty quickly that the girl hasn't spent much time around computers. She can barely use basic typing and spreadsheet programs. I want to ask her about it, but one look at the deep furrows in her forehead as she concentrates on what I'm telling her, combined with the nervous tapping of her nails against the table, and I can tell she wouldn't take it well.

She nods along with everything I explain to her, appearing to take it in and asking questions here and there when she needs something clarified. It takes the full hour, but surprisingly, I don't mind. I'm not a dick, I'd help someone out if they asked for it; but it's usually begrudgingly, and I'm always ready to be done with them so I can get back to my own work. Not today, though. Maybe it was just her citrusy shampoo messing with my head, but I actually enjoyed showing her the ropes, watching her eyes light up when she learned something new, and how she bit the inside of her lip when she was processing what I was saying.

"Thanks," she says, her soft tone sounding genuinely grateful when the bell rings, signaling the end of class. Her teeth once again dig into her bottom lip in what I've learned is a nervous gesture. "For today. I really appreciate it."

"Any time." The words blurt before I've had a chance to process what I'm saying.

Uh, what now? Any time?

I'm not someone who invites people to hit them up when they need help. I like my own company, and spending time with the guys, but that's it. The last thing I want to do with my spare time is spend it with the students in Pac. I already have to show up at social events for appearance's sake. I definitely don't spend one-on-one time with any of them. Yet I've just told this girl, a virtual stranger, that she can ask me for help any time.

God damn, I knew her shampoo had scrambled my brain!

***

The seniors always host the first party of the year down by the lake. It's on the far side of campus to the teacher accommodation and hidden from view of the school by the forest, meaning no one is likely to bust us. Although I'm pretty sure the teachers are all aware of what we get up to out here, and they just turn a blind eye. It's not like they could suspend or expel the entire senior class.

The lake is usually a tranquil spot, away from the usual furor of the rest of campus, but tonight it's alive with teenage energy, everyone buzzing for a good time. We've lit a fire on the pebbly shore—the flames sparking and fanning into the air, flaring like a beacon against the night sky—and dragged a few logs of driftwood around it for makeshift seats. Music blasts over the speaker system and students sway to the beat, while others sit up on the grassy embankment, chatting and drinking. There's a short dock stretching into the water, where a few kids are currently sitting—dangling their feet over the edge—and a boat shed at the other side of the lake.

The party is well underway when Hadley shows up. I notice her as soon as she arrives with the other scholarship students. They all stand out like sore thumbs, with their discounted clothing and cheap makeup, compared to the designer outfits and thousand-dollar shoes the rest of us are wearing.

Even with that distinction, she still sticks out from the others; with her wide eyes, scanning warily over the party, drinking everything in. Not to mention she's the only girl here in a long sleeve top, baggy shorts, and combat boots, her mess of blonde curls blowing freely in the breeze. She looks like a vagrant, yet she appears so much more at ease in what she's wearing than she did earlier in her uniform.

The crowd of them make a beeline for the drink table, and one of them—I think her name is Emily—shoves a drink into Hadley's hand. She sniffs at it before wrinkling her nose, quickly setting it aside when her friend's back is turned. Everything about her is odd. Different. From her unusual behavior to her strange attire, I can't figure her out. I spent all afternoon trying to get a read on her. She came across as nervous sometimes, almost skittish, yet she's abrasive and acerbic. I'm a sucker for a good challenge, and Hadley may have just become my new puzzle to solve.

"Yo. West, man," Cam calls out, pulling my attention away from the girl who has been taking up way too much space in my brain this afternoon.

"Huh?" I snap my head around to look at him before he can catch me staring at her. I can only imagine the ribbing if he caught me looking at the girl he's been talking non-stop about all week—although I don't think he's managed to make much headway with her.

"The girls are here." He sounds as enthusiastic as I feel, however it's strange to hear him so uninterested in a party; but once again, this is a situation where the girl of the month crap isn't as much fun as he expected. Where's the excitement when you have a sure-thing girl? For a chaser like Cam, there's none of the adrenaline rushing energy that comes from flirting with a girl, slowly building up to that moment when you find out if she's going to go home with you. Sure, I don't think anyone has ever turned him down, but there's still none of that anticipation he loves.

For me, I just don't want to be saddled with Brittany all night, or any other girl. I like doing the weird loner thing, watching everyone around me doing their thing. I don't need some chick hanging off me, trying to get my attention. *Ugh, why the fuck are we doing this stupid tradition again? Oh, yeah, because it's expected of us.*

Parties used to be the one time when we could let loose, only inviting people to hang out with us if we wanted to, but otherwise sticking to ourselves. We could afford to drop the masks we wear in public. Not anymore. The rest of the day, I can get away with telling Brittany to leave me alone, but not here. Part of the deal is that they get to sit with us at parties. That exposure is half the reason they so easily agree to be ours—the other reason being the bragging rights. And of course, the faint hope that we might actually want something more with any of them.

"Great." I sigh, putting on a fake smile and heading over to where the guys are gathered round the fire pit. Bianca, Vivian, Melissa, and Brittany, each of our girls for the month, have joined them. Melissa is already in Hawk's lap, looking way too cozy as she runs her hand possessively over his large bicep, and Vivian is sucking face with Mason. I don't get how those two are so okay with all of this. They don't give a shit about those girls. They don't care that those girls don't give a shit about them. But then, it's nothing different from what they've been doing the last four years. I just don't get it; it's not me. I'm not a meaningless hook-up person.

Brittany is sitting on the other side of the fire, glowering in Mason's direction. Or, more specifically, at the girl attached to his face. It should maybe annoy me that she's blatantly eyeing him up, but honestly, I just don't give a fuck. I didn't at the beginning of the week, and with Hadley screwing with my brain today, I definitely don't give a shit now.

Cam seems to be back to totally ignoring Bianca. An impressive feat, considering she's clawing at him like a cat in heat. He's been hot and cold with her all week, but I figured with a few beers in him tonight, he'd be all over that.

"West," Brittany purrs, jumping to her feet when she sees me in her line of vision. "I was wondering where you were."

Grabbing a beer out of the cooler, not bothering to offer her or any of the other girls a drink, I sit down beside Cam, all but ignoring her. It might come across as rude, but in all seriousness, if you give these girls an inch, they'll take everything you own and destroy you in the divorce.

"Why don't you two girls go dance?" Cam suggests, waving aimlessly toward the crowd of students in a bid to get rid of them.

"You want to watch me shake my ass for you, baby?" Bianca purrs, leaning in to lick Cam's ear. *Fucking gross.* I quickly glance away, taking a large gulp from my beer can, trying to ignore whatever she's trying to do—what *is* she trying to do? Ear fuck him? *Jesus.*

"Sure." Cam's tone lacks all of its usual flirty undertones as he pulls away from her, but Bianca doesn't seem to notice any of it as she grabs Brittany's hand and sashays off.

"God, was she always that whiny and clingy?"

"Yes," I deadpan. "Why did you pick her anyway?"

He gives a casual shrug of his shoulder. "I heard she got a boob job over the summer. I was curious to see if her tits would be firm enough that I could stick my dick between them and get myself off."

I roll my eyes at that. *Of course that was the reason.*

"And are they?"

"I dunno, haven't fucked her yet."

That takes me by surprise. Sure, he's got his sights set on another girl, but this is Cam. Even if he's lost interest, he'd still fuck her.

"Huh, I thought you'd be all about the monthly girls." We haven't actually talked about what's going on with him. Honestly, I thought he was just chasing after Hadley all while getting his dick wet in Bianca, but if he's not fucking her, then his head is more messed up than I realized.

"Yeah, me too," he agrees glumly. "And I was." He sighs, frustrated, downing a large gulp of his beer as his eyes scan the crowd until they catch on to what he's searching for. Turning to see, I spot Hadley dancing in a small circle with her friends. "Until I saw her."

"Just fuck her and get her out of your system." I have to push past the uneasy feeling in my gut at those words. I don't know what the hell that feeling is, but it can fuck right off. For Cam, it should be as simple as that. Yeah, okay, it sounds callous, but that doesn't make it any less true. It's what he does—lures a girl in with his charming ways, fucks her, and moves on.

He snorts. "I fucking wish, man, but she seems to be immune to my charms."

That gets my attention as I turn to look at him with wide eyes, my mouth slightly agape. "She's not interested?" Since when does a girl at Pac not want to fuck a Prince? The scholarship girls are much more reserved about it, but I bet if one of us asked them to suck our dick, they'd fall to their knees without a second thought. That's not me talking out of arrogance. I'm just stating a fact.

"I dunno, man." His brow is furrowed, his lips pinched in confusion as his eyes trail Hadley around the party. "I can't work her out."

That makes two of us.

Hawk and Mason finally detach themselves from the girls and move over to join us as Vivian and Melissa go to dance with the other two.

"What are you two moping about?" Hawk asks, grabbing himself a beer, his eyes following Cam's gaze. "Are you fucking serious? You're still caught up on her?"

"What is your problem with her, man?" Cam snaps, finally stopping his stalkerish ways and turning to look at Hawk in confusion. "What happened the other day?"

"Nothing," he snarls. "She was just a bitch."

"Because she didn't fall to the ground, begging for mercy and offering you an apology blowjob, like any other girl would do?" Cam chuckles, shaking his head, diffusing the tension from a moment ago.

Hawk just shrugs, refusing to answer. That's exactly what his problem is. He doesn't like to be challenged, and he's not used to backtalking from girls. I bet he was shocked she dared say anything to him, and now he doesn't know what to do with it. It doesn't help that his head is already a mess with all this family shit we're drowning in. Mason's the only one who seems to be impervious to her particularly unusual brand of charm.

Hadley

Chapter 6

The party is in full swing when we arrive. In fairness, we're over an hour late. Who knew it took girls so long to get ready? I sure as hell didn't. We spent ages in Emilia's room getting all dressed up. Well, she got dressed up—after finally giving up on forcing me into one of her dresses and heels, that shit ain't happening—while I flicked through the collection of girly magazines she had.

Looking out over the partygoers, I notice a crowd of people hovering around the drinks table, chatting, while others grind on one another on the beach, close to a set of large speakers that have been set up with some sort of dance music pumping out of them.

That same magnetism I feel around them has me looking toward the fire pit, finding all four of them perched around it.

How are they able to lure me in and steal my focus in a crowd this size, with all the distractions that come with being at a party? I should be able to distance myself from them and forget they're even here.

"Cheers, girl." Emilia has a huge grin on her face as she pushes a plastic cup into my hand, bringing my attention back to her as she clinks her own cup against mine, taking a large swallow from it.

Sniffing the straw-colored liquid, my nose scrunches as the sweet-vinegary-malt smell invades my senses. *Nope, no thanks.* Not that I'd drink anything with alcohol in it, but I definitely wouldn't touch anything here. I don't know these people. While their first impression hasn't been horrible, it certainly hasn't been warm and welcoming—only the scholarship students really talk to me. Even if it was, life has taught me to keep my guard up and to always be on alert. Never be vulnerable. Never show weakness. Someone is always watching, ready to pounce at the first opportunity. I'm sure as fuck not about to give these rich assholes an opening.

The others quickly down their drinks; and Abigail, Mary, Todd, and Samuel all make their way toward the sea of dancing bodies, laughing, and getting into the partying mood. Emilia hesitates, and I can see she wants to go with them.

"Go," I encourage, ushering her away.

"Nah, I'm good here for now," she promises, pouring herself another drink and standing with me as we watch the party rage around us.

"So, this is a Pac party?"

"Yup," Emilia nods her head, her hips swaying slightly to the beat as we observe the partygoers around us.

"I thought it would be...bigger." Not that I have much to go on, but looking around at students slamming back shots, making out or grinding on one another, I just don't get it. What's the appeal? Nearly every girl is parading around in sky high heels and a barely there dress, just asking for a broken ankle on the uneven pebbles, while the guys not-so-subtly eye up whatever girl they're hoping to get with for the night. From what I can gather, the whole night is about drinking, dancing, and sex. If two people want to fuck, why don't they just do it? Why do they need the liquid courage and the dancing warm-up? If I want a guy, I just go for him.

My gaze inadvertently flits back to the fire pit, watching Cam and West deep in conversation, ignoring everyone else around them. They're both casually dressed in jeans that hug their thighs, and Cam's t-shirt looks like it's been painted on him, every taut line of his muscles evident through the fabric. West has donned a pale gray shirt with rolled-up sleeves, showing off his lean yet sturdy forearms. Forearms shouldn't be attractive, right? I mean, they're just forearms for fuck's sake. Yet, the flash of an image skitters across my brain of him pinning me against the wall with those forearms. *Yes, please.*

No. No. Off limits.

Okay, so maybe I don't just go for it with *every* guy, but the Princes are the exception. They're a complication I can't afford right now. My body might want them, but my brain knows they're exactly what I don't need.

"Having fun?" Michael asks, interrupting my inappropriate thoughts. He'd been hovering nearby, talking to Andrew, but turning to look at him, I see Andrew being pulled into the swelling crowd by some girl with a coy smile on her face, clearly knowing she's going to get lucky tonight.

"Eh, yeah." It's a less than enthusiastic response, but I think I've discovered parties aren't really my thing. Not that I know what my *thing* is. It's not like I've ever had the time or money to invest in extracurriculars, nor the friends to hang out with. When you spend your entire life simply surviving, you don't have time to discover who you are.

"You wanna dance?" Michael asks awkwardly, fidgeting with the tail of his shirt.

"Uh..."

Before I can work out how to tell him no, Emilia is already clapping her hands. "Yes," she shrieks. "That's an excellent idea." Grabbing my hand, I begrudgingly let her pull me into the crowd—it's not like I can refuse. The poor girl has been dying to dance all night, but has been holding off so she can hang back with me. I can sense Michael at my back as we squeeze past bodies until we reach the others in the middle of the makeshift dance floor. Without letting go of my hand, Emilia gyrates her hips, tugging on my arm every now and again to encourage me to move.

Around me, everyone dances to the beat, closing their eyes and getting lost in the rhythm. I can feel Michael's body pressing into my side and Emilia keeps bumping up against me, the crowd pushing us all together.

I try. I honestly do, but I just can't get into it. Not only do I apparently have no rhythm, but I can't seem to lose myself in the music the way they do. Every time I close my eyes I can feel the sweaty bodies shoving against me, the hairs prickling at the back of my neck as unknown hands sweep my body. My heart rate starts to climb, my breaths coming in harsh pants. Tearing my eyes open, I mutter an excuse to whoever hears me before pushing my way through the crowd, ignoring the others calling after me as I run off into the surrounding trees, until the noise of the party is nothing more than a soft drone in the distance, and there is nothing but fresh air and the hidden cover of the surrounding forest.

Pressing my back against the rough bark of a tree, I tilt my head back, taking a few deep, steadying breaths. What the fuck is wrong with me? Why can't I just be like everyone else? Be a typical fucking teenager for once, having fun and enjoying a party?

In the silence, I can feel myself regaining back some control, my heart rate slowing; but I can still feel a buzzing sensation beneath my skin, that nervous energy that only appears when I'm pissed off or stressed out. It's been building within me since I stepped foot on campus, but tonight has pushed it into overdrive, and it bothers me that I was so easily triggered. In hindsight, it was probably foolish of me to think I could simply escape my past and leave it all behind. I may be safe here, but I'm so used to being on the defensive, to expecting the worst. I can't just turn that off, unfortunately. Sighing heavily, I realize I may be more damaged than I ever knew.

A twig snaps somewhere behind me and I spin around, my head jerking toward the noise as I squint through the darkness, trying to see what fuckface is out here with me, destroying my moment of peaceful solitude. *This* is why I can't be like all those other kids at that party. Shitty karma and dangerous situations follow me around like a bad fucking smell.

"Whoa," a deep voice calls out. "It's just me."

Squinting, I can just about make out the faint outline of someone cautiously approaching me. "West? What are you doing here?"

I don't relax my stance, eyeing him warily as he steps closer.

"I saw you run off, I wanted to check on you."

"Oh." I don't know what to make of that. I only talked to the guy for the first time today. Everything I've heard and seen regarding the Princes indicates that I shouldn't so much as look in their direction unless I want to rain down hellfire on myself. Hell, some of the stories Emilia has told me are unbelievable...How in their freshman year they publicly humiliated a senior who wouldn't bow down to royalty that was younger than him; or the student they drove out of school because he made fun of West for being a nerd.

After my altercation with Hawk yesterday, I'd well believe he's capable of everything I've heard, but West was nothing but nice to me today, and the same with Cam, although he definitely has ulterior motives.

It's difficult to make out his features in the dark, shadows dancing across his face, however everything about him says he's not a threat. His hands are tucked in his pockets, his posture relaxed as he strolls toward me.

"Are you?"

"Am I what?"

"Okay?"

"Oh. Yeah. I'm fine." Deciding he's not here to harm me, I lean back against the tree, closing my eyes, trying to find that sense of calm once again. It's no good though, I'm hyperaware of his presence. It's the same awareness as earlier, in class. The seat beside him was the only empty one in the back row, and I wanted as few people as possible to see how hopeless I am with computers. I didn't expect him to talk to me, let alone *help* me. None of the Princes are known for their hospitality. I hadn't counted on the strange nervousness his closeness elicited. And when he wheeled his chair over beside mine? My heart went into overdrive as his clean, musky scent enveloped me.

My eyes pop open as his arm brushes against mine, and I'm surprised to find him leaning against the tree beside me. Heat emanates out from where his skin touches mine, that small bit of contact starting a chain reaction throughout my body, slowly settling me and, for the first time since arriving here, that buzzing feeling dies down to a background hum.

I don't know what these guys are doing to me. I've felt physical attraction before—that sudden racing of your heart and twisting of your gut, the way you can't stop looking at them, picturing them naked. Those feelings are bland and superficial in contrast to the sheer visceral reaction I have to the Princes; the raw, intense awareness I get around them.

Licking my suddenly dry lips, I blurt out, "You, uh, don't have to stay with me. I'm sure your friends, or your, uh, girl of the month, or whatever, are looking for you."

A breathy laugh escapes him. "You looking to get rid of me?"

"What?" I splutter. "No. You, uh...I just don't want you to feel you *have* to stay with me." I actually don't know if I want him to go or not, but he's been nice to me and I definitely don't need to piss off any of these guys by accident.

"Parties aren't really my thing," he casually admits. He's definitely not as social as the others, but I still figured he would be into this whole typical high school bullshit as much as everyone else seems to be.

"Apparently, they aren't mine either." I don't know why I say that. I don't understand why I'm honest with him. Like earlier, asking for his help. It's like I lose my filter when he's around. Something about him comes across as genuine and truthful, making it difficult to be my usual standoffish, bitchy self with him.

"Apparently?"

Eh, fuck. I've already given enough for him to deduce what I mean, so I may as well just blurt it all out. "This is my first high school party."

"Huh." I wait on tenterhooks, waiting for him to say more, only letting out a relieved breath when it's clear he's not going to ask all the obvious questions. Not that I was going to share any more of myself with him. Fuck, even that little tidbit of information has my heart hammering in my chest once more.

We lapse into silence. It's not uncomfortable like the awkwardness with Michael last night, but honestly, I don't know what the fuck to make of it. It's both settling and fraught with whatever this energy between us is.

"I should, uh, be getting back to my friends," I say tensely after several minutes, pushing off the tree.

"Sure." He shrugs, showing no signs of moving himself. Giving him a stiff, curt nod, I stride off, heading back to the party, all the while ignoring the burning of his eyes into my back as he watches me go.

"Hadley!" Emilia calls out when she spots me, swaying in her heels as she stumbles my way. "Where'd you go?" Her words are slightly slurred as she basically hangs off me, draping her arms around my neck.

"Wow, I think someone's had a bit too much to drink." I laugh, wrapping my arms around her.

"You have?" she gasps, staring at me with bright eyes and an unfocused gaze. "Naughty girl," she cackles, throwing her head back.

Jesus, was I really gone long enough for her to drink that much?

"Come on," I urge, "let's get you a seat and some water."

Someone has dug out some old fold-up chairs and scattered them around the fire pit, so I ease her into an empty one, feeling eyes on me from the three Princes seated around us. Everyone else has avoided coming over here all night, but if she passes out on the ground, I'm worried I'll never be able to lift her up.

She's half-unconscious as I glance around the fire pit, finding a cooler filled with drinks, including a couple of bottles of water. Moving over to it, I reach out to lift one, but snatch my hand back at the last second, as the lid snaps shut.

"That's for us, not scholarship trash," Hawk snarls, his ice-cold glare penetrating through me as Melissa—perched in his lap—giggles, like Hawk's pissy attitude is fucking hilarious.

Ignoring her, I return Hawk's scowl with one of my own. "She just needs a bottle of water."

"There's an entire table of drinks over there," he snarks, waving his hand dismissively toward the drinks table. Yeah, but they all have fucking alcohol in them. Trust me, I checked when we arrived.

I sigh heavily, mentally telling myself not to start a fight with this asshole. "They don't have any water," I state, hoping to reason with him. I should have known there was a fat chance of that happening.

"So?" He snorts. "That's not my fucking problem."

My scowl darkens as I stare him down, but he's completely unfazed, unwilling to budge on his decision. I can feel Mason's eyes on me as he and his lap accessory silently watch the interaction. Apparently, neither of them feel the need to speak up or intervene in this ridiculousness.

"She's practically unconscious," I hiss, grinding my teeth as I wave my hand toward Emilia who's slumped over in the chair, her eyes shut. My words are falling on deaf ears, but I'm not about to back down from this shithead; that's exactly what he wants.

Flicking his gaze her way before returning his focus to me, Hawk nods his head slowly, only making me narrow my eyes at him in suspicion. "Okay." Nope. I'm not buying it. I don't respond, waiting for him to tell me what the catch is. "For a price," he adds with a smug smirk.

Pursing my lips, I stare him down, my mind racing through all the possibilities of what he could ask for. "I don't have any money on me."

"I don't want your money," he sneers. "But I will take a blowjob." A shit-eating grin spreads across his face and it takes everything in me not to reach out and slap it off.

What the actual fuck? Is this arrogant dickweed for real? He can't seriously think I'd willingly do that. Melissa throws a pissy look my way, like *I* was the one that just offered *him* a fucking blow job for some measly water. If it wasn't happening to me, the whole thing would be laughable.

"Baby, I can give you a blowjob if you want one," she purrs seductively, not happy at having Hawk's attention directed elsewhere. Her voice is low and breathy as her hand dips down between their bodies to places I don't even want to know about.

"No." Hawk grabs her wrist, halting her movements, his eyes never leaving mine. Deciding he's fucking insane, I tear my eyes away from Hawk's hate-filled, stormy orbs to look at Cam, hoping he will back me up on this. He's been flirting with me all week, making it clear he's more than interested in getting in my pants. Surely, he will tell Hawk to stop being a douche. It's only water, for fuck's sake.

"Dude, it's just water." It's weak, lacking any sort of conviction, but whatever. If it will get Hawk to stop being a cumbucket, then I'll take it.

"She knows the price," he growls. "She either pays it or she can get the fuck out of here."

Of course, Bianca and Brittany come stumbling off the dance floor at that moment, pushing their way through the crowd toward the firepit.

"What are you doing?" Bianca snaps, towering over me in a scrap of fabric that barely covers her...bits. "I've told you before," she hisses. "Stay in your lane and keep your pauper mitts off the Princes."

Seriously? Does she think I'm over here trying to get with one of these assholes? Puh-lease, like I'd ever sleep with any of these arrogant dickwads.

“What’s going on here?” West's deep voice startles me, but before I can explain anything, Brittany practically launches herself at him. “Wes, baby!”

“Don’t call me that,” he bites out, glaring at her. “It’s West. The name’s already shortened, it doesn’t need cut down any fucking further.”

Her eyes widen in surprise, her lip popping out in a pout, but she doesn’t unlatch her death grip from around his neck, and after a second, she shakes it off, giving him a sugary sweet smile again. “Where have you been? I’ve been looking everywhere for you.”

“I’m sure you have,” he grumbles in a low voice, mumbling something under his breath that I can’t quite make out. Something about not being attached to Mason’s face? I don’t understand, and I don’t give a shit.

“I just wanted a bottle of water,” I explain wearily, baffled by how this is turning into such an issue, but he’s the only one who’s been halfway decent to me. Maybe he can convince Hawk to part with a bottle of his precious water.

His eyes flick from me to Hawk before his lips pinch, an apologetic look flashing across his face before he carefully masks it, shrugging his shoulders.

Is he for fucking real?! Fucking jackass.

Fuck this shit.

“I wouldn’t suck your disease-riddled pocket prick if it saved my life,” I snarl, glaring darkly at Hawk before I turn my back on the whole fucking group of them, striding over to where a passed out Emilia sits. I wrap my arm around her waist and haul her to her feet, ignoring the groan of protest from her. *Please don’t puke all over me. I’ll be seriously pissed if you do.*

Feeling each of their eyes on me, I drag her away from the party and back to the dorms, silently cursing each and every Prick with every step. Yes, I may have said it in jest on Monday, but the whole fucking lot of them deserve the title.

With a serious amount of effort, I manage to haul Emilia's dead weight back to the dorms and into her bed, removing her shoes before tucking her in.

"Thought it was a date," she mumbles in her sleep, her words not making any sense.

"What?" I ask, confused. Was she supposed to be on a date tonight? Why didn't she tell me?

"Michael...You."

"What?" I repeat more urgently. What did she just say? She's drunk, she's not making sense, she doesn't understand what she's saying...right? There's no way tonight was meant to be a date. I mean, I'd know if I was on a date, wouldn't I? Would I?

My brows furrow as I think back to last night in the dining hall with him. Was *that* a date? He mentioned the party tonight, but he didn't actually ask me to go with him....but he did ask me if I *wanted* to go. I thought he meant as, like, a group. Did he mean it as a date? If Emilia's drunken self is right, then yeah, that's exactly what he meant. How could I have missed that?

With a despairing groan, I close her bedroom door, slinking across the hallway and silently letting myself into my own room. What a fucking shitshow of an evening.

Hadley

Chapter 7

It's barely eight a.m. but Emilia's drunken words have played on repeat in my head all night. I need to know for sure what she was talking about, because I have enough shit to deal with, with the Pricks, nevermind throwing dates I'm apparently clueless about into the mix.

"What?" Emilia whines when she finally answers the door. She's still in last night's clothes, her dark hair a bedraggled mess, and her makeup smeared across her face. "I'm dying today, come back tomorrow." She goes to shut the door, but I wedge my boot in the opening, preventing her.

She doesn't even seem to notice me doing it, instead staring at the door in confusion before giving up and leaving it open, sluggishly stumbling back over to the bed and collapsing into it.

"Time to get up," I demand. "We have shit to discuss."

"Ugh, no," she mumbles, her voice barely audible through the pillow she's buried her face in.

"Yup," I enforce. "Go shower and we'll grab breakfast. You'll feel worlds better."

She mumbles something unintelligible. I'm pretty sure she's cursing me out, but when she still makes no effort to get up, I decide to add an incentive. "I'll tell you all about my run-in with the Pricks last night."

That gets her attention, and her head snaps off the pillow so fast I'm surprised she doesn't give herself whiplash. "What happened?" she exclaims, her eyes bright with intrigue, her hangover clearly forgotten.

"Go shower, and I'll tell you."

Half an hour later, we're sitting at our usual table with enough food between us to feed a third world country.

"Spill," she demands, nursing her coffee like it's a lifeline.

I quickly rehash last night's events, watching as her eyes grow wider with every word.

"I'm sorry," she apologizes when I'm finished. "That's all my fault."

"What? No, it isn't," I insist, shaking my head fervently. "You didn't make them act like shitheads. That's all on them."

I sigh, pursing my lips as I roll my eyes. "I'm just annoyed that I misjudged Wes so bad. I thought he was a decent guy, but all of them are just as bad as each other."

She gives me a sympathetic look before her brows furrow. "Wes?"

"Ah, yeah," I chuckle. "Apparently he hates it, so I've decided it's exactly what I'm going to call him."

"Even to his face?" she gasps, wide-eyed.

"Yup."

"Girl, you are going to get yourself in serious trouble if you antagonize them."

Giving her a flat look, I brazenly state, "Maybe they should have thought about that before pissing me off."

The look Emilia gives me says everything about how reckless she thinks I'm being, but I'm not one to back down. I'm not going to go after them, but I won't allow them to steam roll all over me either. Enough people have tried to tear me down in my life; I'm not about to let some control-obsessed teenage boys get the better of me.

We're finishing off the last scraps of breakfast, my stomach nearly bursting when I broach the subject of Michael. "So," I begin hesitantly, flicking my gaze up to look at her, "you mentioned something last night."

"Girl, whatever I said, just ignore it. It was the ramblings of a drunken idiot." She laughs, waving me off.

"You said something about Michael thinking last night was a date?" I blurt out before I can talk myself out of it.

She pauses with her mug halfway raised to her lips, her mouth falling open as she stares at me before she cringes. "I did?"

"You did."

She sighs, setting the mug back down on the table. "Eh, yeah. He might have said something to me yesterday about how he asked you to the party, but you never brought it up, and it was clear last night that you weren't exactly on the same page as him."

Burying my face in my hands, I release a frustrated groan.

"How did I not know it was supposed to be a date?" I grumble. "I've been playing our conversation from Thursday night over in my head and, I mean, I may have missed some cues, but it's not like he outrightly said, 'Hadley, will you go on a date with me?' How was I supposed to know?"

She gives an empathetic chuckle. "I dunno, girl. Don't stress, though. I think he realized how clueless you were. He'll ask you again, and next time you'll *know* what he's getting at."

"Wait. What? He's going to ask me again?" I shriek in an embarrassingly shrill voice. I like to think I'm a cool badass bitch most of the time. I've definitely dealt with shit that would have most of the kids in this fancy-ass school shitting their pants, but give me a high school boy that has a crush on me and I don't have a fucking clue.

I lost my virginity last year to some biker dude in a back alley. I never even got his name; and all my *wham-bam-thank-you-ma'ams* since have been the same. I've spent a decent portion of my teenage years in seedy bars and dodgy warehouses, trying to make a buck so I could survive. They don't exactly come with the typical sweet, innocent boy most girls probably end up with for their first time, but, for the most part they know how to use god's gift between their legs.

"Why would he do that? He doesn't even know me," I insist, but even as I say it, the little demon voice in my head argues that I don't know any of the Pricks and I have—had—some sort of strange reaction to them. Now that I've affirmed they're shitheads, I'm sure whatever that was has fizzled out. Even so, I don't know them, and they had that allure over me. I've definitely had several vibrator sessions thinking about Cam and how talented his fingers most likely are. You don't actually have to *know* someone to be attracted to them. Hell, if I've learned anything this past week, it's that you don't even have to like whoever you're attracted to. Hormones are a fickle thing.

Chuckling, Emilia shakes her head, rolling her eyes at me. "The whole point of dating someone is to get to know them. He obviously likes what he's seen so far, and he's clearly attracted to you."

"He is?" How did I not know that? I mean, I know Cam finds me attractive—he's blatantly obvious about it, but I had no idea Michael felt the same way. Maybe I'm just not used to subtle gestures, or the way teenage boys flirt?

When I've picked up guys before, it's always been in dark, dingy bars, with guys willing to sink their dicks in just about anything, so it's not like I needed to have any game or make an impression. Literally, all you had to do was bat your eyes in a guy's direction and he'd drop his pants. When a man did approach me, it was painfully obvious what he was after.

The problem is, Michael wants more than just sex. Even Cam, while all he wants is sex, is problematic. I've never had sex with someone I had to ever see again. Nameless, faceless sex I can do. That's right up my street, but anything more than that, especially dating someone? Spending time with them? That's really not my thing. From what I've learned about Michael, he's quiet, shy, innocent. He's not like me at all.

Emilia must be able to see my internal panic written all over my face as she bursts out laughing. "Girl, you're totally overthinking it. Ask yourself, are you attracted to him?"

I pull up his image in my mind's eye, picturing his short-cut dark hair and wiry frame. He's not unattractive, but there's no swirling in my lower abdomen, no fluttering as my heart rate increases. There's definitely not the same intense, indescribable reaction that I get in the Pricks' presence.

"No. I'm not."

"Then next time he asks, just let him down gently."

We spend the rest of the day spread out on the lawn catching up on homework while enjoying the last rays of sun before the seasons change, only making a move to head indoors when the sun starts to set.

That night we walk over to the rec center with the others for yet another movie night. Tonight is Mary's turn to pick the movie, and she chooses some romcom I've never seen before. Turns out romantic comedies are not my thing—way too sappy and dull. Where's all the action? Not that I get the chance to focus much on the movie, with my stomach in knots, worried Michael is going to want to talk to me. I haven't worked out what to say to him yet. I don't want to hurt his feelings, or say the wrong thing. The tension only drops out of my shoulders when we say goodnight to the guys, Michael giving me a soft smile when we part ways.

***

“Hey, girl,” Emilia greets, dropping into the chair beside me at our usual table in the dining hall. “Everything okay?”

“Yeah,” I assure her. “I just couldn’t sleep, so I thought I’d come for breakfast early.” I tossed and turned all night, not that I usually sleep all that well, but last night was particularly bad.

Every year has a time slot for breakfast, with seniors getting the last one right before classes begin. Most students turn up not long before class, which, unsurprisingly, is also when the Pricks tend to arrive, so this morning I decided I was in no mood to watch their usual routine, and made sure I was here just as the slot for seniors began.

I messaged Emilia before I left so she would know where I was if she came looking for me, which, it seems, she did.

“If you’re worried about the Princes…” she begins, but I shake my head, cutting her off.

“I’m not. Not really. I’m not afraid of them, I just don’t want any of their drama. I’m here to do the work, so I can have the future I want. I’m not about to let wayward hormones or devilishly handsome teenage boys interfere with my plans,” I joke.

“Right.” She laughs before growing serious. “But after Friday, Hawk’s going to be pissed.”

He’s pissed? *I’m* fucking pissed!

I shrug my shoulders, not giving a shit about how he’s feeling. “So? He can be pissy all he wants, so long as he leaves me alone.”

She sighs, resigned. “Just don’t do something that will only get you into more trouble with them.

The hall slowly fills up over the next half hour and just before the time the Pricks usually arrive, I slide out of my seat, deciding I'd rather be ridiculously early to English than have to force myself not to spend all of breakfast watching them.

I saunter through the relatively empty corridors, slowly making my way to Mr. Greer's classroom, and by the time everyone else filters in, I'm sitting there, ready to begin.

Bianca throws a glare in my direction as she enters, but I pay her no mind. What the fuck is her problem, anyway? Is she seriously still annoyed about last week? Has Cam not fucked her good enough to forget about it?

"Morning, beautiful," Cam purrs as he slides into the seat beside me. Ignoring him, I stare pointedly at my black tablet screen until he sighs. "Okay, I get it, you're pissed." After a moment's hesitation, when he still gets no response from me, he continues, "It's complicated."

"Complicated?" I snort, turning to face him. "It was a bottle of water."

"It wasn't about the water. I mean, it was...but it wasn't."

He's not making any sense and I just roll my eyes at him, returning my attention to the desk once again.

"Look," he begins, leaning in so no one around us can overhear our conversation, "it was about more than just the water. In front of everyone else at this school, we have to present a united front. Yes, even over something as stupid as a bottle of water." He tacks on before I can interject. "With the girls watching, there was nothing I could do."

I give him a disbelieving look out of the corner of my eye. "So, you're saying if the girls weren't there you'd have given me the water?"

"I'm saying it wouldn't have been such a big deal," he responds immediately. He sounds sincere, but he could simply be telling me what he thinks I want to hear.

"Unfortunately, words mean nothing when you can't back them up," I retort, not trusting a thing he says.

I'm still side-eyeing him, watching him closely, so I catch the pained expression that flashes across his face before he masks it. "For what it's worth, I'm sorry. Hawk was being a dickhead for no good reason. You managed to piss him off good with whatever happened between you in the hall last week."

My head snaps around so I can glare at him. "Nothing happened between us," I bark. "Just because I didn't back down from him like everyone else here does, doesn't give him the right to act the way he did."

Cam just nods his head, not saying anything, and thankfully the teacher brings the class to order, beginning the lesson before I can do something stupid like strangle him with my bare hands in front of all these witnesses.

For the next hour, I feel Cam constantly glancing my way, his leg bouncing annoyingly under the table. I can tell he wants to say more, but he has the foresight to realize I'm not in an understanding mood.

"Don't forget you need to be working on your projects outside of class hours," Mr. Greer calls out as the bell rings and everyone starts packing up. Fucking hell, how did I forget about the damn project?

"Meet me in the library after class tomorrow," I tell Cam as I shove my things back in my bag, walking off before he can argue with me.

"Damn girl, that looked intense," Emilia says, catching up to me in the hall. I just shake my head, not wanting to talk about it. I don't have any of them in the rest of my classes today and I refuse to spend one more moment talking, or even thinking, about them.

"It was nothing, just sorting out our English assignment."

"Uh-huh." She lets the topic slide and we soon part ways as she heads off to music and I go to my math class.

The next afternoon, I push open the library door, walking past the manned front desk and spotting Cam sitting alone at a table in the far corner of the room. I make my way through the large, circular tables, some of which have students working away at them, letting the hush of quiet conversations wash over me as I drop into the chair beside him.

"Hadley," he purrs, his voice thick and raspy in a way that makes my insides do stupid things. "Looking fine as always." He's clearly back to his usual flirty ways, his remorse over Friday long forgotten.

"We need to sort this assignment out," I snap, getting straight to the point. "Did you read the book?" It's the only thing we've managed to sort out so far, although I don't for one second believe he's read it.

"Of course I did!" he gasps in mock outrage, his hand clasping his chest. I don't believe him, but whatever. As long as he does his half of the work and it's solid enough to pass, I don't give a fuck.

"Okay, I'll write the critical analysis of the book, and you can compare it to others from that time period."

"I'll do whatever you want me to do," he replies, his tone suggestive.

For fuck's sake, Hadley, don't fall for it. Remember, he's a dickwad.

Glancing at him, I bite my lower lip as I cross my legs, 'accidentally' grazing them against his as I lean in. A sense of satisfaction courses through me as his pupils dilate, eating me up. Giving him my best seductive look, I lower my voice and breathe out, "I want...you to write your half of the book report." Pulling back abruptly, I lift out my notebook, flicking through the notes I made while I was reading the book.

I can feel Cam gaping at me before his wits finally return to him and he barks out a laugh, shaking his head like he can't believe he fell for my act before pulling out his tablet and finally getting into the assignment. We work in silence until someone drops into one of the spare chairs at the table.

"What are you doing here?" West asks in a suspicious tone, like I'm doing something I shouldn't be. We haven't spoken since the party, not that I have anything to say to him. Glancing at Cam's work, he returns his gaze to me. "You're not doing his homework for him, are you?"

"What?" I can't do anything but gape at him. Why would he even think that? "Definitely not, *Wes*," I snark, not appreciating the inference that I'd willingly be someone's homework bitch.

His eyebrows raise in surprise, his lips pinching at my new name for him. He didn't like Brittany calling him that at the party, so I'm betting he won't be too pleased at me using it either, but I sure as hell won't let his pissy personality put me off.

"We're working on an English assignment together," Cam explains.

"Of course you are," West drawls. "Just don't forget about Bianca. Whatever you're doing, you should keep it on the down low."

"Excuse me?" I sneer, pissed off at his insinuation. Even worse than people thinking I'm Cam's homework bitch is people thinking I'm his side piece. Regardless of how unofficial he thinks his monthly girls are, he is basically publicly dating Bianca, and I don't want to be anyone's dirty little secret. "We're not *doing* anything." When he just continues to look at me, like I'm bullshitting him, I spell it out for him, "I'm not fucking sleeping with him."

After another long, intense stare, West shrugs, offering a half-assed apology. "Sorry, that's just his MO."

"Dude," Cam hisses. "Shut the fuck up."

I'm clearly missing something between them, but whatever.

"You really think after your dickish behavior at the party last week, I'd be interested in any of you?"

"I apologized for that," Cam exclaims.

"That doesn't make it right."

West leans in closer, casting a surreptitious look at the other students around us before saying, "Look, we have to put up a united front when we're around others. We can't let anyone see any rifts or disagreements. It's nothing personal."

I just shake my head, not understanding him. It's basically the same crap Cam spouted, but I really don't get this whole social politicking. Who cares if they all agree or disagree on something? What does any of it really matter?

Ignoring the pair of them before I end up doing something I regret, I get back to work until two more assholes join us at the table.

Yay, the gang's all here now.

Mason stares at me with his sky-blue eyes for a long moment, but doesn't say anything before glancing away. He's the hardest one to gauge. I never know what he's thinking. Sometimes I catch him staring at me, just like he was doing there now, but I don't know what to make of it. Hawk, on the other hand, glowers at me. "What is *she* doing here?" *Fucking asshole.*

"We're working on a project together," Cam reiterates, barely sparing Hawk a glance, completely unfazed by his attitude.

I really don't get what his problem is. He doesn't even know me. He can't seriously be that annoyed over our run-in last week. What mentally stable person holds such an intense grudge over a complete accident?

I've been watching him closely since the party, and he's the grumpiest dickhead I've ever met. He's surly, and he snaps at pretty much everyone around him. I don't know how Melissa puts up with him—although from what I've seen, they do nothing but make out and grope each other when they're together. I guess he can't say something shitty when her tongue is rammed down his throat.

The four of them settle down to get busy with their own work, occasionally sharing the odd comment before lapsing into silence again.

After about an hour, a rustling noise gets my attention and I look up as Cam empties an entire bag of skittles into the middle of the table.

Seeing the confused look on my face, he gestures to the pile, "Help yourself."

Leaning forward, I stretch my arm across the table until I can grab a couple of green skittles, but a hand snaps out and grabs my wrist before I can pull it back.

"The green ones are mine," Hawk snarls.

Fuck me, are we seriously doing this shit again?

Staring at him with wide eyes, aware of everyone around the table watching us, I give a hesitant nod. "Okay."

Releasing my hand, I make as though I'm going to set the candy back on the table, but at the last second, I pick up the last few green ones and shove all of them into my mouth before anyone can stop me, flashing Hawk a toothy grin across the table.

"Mmm, yummy. The green ones are my favorite."

The table is deathly quiet for a second before Cam bursts out laughing. "Fuck, I can't believe you did that, he's definitely going to kill you now."

I give a shrug of my shoulder, which only serves to annoy Hawk further as his hand clenches tightly around his stylus, threatening to snap it.

"There are plenty of other flavors," I appease, waving toward the candy.

"He only likes the green ones," West explains.

"Huh." Well, you snooze, you lose.

Hadley

Chapter 8

The rest of the week passes in a blur of school work. There're literally not enough hours in the day to do everything they ask of us. Plus, Hawk has taken to openly glaring at me when we pass in the halls, and students are starting to whisper.

“What's going on with you and the Princes?” Abigail asks on Saturday night at our weekly movie night.

“Nothing.” I shrug, not really wanting to get into it.

“There must be something,” Samuel insists. “Bianca is going around telling everyone you're trying to steal Cam from her, and Hawk looks at you like he wants to rip your head off.”

“Bianca is what?!” I gasp. How have I not heard of this? As for Hawk, well, that makes two of us.

"Sorry, girl," Emilia says sympathetically, cringing when I turn to look at her. "I heard it for the first time today. I was going to tell you later."

The audacity of that bitch!

"For the record, I am *not* trying to steal Cam from her. She's just annoyed that we're working on an assignment together." We've spent all week in the library, trying to hammer out this project, but unless it's work related, we don't talk. He finally seems to have coped on to the fact I'm angry with him.

"Pfft." Samuel snorts. "Cam never does his own work. If he's spending time with you, it's because he wants in your pants."

"Samuel," Mary scolds. "You don't need to be so crass about it."

"What? It's not like it's not true." He shrugs unapologetically. "She's good-looking. Of course he'd try it on the new girl."

"It's really not like that," I assure them, but based on the dubious looks I'm getting, no one believes me.

"Well, what about Hawk?" Mary asks.

Rolling my eyes, I rehash my run-in with Hawk last week. By the end of it, everyone except Emilia, who has already heard the story, is gaping at me.

"It was just an accident," I reiterate, confused by their expressions. Why is everyone making such a big deal out of this? So what?

"You're so screwed," Mary gasps. "You better keep your head down and stay out of the Princes' way."

"Why?" I don't get it. Emilia has expressed concern several times, and begged me not to antagonize them, but seeing everyone else looking worried has me on edge. "He's just one person. What can he possibly do?"

With wide eyes, Abigail shakes her head. "Nu-uh, if Hawk decides he doesn't like you, you're done for. Last year, Greg knocked into Cam while he and his friends were messing around on the lawn. He knocked him to the ground, but that was it. It's not like he hurt him or anything, but all four of them ganged up against him, claiming he had disrespected them. He was gone by the end of the month."

"What do you mean he was gone?" They can't have that power. What could they possibly do to him?

"He left. Dropped out of school."

As if that isn't disturbing, Samuel adds on, "If you do anything to one of them or if one of them decides they don't like you, the others will back him up. They support each other in everything."

Remembering the way the others sided with Hawk over the whole water incident, and West's words about presenting a 'united front', their meaning is suddenly clear.

"I have no intention of pissing Hawk off any further," I assure them all, making a mental note to try and stick to that promise. I plan on staying as far away from him as possible—we only have one class together, so it shouldn't be that difficult.

We all settle in to watch the movie after that, but there's a tension in the air that wasn't there before and when we're walking back to the dorms, Michael, who hadn't said a word all night, falls into step beside me.

"You need to be careful around the Princes," he warns. "I don't want them starting a witch hunt against you."

I give him a soft smile. He really is a sweet boy, a good person, not at all like the complicated, convoluted Princes. If only I could be attracted to him like any normal girl, but I think the last of my sanity left me the day I entered Pac Prep.

"I can look after myself," I assure him.

"I'm sure you can," he agrees. "Just...don't trust them. They don't care about anyone but themselves."

"I don't," I promise just before we part ways.

***

It's late on Sunday night when the sound of my tablet vibrating from within my bag distracts me from the business homework I'm finishing off. Fishing it out, the notifications show a new message from Cam.

Everyone has phones here, but they seem to prefer using the school's own messaging app on the tablet to communicate with one another.

Cam: *Are you up?*

I consider ignoring him. It's after midnight, for all he knows I could easily be asleep by now, however the tablet goes off again, vibrating in my hand as another incoming message pops up.

Cam: *I'm stuck on our English assignment.*

He's probably lying to get me to show up. We basically had the whole thing wrapped up last week, but it's due tomorrow and I've put a lot of effort into my half of it, so I don't want his annoying ass dragging my mark down.

Me: *Meet me in the dining hall in 5.*

It's the only part of campus open at this time of night, and I'm sure as hell not going to bring him here. Stuffing my feet into my boots, I cast a quick glance in the mirror, my lycra leggings and hoodie more than sufficient, given the late hour. The tablet chimes again as I walk out of my room.

Cam: *Already here.*

Pulling open the door of the dining hall, the place is empty, except for Cam sitting at the Pricks' usual table at the far side of the room. Going over to the coffee bar, I make myself a strong coffee and drop into a seat opposite him, taking a second to see what the view of the hall is like from here. I'm taken by surprise to see it looks exactly the same as it does from the scholarship table. I don't know what I thought it would be like, but it's disappointing.

"Not what you expected?" Cam asks, watching me closely.

"No," I admit. "I thought it would be...different." I guess I thought it would be more impressive? That I'd feel more important?

"Yeah." Cam sighs. "Everyone thinks that."

Turning to face him, he looks completely different than he does during the day. Sure, I've seen him and the others here late at night before, but I'm usually sneaking furtive glances their way, never really able to check him out this closely. His blond hair is rumpled, like he's been running his hand through it all day, and his baby blue t-shirt strains against his defined muscles, giving me an up-close and personal view of just how ripped he is underneath his uniform.

"But if they knew what it was really like to be us, they'd quickly change their mind."

His words remind me he's not just a slab of meat for me to drool over, especially when he's being strangely open with me. Looking past his insanely good looks, I can see how tired he is, like life has worn him down, but how can that be possible? Don't guys like him have everything? I mean, look around us. He's basically the king of this campus. He can do whatever he wants, get any girl he wants. His family is loaded, so it's not like he ever has to worry about supporting himself or even finding a job. How much easier could his life get?

I really don't have any sympathy for him, yet that haunted look in his eyes resonates with me, suggesting there's something I'm not understanding, something about who he and the others are that I'm not seeing.

"What's it like to be you?"

The corner of his lip tips up in a smirk as his barrier slides back into place, cutting me off from whatever it was I was seeing. "Let's just say it's not all parties and pussy."

I don't know what to say to that. From what I can tell, that's exactly what it looks like.

Sensing he won't tell me anything more, I change the topic. "What do you need help with?"

Without a word, he taps on his tablet, turning it around so I can see. "Can you just read over these few paragraphs, I'm not sure I've got it quite right."

I'm taken aback, not expecting him to actually want to discuss homework, certain this whole thing was a ploy just to get me alone.

"Uh, yeah. Sure."

Pulling the tablet toward me, we sit in silence while I read over what he's written, becoming more impressed by the minute. Not only has he done the work, but he's done one hell of a job.

"Cam, this is really good," I praise him. "I'd maybe swap these two paragraphs around, but other than that, it reads really well."

Nodding his head, he does as I suggest, re-reading it. "Yeah, thanks. That reads better."

Sipping on my coffee, I nod in acknowledgement, not knowing what to say. There's something about him tonight. He's different than normal. He's dropped the flirty air and seems more vulnerable.

"Why did you come to Pac?" The question catches me by surprise, but of course, someone like him doesn't understand the desperate need to escape your current situation, to want to be better, do something *more* with your life.

"I couldn't live the life I saw unfolding before me," I respond honestly. "I needed to escape, to find who I am and lay out a future for myself that I want, that I can be proud of."

He nods, like he understands what I'm saying, but I don't know if he really gets it or not.

“I hope you find what you’re looking for.”

Scanning his face, I see nothing but sincerity there.

“You and the others, how long have you been friends?”

“Our whole lives. Our parents are all friends, and our families co-own a business. We all grew up in the same community.”

“Huh. That must have been nice.”

“It was,” he agrees absently. “You might not believe it, but Hawk was a surly asshole as a kid.”

“No way!” I gasp in fake shock. “I can’t imagine that, he’s such a cheery guy.”

“Ha, right?” Cam laughs, his face lighting up with whatever memory he’s thinking about. “When we were about nine or ten, I poured blue dye in his swimming pool.” He barely gets the words out between fits of laughter. “The asshole was blue from head to toe for nearly a month. He looked like a smurf.”

“Oh my God.” I laugh along with him, not requiring much imagination to picture Hawk raging up a storm.

“It didn’t matter what his parents did, they couldn’t get it to wash off. We were always pulling pranks like that on each other.” There’s a fond smile on his face as he falls into the past, recalling old memories.

“And your parents were okay with stuff like that?”

He shrugs his shoulders. “None of them are really around all that much. So long as we don’t publicly humiliate them, and agree to work at the firm when we graduate, they generally don’t care.”

“Do you want to go into the family business?”

“Not particularly. None of us really do, but it’s not something we can simply turn down.”

"How come? There are people out there that would sell their souls to be given such an opportunity."

He releases a defeated chuckle. "God, I probably sound like an entitled jerk right now."

"You don't," I assure him. When he just gives me a dubious look, I release a chuckle. "Yeah, okay, maybe a little."

Barking out a laugh, he gives me a small, genuine smile that's so much more enticing than any flirty grin he could throw my way. It's real, and it feels like some sort of achievement, like, in a rare moment of openness, he's showing me his true self.

"It's just..." He trails off, struggling to find the right wording.

"Complicated?" I supply, recalling his words when he tried to explain why he behaved the way he did the night of the party.

"Yeah." He sighs. "I know you don't get it, and I can't explain it to you. There's a lot of pressure on us from our parents and we..." He once again trails off, sighing as he runs his hand through his hair in frustration, unsure of his next words.

Seeing how much he's struggling, wanting to remain loyal to his friends, I shake my head. "You don't have to explain yourself to me."

Giving a sharp nod of his head, understanding passes between us.

"I guess I should let you get some sleep." He gives me a soft smile, picking up his tablet and getting to his feet. Following him, we walk to the door, but he pauses before pushing it open.

"You know, you're different from anyone else here." That same raw honesty is clear to see in his eyes as they roam over my face, like he's trying to memorize my features.

"How so?"

"I can guarantee you, if asked why they were here, none of them would say they wanted to become someone they could be proud of. They might not say it out loud, but everyone is here for selfish reasons. Whether it's money, familial obligation, or to find a rich husband, not one of them would give me the answer you did."

I don't know what to say to that. I'm not sure I agree with him, I've gotten to know Emilia and she's the least selfish person I know. She's only here so she can provide for her mother. Isn't that the same with all the scholarship students? Sure, I've heard some of them discussing how, thanks to Pac, they have acceptances to top line colleges, and talking about high-flying careers, but isn't that all part of bettering themselves? They just seem to have more of an idea as to what they want to do with their futures. I know I don't need a kickass career and money in the bank. I just want to be free to be me, to earn enough to be comfortable and be happy doing it, but beyond that, I haven't really figured my shit out yet.

***

On Monday night, I once again find myself walking toward the dining hall. I'm telling myself it's because I want some ice cream, but there's this pathetic little part of me that's hoping I'll run into Cam. Despite how much I try to tamp it down, part of me can't stop obsessing over him. That moment we shared last night seemed to change things, and today he was different. Don't get me wrong, he was flirting away in his usual fashion, but it felt more genuine than it did before. Like he wasn't just doing it because he's 'the flirty guy', but because he had a true interest in me. I'm most likely reading way too much into it, but the riot of butterflies in my stomach and this incessant need to watch him won't let me get over him.

Pulling open the dining hall door, I pause in the entrance. Cameron Rutherford is sitting at the *scholarship* students' table. Skipping the coffee this time, I head toward him.

"Well? Is it what you expected?" I ask, reiterating his words from last night.

"No," he admits, giving a small shake of his head. "It's better."

His words take me by surprise, something he must be able to read on my face, as he explains, "You're more hidden back here. It doesn't feel like you're on display the same way our table does. Back here, you're just a faceless person in the crowd. There's something to be said for not having people watching you all the time, judging your every move."

I have nothing to say to that, but Cam doesn't let us sit in silence for long.

"I wasn't sure if you'd show up."

Licking my lips, nerves flit through me. I don't know what we're doing here, flirting with danger. Neither of us should be doing this—whatever *this* is. It's asking for trouble.

"Tell me more about you and the guys growing up."

"Why?"

Shrugging my shoulders, I give him the honest truth. "I never had siblings, or anyone to muck around with. I guess I wanna hear what it was like to have that."

Nodding his head in understanding, he thinks for a moment before his lip lifts in a small smile.

"Our parents own summer houses up in the mountains, right by a lake. Every year the guys and I head up there for a few weeks, just to get away for a bit.

"A few years ago, we were out swimming in the lake, fucking around as usual. West was always more hesitant than the rest of us. It would take forever for us to coax him into the water. He was terrified of getting caught up in the reeds."

A sly grin crosses his face and I can immediately guess what he did. "You didn't?" I chuckle.

Cam lets out the most genuine, carefree laugh I've heard from him yet. "Oh, I did." He chuckles, bobbing his eyebrows. Everything about him screams mischief. I can only imagine he's kept the others on their toes all these years.

"Anyway, we finally got him out to the middle of the lake and while Mason and Hawk distracted him, I ducked under, grabbing a hold of his feet. Man, he screamed bloody murder, kicked me right in the face too. I had a shiner for weeks after that."

"Sounds like you deserved it." I laugh along with him.

"I love that lake, it's where I learned to swim. I've some of the best memories of my life up there."

"Do you still swim?"

"Yup," he says proudly. "I'm captain of the swim team. If all goes well, I'll be heading to the State Championships this year."

"Wow, that's incredible." I don't really know what that means, but it's clearly something he's excited for and cares a lot about.

"Your parents must be so proud of you."

"Yeah." He snorts. "I'm sure they're super proud." The words drip with sarcasm, my eyes narrowing in confusion. How could parents not be proud of a son like Cam? He's clearly liked, more so than the other Pricks. He does well in school and he's good at sports? What's not to be proud of?

"My parents couldn't care less about me," he admits after a moment. "My father is never around, unless it's to come to my competitions, but it's just so he can remind me that *Rutherfords are winners.*"

The lightness in his eyes from earlier is gone, his laugh lines faded, his face withdrawn as he stares glumly at the tabletop.

"I'm sorry." My voice is soft as I reach across the table, giving his hand a quick squeeze, ignoring the way his skin feels against mine and how even that simple touch causes my breath to hitch, my heart hammering in my chest.

For the rest of the week, every night at midnight, I pull open the dining hall door to find Cam waiting for me, even though every alarm bell is going off in my head, telling me I shouldn't be encouraging this.

On Friday night, I step into the hall, once again expecting to find him there...only the room is empty. *Huh.* Grabbing a tub of ice cream—this time deciding to try a cookies and cream flavored one—I take a seat at the scholarship table, where I usually find Cam sitting, ignoring the sinking pit in my stomach at the thought of him not coming.

It's nearly an hour later—I know, I shouldn't still be sitting here, it's pathetic—when the door creaks open, but it's not who I was expecting.

Mason storms into the room, stomping toward the freezer, lifting out a bag of ice. Turning around to head back out, he freezes in place, spotting me. Yeah, I must look like a weirdo sitting here alone in the middle of the night.

"What are you doing here?" he demands, his voice coming out as a growl as I climb to my feet.

"Just enjoying some late night ice cream." Holding up the empty tub for him to see before I deposit it in the trash, I glance down, noticing his knuckles are all scraped and covered in blood. "What are *you* doing here?"

"That's none of your goddamn business," he snarks, his temper clearly not much better than Hawk's.

"Whatever." I shrug. "But you're going to have a hard job holding that ice to both sets of knuckles at once."

He makes no effort to move or respond, simply continuing to stare at me with a mixture of hate and confusion. I can practically hear the static intensity of the energy around us, like an invisible force pushing us together.

After a moment, I sigh, rolling my eyes. "Come here." Before he can refuse, I snatch the bag of ice out of his hand and grab some napkins, walking over to the closest table. Opening it, I wrap a few cubes of ice in the napkin, giving him a look that says 'what are you waiting for?' when he remains frozen in place. It takes a moment before he unglues his feet from the floor, coming to sit on the opposite side of the table, facing me.

This close, I can see the flecks of blood dusting his knuckles, both hands looking worse for wear than they did from further away. With both his hands lying flat on the table, I press one of the ice-filled napkins against his knuckles, a startled gasp escaping me when our skin touches, a static charge jumping between us before he pulls his hand back slightly, breaking the contact. With wide eyes, I stare up into his bright blue ones, swirling with confusion that's matched by the intense way he's looking at me, like I'm an enigma to him, his brows pulled down as he tries to suss me out.

Coughing to clear the lump in my throat, I murmur, "Sorry," making sure I don't touch him as I once again place the napkin on his knuckles before doing the same to his other hand.

It's only once I no longer have something to keep me occupied I realize how fucking awkward this is. I don't even know this guy, and I'm beginning to feel like a bug under a microscope with the way he keeps staring at me. *I can't be that bloody interesting to look at.*

After an awkward fifteen minutes where neither of us says anything, I remove the ice from his knuckles, using the now wet napkin to wipe away the blood until they almost look good as new.

Licking my dry lips, I keep my focus on gathering up the napkins and grabbing the bag of ice. "There you go. All done."

He *still* says nothing and, after another uneasy moment, I give a stiff nod and get up, dumping everything in the trash and head out, leaving the mindboggling Prick behind.

The next morning, I wake up to a new message from Cam.

Cam: *Sorry about last night. Something came up.*

Why do I get the impression that 'something' is the same reason Mason's knuckles were busted?

Hadley

Chapter 9

My least favorite class of the week is gym. From the grumblings of the other girls in the changing room, I'm not the only one. The problem is, it's not the actual physical exercise I dislike. I enjoy the class, although, apparently parents kicked up a fuss about their little princesses having to appear a sweaty mess in front of the boys in our year, so now the girls do yoga and pilates, while the guys get to do whatever they want, basically. Even so, it's still enjoyable.

No, my problem is with the pre-and-post-gym changing routine. I always make sure I arrive early, ducking into a stall to change into a baggy top and yoga pants before anyone else shows up, and thankfully gym is the last class of the day, so as soon as it's done, I grab my stuff and get out of there, showering back in the dorms, instead of in sight of the rest of the girls.

As I grab my clothes from my locker, I can hear the other girls whispering, wondering why I'm so weird. Just because I don't have the same desire to strip in front of them all and have them judge me, picking out their perceived faults and laughing at them. Emilia, Mary, and Abigail quickly copped on to my strange routine, but thankfully they haven't said anything about it. They seem to be the only ones though, as each week the whispers become more and more prominent.

"What is she hiding?"

"Why does she refuse to shower?"

"I bet she's got, like, a horrible skin condition or something."

For the most part, I tune them out. Who cares what they say? They're vapid girls with nothing better to discuss. Unfortunately, Bianca has decided to make it my problem, as she and the other three girls of the month block my escape out of the locker room after class.

"Where are you always running off to after gym?" she snarks, her arms folded across her chest, pushing up her tits that are already barely restrained by the thin, stretchy fabric of her sports bra.

"Why do you care?" I sigh, not in the mood to deal with this today. At this point, the entire school thinks I'm fucking Cam, and based on the dark looks being thrown my way, no one is too happy about it. I'm seriously starting to think I should just fuck him. If I'm going to be accused of doing just that, I may as well get something out of it, right? "Making sure I'm not running off to see Cam?"

Her face darkens at that thought, her eyes drilling into me. I don't know if she actually thinks I am sleeping with him, or if it's just a rumor she started to gain some sympathy.

"Stay away from Cam," she snarls. "He's mine."

"Yeah." I snort. "For like another week, but then some other girl is gonna be warming his bed at night."

Her lip curls up in disgust, but she doesn't argue with me, knowing I'm right. Instead, she takes a step forward so we're toe-to-toe. "Maybe so, but it will never be you."

What she doesn't get, though, is that I have no real interest in Cam. Yeah, he's smoking hot, and one look in my direction has my body fired up and willing to do whatever he wants to me, but I don't want to *be* with him. I'm not made for the rich, pampered life that would come with being with someone like him. I don't want the spotlight on me, all that attention. While it seems to be what most of the girls here are after, it's not me. I live in the dark, move silently in the shadows. It's where I'm comfortable, where I belong.

My casual shrug seems to do nothing but confuse her, as she most likely expected another snarky retort, but I don't have space in my life for such petty drama.

I move to step around her, but she snatches my wrist, her nails digging into the skin. "You're reaching above your station. Stick to the scholarship boys. Trash should only date trash after all."

Throwing a final glare her way, I yank my hand out of her grip—she should be fucking thankful that's all I do—and storm out of the locker room, leaving the lot of them whispering behind me.

I'm still in a rotten mood the next day when I arrive at computer science, not helped by the fact I *hate* this class. I have no fucking clue what I'm doing and the online lesson plans may as well be written in French for all I can comprehend of them. So it's safe to say this class is kicking my butt.

I've actively avoided sitting anywhere near West since the party, but today I have to suck it up and ask for his help because I'm seriously at risk of failing if I continue on the way I am. Why it's compulsory to have at least a basic level of understanding in this crap is beyond me. What the hell am I ever going to do with spreadsheets? And I can't see myself doing a job where I have to give presentations. As far as I can tell, this whole course is just a headache. Nevertheless, it's one the school has mandated as necessary to pass before graduation.

Throwing my shoulders back, I make a beeline for West, claiming the seat beside him, the same one I sat in on the first day. I can tell by his tense posture he knows I'm here, but he doesn't look away from his screen, his fingers flying over the keys as he types what looks like gobbledygook into some sort of program. He's definitely not following the same beginner's lesson plan I am.

"Hey," I begin hesitantly.

"Oh, so you're talking to me again?" he snarks, his eyes never leaving the screen.

"I was never not talking to you. I was just angry with you, which I had every right to be, by the way."

"Your temper is as bad as Hawk's," he grumbles, clearly not realizing how fucking insulting that is.

Gritting my teeth, I attempt to overlook it. *Remember, you need his help.*

"I was wondering if you could maybe help me?" I ask in my sweetest possible voice. Adding my best attempt at an innocent smile, too, when he glances my way. It must come off as more of a grimace if his suspicious look means anything.

"With what?" he asks dubiously.

"All of this," I gesture to the computer. "I'm gonna fail if I don't start improving."

After a long, tense moment of silence, where he attempts to ascertain if I'm lying or not, he finally lets out a breath. "Fine, what lesson have you made it to?"

"Eh, lesson two."

"Two?!" His eyes widen in surprise, his lips pursing. "So you haven't managed to do anything since our first class?"

"Hey!" I defend myself. "It's hard when you're trying to teach yourself."

Rolling his eyes, he waves toward the screen, "Alright, sign in and I'll help you."

With a pep in my step, I jump to action, swiveling toward my computer and logging in. I can feel his eyes on me and I once again feel that sense of calm he evokes in me as he rolls his chair over beside mine. My body has never settled the way it does when he's around. I'm always on alert, ready to jump into action. Life has taught me to be that way; yet with him, all of me relaxes, my body like a purring housecat around its master.

For the next hour he takes me through the lesson plan, and I pick up on things so much quicker when he explains them than I do just reading the document. His passion for computers comes across with every word he says, every carefully thought out explanation, and instead of the class dragging like it usually does, the hour flies by. I'm still convinced I won't need to know half this crap, but at least I understand what I'm doing now.

I'm so focused on my task I barely notice the bell ringing. Grabbing my bag, I get to my feet. "Thanks, *Wes*," I throw over my shoulder as I leave the classroom, smirking at his glower before rounding the corner and disappearing out of sight.

***

The bright light of the alarm clock taunts me, silently mocking me and my inability to sleep. I've always been a bit of an insomniac, lucky if I manage to get four hours sleep. It's the only reason I've been able to stay on top of the workload since I got here; but thanks to Hawk's continued glares and Bianca spreading gossip, sleep has been non-existent.

Seeing that it's already four a.m., I give up on trying to get some rest. It doesn't matter that I keep closing my eyes, focusing on my breathing and blocking out the errant thoughts that keep probing at the corners of my consciousness. My body won't lie still; it won't switch off.

I've been so busy adjusting to my new routine here I haven't kept up with my regular exercise. Working out every day is something that was ingrained into me from a young age. I'd start my day with some simple stretches, followed by a five-mile run and a second cardio or weights session later in the day. I used to hate it, but being without that routine recently has thrown me off-kilter. My body feels sluggish and out of sorts.

Deciding to get back to it, I toss back the covers, quickly donning a sports bra, lycra shorts, and my ratty sneakers.

Throwing a loose t-shirt over the ensemble, I pull my hair up into a messy ponytail, grab a bottle of water and my gym bag and head out the door. It's still dark out as I cross the campus, soaking up the pre-dawn silence. This is my favorite part of the day, before the rest of the world wakes up. It's so at odds with the usual noise and chaos of the campus.

Entering the sports complex, I follow the signs for the gym, stepping into the dimly lit, empty room. I don't bother to turn on any more lights, preferring the half-light atmosphere as I cast my eyes over the various machines, weight benches and yoga mats before striding over to the heavy punching bag hanging from the roof in the far corner of the room. Dropping my stuff on the floor, I pull off my t-shirt and tug on a pair of fingerless boxing gloves, flexing my fingers to stretch the leather over my knuckles before swinging my arms to loosen the muscles, doing a few jumping jacks to warm myself up and getting into position in front of the bag.

With my weight centered and my arms raised, my thumbs un-tucked, and my fists clenched tight, I pivot on my back foot, pushing my body forward and driving my fist into the bag. It swings slightly, absorbing the impact from my knuckles. Even that one hit has the strange buzzing sensation I've been feeling recently beginning to ease, quickly replacing it with adrenaline as I settle into a punishing rhythm.

Jab. Cross. Hook

Repeat.

I lose all track of time as my whole world narrows down to that small sequence of movements. Nothing but the sound of my labored breaths and the satisfying snap as my punches land perfectly on the leather material.

I hit the bag over and over, giving it everything I've got. Pouring every ounce of frustration, anger, and determination I have into each and every punch until I'm an exhausted, sweaty mess. Even then, I keep going.

You don't stop until I say you can stop!

The angry bark echoes in my mind, taunting me as I continue to pummel the bag, fighting past the weariness settling into my arms.

I'm reaching my limit when I first sense I'm no longer alone, that ingrained feeling of being watched crawling over me. Not letting him know I'm aware of him, I continue on with my routine. Jab, cross, hook. Jab, cross, hook. But my attention is no longer on the movements, it's entirely focused on him. I'm expecting him to do something, but I don't sense him getting any closer to me. Nor do I hear him moving over to any of the gym equipment. *What the fuck is he doing?*

"Are you just going to stand there and watch me like a creep, or are you going to work out?" I pant, not bothering to turn around.

I knew it was him the second he entered the room. The crackle of electricity zinging through the air was a dead giveaway. Over the years, I've trained myself to pick up on the subtle changes that occur in the air when someone is nearby. I've learned to listen to my basic instincts, to pay attention when the hairs at the back of my neck stand up, or the feeling of eyes digging into the back of my head. Those instincts have saved my life more than once.

It's more than just being aware of his presence, though. It's like my body is primed to respond to him, to all of them. I don't just sense that *someone* is in the room, I instinctively know it's one of *them*. What's more, I can tell *who* it is. I don't even need to look over my shoulder to know Mason's been silently watching me for the last few minutes.

It's the same with all of them. Cam has my body instantly going into overdrive when he's nearby. Just the feel of his eyes roaming over me has my pulse thudding and my breath stuttering. He's pure sex appeal, and damn, when he's around me, I just want to tear his clothes off and fuck his bloody brains out.

With West, it's how his presence settles me in a way nothing else ever has. Even exercising only dulls the buzzing to a faint background noise, but when he's around, everything within me hushes. It all quietens, as though I'm responding to his steadiness. He dons an impassive expression, like he doesn't give a shit about anything around him, but I'm beginning to suspect he's just quietly confident that nothing will surprise him, that he can solve any problem thrown his way. That certainty resonates with me.

Hell, even Hawk's presence affects me. Not in the same way as the others. No, his is much more volatile. He just has to enter a room and he has unadulterated hatred pounding through my veins, and I instantly want to claw his eyes out. And that's before he opens his mouth and says something that makes me want to rip his nut sack off and shove it down his throat. Just thinking about that asswipe has me punching the bag harder, pretending it's his face I'm smashing my fists into.

For Mason, I can feel his penetrating gaze on me as soon as he enters a room. He's always silently watching me, making me feel like he can see right through me. With just one look, he tears through every barrier I ever erected around myself, leaving me exposed and completely at his mercy. Everything between us is more subtle, but it's no less intense. When our skin touches, it's a jolt of energy, like I've just stuck my finger in a live socket. He makes adrenaline rush through my system, heightening my senses. I can practically taste the tension in the air around us. I'm just not sure if it's sexual on his part, or something else. Hell, it could be pure fucking hatred for all I know. He's impossible to get a read on. It could honestly swing either way. I know *I* can't deny he's hot as fuck. With his broad, muscular frame and those thick biceps, how can I not picture his large palms squeezing my ass as he easily pushes me against the wall, punishing me with every savage thrust of what I am certain is a humongous dick. The type that eviscerates women and ruins them for all other men.

Now I'm hot and bothered, and it's got nothing to do with my morning exercise. Thank God, Mason, who is still watching me from the doorway, can't tell what I'm thinking. There's no way he can know my red face is because of my dirty thoughts. That's the only reason I'm comfortable dropping my fists, spinning around to glare at him. *Why the fuck is he just standing there watching me like a creeper?*

I try my damnedest to ignore the way his heated eyes trail over my exposed thighs and naked torso, pausing on my heaving chest before meeting my face, thanking the lucky stars above I never turned on the lights. In the half-darkness, he won't be able to see my imperfections.

Realizing he never answered my question, I scowl at him. "Can I help you with something?" I bite out. My sharp words, combined with the death glare I'm giving him, must knock him out of whatever trance he's in because he quickly dons his usual look of indifference and stomps over to the weights bench, effectively dismissing me. Of course this asshole gets an early morning gym session in before class, ruining the little bubble of peace I'd created for myself. I should have expected him to be here, he looks like he fucking lives in the gym.

I watch as he silently sets himself up, loading more weight plates onto the bar than any normal human should be able to lift before getting comfy on the bench, planting his feet firmly on the ground and starting into a round of bench presses, confident enough in his strength that he doesn't need anyone to spot for him. *Talk about arrogance.* I'm sure as fuck not going to save his sorry ass if he drops all that weight on his chest. Not that I could possibly lift what looks like the equivalent of a small car in weights off of him if I tried. I'd need to be fucking superwoman to do that shit.

Once I'm satisfied that he's done paying me any attention, fully focused on his workout, I get back to mine. Now that I'm no longer in the zone, I can feel the ache in my fingers and the stiffness in my hands from taking out all of my pent up anger on the punching bag.

Despite how hard I've been going at it, I can still feel that restless energy inside me, itching for more. Checking the time on my phone, it's still early. Class isn't for another few hours, and I'm still too worked up to go back to my room. Besides, I can't let this fucker think his presence here is enough to send me running.

Downing half my bottle of water and wiping the sweat off my forehead, I move over to the treadmills, carefully selecting one that doesn't give me a direct line of sight to Mason—I don't want him to think I'm fucking watching him—but also enables me to keep an eye on him out of the corner of my eye. Most likely, he's just here to work out. He seemed surprised to find me here, but the four of them are a conundrum I don't understand, and I can't afford to risk turning my back on any of them.

Setting a fast pace for myself, I sprint along on the machine and it doesn't take long for a new layer of sweat to coat my skin, my breaths becoming labored as I push myself harder than I probably should, considering I've neglected my regular running routine for the last few weeks. I'm a panting, sweaty mess when I climb off the machine an hour later, my legs like jelly as I slowly make my way over to where I left my towel and water. I've been slyly watching Mason out of the corner of my eye, but he hasn't done anything other than cycle through various weight-based exercises, occasionally pausing between reps to stare at me, with that same strange expression on his face that he had when he walked in. I don't know him well enough to understand what he's thinking. Hell, I don't know the guy at all. He could be picturing me naked or imagining the thousand different ways he could kill me and dispose of my body before anyone would even know I was missing. Choosing to put him out of my mind and in desperate need of a shower, I grab my stuff and head out of the gym, not looking back at him as I leave.

Mason

Chapter 10

She's fucking everywhere I go. Everywhere, even the fucking gym! The one place that gives me some peace, and she's fucking there, ruining it. What the hell is she even doing here so early?!

I'm stuck, frozen in the doorway, watching her pummel the shit out of the heavy bag. I can feel the rage coursing through her from here, every move carried out with perfect precision as she throws her entire weight into each punch. Taking in her form, her straight back and wide stance, the accuracy of her hits and the sound the bag makes when you hit it just right, it's obvious she's had training. I had no idea she was a fighter, not in the physical sense. She's shown she can fight back with words, but she never resorts to physical violence.

As my eyes roam over her lithe body, taking in her sweat soaked skin and heaving chest, I can feel my traitorous dick hardening in my shorts, not giving a single shit that this girl is off-limits.

The black marks of a tattoo curl around her hip, dipping beneath her shorts. Black lines that swirl up her side until they form an abstract image, some sort of a bird, over her ribs.

Her tits look fucking incredible in that little bra thing she's wearing, rapidly rising and falling from the exertion of her workout. I've never really paid much attention to her tits before. Don't get me wrong, I noticed she had them. They're large and perky, and would look fucking perfect with my dick shoved between them as I come all over her face. Sadly, she usually has them hidden under her uniform, or the unflattering tops she wears, that have apparently been hiding her hot-as-fuck body from the world. Such a fucking travesty. Someone with a body like hers should walk around naked all the time. It's a work of fucking art. She's skinny, but not the same kind of skinny as the other girls at Pac. It's got nothing to do with not eating and everything to do with how she's honed her body into a weapon. She's pure strength and muscle with her taut abdomen and powerful thighs. She's an athletic missile ready to rain down shit on whoever crosses her.

Her sharp words snap me out of my trance, pulling my gaze from her limber body up to her glowering eyes. The icy glare she's throwing my way reminds me that, although she may look like every one of my dirty fantasies, she's untouchable. Hawk has got a fucking bug up his ass about her; besides, I'm pretty sure she can't stand any of us. She certainly doesn't have the same level of respect and fear for us that everyone else around here has. Although the way she looks at Cam sometimes, it's clear she's attracted to him, and I definitely caught her checking me out this morning. She might not like us, but she fucking wants us.

Regardless, she might be a hot piece of ass, but she's a distraction none of us can afford right now. Between school and our fucked-up families, we have enough shit going on. Hawk's right, we can't have a girl coming in and disrupting the balance, messing with our heads when we need our focus now more than ever. Guess I'm just going to have to continue getting my jollies from whatever mediocre girl of the month. It's bad enough that Cam has his sights on her. If she would just give in and fuck him, like I know she wants to, he'd get over her, like he has with every other girl. This back and forth she's got going with him is only creating more problems. He's fucking infatuated, and that's something we sure as hell don't need right now.

With that reminder, I wipe all traces of emotion from my face, not bothering to answer her as I quickly turn away before she can see the hard-on I'm sporting, and make my way over to my usual spot, pushing myself harder than normal, not leaving the gym until my arms and legs feel like wet noodles.

"Damn, man, isn't the gym supposed to make you all zen or some shit?" Cam chuckles as I blow back into our apartment, somehow more worked up than I was before I left this morning. All four of us have the top floor of the boys' dorms. We had the whole place renovated the summer before freshman year, so it has an open plan kitchen and living space, four large bedrooms, and we updated the shower room.

It might sound crazy for four fifteen-year-olds to be able to do all that, but we were Princes the second we arrived on campus. A stupid-ass title, but whatever. We trumped every senior student. Of course, not everyone just rolled over and accepted that. It wasn't easy for the previous reigning seniors to give up their crowns, so to speak. But they were rulers because of their popularity. We rule by blood, by title. Our families are the founding families of Pac Prep. Every Hayes, Davenport, Rutherford, and Warren before us has ruled this school.

We had to stand up for ourselves, fight for our place, but one thing our families taught us is how to be ruthless, to take what's ours. People quickly learned not to mess with us and since then we've been both revered and feared, a healthy combination.

Things have been pretty smooth sailing for the last four years. We can do what we want, fuck who we want, have whatever we want. But now that senior year is here, we're all starting to feel the tension. Where every other student is filling out college applications and preparing for the time of their lives, we are preparing to be inducted into the family business. There's no college education for us, no fraternities or keg parties. Only a boring pre-planned future at our parents' company.

Where our futures should be a vast expanse of the unknown spread out before us, we each feel like all the doors are slamming shut in our face, and our world is closing in around us. The fear that, someday soon, we will be just like our parents, is riding us hard.

It wasn't always this way. Sure, we've never wanted to be like our parents, but until last summer we were content with our lot in life. We accepted the future our parents had laid out for us.

But, fuck, everything changed this summer. Everything we thought we ever knew went up in smoke. The carefree life we've lived so blindly in came crashing down around us.

Learning your parents aren't who you thought they were is always a bitter pill to swallow. Hawk took the news the hardest, and has been burying his anger in fights and pussy. Out of all of us, he thought he had relatively decent parents. The rest of us learned early on what assholes our parents were, so while still a shock, it wasn't a complete surprise.

Ignoring Cam, I storm into my bedroom, slamming the door behind me. Despite the fact I put myself through a vigorous workout this morning, I can still feel all this pent up energy thrumming through me. I couldn't fucking concentrate with her so close. Even after she left, I could still fucking smell her in the room.

I don't fucking understand it. Ever since that day in class, when I first saw her, I haven't been able to get her out of my head. I don't even know what it is about her that has caught my attention. She has this prickly attitude that's designed to keep people at arm's length—anyone who's paying any attention can see that—yet, underneath it all, I can sense there's something more. There's something that resonates with me on a primitive level, not that that makes any fucking sense. It's kind of like my soul recognizes hers? I don't fucking know. It's confusing as hell.

I don't usually like other people. I have my boys, sure. We grew up together. We know everything there is to know about one another. But other people? Not my thing; and they don't understand me either. Neither do girls. They assume I'm not interested because I don't talk much, and my size tends to send most of them running for the hills. But something about *her* is different. I haven't been able to take my eyes off her. Not that I mean to, my eyes seem to gravitate in her direction whenever she's around. I don't have any fucking say in it. I'll be working away, minding my own business, and the next thing I know, I've been staring at her for god knows how long, my work long forgotten.

Sometimes, when I'm watching, it's like her mind is off somewhere else. There's a vacancy in her eyes. It's in those moments that my connection with her is the strongest. It's almost like I can sense her pain or some shit, like it's similar to my own.

A harsh bang on the door snaps me out of my funk. "What?" I growl.

"We've gotta go," Cam calls out, pausing a moment on the other side before I hear his footsteps as he walks away.

Fuck, I'm still far too worked up to make it through the day like this. I'll kill the first asshole that so much as looks at me wrong. Grabbing my bag, I head out the door, the four of us making our way toward the dining hall.

"I'll meet you inside," I call out, walking past the entrance, toward the girls' dorm.

"What the hell, man?!" Hawk shouts after me. "It's changeover day!"

"I'll be there, I just need to sort something out first."

I hear him grumbling behind me, but I don't slow down or turn around. I need to release this feeling inside of me. Now. If I go into that hall, with all those insipid fucking assholes watching my every move, I'm going to do something I regret.

Throwing open the door to the girls' dormitory, it bangs off the wall. The few girls in the foyer jump, looking at me with wide eyes, but I ignore them all as I take the stairs two at a time, making my way to the fourth floor.

Girls flatten themselves against the wall as I stride past, stopping outside a now familiar door and banging on the wood.

"What the...What are you doing here?" Vivian gasps. I don't know why she bothers, though. She knows the routine by now. I've never shown up looking as enraged as I feel right now, but even so, if I'm here, she knows why.

Pushing past her, I barge into her room as she closes the door. "Desk," I bark out, unbuckling my belt and popping the top button of my slacks. Moving past me, she perches on the edge of the desk, her ridiculously short skirt giving me a flash of her bright pink thong. "Turn around."

"Can't we do it my way this once?" She might think her pout is cute, but it makes her look like a child—a creepy as fuck one with all that makeup gunk on her face.

"No," I snarl, getting impatient.

Huffing, she finally does as she's told, bending over the desk as I dig a condom out of my pocket, rolling it over my hard dick. Pushing into her, I feel absolutely nothing. She used to at least feel good, but now she does nothing for me, and her fake pornstar moans only aggravate me further as I pound into her hard enough to hurt.

"Oh yeah, baby, give it to me," she moans in a breathy voice, her grating tone doing nothing but making it harder for me to pretend it's someone else I'm fucking.

"Shut. Up," I hiss through gritted teeth. Instead of the anorexic-looking brunette bent over the table, I picture an athletic blonde, authentic wanton moans escaping her plump lips as I hammer into her tight cunt. I only have to imagine myself fucking Hadley for a few seconds before that tingling feeling at the bottom of my spine ratchets up and I finally explode into the condom.

For the first time since seeing her this morning, I finally feel at ease, my whole body relaxing as I pull out, throwing the condom in the trash can and tucking myself away.

"Mmm, that was so good, baby." I don't even know if she came, nor do I give a shit.

I've just reached the door when she calls out, "Wait, are you at least going to pick me again?" The hopeful tone in her voice is fucking pathetic. Does she seriously think this means anything more than exactly what it is—a month long fuck buddy?

With my hand resting on the doorknob, I snap out, "No," not bothering to turn around before opening the door and leaving her behind, finally feeling like myself again.

Breakfast is well underway when I arrive in the dining hall, ignoring Hawk's scowl. He's always been a grumpy bastard, but it's gotten so much worse since the summer. He's always loved the control he has over the school, the way the other students cower to him, but it's become something he craves. The slightest hint of defiance and he'll ensure he squashes it, likely leaving whoever pissed him off fearing for their life. Not that he's ever had much control over his anger. Even as a kid, he would throw a motherfucker of a tantrum over the slightest thing.

Of course, Hadley is the one person in this place who doesn't flinch in the face of his rage. Instead of taking his anger as a warning, she seems to see it as a challenge, something to fight back against. Needless to say, her unwillingness to submit has only infuriated him more, and it's only made worse by whatever is going on between her and Cam. He thinks we don't know he's been sneaking out at night to meet her, but we all know. Fuck, I had to talk Hawk down from storming in there and tearing her fucking head off. Seriously, if she doesn't sleep with him soon so he can get over her, I don't know what the hell is going to happen.

Just like last time, Hawk gives us *the look* and we get to our feet, the room dropping silent in an instant. The buzz of excitement is suffocating as the girls all touch up their makeup and make sure their hair is sitting perfectly. The only girls who aren't preening are the scholarship ones. In fact, I'm pretty sure I catch Hadley rolling her eyes, sharing a comical look with the girl beside her. Sure, she's a scholarship student, and she knows she can't be chosen, but it's interesting to see how unimpressed she is by this whole farce. While the other girls at her table might not show the same level of excitement as the rest of the senior girls, I'd have to be blind to miss the wanting glint in their eyes. Despite knowing they can't be chosen, they still *want* to be. But not Hadley. She looks like she couldn't imagine anything worse.

When it's my turn to step forward and select a girl, my eyes run over the sea of batting eyelashes and coy smiles until I find someone suitable. Cora Farber. She's got medium length, blonde, curly hair, and a bit more meat on her bones than Vivian had. She's not quite right, but she'll do. I make sure to keep a table between us when I point to her so she can't get any ideas about jumping all over me, and thankfully she stays seated as she squeals in excitement. I struggle not to roll my eyes at the whole scene as I stomp back to my seat and sit down, glad to be done with my bit as Cam steps forward to put on his usual performance. He does the same song and dance as last time, but I notice he doesn't have the same enthusiasm as before, and I don't miss his less than subtle glance toward the scholarship table before he finally points to Missy Barton. It doesn't take West long to pick someone and the four of us make our exit, leaving the hall in an uproar of excited squeals and murmurs.

The week drags by the same as every other week, except Friday is Cam's first swim meet of the year. He's determined he's going all the way to the State Championships this year, and anyone who's seen him in the water knows without a doubt he will. Not only does he love the sport, but he's fucking incredible at it. He would have an impressive future on the Olympic team if it wasn't for our shithead parents and the legacy we have to maintain by following in their footsteps.

He's completely focused as he stands at the edge of the pool alongside the other swimmers—waiting for the whistle to blow—and when the race begins, he's the first one to hit the water, quickly getting out ahead of everyone else, a distance he easily maintains as he reaches the far side and swims back to the start. He wins the race by a landslide, a huge goofy grin on his face as he seeks us out in the crowd, lifting his arms in the air.

Swimming is one of the few times he lets his true self shine through. He loves the sport; the competitive nature, the energy that comes with winning. The smile only drops from his face as his father moves toward him. Of course he's here. He never misses a race, but we'd hoped since it was only a district meet, he wouldn't bother showing his face. The two of them exchange words—well, from the looks of it, Mr. Rutherford does most of the talking, Cam occasionally nodding his head, his face pinched in annoyance. After a few moments, his father gives a final nod, storming out the door, leaving Cam glowering behind him. I'd be surprised if he can't feel the heat from Cam's hatred burning holes in his back as he leaves.

We quickly scramble from our seats, making our way down to the pool, all three of us with grins on our faces, offering our congratulations in an effort to put that smile back on his face.

"Come on, man," I slap him on the back, jerking my head toward the exit. "Let's get the hell out of here, we've got some celebrating to do."

Hadley

Chapter 11

Over the next week, things fall into a regular rhythm. I make an effort to stick to my normal gym routine—it eats significantly into my studying time, but it prevents at least one kid from ending up with a broken nose when they call me a slut. I thought that shit would die off when the Pricks all chose new girls, but it's only gotten worse. The only problem is that Mason shows up at five a.m. every morning to get his workout in too. Neither of us says anything, not even acknowledging the other's presence, but I'm aware of his every move.

On Tuesday, Bianca and Cam's new girl, I think her name is Missy, corner me between classes.

"Bianca." I sigh, as the two of them step in front of me. I'd stayed late to discuss my history assignment with Mrs. Beaufort, so now there's hardly anyone in the halls, apart from the three of us. "Aren't we done with this? You're no longer Cam's girl. Shouldn't you be taking issue with Missy, who's *actually* fucking Cam, instead of with me?"

The two girls scowl at me, and seriously, I can't understand their problem. "I won't let you do to Missy what you did to me."

"And what exactly was that?"

"You took him! He was supposed to be *mine* for the month, and you stole his attention. He didn't want anything to do with me!" Her last sentence comes out in a broken sob, the tears gleaming in her eyes. I almost feel bad for her, but if Cam didn't want to spend his time with her, then that's between them. It has nothing to do with me. It's not my fault if he started chasing after me while he was with her. The guy is clearly a player, I picked up on that on day one, so surely she knew what he was like. Besides, from what I've heard, it's not like there is any exclusivity clause in this whole antiquated tradition. Not that I've actually done anything fucking wrong here. "The other Princesses and I won't let you do it to anyone else."

"I'm sorry?" I struggle to hold back the snort threatening to spurt out of me. "You and the what?"

"The Princesses," she states with so much seriousness that I'm biting my lip hard enough to break the skin in an attempt to keep my composure. "The other girls that the Princes have chosen." She says it like that isn't the most ridiculous thing I've ever heard.

"The Princess Club?" The snort I was holding back bursts free. "What, like the mile-high club? You fuck a Prince and you get a badge or something?"

Neither girl seems to find the whole thing as funny as I do, glowering at me with unimpressed looks until I roll my eyes.

"You have to be *chosen*," Missy emphasizes. "Trash like you could never be a Princess."

Aw damn, but I always wanted to be a Princess.

Does this idiot seriously think I want to be part of their stupid club?

"Missy." I sigh wearily. "I'll say the same thing to you, that I said to Bianca. I'm not interested in stealing Cam from you. I suggest you learn from her mistakes and instead of worrying about me, focus on your relationship with Cam."

Neither girl seems to know how to respond to that, so while they both gape at me, I step around them, having had enough of this pointless conversation, and head on to history before I miss the whole damn lesson.

What I said to Bianca and Missy is true, I don't have any interest in being a part of their stupid club, but I continue to meet with Cam every night in the dining hall, where he regales me with stories of his childhood. He doesn't talk much about his parents or the company he and the others are supposed to take over, so we end up mostly sticking to lighter topics of conversation. Every now and again he probes into my past, wanting to know more about me, but I manage to distract him, avoiding having to share much of myself with him.

It's late on Sunday by the time I leave the library and the sun has long since set, the glare from the pathway lamps my only source of light as I step into the cool, quiet night air. I was the last one left by the time I packed up my things, and I'm supposed to meet Cam any minute now. I'm pulling the door to the front entrance shut behind me when a brutal force crashes into me, throwing me against the solid wood; a large body pressing up against me before I can bring my fists up.

Glancing up, I stare into the fuming eyes of Hawk. *Great, just what I need today.* His arms are outstretched, his hands pressed firmly against the wooden door beside my head as he glares down at me. His stony expression and icy eyes are menacing, and I have to push back some dark memories, forcing myself to stay in the present.

The corner of his lip curls up in disdain as he snarls at me, "I don't know what the fuck you think you're doing with Cam, but leave him the fuck alone."

I don't react as all the different ways I could get him to back the fuck off flick through my mind. A well placed punch to the kidney always does the trick. Or a knee to the balls; although he's a little too close to guarantee a direct hit.

"I don't like you, and I sure as fuck don't trust you. I don't know what you're playing at, but I won't stand by and let you screw with his head."

"I don't—"

"Bullshit," he snarls. "You taunt and tease him. You have him chasing after you, going to secret little midnight meetings with you—yeah, don't think I don't know about that. If you wanted him, you'd just fuck him. I don't know what it is, but you're up to something, and I won't let you mess with him anymore."

He pins me in place with his penetrating stare, the faint light enough to discern the glow of hatred in his eyes. Having apparently said his piece, he stands up straight, giving me one last glowering look before stalking off into the night.

What a fucking douche.

His blitz attack has the adrenaline thumping through my veins, my hands shaking as I try to steady my nerves. Taking several deep breaths, I slowly exhale until my heart no longer feels like it's trying to break free from my chest. Once I feel calm again, I scurry down the steps and head toward the dining hall, pushing open the door. Hawk might have caught me off guard tonight and given me a scare, but he's going to have to do a lot better than that to get me to fall in line.

***

"You have to come! You haven't been to one since the first party of the year," Emilia whines on Friday night.

"I'm just not feeling it tonight," I repeat for what must be the fifth time. When she continues to look at me like I'm deliberately being difficult, I tack on, "I just don't think parties are my thing."

I've managed to worm my way out of the last couple with one excuse or another, but Emilia isn't hearing any of it tonight. Pushing out her bottom lip and searing me with those goddamn puppy dog eyes, I can't help but roll my eyes at her antics. She's pulling out the big guns—how the fuck can I say no to that?

Gritting my teeth, knowing I'm going to regret it, I grind out, "Fine."

"Ahh," she squeals, throwing herself into my arms. "We're going to have a great time. Wait 'til you see."

"Uh huh." I really don't agree with her view of tonight, but I guess if I'm going, I may as well make the best of it and try to enjoy myself.

"Here, wear this. You'll look fucking fine in it." Emilia throws a tiny piece of black fabric at me that I manage to catch before it hits me in the face.

"Uh, no. No way am I wearing that!" I insist, holding it out in front of me. Without even trying it on, I know it will barely cover my ass. Thankfully, the neckline is high so my tits wouldn't be on display for everyone to gawk at, but even so.

"Come on," she whines, and I can already see her lip starting to pop out in a pout.

"Fine," I cave, knowing it's just easier to give in. "But you have to turn around."

Rolling her eyes and sighing, she turns around, giving me a modicum of privacy to change. "I've never known a girl to have such issues changing in front of other girls. Especially one that has as hot a body as you have."

Not responding, I quickly strip off my clothes, pulling the dress on over my head, ensuring it covers my ass as I glance in the mirror, adjusting the neckline slightly before pulling my hair over my shoulders, attempting to flatten the curls. I like the little short sleeves that cover my shoulders and the fact it isn't backless like a lot of dresses the other girls wear. When I'm happy, I call out, "Okay, you can turn around now."

"Damn, girl, you are smokin'...but those boots? Hell no. Here, try these on with it." Emilia holds up a pair of stiletto heels, but I'm already shaking my head, adamant that I won't be wearing those death traps. Not tonight, not ever.

"Not a chance," I assert. "You'd have to pin me down and strap them to my feet, and there's no way I'm letting you do that."

She roars with laughter, dropping the heels with a shrug, thankfully not pushing the matter. Pulling another dress out of the small closet, she strips down, not having the same issues with walking around in only her underwear that I do. She slips into a dark red dress similar to my own, except, more revealing, with a plunging neckline, finishing the outfit off with a pair of heels. I can't deny she looks amazing, her black hair and tanned skin contrasting perfectly with the dress and shoes.

"Don't we look pretty fucking hot?" She laughs, dragging me over to stand beside her in front of the mirror. I have to admit, I don't look half bad. The way the dress hugs my curves, highlighting my narrow waist, it makes me look older somehow, sexier.

"Here, sit." Emilia pushes me into the chair at her desk where she has set up all her hair and makeup stuff for tonight. "I'll see what I can do with those curls."

An hour later, I'm probably more primped than I've ever been in my life. My hair has so much hairspray in it, I could probably hang upside down from a tree and it wouldn't move an inch. Despite that, though, Emilia did a pretty amazing job with it. I usually just let my hair drip dry, accepting that it's going to be a frizzy mess of curls, but she somehow managed to get them all to behave and with some product and a curling wand they now sit in beautiful sleek ringlets down my back.

Regardless of how amazing I think I look, though, I'm already bored with this party. As I predicted, it is no better than the last one. Worse even, since this stupid dress keeps insisting on riding up my ass. I mentally curse Emilia out for guilting me into wearing the damn thing as I pull it down for the hundredth time, glancing around to check no one is watching me wrestle with it.

Everything looks just the same as the last party. The Pricks are once again congregated around the fire with their new girl of the month, while the rest of the year is spread out along the beach, most of them already looking worse for wear. I just don't understand what the fascination is with getting rip roaring drunk and stumbling all over one another. Maybe it's because I've never been able to let my guard down enough to just live in the moment, but the thought of not being in complete control, of not being aware of everything going on around me, sounds terrifying.

"You don't exactly look like you're having fun," Michael jokes, coming up beside me. Emilia was whisked off to the dance floor with Andrew as soon as we arrived. I'm pretty sure he's got a bit of a crush on her. Recently he's been sitting beside her at our weekly movie nights and walking her to classes. It's adorable to watch, and based on the way her cheeks flush and she gets all flustered when he's around, I'd guess she likes him too.

"Ha, yeah. I'm not really a party person."

"We could—"

A commotion over by the fire pit cuts off Michael's words as yelling, loud enough to be heard over the heavy bass of the music, reaches our ears. The whole party seems to come to a standstill, everyone turning to watch the unfolding drama. Emilia comes stumbling over from the dance floor, excitement dancing in her eyes as she drags me forward toward the scene. "What's going on?" I whisper-yell as we move closer, shoving our way through the crowd until we can get a good look at what's happening. All four of the Pricks have gotten to their feet, standing with the fire at their backs, looking like the kings of hell as they face off against a bunch of jocks. Running my eyes over them, I count eleven guys, wearing jerseys, who I'm guessing make up the school's football team.

"What the fuck is your problem, Deke?" Cam growls, glowering at the guy standing front and center. He's tall and muscular with styled brown hair and a cold look in his eyes. He's nearly as tall as the Pricks and as broad as Hawk. Based on how the rest of the team swarm around him, I'm guessing he's their captain.

"You're our problem," he snarls. "None of the girls are interested in us 'cause they're all holding out for one of you assholes to pick them."

"Watch your mouth," West barks, the hostility in his tone and the dark look on his face taking me by surprise. I've never seen him confrontational before. Unlike the others, he goes out of his way to fade into the background, never seeming to have an issue with anyone around him. The West standing up there right now is very different to the everyday West I've been watching far too intently for the last few weeks.

"You can't blame us if your usual groupies want an upgrade," Hawk drawls, a confident smirk lifting his lips. "Not our fault if the steroids have shriveled your dicks so much you can't satisfy them."

"You piece of shit," Deke growls, taking a step toward the guys, his boy band stepping forward too, backing up their leader.

Hawk and the guys quickly adjust their stances, Mason stepping forward so he's chest to chest with the captain. Both boys are as tall as each other, but seeing them standing facing one another, it's clear Deke is nowhere near as broad or as muscular as Mason. Don't get me wrong, as a football player, he's stacked. It just doesn't compare to Mason, or the rest of the guys. Even West, despite being scrawnier, looks more formidable. It must be some sort of air that comes with knowing you're invincible. In any other high school, Deke would probably be the typical reigning king, but here, he's just another rich asshole in a sea of wealthy kids.

The two of them face off, the entire audience holding their breath, waiting anxiously to see what's going to happen next. West steps up beside Mason, his gaze focused intently on the captain, sizing him up. I find myself, along with everyone else, leaning in to listen as his lips part, "Think very carefully about your next move, Deke. We'll tear you to shreds—and I'm not just talking about a social beat down in front of the entire senior class." West tips his head to the side and Deke turns to look at us all, his eyes widening as he finds us watching them closely, wondering what his next move will be. "You and I both know Mason here could beat the crap out of you. You think you're having difficulties getting girls now? Wait until that ugly mug of yours is all purple and swollen." I've never heard West talk like this to anyone. Never even knew he was capable of it, but the vicious smirk as he tears Deke down in front of the whole class says everything—he's fucking enjoying himself.

Where the other three—particularly Mason and Hawk—get their kicks out of beating the shit out of disrespectful students, West gets his from eviscerating them with his sharp words.

With a shit-eating grin on his face, Hawk steps forward, joining the other two. "Not to mention, one word to the coach and, just like that, you'd be off the team. You'd probably lose your football scholarship to Arizona State, too."

Deke is looking less and less sure about his stance with every word, his eyes flitting nervously around the crowd, hesitant to back down and look weak in front of his team and the rest of the school, but equally realizing he hasn't a hope in hell of defeating these guys.

"Back down, Deke. Don't throw away your entire future over some pussy. There's a time and a place for this, here is not it." West's final cryptic words get through to him, and with an incomprehensible snarl, Deke stomps away toward the far side of the lake, the rest of the team following after him like good little lap dogs.

As soon as the tension dissipates, the rest of the class break out into murmurs and it's only then that I realize someone must have stopped the music at some point. With the action over now, the music starts up again and people are quickly sucked back into the party, the drama forgotten for now.

"Wow, that was tense." Emilia chuckles. "But damn, what a showdown that would have been if Deke and Mason had gotten it on, right?"

"Sure," I say distractedly, my focus still on the four guys as they huddle together whispering quietly to one another. Almost as though he senses me watching, Mason's head whips up, his gaze instantly zoning in on me.

"Shit," I murmur, ducking my head and breaking eye contact with him, pulling Emilia through the crowd away from the Pricks.

Once we're safely on the far side of the beach, we drop down onto the pebbly shore. We're a bit of a distance from the main party, the thud of the music not as deafening over here, making it easier to talk to one another without having to shout.

"So...Andrew?" I glance at Emilia, a sly grin lifting the corner of my lip as her eyes widen in surprise. Yup, I might not be tuned into my own love life, but I've been paying attention to hers.

"You've noticed it too?" She groans into her hands.

"Yup. What's going on there?"

"Nothing...Something, maybe. I don't know." She lets out a heavy sigh. "He's been so sweet this week, but I don't know what it means."

"Oh, he definitely likes you." I laugh as she turns to face me, her lower lip caught between her teeth.

"You think so?"

"Oh, yeah. He's been following you around like a lost puppy and he's constantly glancing at you at breakfast."

Her cheeks glow pink and I can see excitement brimming in her eyes.

"You like him." It's not a question; it's clear to see on her face that she does, but she nods anyway.

"Yeah. I mean, I always thought he was cute, but we've only ever been friends. I didn't know he was interested in me like that."

"Girl, he'd have to be deaf, dumb, and blind not to be interested in you," I say, bumping my shoulder against hers. "You're awesome."

Hadley

Chapter 12

Dumping my bag on a spare table in the library, I pull out my tablet and workbook, ready to get stuck into yet another night of studying. If I didn't know any better, I'd swear they were trying to kill us through sleep deprivation. How does everyone else manage this workload?

Wrapping up my history homework, I move on to the next English assignment Cam and I have that is due next week. We need to compare and contrast two books from our reading list. Already knowing what book I want to use, I get up and go in search of it, walking amongst the stacks until I find the aisle I'm looking for, pausing when I see West blocking my way as he scans the shelves in front of him.

I'm honestly not sure what to make of him. He's been a lifesaver, helping me with computer science, but we never talk about anything personal so, despite us spending an hour a week together, I don't feel like I know him at all. He's quiet and nerdy, more interested in his studies than girls and social etiquette, yet I've seen that same flash of violence that Hawk and Mason, and even Cam, have.

Pretending he's not there, I saunter down the aisle in search of the book I'm looking for, ignoring when he notices my presence, his head turning slightly as he watches me approach. Finding it on the top shelf, I stretch up onto my toes, but I don't have a hope of reaching it. Glancing around for a stool or ladder or something, I see absolutely nothing. *How the hell do other students get books on the top shelf?*

Eyeing the bookcase, I figure I can easily climb up and grab the book. Wedging the tip of my boot in a gap on a low shelf, I haul myself up, until I'm several shelves off the ground and can grab a hold of the top shelf. With my free hand, I reach out to pluck the book, but just as my fingers touch the spine, my boot slips and I lose my footing.

"Aah." A small gasp escapes at the sudden movement, my hand instinctively clasping tighter around the shelf as I slide down the bookcase. Before I can regain my footing, an arm winds round my waist, catching me before I hit the ground, pulling me in against a hard, warm body.

"What are you doing?" a gravelly, breathy voice whispers in my ear. Holy shit, does he normally sound so irresistible? His voice belongs in an audiobook. It would have women everywhere panting. The timber alone has me close to orgasm.

“I needed a book,” I respond, my own voice coming out husky.

West stretches above me, keeping one arm wrapped around me as his tall frame and long arm enables him to effortlessly reach the top shelf with his free hand. The move has him towering over me even more, penning me in, enveloping me in his clean, musky scent. His nearness is scrambling my brain, though, doing all sorts of stupid things to it.

“This one?” he asks, the rumble in his chest making my panties damp as it vibrates through me. I'm not capable of doing anything other than nodding as he grabs the book I was after, lifting it down.

“Thanks,” I murmur, taking the book from him. He holds on to it for another moment, neither of us moving. I can feel his breath on my cheek as he dips his head, inhaling the smell of my shampoo.

“You're welcome,” he eventually whispers, slowly sliding his palm across my abdomen, like he's putting off letting go of me. *But that would be crazy, right?* Giving my hip a final squeeze, he steps away, the cold air replacing his heat at my back. I hear his footsteps as he walks off, but I don't look around, trying to calm my racing heart rate and understand what the hell just happened.

By the time I make it back to the study area, Cam has arrived, his stuff spread out over the table I was sitting at. As I head toward him, I scan my eyes around the room, searching for West or the other Pricks, but I don't see any of them. *Strange.*

“Hey,” I greet, settling back into my chair, finding Cam reading through the few notes I've taken in my notebook.

"Why do you write it down in your notebook first, instead of using the tablet? It'll take you twice as long to do the assignment that way." Cam laughs. Things have come a long way since we were handed our first assignment. Don't get me wrong, he still spends most of our time together flirting and driving me to distraction, but it's different than before, and I've let go of my anger over the first party of the school year. I'd say we're almost...friends? Maybe? I'm not sure you could put a name on what we are. *People-who-are-friendly-but-also-have-an-insane-sexual-attraction-to-one-another? Hmm, that's a bit wordy.*

"Because it takes too long to write it on the tablet," I tell him. "By the time I've written a sentence, I've forgotten where I was going with it. At least this way, I get it all down while it's in my head, then I can just copy it across."

He shakes his head, rolling his eyes like I'm deliberately being difficult. "If you actually tried, you'd get better at it."

"Why?" I argue. "No one in the real world uses that crap. It's all pen and paper beyond these hallowed halls of yours."

Holding up his hands in defeat, he concedes. "Do it your way."

We settle down to work after that, getting an outline and draft written for our assignment. It's late by the time we finish up and, glancing around, it appears we're the last ones left in the library. I lean over the desk to grab my things and put them in my bag when a presence behind me has me straightening and spinning around. Cam is standing right in front of me, his tall frame towering over me. I have to tilt my head back so I can see his face, the move bringing our lips within inches of each other.

"You're killing me, you know," Cam murmurs, his eyes roaming over my face, the brown flecks of his irises holding me captive. "I can't tell if you like me, or if you seriously think we're just friends. There's no way you don't feel this tension between us, right?" He lifts my hand, placing it on his chest so I can feel his heart hammering against his rib cage. "Do you feel what you do to me?" As though the racing of his heart beneath my palm isn't enough, he rests his hand on my hip, the pads of his fingers pressing into my skin as he grinds his hard cock against my thigh. The action has my chest heaving, heat coiling in my lower abdomen. "Do I do the same to you?"

My mouth is too dry, my head too fuzzy, my senses intoxicated with his apple and lotus scent. I can't think past the feel of his hard body pressed against mine, his dick grinding so close to where I need him most. He places his palm over my chest, as though needing to feel for himself just how badly he affects me, before slowly sliding it up until his thumb rests over the pulse in my neck, likely feeling it thumping beneath his fingertip.

His eyes dart between my eyes and my lips, as I watch him intently, waiting on tenterhooks to see what his next move is. I can no longer deny that I *need* to know what his lips feel like pressed against mine. That voice in my head, telling me this is a bad idea, that it's a line I shouldn't cross, is barely more than a whisper at this point.

I see it when he makes his decision, his hand sliding around the back of my neck, his thumb pressed against the underside of my chin, tilting my head as his lips brush over mine in a barely there kiss, testing the waters.

I gasp at the contact, that small touch affecting me more than any kiss has before. Our lips meet again, more firmly this time, his tongue flicking out to run along my lower lip. Opening beneath him, his tongue dips into my mouth, gliding slowly over mine. Everything about him is unhurried, deliberate, like he's thought about this a thousand times, and now that it's happening, he's going to savor every moment.

He pushes his hips against mine, leaning over me, pressing me into the table until I'm perched on the edge. My fingers thread through his short, soft strands as I pull him harder against me, every lustful feeling I've been trying to ignore rising to the surface.

He wedges himself between my legs, his hands slipping up my bare thighs until they dip under my skirt, his fingers trailing along the lining of my panties. My hips tilt up, telling him exactly where I need him. I feel him smile lasciviously into the kiss, his hand dipping between my legs. His fingers graze along the front of my panties before his thumb presses on my bundle of nerves, making me gasp into his mouth.

"Mmm, baby, you're so damn wet for me."

Pushing my panties aside, he slides his fingers through my pussy lips, pushing them inside of me. I pull my lips from his, my head falling back as I moan, my fingers digging into his shoulders. He moves to run his lips down my neck as his fingers expertly slide in and out of me, curling so he hits that perfect spot every time.

It doesn't take long until I'm a panting mess beneath him. Just when I think I'm about to combust under his touch, he pulls out of me. I growl at the sudden emptiness, but he simply gives me a coy smirk as he pushes my legs further apart, getting to his knees in front of me. Fuck, staring down at him kneeling in front of me, it's breathtaking. I feel powerful, like a fucking goddess he's about to worship with his hot mouth.

He stares up at me, his tongue flicking out, circling my clit. “Holy hell,” I breathe, bucking against him. I press my hands flat against the table behind me, leaning back as he flattens his tongue, pressing it firmly against my already sensitive bundle. I can feel the familiar coiling in my stomach as he pushes two fingers inside of me once again, this time setting a faster rhythm that his tongue easily meets.

“Cam,” I moan, just as that coiling in my stomach explodes, fire running through my veins until my fingers and toes tingle with a tantalizing orgasm.

He laps up every drop before fixing my panties and pulling down my skirt, leaning over me, pressing his lips to mine. I can taste myself on him as he pushes his tongue between my lips, entangling it with mine, our combined taste flooding my mouth.

“I knew you'd taste fucking delicious.”

We don't hang around for long after that, quickly grabbing our things and heading out. As we reach the door, I glance back, checking I didn't leave anything on the table when movement out of the corner of my eye grabs my attention. My heart skips a beat at the thought Cam just went down on me and someone was around to hear it, but when I glance toward the movement, my breath catches in my throat, my eyes widening as they meet West's. It would be impossible to miss his heated stare or the hard on in his pants as his gaze holds me frozen in place. Something passes between us. It's nothing like the usual calmness I feel in his presence. It's hot and energetic, palpable in the air between us. Before I can think too much about it, Cam calls my name, breaking the moment between us. Pulling my gaze from him, my mind is a jumbled mess of questions as I distractedly follow Cam outside.

***

The next night, I'm in Emilia's room as she gets ready to go on a date with Andrew. He asked her out last weekend and she's been talking non-stop about it since.

"What's going on with you and Cam?" she blurts out, her gaze focused on the mirror as she does her makeup.

"What do you mean?"

Turning to look at me, she lifts an eyebrow, silently saying, *are you serious?*

"Nothing." I shrug, ignoring the tingling between my legs from our library session yesterday. That was so fucking hot and I'm more than ready for round two.

"Look." She sighs, turning around, giving me a serious look. "I'm only bringing it up because the others have noticed and, well, they're worried."

With furrowed brows, I ask, "Why?"

"Because we make a point of staying out of their way, of keeping our heads down and just getting on with the workload. It's an unwritten rule that we don't get in their way and they won't make life difficult for us. But you're breaking all the rules."

"I..." I begin, not even sure how I was going to argue with that. She cuts me off anyway by raising an eyebrow.

"He's been hitting on you since the first day, and now you're telling us you're friends? But the Princes don't do friends, and Cam definitely doesn't do friends with girls."

My silence says everything to her. I never told her about my late night chats with Cam, but based on the hurt in her eyes, I should have said something. I tried to bring it up a time or two, but every time, I couldn't get the words past my lips. I'm not used to having a girlfriend or talking about this stuff. It's not natural for me to just tell other people about my private life.

"I'm sorry," I murmur, guilt hitting me hard.

She waves me away, finishing up with her makeup and coming to sit beside me on the bed. "It's fine. Forget about it. I know you're a private person. I copped on pretty quickly that you don't like to talk about yourself. Do I wish you felt like you could have told me? Hell yes, but I can't be pissed at you just because it's not your nature to share things. Now, how do I look?"

She jumps up, doing a little twirl in front of me, her purple skirt spinning out. In cute ankle boots and a leather jacket, she looks gorgeous.

"Andrew's brain is going to short circuit as soon as he sees you." I laugh, making her grin wider.

Shortly after that, she leaves for her date, and I head out to the gym to work out my frustrations, running myself ragged before calling it a night. Flicking off the light switch, I exit the gym, finally feeling relaxed for the first time all day. How come it takes me to be so physically exhausted I can barely walk or think straight to feel at ease?

I'm slowly dandering up the path toward the dormitories when movement out of the corner of my eye catches my attention. It's well after midnight, no one else should be out here. Hell, I shouldn't even be out here right now.

The lights along the path turn off at midnight—some sort of stupid notion that students are unlikely to stay out until all hours of the night if there are no lights on the path—so it's pitch black out, but I can see the faint shadow of people moving amongst the trees.

Pausing, I stop and watch, seeing silhouettes flitter amongst the treeline as students in pairs, or individually, slip into the forest. Confused about where they could be going, I stand stock still in the middle of the darkened path until I don't see any more movement, then I abandon my plan of heading back to my room and instead make a beeline to where the other students disappeared amongst the trees, curiosity getting the better of me.

Reaching them, I slip into the forest, moving carefully over the uneven terrain. What the hell are people doing out here in the middle of the night? Most parties are thrown in the dorms or down by the lake, and I hadn't heard anything about a party going on tonight.

I traipse through the dark, silent forest for several minutes before noise up ahead draws my attention. Moving closer, light starts to filter through the trees and I can hear people cheering. *Huh, maybe it is a party.*

A clearing opens up in front of me and I can see a crowd of boys forming a large circle in the middle of it. Someone has strategically placed flashlights amongst the crowd, providing an eerie glow and casting shadows that make the whole scene appear macabre.

Another roar goes up from the crowd, and, peering through the bodies, I can just about make out two boys in the middle of the circle. Both of them are topless and covered in sweat as one of them helps the other to his feet. One kid has a cut above his eyebrow and if I squint, I think I can make out bloody knuckles. *Is this some sort of amateur fight club? How rich kid of them.*

The cheers from the crowd die down as Hawk raises his hand in the air. For the first time, I notice the four of them standing at the far end of the circle. I don't know how I missed them initially. They somehow tower over the other students, their demanding presence and steely aura drawing everyone's attention.

Mason strides forward into the makeshift ring in only a pair of boxing shorts. His head is held high, confidence oozing from every step. And why shouldn't he be confident? He's by far the largest guy in our year. He could break some of the scrawnier ones in half without breaking a sweat. No one immediately steps forward to challenge him and, as he surveys the crowd, some of them even take a step back.

"Don't make me pick one of you pussies," he bellows.

After another moment's tense silence, someone steps forward. I can't initially make out who it is, but with another step, the lights glances off his face and I get a clear look. Deke. Of course it is. After the verbal beat down West gave him at the party, I bet he's been waiting for this opportunity to get some payback.

A cruel smirk cuts across Mason's face as he cracks his knuckles, making it clear he's going to enjoy destroying him.

Tearing his top over his head and piercing Mason with his own dark look, Deke flexes his muscles, widening his stance and preparing to face off against the muscle machine that is Mason. With both of them crouched low, ready to pounce, they stand and glower at one another, waiting for some sort of signal.

After a tense moment of silence, Cam barks out, "Go," and the two of them launch themselves at each other.

Deke is all pent up anger and aggression, his hits sloppy as he attempts to pummel Mason, who, in stark contrast, delivers punishing blows to Deke's midsection, making every hit count. It's painfully obvious that, of the two of them, Mason is the fighter. His punches are well aimed and intended to inflict pain, whereas Deke is just punching whatever part of Mason is closest to him. There's no skill or tact in his movements, no forethought to his hits. It's an unexciting match that quickly ends with Deke laid out on the floor, barely moving. I scan my eyes over the other kids in the crowd and quickly deduce that none of them would make for an enthralling fight, except maybe Mason and Hawk. I'd quite happily watch Mason beat the crap out of Hawk. Give me a seat and a cold can of coke and I'll watch that shit all day.

A couple of other football players step forward to help a groaning, half-unconscious Deke to his feet while Cam claps Mason on the back, a dark grin on his face. Glancing at the other Pricks, I notice all of them are wearing matching sinister expressions, only made more terrifying by the half-light of the flashlights. Not wanting to hang around and risk getting caught, I slip into the darkness of the surrounding forest, silently making my way back to the dorms, replaying what I just saw in my head, unable to forget the sadistic looks on all of their faces.

Hawk

Chapter 13

Storming back into the apartment, I slam the door behind me. Senior year is supposed to be *the* year, but mine is going to shit faster than I can blink. As if it isn't bad enough I found out my parents aren't who I thought they were, but some new girl has to show up, defying me at every turn and messing with Cam's head. Why the fuck won't she just bow down to us? Every other girl here either worships the ground we walk on, or is too afraid to come near us. Why the fuck can't she just fall into one of those categories?

Striding over to the fridge, I lift out a beer, twisting off the lid and bringing the cool bottle to my lips, my eyes drifting shut as I gulp down half of it. *If only alcohol was the answer to all of my problems.*

Finishing off the beer, I dump the bottle in the trash, striding across the living space to the bedrooms. I seriously need to wash this day off me, or fuck it out of me. Maybe I'll stop by Tina's tonight. God knows, she and the last girl of the month have been taking the brunt of my anger.

Walking past Cam's door, the creak of a floorboard from within his room halts my steps and I eye the closed door with confusion. I didn't think any of the guys were back yet, and Cam is usually the first one out of his room when anyone comes home.

Cautiously, I wrap my hand around the handle, slowly turning it. My muscles are tense, my body on alert and ready to confront whatever I'll find on the other side of the door. As it silently swings open, my eyes widen in surprise as an annoyed-looking Hadley is revealed, standing boldly in the middle of Cam's room.

"What the fuck are you doing?" I bark out, quickly scanning my eyes around the space, trying to determine if anything is out of order, before returning my glare to her. Cam's room is such a mess, it's impossible to tell what she was doing in here. Her spine straightens as she grinds her jaw, returning my glare, like I'm the one in the fucking wrong here. Where the hell does this girl get off, thinking she can do whatever the fuck she wants?

"Cam accidentally lifted my notebook the other day. He said I could stop by." The words come out confidently. No hesitation or stumbling, and she maintains direct eye contact. She's certainly not acting like someone caught in a lie.

"And you just thought you'd show up when none of us were here?" I question. "How did you even get in?" Despite her nonchalance, nothing is adding up here.

"You must have left your door unlocked." She shrugs. "I called out, but no one answered. I figured it would be on his desk or something and it would be no big deal, but I can't seem to find it."

I narrow my eyes on her, flicking them toward his desk, but I don't see anything that either corroborates or contradicts her story. Regardless, I don't fucking believe a word she's saying. I honestly can't put my finger on it, but something about her rubs me up the wrong way. I just don't like her snarky personality, or her shitty temper. She's constantly glowering at one of us, never giving us the fucking respect we deserve. The only person she seems to halfway like is Cam, which really just makes her seem more suspect. Not because she likes Cam, he is the most likeable one out of us all, but he's still as much of a dick as the rest of us. Yet she overlooks that quality in him, while berating the rest of us. It makes no sense.

"What's your angle?" I ask, unable to figure her out.

"Huh? What do you mean?" Her eyebrows are scrunched together in confusion, but I don't miss the spark of...something in her eyes. Knowledge, maybe? I'm not sure.

"I don't know what you're after, but Cam's not stupid, and you sure as hell don't want to cross any of us." I pin her with a fearsome glare. One I learned from my father that I *know* can have grown men shitting their pants and running off to do whatever you want. "Some scholarship kid like you?" I sneer, dropping my gaze to take in her unimpressive appearance. "We'll fucking destroy you." I expect to see fear and shock in her eyes.

It's the normal response. Instead, I'm met with a steely resolve, a sly smirk lifting the corner of her lips.

What the fuck? What is wrong with this girl?

She takes several slow, deliberate steps toward me until we're only inches apart. Pressing up onto her toes, closing the height difference between us—not that it does much good, I'm still nearly a foot taller than her—she glares right back at me. "I'd love to see you try," she retorts confidently, my steely gaze and dark tone not affecting her. She fearlessly pats me on the shoulder, her arm brushing mine as she steps around me, striding out of the room. By the time I've worked out what the fuck just happened, she's long gone from the apartment.

I'm pacing back and forth across the open living space when the others come in. After she left, I had a good look around Cam's room, but nothing was out of place and I couldn't find anything obvious that was missing.

"Dude, what is eating you?" Cam chuckles as he collapses onto the leather sofa. West eyes me warily as he lowers himself into an armchair, bringing his leg up, crossing his ankle over his knee. Unlike Cam, he's much more refined, his movements carefully thought out instead of slumping into his chair in a boneless heap.

I stop my pacing as Mason joins us, facing all three of them as I tell them about Hadley.

"I'm telling you, I don't trust her," I growl, getting annoyed that none of them seem to think her intruding on our space is a big deal. Cam just shrugged me off when I told him I found her in his room.

"She was just getting her notebook," he says easily. "She told me she'd be stopping by."

“She wasn’t looking for any notebook,” I snap. He wasn’t there, he didn’t see the look in her eye, hear the defiance in her tone. I might not know for sure that she was up to something, but call it gut instinct. She was too calm, too confident considering I’d just caught her red fucking handed. An innocent person would have shown a healthy dose of fear at being caught—not that any other Pac student is stupid enough to even think about coming into our personal space. “She was searching for something.”

“Searching for what, man?” Cam sighs. “Unless she wanted condoms or something from my porn stash, there’s nothing to find in my room.”

I throw an exasperated look toward the other two, needing some sort of back-up here. One of them has to be on the same page as me. They at least appear to be thinking over what I’ve told them, even if they aren’t as angry about the whole thing as they should be.

“She said we left the door unlocked?” Mason questions, his brows furrowed, deep in thought.

“Yeah,” I nod, “but there’s no way any of us would do that.”

West nods in agreement, remaining silent as he processes everything.

“I wouldn’t,” Mason agrees.

“Same,” West concurs.

All three of us look in Cam’s direction.

“I don’t know,” he moans. “I mean, maybe. I might have been distracted when I left this morning. It’s possible I forgot to lock up.”

"Dude, what the hell?" Mason grouches, throwing his hands up in frustration, pinning Cam with an angry look.

"Say she *was* looking for something," West pipes up, playing devil's advocate. "What would she expect to find in Cam's room?"

Fuck. "I don't know," I grumble. This is the problem. She's up to something, and I fucking know it, but I don't know what she's up to, or why.

"See," Cam states, waving his hand in my direction.

"She's a scholarship student, she could be after money or anything," I spit back, scrambling to think of some reason she could have been in his room.

Cam raises his eyebrows at me, giving me a *'are you fucking serious'* look. "She wouldn't risk her scholarship for some petty cash, and there are definitely easier students she could target than one of us," he reasons.

"I'm just saying, it couldn't do any harm to at least keep an eye on her," I say, pointedly looking at Mason and West to back me up in this, since Cam's clearly thinking with the wrong head right now.

"Dude, you haven't liked her since she crossed you in the hallway." Cam sighs wearily, clearly done with the conversation. "Just let it go."

"I mean, it couldn't hurt," West points out, backing me and earning a glare from Cam. "If nothing comes of it, we'll leave her alone and you can do whatever you want with her."

Cam sighs, rubbing his hand over his face. "Look, man," he says wearily, leaning forward in his seat, fixing me with a serious expression, "you're under a lot of stress right now. We've got a lot going on. It makes sense that you're looking for someone to offload all your issues onto, but, man, it can't be her. I actually like this chick."

With a heavy sigh, I run a hand through my hair, tugging on the ends in frustration. "If she's got nothing to hide, then it won't matter," I reason, piercing him with a deadpan look until he concedes.

"Fine," he growls. "But, honestly, I think you just need to get over it."

"I don't trust her," I grumble, repeating myself for the umpteenth time. "And she's got anger issues."

"So?" Cam snorts, looking at me like I'm crazy. "So do you."

"Man, she's basically the vagina version of you." Mason chuckles.

"Pfft, no, she's not. She's got no respect, and she shits a fucking brick over the slightest thing."

Mason raises an eyebrow in a 'are you for real?' gesture, only annoying me further.

"And she's always got a smart remark."

"Again, so do you." Cam rolls his eyes, but the corner of his lip lifts in a small smile, his annoyance over our conversation fading.

Sighing heavily, I drop into an empty chair. "I just don't like her," I grouse. I might be able to talk Mason and West into being wary around her, but I'm going to need something more in order to make Cam see her for who she really is.

Letting out a bark of laughter, Cam retorts, "You don't like anyone."

***

The school throws a Halloween party every year. It's usually a complete bore, only the freshmen enjoying themselves while the rest of us make a quick appearance before heading to the lake to get started on the after party.

The campus has been abuzz with excited chatter all week. All anyone can talk about is their costumes for tonight.

"I don't understand why we can't do a couple's costume," Tina whines that morning at breakfast. It's the gazillionth time she's brought it up this week. You'd think my adamant refusal the first few times would have made it clear to her, but apparently not.

"Tough," I growl. How do these girls not understand that just because we're fucking them, it doesn't make us a fucking couple? It's sex, and a tradition we're forced by legacy to obey. I'm all for the anytime hook-up. It's great not having to put any effort into flirting with a girl or spending all night laying on the charm so she'll let you into her pants. Knowing I can just turn up at Tina's door any hour of the day or night and fuck her until I've exhausted my frustrations is perfect, especially with the amount of rage constantly coursing through me these days. It's saved more than a few asshole kids from having the shit beat out of them for pissing me off.

But dealing with the girls' whining is fucking exhausting. Thank fuck we get to switch them out every month. By the time they settle into their role and build up the confidence to get so annoying, it's nearly time to move on to the next girl.

Tonight we'll have to spend time with the girls as part of the tradition, but that doesn't mean we have to wear whatever costumes they want, or arrive with them. They get to be seen hanging out with us, and usually they get to leave with us, but that's it. Besides, I've something else planned for tonight, something much more important than some stupid costume.

The day passes in a blur, everyone too distracted to focus on classes and that night, when the party is in full swing, we throw open the doors to the dining hall, all eyes falling on us. Cam is standing on my right, wearing nothing more than a pair of tight swimming trunks and flip-flops, with a plastic Olympic medal swinging from his neck. Apparently he's some famous Olympic swimmer.

Wearing all black and wearing a trench coat and boots, I'm dressed as Neo from The Matrix, deciding to go old-school with my costume this year. When I was a kid, one of my nannies was obsessed with Keanu Reeves. I don't remember how many times I sat and watched The Matrix with her when I should have been in bed, asleep.

Beside me, West is dressed in a fancy suit with a weird ass hat on his head. I honestly have no idea who he's supposed to be. He tried explaining it to us, but it still made no sense.

On the other side of him, Mason is dressed in his usual casual attire of a muscle top, gray sweats and a blank expression, dressed up as himself apparently.

Scanning my eyes around the room, I take in the tacky orange and black balloons, the fake cobwebs strung up around the lights and windows. All the tables have been removed, opening up the space for students to dance, the buffet table overflowing with trays of Halloween-themed food and bowls of blood-red punch. There are students dressed in all sorts of weird and slutty costumes, dancing to the music on a makeshift dance floor or congregating in groups around the outskirts of the room.

Each of our girls of the month push their way through the gaping crowd, Tina coming to latch onto my arm, a seductive smile curling her lip as her eyes roam over my outfit. She's dressed as a slutty nurse or something, honestly, all I really notice are her pushed up tits that are practically falling out of the white tube top she's wearing. Hell yeah, I'm so ready to watch them bouncing up and down while I fuck her brains out.

"Mmm, baby, you look so good," she purrs, running her hand down the front of my shirt. "Why don't we start this party off right?" She bites down on her lower lip, a coy look in her eye as her hand grazes across the front of my pants, giving my balls a squeeze. *Fuck yes!* Checking my watch, I've got some time before they announce 'best costume' and the real fun can begin.

Giving her a dirty grin, I let her drag me back out the door and around to the back of the building.

An hour later, the music cuts off as Mr. Phister calls the room to attention, a microphone and envelope in his hand.

"Alright," he calls out. "I hope you've all had fun tonight, but now it's time to find out which lucky student has won this year's 'best costume'. The winner will get to choose the theme for the Valentine's Day dance and head up the party planning committee."

I roll my eyes. Who really gives a fuck about picking the theme or standing over a bunch of other students, making sure they pick streamers instead of balloons, or that the color they choose for the tablecloths is right?

Before Mr. Phister can announce the winner, I shove Tina off my arm, striding through the crowd, ignoring the confused looks on the other guys' faces.

Stepping up beside the headmaster, I say, "If you don't mind, Thomas, I'll take it from here," loud enough for the surrounding students to hear us, taking the microphone and envelope from him.

He gapes at me with wide eyes for a second before giving a hesitant, sharp nod, scurrying off to the side as I face the crowd, a cruel smirk on my face.

"Let's find out this year's winner then," I announce into the microphone, opening the envelope and glancing at the name printed on the page. "And the winner is...Abigail Cole."

I keep that same grin on my face as the crowd breaks into hushed whispers, everyone looking around them in confusion. A quick glance around the room is enough to know how much some of these kids spent on their costume, and let me tell you, the scholarship students never win. They don't stand a chance, so the fact one of them has just won is unheard of.

The students near the scholarship kids all seem to take several steps back, a gap opening up around them as they all look at each other with confused and wary glances.

"Don't be shy now, Abigail. Up you come." I wave her up onto the stage and, with one final wide-eyed look at her friends, she takes a hesitant step forward, then another, clearly seeing that she has no other option but to come up here. *Good girl. It would only have been worse for you if I had to come and get you.*

When she's finally standing beside me, an anxious look in her wide eyes that speaks right to me, feeding the inner part of me that lives off her fear, I wrap my arm around her shoulder, preventing her from running off. The poor thing looks like she's about to faint; she'll definitely bolt at the first opportunity if I don't stop her.

"Well, what do we think of Abigail's costume?" I ask the crowd. "Is it worthy of a win?" More whispered murmurs, a few people shaking their heads, but no one speaks out to confirm or deny.

"I don't think so," I answer my own question, glancing over her thrown together outfit. I don't even know what the fuck she's supposed to be, although at least she made an effort, unlike Hadley. I spotted her earlier, dressed in her usual attire of worn jeans, baggy top, and boots, having made no effort for tonight.

"I don't think scholarship students should be allowed to enter at all," I continue, speaking into the microphone. "Don't we give them enough? They are already getting an education that *our* families are paying for, with *our* hard earned money." My fingers dig into Abigail's skin, holding her in place as she subtly tries to shake off my grip and escape. "They shouldn't be given the opportunity to steal what is rightfully ours by birthright. They should cower in our presence, thank us for simply letting them walk these halls with us."

The murmurings are louder now, more than a few students nodding their head in agreement. Whether they actually agree or they're just too afraid to disagree with me, I don't really give a fuck.

Pushing the girl away from me, she stumbles, scurrying through the crowd as tears run down her face, not stopping until she crashes into some guy's arms.

"Take this as a warning," I say, my steely gaze intent on the group of scholarship students. "If you mess with us, you *will* get burned." I stare at Hadley, making it clear to her that this is all her fault, this show is for her benefit. She better heed my warning.

Hadley

Chapter 14

"That was all because of you," Abigail cries, whirling on me. Her makeup is smeared, black tracks from her mascara running down her face as Todd hugs her against him, the others standing in a semi-circle around them, all of them wearing tight expressions as they look at me.

"Me? That wasn't...I didn't..." I trail off, not knowing what to say.

She shakes her head, not wanting to hear my excuses.

"No. Everything was fine before you showed up. They left us alone." She sobs against Todd's chest. There's an unfamiliar tightness in my chest, guilt eating at me as I watch her fall apart. "As long as you continue to piss them off, just stay away from me."

She buries her face in Todd's chest and he wraps his arm more tightly around her, throwing a glower my way before whispering in her ear, the two of them walking off toward the dorm.

"She's right," Samuel speaks up, drawing my attention his way. "I think I speak for all of us when I say, stay away from us. All of us." Everyone but Emilia nods in agreement, even Michael gives a hesitant jerk of his head, his lips pursed.

My eyes fall on Emilia as the others give me a final, hard look before turning their backs and walking off. Emilia's the only one who looks at me with sympathy and pain, but she doesn't say anything, looking torn between staying with me and following the others.

"Emilia, are you coming with us?" Samuel calls out.

"I told you they weren't worth messing with." Her voice is choked, tears gleaming in her eyes as she gives me a final empathetic look, her face pinched before turning on her heel and walking over to the others.

A sea of emotions flows through me as I silently watch them leave; rage, pain and sadness swirling around like a tornado inside my gut. I'm torn between going after them and apologizing, and storming back into that hall and eviscerating Hawk. Did the others know what he was going to do? I didn't see their faces, too enraptured by the show of devastation Hawk was putting on for everyone.

Closing my eyes, I release a deep breath, weariness creeping into my bones.

"Are you okay?" Cam's soft tone only heightens the exhaustion. How did everything get so complicated? Coming here was supposed to make my life better. It should have been easy.

Turning around, I slowly take him in, trying to read from his face if he was involved in tonight's fiasco.

"What the fuck was that in there?" I sigh, waving toward the dining hall.

His lips are pressed tightly together as he gives a quick shake of his head, a gesture that doesn't really tell me anything.

"He was pissed about finding you in the apartment."

For real? What right does that give him to do what he did?

I stare at him incredulously for a moment, not understanding him at all.

"So he took it out on Abigail? She never did anything to him!" My voice rises as anger sparks within me. "She didn't deserve what he did to her tonight; none of them did."

"I know." Everything about him is too calm, too at odds with the raging storm within me.

"But you never stopped him."

He shakes his head again, his shoulders dropping. "We didn't know he was going to do that."

My eyes narrow as I scrutinize him, carefully trying to suss out if he's telling the truth or not. His open expression, his uncrossed arms and steady eye contact say he's not, but just because he doesn't know about it doesn't mean he won't have Hawk's back if he goes after the others to settle his score with me.

He's got my head all twisted, trying to work out where he stands. It's too much. I can't handle any more tonight.

I shake my head. "I've gotta go."

The words are barely out of my mouth before he takes a step forward as though to stop me, but I quickly raise my hand. "Don't. Please. It's been a long night, I just wanna go to bed."

With a pained expression on his face, he gives a sharp nod and I turn on my heel, my gut swirling with upheaval as I walk back to my room, regretting ever leaving it tonight.

I toss and turn all night, sleep evading me. Any time I do get over into a semi-sleep, it's filled with nightmares. Hawk's face combined with *their* voices. Every time, I wake up in a cold sweat, my heart racing, and in the early pre-dawn hours, I give up on sleep and decide today I'll have to function off coffee alone. At least no one will be in the dining hall this early so I can avoid the judgmental looks and whispers from the other students, and the awkward glares from the friends I had there for a little while.

Pushing the door open and stepping into the hall, I cast a quick glance around the room, expecting it to be empty, but I pull up short when I see West sitting at his usual table, alone. Why is one of those assholes always in here? They have that fancy-ass apartment with a kitchen and everything; they don't even need to fucking be here. Can't a girl catch a break for once?

Ignoring him, I make myself a coffee, ordering some breakfast. I hesitate as I glance over the tables, though. I'm probably not welcome at the scholarship table anymore, but I'm pretty sure I wouldn't be accepted at any of the others, either. Deciding it's not an issue for today—I'll be long gone before anyone wakes up and takes offense to my seating arrangements—I stroll over to my normal table and sit down.

My ass has barely hit the seat when West gets up from his chair. Instead of heading for the door like I was hoping, he comes toward me, sitting down in the chair opposite mine.

"What do you want, Wes?" I sigh, not mentally fortified yet to get into an argument with him. Could he not have let me get caffeine in my system first?!

"Hawk said he found you in Cam's room the other day."

My eyes immediately snap up to him, narrowing in suspicion. Cam indicated as much last night—not that I'm surprised Hawk told the others.

"What were you doing?"

His tone is more curious than accusatory, which is the only reason I engage him.

"Like I explained to Hawk, I was looking for my notebook. Cam must have accidentally lifted it. The door was unlocked, and I figured it wouldn't be a problem, but clearly, I was wrong. Next time I'll just leave it."

"Next time?" His brows pull together in confusion. "What exactly is going on between you and Cam?"

"Nothing," I insist, trying really hard not to think about what he did to me on that library table. But then I remember...West was watching us. My cheeks heat at the memory.

"You know, Cam is only interested in girls until he gets what he wants, then he drops them like yesterday's trash."

"Careful, *Wes*, you're sounding awfully jealous."

"Please." He snorts, his gaze not quite meeting my eye. "I'm not. I'm just letting you know how it is with him."

"Well, consider me warned."

He eyes me up for a moment before nodding.

"About last night..." He trails off, silence filling the space between us as he finds his words. "Hawk shouldn't have done what he did."

"But you're going to have his back anyway." I sigh. I can see it in his eyes. I don't even need him to confirm it.

"We're a team," he justifies. Something that I just don't understand. I'm more of a lone wolf myself. I play the game by my own rules, never answering or relying on anyone else.

After breakfast, I pull up my big girl panties and knock on Emilia's door, not happy with the way we left things last night. She was the first person here to be kind to me, and she's been an amazing friend. I don't want to see that end the way it did last night.

I can hear her shuffling around in her room before the door creaks open a crack, revealing a still half-asleep Emilia in her bunny rabbit pajamas and fluffy slippers.

Her eyes widen as she looks at me. "Oh, hey," she says awkwardly, none of her usual morning loveable grumpiness to be seen.

Licking my lips, unable to stop myself fidgeting with the hem of my top, I say, "I was, uh, hoping we could talk…about last night?"

She cringes, breaking eye contact with me. "I don't think there's anything to talk about," she mumbles, staring pointedly at her feet.

"Seriously? You don't think we need to discuss what happened?" I know her and the others are pissed at me, and I get that, but it's not like I *knew* Hawk would do that. If I'd known…

"Hadley." Her voice is strained, emotion heavy in that one word. "None of us can risk having the Princes, or anyone else in the school, ganging up on us. We just want to get through the year without any issues. I…I'm sorry, but we can't afford to gamble with our futures."

Before I can argue further, she closes the door in my face, the click of the lock engaging like a death knell on our short-lived friendship.

With a heavy heart, I let myself back into my room, anger and agitation making it impossible to sit still or focus on school work. Glancing at the clock, it's still early morning, so I grab my gym bag and head back out. I wasn't feeling it when I first got up, but maybe a physically exhausting workout is exactly what I need to stop me obsessing over everything.

Over the next hour, I pummel the shit out of the heavy bag, my arms exhausted and my hands aching by the time I switch over to the treadmill, setting a fast pace so all I can focus on is putting one foot in front of the other. Mason entered the gym not long after I did, but he at least had the decency to stick to our silent agreement of not talking. He went straight over to the weights corner and has barely spared me a glance since.

The sweat runs into my eyes and I wipe it away with the towel, faintly aware of the sound of Mason putting the bar back on the rack. Instead of starting into his next round of pull-ups like he's supposed to do, he crosses the floor toward me. It's clear he's got questions on his mind, and he looks determined as hell to get answers. His whole appearance gets my back up and I'm immediately on alert as he stops in front of me.

"What's your deal?"

Not slowing my pace, I glare at him. "What's yours?"

The wankstain ignores me, his eyes narrowing as he tries to figure me out. I'm pretty sure it's something he's been trying to do since that day in business class. He hasn't managed it so far, so I doubt he's suddenly going to piece me together now.

Ignoring me, he runs his eyes over me, taking in the loose t-shirt sticking to my sweaty skin and my tight shorts, his gaze lingering on the flexing muscles of my thighs as I maintain my fast pace.

Returning his gaze to my eyes, he cocks his head.

"Poor parents?"

I don't give him anything, my face a blank slate.

"Absent parents, then?"

Still, I give him nothing, but my silence seems to be enough of an answer itself.

His eyes narrow and I can see the cogs turning in his head.

"Foster parents?"

I make sure my face remains a rigid mask, no part of me giving away any indication of who I am or where I come from to this probing asshole.

Yet, his lips pinch, and he nods his head.

"So that's why you're here? You're escaping a shitty foster home?"

How the fuck does he know any of that? I *know* my features are unreadable.

Slamming my hand down on the stop button, I hiss out, "What the fuck do you want?"

"I want to know what you're doing with Cam." His voice is steady, but there's a slight rumbling in his chest, giving away the fact he's not as indifferent as he's making himself out to be.

"What is everyone's obsession with Cam?" I snarl, jumping off the treadmill. "He's a big boy, he can look after himself." I run the towel over my face and the back of my neck, pushing past Mason to get to my bag. "I highly doubt you all take such a keen interest in every other girl he chases after, so why me?"

"Because," he growls out, his hand snatching out, his fingers wrapping firmly around my arm, pulling me back toward him, "there's something different about you."

I stare up at him in confusion, taking in his beautiful baby blues that are swirling with just as much chaos as I feel. What the hell does he mean by that?

***

That afternoon, Cam has a swim meet, and like the love sick idiot I am, I show up, hiding at the back so he, and anyone else, can't see me. I'm not ready yet to face the backlash from the rest of the school. I just want to be left in peace to see that light Cam had in his eyes when he talked about swimming. I've never felt the passion for anything that he has for the sport. I guess I'm curious what it's all about.

I can feel the vigor in the air as soon as I enter the room, the stench of chlorine combined with the buzz of excitement and nervous energy. Watching him in the water, he's like an art form come to life. He's captivating; mesmerizing to watch. I can't tear my eyes away from him. I'm not even aware that he's won—hell, I don't even register the others in the water—until someone claps him on the back.

The second his race is over, I slip away, wandering around the empty hallways until I find the entrance to the changing rooms. I'm not sure what I'm doing here, what I'm hoping to achieve. It's like I'm a puppet being pulled on by a string, some greater force leading me to this moment. Only I'm not sure what I'm supposed to do next.

Cam

Chapter 15

"Rutherfords are winners. You better not let me down out there today," my asshole of a father reminds me once again, before stalking off, leaving me to warm up beside the pool. Like I don't fucking know already that Rutherfords don't lose. He's always been a belligerent asshole, but he's gotten worse the last few months. I have no idea what's going on with him, but he's fucking unbearable, and that's saying something since I could barely tolerate his presence before.

Thank fuck I hardly have to put up with him, except at these stupid competitions. It's almost enough of a reason to quit, but swimming is the only release I have, other than sex. Not that I'm getting much of that lately.

Since Hadley showed up, my dick has been on the fritz. I mean, I get it. She's hot as sin and that mouth...fuck, I can picture her doing so many things with that mouth. Not only is she hot, but her feisty attitude and the way she talks back is apparently my thing. Who knew? I hadn't realized how fucking bored I was with girls willing to do anything we wanted. None of the rest of them have any backbone. They are too terrified to stand up to us, or too eager to suck their way to the top that they just don't care. Either way, I was bored out of my fucking mind, and I didn't even know it. Not until Hadley showed up and made me realize what I've been missing out on. The feisty blonde with combat boots and a snarky mouth is a hot little challenge I didn't know I needed in my life. Things have been so much more interesting around here since she arrived.

Just my luck though, that Hawk has gotten himself in a fucking tizzy over her. I don't think it's because he's attracted to her, although sometimes it's seriously hard to tell with him. I swear, I've caught him fucking girls before and, honestly, it's impossible to tell if he's actually enjoying himself or hate fucking them.

When it's time for my race, I step up to the side of the pool, curling my toes around the edge of the concrete. I cast my eyes out over the crowd, quickly skimming over my father's sinister presence, spotting the guys cheering me on, like they always do on competition days. My eyes continue to search the stands, looking for a particular blonde. It's stupid. I know she won't be here, especially not after last night. Why would she be? I'm not even sure why I want her to be here. That's like girlfriend territory. Not something I do. Ever.

Yet, I can't ignore the disappointment I feel when I don't see her. Shaking off the feeling, I focus back on the water. Arching my body into the perfect dive pose, I steady my heart rate, focusing every one of my senses on the race in front of me, preparing myself for the loud blast of the whistle.

When it finally sounds, I push off with my feet, smoothly plunging into the pool. I've spent years honing my body, turning it into a machine that can move effortlessly through the water, barely causing a ripple. Kicking with my feet, I travel half the pool underwater before finally emerging. Gulping down a lungful of air, I skillfully glide through the water, propelling myself forward with my arms.

As I approach the far end of the pool, I duck under the water, tucking my head and flipping myself around so I'm facing the direction I just came from. Kicking off from the side of the pool, I speed back to the far end. Quickly traversing the distance, my hand slams down on the concrete as cheers ring out from the crowd in the stands.

Glancing back at the other competitors, I see I won by a decent bit, and, looking up to the timer, a large grin crosses my face as I fist-bump the air. I'm going to the State Championships, baby, and that race was my best time yet. Hell yeah!

That should keep my father off my back.

Pulling myself out of the water, I shake hands with the surrounding coaches and other competitors, politely accepting their words of congratulations.

"Well done, son," my father praises, his hand squeezing my shoulder, his shitty attitude from earlier now gone, replaced with a proud smile, like my achievements somehow reflect positively on him. I know he's not actually proud of me. He couldn't give two shits about me or my accomplishments. He's barely present in my life, except to dictate what I should and shouldn't be doing with it. Even growing up, he was barely around, and when he was, his mind was elsewhere. Who the fuck knows where, but it sure as hell wasn't at home with his family.

"Thanks, Dad," I respond, giving him a tight smile. Seeing the guys emerging through the crowd, I shake off my dad's hand. "I better go, the guys are waiting."

"Of course," he agrees, nodding his head, but he doesn't step aside to let me pass. Instead he stares at me intently, his penetrating gaze seemingly seeing right through me. "Enjoy these last few months of freedom, son. You'll be graduating soon and we need you to step up into the role we have set aside for each of you at the company." On that ominous note, he strides off, taking with him all of my joy from a moment ago.

As the guys approach, I plaster on a fake smile, accepting their congratulations before making my excuses to go shower.

***

Turning off the hot water, I step into the locker room. I always wait until everyone else has left before showering off the chlorine. Sure, the post-race locker talk is invigorating, but I love this moment of quiet reflection after a competition, where I can replay every moment and analyze every second.

I'm running a towel through my hair when I hear the door open. Assuming one of the other guys has forgotten something, I don't bother to turn around, but when no one says anything, I glance over my shoulder, freezing when I see Hadley standing just inside the door.

Her eyes drop to take in my naked chest, the towel wrapped loosely around my waist, and she runs her tongue along her lower lip, her eyes becoming heated as she drinks me in. Fuck, seeing her turned-on like that is crazy hot. I don't know what it is about her, but she has my dick all tied up in knots. I barely even know her, yet something about her constantly draws me in.

Maybe the guys are right when they say I'm all about the chase. There's something thrilling about going after a girl, but the ones here give in too quickly. One wink in their direction and they are practically ready to spread their legs for me. It's too easy. Hadley isn't anything like that. She's the perfect challenge. I know she wants me, but the push-pull dynamic we've got going on is infectious. I can't get enough of it. But it's more than just chasing after her. I can feel it. There's a hell of a lot of sexual chemistry between us, but there's also something more, something deeper.

"What are you doing in here?" I ask, my voice husky. Her short skirt shows off her toned, milky thighs, her white shirt clinging to her tits, sending all my blood due south. I couldn't talk my dick down even if I wanted to.

"You were great out there today," she murmurs, ignoring my question as she stares transfixed at my chest.

Her words catch me by surprise. I hadn't realized she was in the crowd. I didn't see her, and honestly, I never expected her to be there. After Hawk's one-man show last night, I'm shocked she's even speaking to me.

"You were watching?"

She shrugs like it's no big deal; her gaze darting nervously around the room like she's embarrassed, but a seed of warmth sparks within me at the thought of her cheering me on from the stands. Sure, the guys always show up, and of course girls do too, but I've never actually wanted a girl there before. "Had to see what all the fuss was about."

I move quicker than I've ever moved before—which is saying something, considering how lean and agile I am from years of swim training. My lips crash down on hers, my hands wrapping around her waist, neither of us giving a shit that I'm getting her wet.

I've never felt so drawn to another person. It's like the shit in the movies where they have this undeniable chemistry. I never thought that crap was real, but there's no denying the pull she has over me, drawing me in like some sort of succubus.

Her tiny hands roam over my pecs, squeezing my shoulders and running down my back. Every part of me she touches lights up like a fucking Christmas tree, demanding more.

I shove her blazer over her shoulders and down her arms until it pools at her feet, reaching around to grab two handfuls of her ass cheeks and pulling her in against me as I grind my dick against her core. Groaning, she breaks our kiss, her head falling back as she arches into me, the movement exposing her neck. Her hands grip onto my shoulders and I dip my head, kissing and sucking as I use my grasp on her ass to lift her up, pressing her more firmly against the locker room door as she wraps her legs around me. I know I should take the time to strip her naked, lay her out and feast on her, but I'm too fucking desperate for her. I just need to be inside her. Next time,

I'll make sure I lick every part of her before I have her screaming my name.

Using the heel of the weird-ass combat boots she wears, she dislodges my towel, my dick springing free and immediately nestling itself between her spread thighs. Reaching between us, I run my finger up the front of her panties, groaning at how wet she is, loving her soft moans as she tilts her hips, increasing the friction of my finger and silently demanding more.

Giving her what she wants, I press down on her clit, rubbing tight circles until she's panting heavily. "Oh, Cam," she cries out, her grip on my shoulders almost painful as her fingernails dig into my skin. Slipping my fingers underneath her panties, I slide them through her pussy lips, sinking two fingers into her.

"Fuck," she moans, her hands sliding up into my hair, grabbing the strands and slamming her lips down on mine, using her grip on my hair to angle my head just how she wants it, her tongue sweeping deep into my mouth. My lips slide over hers, sucking her in further as my fingers pump in and out of her, the pace matching the clashing of our tongues. Her cunt clenches around me as her hand trails down the front of my chest, reaching between us until she's holding my cock in her hand.

She gently squeezes it, causing me to groan into her mouth as our kiss turns fierce, both of us getting lost in the passion. Her hand slides up and down my dick, providing the perfect amount of pressure. Fuck, most hand jobs are just meh, nothing to get excited about unless you're a pre-teen virgin, but holy hell, just the feel of her hand wrapped around me has my balls drawing up, that tingling feeling reverberating through me.

She tears her lips away from mine, her head falling back against the door. "Fuck, Cam, I'm going to come." Her eyes drift closed, her hand still pumping my dick as I circle my thumb over her clit and curl my fingers over that magical spot.

"Fuck. Fuck. FUCK," she cries, her pussy clamping down on my fingers, her juices dripping down my hand as she comes.

Pulling them out of her, I bring my fingers to my lips, sucking them into my mouth and groaning at the taste of her on my tongue. Her pupils are blown, and she watches transfixed as I lick her off me.

"Mmm, baby, you taste so good."

She licks her lips, her teeth digging into her bottom lip, her chest rapidly rising and falling with her heavy breaths.

"Cam," she breathes. "Condom." It's a husky demand, overflowing with hunger and carnal need.

"Yeah, baby," I agree, my lips meeting hers as I wrap my arms around her thighs, carrying her over to where I left my stuff. Dropping her to her feet beside my locker, I dig in my bag until I find a condom. She snatches it from between my fingers, tearing it open and rolling it down my dick before I've even comprehended what's happened. Damn, I love a girl who isn't afraid to go after what she wants.

Towering over her, my forearm leaning against the metal locker above her, I tuck my fingers under her chin, lifting it so she's looking up at me. I don't think I've ever wanted a girl more than I do in this moment. With raw lust in her eyes and heat on her cheeks, she looks fucking incredible. Dick-blowing. Literally.

My hand slides round the back of her neck, my lips descending on hers, loving that she can taste herself on me. She moans into my mouth, her tongue sparring with mine as we swiftly fall into that all-consuming heady sensation of being wrapped up with someone physically.

She lifts her leg up, hitching it over my hip, the heel of her boot digging into my ass. Lifting my arm off the locker, I run it up her thigh, tucking her panties to the side before holding her leg securely in place as my cock stands at attention, aimed perfectly at her center.

Nudging at her opening, I slowly sink into her, our kiss breaking as we are both overcome by pleasure. My eyes drift shut and I groan at the feel of her wrapped around me, her sweet heat like fucking ecstasy as I bottom out.

"I knew you'd feel fucking incredible," I breathe, my forehead pressed against hers.

Tilting her head, her lips brush over mine as I pull back. My hand clamps tighter around her thigh as I push into her again, savoring the feel of her clenching around me. Maintaining a slow pace, I thrust in and out. The tingling at the base of my dick spreads to my spine and I know I'm close to blowing my load, but I'm so not ready for this to be over yet. She feels far too fucking good.

Linking my fingers with hers, I pin her hand to the locker above her head. Holding her thigh in my large palm, I pick up my speed, ramming in and out of her, her soft moans of pleasure pushing me on as I bury my face in her neck, sucking and biting at the soft skin.

I can feel her clenching around me, her soft cries letting me know she's close to coming. Inching my fingers up her thigh until I can feel her puckered hole, I dip lower, feeling my slick dick sliding in and out of her. Collecting some of her juices, I circle my finger around the rim of her hole, feeling her soft gasp against my cheek as she realizes what I'm doing.

I've barely pushed the tip of my finger inside her when she cries out, her walls slamming down around my dick in the best way, breaking through the last bit of resistance I had as I let go, grunting out her name as I go over the cliff with her, into orgasmic bliss.

We stay like that for a long moment after, both of us breathing heavily as we come back to reality. With my head still buried in her neck, I kiss her skin again, not wanting to leave this moment of contentment.

Eventually, though, she shuffles, and I have no choice but to lower her leg, pulling out of her. I keep the rest of my body flush with hers though, my hand wrapping itself in her hair.

"That was definitely not a one-time thing," I promise. "I'm nowhere near done with you."

***

It's changeover day again. I can't say I paid any attention to Missy last time, and why the fuck would I when I can be chasing someone like Hadley? And holy fuck, was she worth it! I knew it the second I slammed myself balls deep inside of her—she's so much more than a simple fling. I don't know what the fuck she is or what it means, but I want to do it again and again.

That's why I've made my decision. Hawk's going to shit a brick, and West and Mason might be pissy about it, but I don't give a damn. It's the right thing to do.

The four of us stride into the dining hall and all eyes turn our way, everyone following our every move as we make our way to our normal table. I hate that we have to eat here every morning. We have our own damn kitchen, yet we have to come down here to appease the masses. It's a control thing, to remind the school who owns it, but I'd much rather have breakfast in our apartment every day, away from prying eyes.

After breakfast, all of us get to our feet. That buzz of excitement I felt the first month is back, and I can barely stand still as I wait for Hawk and Mason to take their turns. Mason once again picks out a curly-haired blonde, and I can't help but notice the similarities to Hadley. Is that just a coincidence? He barely knows Hadley. In fact, I don't think I've ever even seen him talk to her. Yeah, they've sat at the same table in the library once or twice, when the two of us have been working on our English assignment, and we all have business class together, but other than that, I don't think they ever cross paths, and he's never mentioned her before.

Realizing it's my turn, I shake myself out of that weird train of thought and circle round to the front of the table. Unlike the last two times, I don't make a whole song and dance out of the thing. I know what I want this month, and I'm not about to let another second pass without her.

Stepping into the middle of the room, I turn to face her, looking directly at her as I call out her name. "Hadley."

Hadley

Chapter 16

"Hadley." That one word, my own goddamn name, obliterates the last shred of peace I had constructed for myself here at Pac Prep.

I slowly turn in my seat until I find Cam standing in the middle of the dining hall with a stupid-ass grin on his face, looking proud as shit. God damn, I just want to strangle the sexy idiot. He's got no idea the damage he's just caused.

Meeting his eyes, I try to communicate how sorry I am. I don't mean to hurt him, but that's exactly what I have to do because there is just no fucking way I can be a girl of the month. I don't even agree with the fucking concept, and I thought the idiot knew that.

Rising to my feet, I steel my spine, running my tongue along my suddenly dry lips. I cast a glance around the rest of the hall, ignoring Hawk's murderous glare and Mason's tight expression.

"No." The word comes out like a whip, swiping the excited look from Cam's face as it falls, shock and hurt evident for only a second before he composes himself, donning an impassive expression.

"You can't say no," Hawk barks out, surprising me. I thought he, of all people, would be more than happy for me to turn Cam down. He's been telling me to keep my distance for weeks now, and when I finally do as he asks, he's not happy? *Fucking infuriating shithead.*

"He's right," West agrees. Of course he does, because when one of them decides something, the rest of them immediately jump on board and back them up.

"*He* can't choose a scholarship student," I retort.

"Also true," West nods, his brows furrowing as he tries to work out which is the bigger issue—Cam asking out a scholarship student, or a girl turning him down.

"Who says I can't say no?" I question, adamant that regardless of whatever they say, I am *not* becoming a girl of the month. "Just because a girl has never said no before, doesn't mean it's not allowed."

West nods his head, that small movement allowing me to release the tense breath I'd been holding. He leans in to whisper in Hawk's ear, the two of them having a private conversation. I can't make out any of it, but I keep my eyes locked on them, refusing to look in Cam's direction and see the pain and confusion written all over his face. Why the fuck didn't he just talk to me first? I could have explained myself to him in private and saved both of us from this embarrassment.

“We need to discuss it,” Hawk finally says, addressing the room. “We will have an answer for you by tomorrow.”

What the fuck does that mean?!

Before I can argue, West steps forward, quickly picking a girl and dragging a still frozen Cam back toward the table. Cam shakes him off halfway, though, storming out of the room.

With shaky legs, I sit back down at my table. I've been sitting alone since Halloween, but I can't help glancing toward where the scholarship students sit, finding all seven of them are gaping at me with mixed looks of awe, shock, and displeasure.

Fuck my life.

***

“What the hell was that?!” I demand, sitting down beside Cam. I deliberately left the dining hall as soon as I finished eating, hoping to track him down before class. I looked everywhere for him before giving up and coming to English early; and apparently he's been here the whole time.

He doesn't even look at me or acknowledge I've spoken.

“Cam! Why didn't you tell me you were going to do that?”

“What does it matter?” he snarls, his head snapping my way so he can glare at me. “Would you have given a different answer if I'd consulted you first?”

“No,” I respond truthfully. He gives a tight nod of his head, his gaze dropping back to his table.

“At least tell me why.” His voice is quiet now, sad, and it only breaks my heart for him. I never wanted this to happen, but there was no way I could say yes; submit to someone like that, give them that power and control over me, not when I'm here to gain my own freedom, to live my own life.

"I...It's complicated." I sigh weakly, rubbing my hands over my face in frustration, unable to explain any of it to him. "It has nothing to do with you, though. I just...couldn't say yes."

We lapse into silence, neither of us speaking again as the class fills up and Mr. Greer begins today's lesson. The air between us is fraught with tension and the second the bell goes, Cam darts out of his chair like it's on fire, storming out of the room.

The rest of the day goes by in a blur, but I don't miss the glares thrown at me by the girls, everyone whispering, trying to work out why Cam would choose me. They aren't the only ones asking themselves that question. I can't understand why he would do that, why he would openly acknowledge there's anything between us. Of course, the guys seem to have decided it's because I'm good in bed and catcalls have been following me around the halls all day. It takes everything in me not to lash out at one of those motherfuckers, but I can't afford to lose my spot here and *that* is the only reason several of them aren't sent to the hospital today with fractured arms or broken noses.

That night I've just flicked the desk lamp off—having crammed enough school work nonsense into my brain for the day—and I'm getting ready for bed when my tablet goes off. Ugh, who could be messaging me so late? The only person who ever did was Cam, and somehow, I doubt he's sitting in the dining hall wondering if I'm going to show up for our usual midnight date.

Hawk: *Dining Hall. Now.*

Seriously? Does he think I'm some sort of lapdog who's just going to come when ordered?

The device vibrates with another incoming message.

Hawk: *Don't make us come get you.*

Well, I sure as hell don't need them turning up at my door and disturbing the whole dorm at this time of night. God knows there's enough drama involving me at the minute, I don't need to add to the rumors.

Not giving a flying fuck that I'm wearing a pair of boxer shorts, I throw on a hoodie and stuff my feet back into my boots, cursing out every single Prick as I storm out of the dorms and over to the canteen, throwing the doors open and glowering at the lot of them as they sit at their usual table. It's well after midnight, yet each of them looks better than the last. How is that fair?

Hawk's scowl only deepens as he takes in what I'm wearing, while Cam's face pinches when he sees me. I have to admit, that hurts a little and I quickly glance away, finding Mason staring at my legs, and West with a slight blush in his cheeks which he hides by ducking his head.

"What is this about?" I bark, sitting down on the opposite side of the table, feeling all of their eyes on me. It's unsettling, and I struggle not to squirm under the weight of their gaze, but I'm not about to let them know how on edge I am about all of this.

"It's about what happened today." Hawk's growl makes it clear he's still fucking pissed about this morning. *Yeah, you and me both, buddy.* "You can't say no."

"Excuse me?" My eyes snap to his. He's got to be fucking joking, right? "In case you missed it, I already did."

Cam mumbles something under his breath that sounds suspiciously like *nobody could have missed that,* but Mason jams his elbow in his ribs, shutting him up.

"We'll announce it to the school tomorrow. You'll be expected to sit with us at breakfast, come to parties with us, and basically do whatever we say. You belong to Cam, so he's the only one who can fuck you, but it's in your best interest to just do as you're told."

Slamming my hand hard against the table, I jump to my feet. "I belong to no one," I snarl back, having barely heard the end of his sentence over the rage building inside me and the panic swirling in my head. I'm pretty sure most of it is shit he's just tacked on for me. Outside of breakfast and parties, I rarely see the girls with the guys, unless they're willingly draping themselves all over them. But then I guess I'm the exception to all the other girls. The only one who doesn't want to be here.

A slow, cruel grin spreads across Hawk's face and I swear to fuck, if it's the last thing I do, I'm going to wipe it off him. Make it so he can never fucking smile again. "You do now, trash. Now run along, and don't be late tomorrow. You wouldn't want to miss your first breakfast with the Princes now, would you?"

My hands clench into tight fists as I grit my teeth, fighting back the urge to dive across the table and strangle him with my bare hands. Violence isn't the answer, and it will only get me kicked out of here. No, I have to play this smart. If he thinks he can forcefully keep me around, then fine, I'll make every second a living hell for each of them.

With my lip curled up in disgust, I flick my gaze between them, silently communicating the promise of pain, death, and destruction. Hawk only smirks back, rising to the challenge, while Cam still looks pissed. I'm beyond giving a shit that I hurt his feelings, though. Boo-fucking-hoo. Grow the fuck up and get over it. Mason is as impassive as ever, his penetrating gaze analyzing my every movement. I swear he can read every murderous thought flitting through my mind right now. West is the only one who looks uncomfortable, unwilling to meet my gaze.

"Fine," I snarl through gritted teeth. "But if you think you're going to get to me, you should know, I give as good as I get." With that, I turn on my heel and storm out of the hall without a backward glance.

***

I toss and turn all night and the next morning I'm a ball of nerves, my hands shaking frantically as I struggle to button my shirt. Closing my eyes, I take several deep breaths, trying to steady myself. I'm being fucking pathetic. This is nothing I can't handle. Hell, this doesn't even make the top ten of fucked-up shit I've survived. I can do this. I'm going into battle and I need to fucking prepare myself.

Snapping open my eyes, I'm pleased to find my old mask in place, the one I tucked away when I walked through those gates. This old thing has gotten me through everything I've had to face so far in life; I know it won't let me down now.

There's only fifteen minutes left of breakfast when I storm through the dining hall doors, a look of thunder on my face. If I'm going to do this, I'm going to make it very damn clear I'm not fucking happy about it, and hopefully, the dark scowl on my face will be enough to deter some of the weaker kids from thinking they can gossip about me.

"Ah, there she is," Hawk calls out, a shit-eating grin on his face that I can't fucking wait to rip off. "Come sit with us, Hadley."

As if I have a fucking choice.

Casting a quick glance out of the corner of my eye toward the scholarship table, I find all eyes on me, Emilia's mouth agape as she watches me cross the room to the Princes' table, sitting down beside Cam.

"I ordered you breakfast since you're late," Hawk says in a sickly-sweet tone. Looking down at the plate, there's a slice of grapefruit in front of me. That's it. One measly slice of fucking grapefruit. Thankfully, I didn't undergo my usual exercise routine this morning, otherwise I'd be fucking starving, but even so, who the fuck can live off that all morning?

Gritting my teeth, I don't bother to acknowledge Hawk, pretending I'm not insulted by the lack of food, and instead picking up my fork and digging in, ignoring everyone's eyes on me. No one says anything else to me for the rest of breakfast, the others too caught up in talking to their new girl, while Cam does his best to pretend I don't exist. He doesn't even glance in my direction, and it's the longest fifteen minutes of my life; but fucking finally, people start to filter out to class and the Pricks get to their feet. The second I can, I get away from them, and other than having to endure their presence in business class, I spend the rest of the day ignoring their existence.

Of course, it's much harder to ignore the rest of the school, and Bianca and the other Princesses corner me that afternoon. Scanning my eyes over their scowling faces, I notice the group size has grown, the club having welcomed each new set of girls into their ranks. Somehow, I don't think they are here to give me my induction talk and welcome pack.

"How the fuck did you make Cam do that?" Bianca demands. She stands front and center, clearly the ringleader of this little band of fake royalty.

"I didn't make Cam do anything," I retort, crossing my arms over my chest.

"Then why would he choose you?" Missy's eyes run over me with confusion, like she can't understand what Cam could find so appealing about me.

"Why would you say no?" another girl demands. I think her name was Cora or something.

I scan my eyes over all of them, seeing the same question in each of their eyes. "Because unlike you, I didn't dream of growing up, finding a Prick and living unhappily ever after," I snap, pushing through the crowd of desperate girls that are never going to understand why I'm not exactly like them.

"You're *never* going to be one of us," Bianca calls out behind me, causing me to pause, turning around to face her with an incredulous look on my face.

"Bianca, understand this," I say evenly, "I don't *ever* want to be you."

As I turn away, I catch Mason standing in a doorway, watching the whole thing like some creeper in the shadows. I only stare at him for a second before forcing myself to look away, storming on down the corridor.

The rest of the week goes by in much the same way. Cam doesn't say a word to me, Hawk takes far too much pleasure from the cheap shots he fires my way, and he's somehow managed to get the kitchen staff to only bring out fucking grapefruit for me every morning, even if I order something different. I've had to stock up on snacks from the shop in the rec center so I can eat something halfway decent in the mornings before I have to go to the dining hall, but, man, I fucking miss the pancakes.

The worst part of it, though, is that the scholarship students barely look at me. Any time I smile their way or dare to wave at them, they duck their heads and glance away, ignoring me. What hurts the most is Emilia's absence. I miss our easy friendship and her daily chatter.

On Friday, I show up early for computer class so I can sit as far away from West as possible, fully intent on going back to my original plan of teaching myself how to use the stupid software on these machines. Eating breakfast with them is enough torture, and while I know Hawk is the one behind most of this shit, the fact the others just go along with it pisses the hell out of me.

Picking a seat on the far side of the room, I log in and open up today's lesson plan, only to be disturbed when someone sits down beside me. His familiar scent washes over me and I snap my head around to glare at him. "What are you doing over here?"

Both of his eyebrows jump up, his surprise at my anger only infuriating me more. How can he not expect me to be pissy with him? I've had the week from hell, thanks to him and his stupid friends.

"I thought you needed my help."

"I'm sure I can work it out by myself," I snap, ignoring the little voice in my head that reminds me I tried to do that before and failed epically.

"Sure you can." He snorts. I don't respond as I mentally count backward from ten so I don't smash him over the head with my mouse. "Look." He sighs. "How about we leave all that crap outside the classroom?"

"You mean the crap where you're forcing me to be one of your stupid girls? That crap?"

Ignoring my attitude, West asks, "Why did you say no to Cam anyway? I thought you two were a thing."

Huh, why did he think that? Did Cam say something? Shame he couldn't have talked to me about us too, before making such a public and antiquated declaration.

"You can't just go around claiming girls and demanding they be yours, *Wes*. People are not possessions, you can't treat others like livestock to be traded at will."

A tense moment of silence fills the air between us as I wait for the verbal lashing that I've overstepped my mark, but instead, he surprises me. "You're right," he easily agrees. "I can only imagine how it looks to someone who hasn't grown up in our world, but it's tradition. Despite how it might look, it's bigger than us. We actually have very little say over any of this. Did you know most of the senior girls were enrolled here because of us? Because *we* were here. Everyone who's anyone in our circle knows the tradition. They enroll their daughters in the hopes they'll snag themselves a Prince for a husband. It's all part and parcel of being in the upper class. Hell, each of us will probably marry one of those girls someday. You're the first person I've heard of to fight back, to *ever* say no."

I take a moment to think over his words, navigating my way through the various bomb drops. Parents pimping their daughters out, the Pricks marrying girls they don't have any respect for. I thought the life I left behind was pretty fucked up, but this one is quickly coming in at second place.

"I just don't understand how you can be happy with any of that. How can you be okay with knowing girls are being pushed to be with you? How can you be happy spending your life with someone you don't even seem to like?"

"Happy?" West laughs, but it lacks any humor. "Who said anything about being happy? Despite what people think, happiness and money do not go hand in hand. You do what's expected of you, because that's what every generation before us has done. As for the girls...well, you've seen them. Do they look like they're being forced to you?" He has a point there. The girls are all champing at the bit to be with the guys of their own free will. "They want us as much as their families want them to be with us; because we're rich and powerful."

"Doesn't hurt that you're all built like gods," I joke, but it falls flat when West simply stares at me, surprise and confusion flitting across his face. I'm not sure what has him stumped, though. Surely he knows how hot he is?

After a moment he shakes himself out of whatever he was thinking, clearing his throat. "I'm sorry you got caught up in the middle of all of this. I don't know what's going on with you and Cam, but I know he's hurt, and he's going to take it out on you. Hawk's also going to do everything he can to make your life hell for the next month. There's nothing I can really do to stop either of them. All I can do is promise that, in here, we can continue on like normal; leave all that shit at the door."

I look deep into his forest green eyes, wanting to believe him. In my head, there are two very different versions of West, the one he shows the world—the one he is when he's with the others—and this soft, gentle version that he is around me. I want to believe the version he shows me is real and not a ruse, but if I've learned anything these last few months, it's that I can't trust any of them. However, despite what I *know*, I *want* to believe in him. It's for that reason that I slowly nod my head in agreement. "Okay. We'll leave the rest of the world outside."

Hadley

Chapter 17

Hawk: *Get your ass to the lake! Now!*

West: *It will be easier if you don't fight it.*

Hawk and Cam are both assholes, and clearly, West doesn't know me at all. I've been hiding out in my room for the last hour, trying to ignore the incessant buzzing of the tablet. There's a party tonight and according to Hawk, attendance is mandatory.

With a groan, I get to my feet, rifling through my meager belongings. Finding the oldest, rattiest, pair of shorts and a t shirt with a middle finger on it, an evil grin lights up my face. Well, if they insist on my presence, I'm at least going to dress how I want.

Twenty minutes later and I'm strolling down the embankment toward the fire pit where, as per usual, the four of them are chilling. Mason and Hawk have this month's girls on their laps. West's girl clings to his arm, trying to get his attention, but her gaze flicks jealously between Mason, Hawk, and Cam. What the hell is her problem? West is a fucking catch, you know, if you're into stupidly rich, pampered boys. The bitch should appreciate what she has.

Glancing Cam's way, I expect to find him with the same sullen look he's worn all week, but instead he's hitting on some chick I don't recognize. *Is he for fucking real?* I guess this is what West meant when he said Cam would take his hurt out on me, and, damn, the spike of jealousy that zings through me only annoys me further.

"What the fuck are you wearing?" Hawk snarls, tearing his lips away from what's-her-name. "You look like a fucking homeless person."

I mock gasp, bringing my hand up to my chest. "What? But these are my best clothes. Only the finest for a Pac party, right?"

Rolling my eyes, I snatch a water bottle out of the cooler and drop into a seat on the other side of the fire, as far from Hawk and Cam as I can get. Stretching my legs out in front of me, I cross my boot-covered feet at the ankle, looking chill as fuck as I unscrew the water and take a long gulp.

"You're an extension of us, now. You have to dress the part."

The look I give him says everything about how few fucks I give about what he wants, but of course his snarking has drawn the attention of the other girls around the fire.

"Eww." The girl Cam was flirting with scrunches up her nose in disgust. "Where did you even find those?"

I turn to look at her in confusion. "They were a gift, Stew gave me this hoodie."

"Who the fuck is Stew?" Hawk growls.

"The homeless man who let me share his cardboard box house with him for a few nights." Okay, so not quite the truth, but the gasps of shock and looks of disgust are so totally worth it.

"If you wear that shit around us again, I'm going to strip it off you and burn it. See if you like walking around naked." Hawk's snarl is deadly serious. If he so much as laid a hand on me, I'd make him regret it, but the thought of ending up in only my underwear in front of all these assholes has a skitter of fear running up my spine. *No fucking thanks.*

It's not long before Cam takes off to dance with the brown-haired bimbo he's been flirting with all night. Not that I notice. Hawk is practically fucking his girl in front of us all, while Mason and West talk quietly, both of them ignoring their girls. It's strange. While West frequently pays little to no attention to his girl of the month, it's the first time I've seen Mason ignoring his. He's usually all over that, but since I sat down, he's barely looked her way.

Spotting Emilia and the others over by the drinks table, unease swirls in my stomach. Heeding their words, I haven't talked to any of them since Halloween, and I miss hanging out with them.

"Where the fuck are you going?" Hawk's growl has me realizing I'm on my feet, as though I was going to go over to them. Which is stupid—they wouldn't want me anywhere near them.

"For a walk," I lie, needing some sort of excuse to cover whatever I thought I was doing.

"No, you're not. Sit your ass down and shut up."

I grind my teeth together, my hand clenching around my water bottle until it crinkles under the pressure as my sadness is quickly burned away in the heat of my anger.

"I'm not about to sit here and watch you attempt to fuck what's-her-name with your stunted dick. Trust me, you don't want anyone to see her fake as fuck orgasm."

With a venomous snarl, he gets to his feet, dragging blondie with him as he takes off into the forest. Only when he's gone, do I let out a laugh, shaking my head.

"Why do you have to wind him up like that?" West asks, reminding me there was an audience for that little showdown.

Shrugging, I take another sip of water. "He makes it way too damn easy."

He shakes his head, getting back to his conversation with Mason while I sit and watch the scholarship students partying at the far end of the beach. After a while, my gaze comes back to Mason and West. The girl Mason chose, I think her name is Tiffany, has gone off to dance nearby, but every now and again she glances in this direction, scowling when she discovers Mason isn't watching her. On the other hand, West's girl stares star-struck at Mason.

"Why the fuck are you staring at Mason?" I bark at her, drawing not only her attention but also Mason and West's.

"What? I wasn't—" she splutters.

"Yes, you were. You have been all night. If you don't want to be with West, then you should have said no."

"Like you did?" she snarks, spitting fire at me.

"At least I'm not pretending to like one guy while eye fucking his best friend."

With a glowering look she storms to her feet, taking off toward Tiffany, dragging her deeper into the crowd and out of view. Two for two. I wonder who I can piss off next.

"You're on fire tonight, aren't you?" West deadpans, the pair of them still looking at me.

I shrug my shoulders in a *what can you do* gesture. "Hey, you guys are the ones that wanted me to come. Maybe next time you'll think better of it."

***

On Sunday, I get a notification on my phone that there is a parcel waiting for me in the post room. When I arrive, I find a stack of garment bags, each one containing a dress. *What the hell?* There are enough dresses to fill my entire wardrobe.

After getting help to carry them all back to my room, I flick through each bag, lifting out the dress and giving it a critical look before hanging it up. Each one falls to my mid-thigh and all of them are relatively conservative. No plunging necklines, and none of them are backless. Nothing like the strips of fabric the other girls wear. The most daring they get is a split up the side that I'm certain will show my panties. That I can totally live with.

I'm about halfway through the bags when I find a note stuck to one.

This should keep Hawk off your back for a while. W.

West. Why would he help me out, though? Not having any answers to that, I ignore it, instead focusing on my pretty new dresses. I've never had anything like them before. Nothing designer, nothing that was just mine. I can't stop running my hand down the soft fabric, a goofy smile on my face as I continue through the pile. I now have enough dresses that I could probably wear a different one to each party for the rest of the year and still have some I've never worn. That's crazy, right?

On Friday night, after yet another un-fun week of grapefruit slices, girls calling me a slut, and trying to avoid spending any more time than necessary with the Pricks, I'm dressed in one of my new dresses, strutting across the sand toward the fire pit. I have to admit; I feel like hot stuff right now.

All four boys are in their usual seats around the fire, but what's surprising is that they're alone. No girl of the month, or any other girl, in sight. Maybe that means they will let me off the hook for the night.

They all glance my way as I approach, various looks flitting across their features. While I see heat and surprise in Mason's, West looks almost smug, an unusual look on him. Cam takes one heated look at me and storms off. It's been yet another week of silence and avoidance from him, so I can't say I'm surprised. Hawk, as per usual, has his characteristic scowl firmly in place.

"Better," is all he says, barely glancing at the dress. "But you forgot the shoes."

"Nope, I didn't." I stick out my leg, shaking it in front of him so he can see my usual, impossible to miss, scuffed, chunky boots, enjoying the disgusted sneer that curls his lips.

"Heels go with dresses, not those monstrosities."

"Trust me, Hawk," I say sweetly, giving him a blinding, innocent smile as I drop into Cam's empty chair beside him. "You don't want me to wear heels."

His eyes narrow at me in suspicion. "Why is that?"

I make sure to keep my sugary sweet smile in place. "Because I won't be able to stop myself from stabbing you through the eye with it."

Unimpressed, he glowers at me, and I swear I see West covering a laugh behind his hand.

"Beer?" Mason offers, stretching across to lift himself one.

"No thanks, I don't drink."

"You don't? Ever?" His eyebrows lift in surprise as he cracks the tab on the beer.

"Nope. Never."

"Huh. How come?"

I shrug my shoulders, not wanting to get into any of it. "I just don't. It's not my thing."

"What *is* your thing?" Hawk sneers. "You don't like parties, you don't drink, what the fuck do you like doing?"

"I like pissing you off," I retort sweetly. This time, both West and Mason snort, and Hawk turns his icy glare on them.

***

The same sort of truce I have with West in the computer suite seems to apply to my time in the gym with Mason where we both pretend to not notice the other as we go about our morning routine, but for the last two weeks, he's managed to secretly sneak a high carb, high protein snack bar—one of the fancy, expensive ones—into my gym bag without me noticing. I feel like I watch his every move so I've no idea how he's managing it, but it's so much tastier than the cheap, unfulfilling shit in the shop, and Hawk still has the kitchen staff giving me only grapefruit for breakfast so I'm not about to argue.

I seriously don't understand it. He's not around when I eat the rest of my meals and the kitchen staff bring me whatever I order, but he's intent on pissing me off every morning by dictating what I eat. What he doesn't realize is that, every morning, as I tuck into my measly slice of fruit, I'm imagining all the horrific ways in which I'm going to get him back.

I'm putting my gym gear back in my bag after my workout when my tablet goes off in my bag and, pulling it out, I find a new message from Cam.

Cam: *Library.*

God, I'm getting seriously fucking sick of these demands. First Hawk, now Cam. I almost preferred it when he was ignoring me.

Grabbing my backpack, I take off for the library. Part of me fucking hates the fact I'm going to them as though summoned, but while I might be playing along, I've been using the time I spend with them to learn what I can about them. They think they hide themselves behind their public personas but they don't realize how much they let slip; the small things about themselves that most people probably wouldn't pick up on, but I do. I note every part of themselves they unwillingly offer me.

Entering the library, I don't see Cam, or any of the others, at their usual table at the back of the room. Glancing around, I don't see them anywhere. *If this is some sort of fucking joke...*

Someone waving catches my attention and I turn my head to find some dark-haired girl I don't know waving me over. Cautiously, I approach the table, not able to work out what is going on.

When I just stand at the table, looking down at her, she must cop on that I'm not going to sit down.

"Oh, uh," she stumbles, flustered. "Cam wanted me to give you this." Eyeing the pages she's holding toward me, it's Cam's half of our English project. *Seriously? He's getting minions to deliver his assignments to me? He could just have emailed the damn thing.*

"Why isn't he delivering it himself?"

She must not have expected me to question her as her eyes widen in surprise. "I don't know. He just told me to tell him when I was done and he'd get you to come pick it up."

Hold up. What did she say?

"When you're done with it?"

"Yeah." She's looking at me like she can't understand my confusion. With her hand still outstretched in a desperate bid to get me to take the pages, I glance over the work. It's painfully obvious this is not Cam's writing. What Cam wrote for our first assignment got us an A+, but this drivel is barely passable.

"You wrote this?" Obviously she did, but I want her to confirm it.

"Yeah." She smiles brightly, clearly proud of the job she did. She really shouldn't be, though. If this is who Cam has been using to do his work for him, it's no wonder Mr. Greer looked at us with suspicious eyes when he handed back our last two assignments.

"I'm not taking that," I state bluntly, gesturing to the pages, and she finally drops her arm, gaping at me.

"Wh...what? But you have to."

"I don't *have* to do anything," I growl. Why the fuck is everyone making decisions for me and telling me what I can and can't do? I'm getting seriously fucking sick of it. This is not what I signed up for when I came to Pac. "Why would you do his work for him?"

She shrugs her shoulders. "He said he would pick me next month." The hopeful gleam in her eyes makes me bite back my words before I can snark out something insulting. I should have realized that was the reason.

Shaking my head. "It's really not worth...all of this." I wave my hand at the table where she's got textbooks open and was taking notes when I arrived. I want to tell her it's not worth the hit to her dignity, the selling of her pride, but I don't know her and I'm pretty sure anything I say will only come across as judgmental and bitchy. If she's going to be another Princess, I should probably at least try to not piss her off.

Turning on my heel, I head back toward the exit, ignoring her spluttered protests, but as I reach the door, a hand wraps around my wrist, yanking me away from it as I stumble.

Spinning around, Cam is dragging me into the stacks and when I pull my arm back, trying to break his hold on me, he tightens his grip, my teeth gritting as my bones grind against one another.

When we're safely hidden from prying eyes, he lets go, using his larger body to push me against the shelves, glowering down at me with fire in his eyes. This is the first time he's so much as looked at me in the last two weeks and, despite how angry he is with me, and how frustrated I am with him, my body reacts instinctively to his nearness, remembering what it felt like to have him pressed up against me last time.

Staring unblinkingly into his eyes, I can see he feels it too. Buried underneath all that anger, he still feels what I feel—the intense physical response we have to one another.

"Go back and take the assignment from her," he growls, his voice a deep rumble that sounds barely human.

"No."

His eyes narrow at my defiance, his jaw clenching.

"I'm not handing in something that isn't your work," I boldly tell him, not letting his icy glare scare me. "Do the damn assignment yourself. And don't use some lackey to give it to me. I know you have a set of balls, so fucking use them."

His nostrils flare, the brown around his eyes a thin ring as his pupils enlarge, his face darkening with rage.

His hand wraps around my throat, a move that takes me by surprise as his fingers press into the skin on either side of my neck. I can feel the strength in his grip as his fingers flex, the intermittent loosening and tightening of his hold as he struggles to decide what to do.

With a savage growl and a final squeeze, he drops his arm, storming away without a backward glance, leaving me sagged against the bookcase as I try to control my breathing.

Hawk

Chapter 18

Still half asleep, I rub at my eyes, running my hand through my hair as I look at myself in the mirror. Reaching out for my toothbrush, I glance down as my fingers touch nothing but air. *What the hell?* I swear it was here last night when I went to bed.

As I glance around, I don't see it anywhere. Grumbling under my breath, I turn on the shower and step in, letting the hot water flow over me. I can look for the damn thing when I'm done. Tilting my head back, letting the water splash into my face and over my hair, I blindly go to grab the shower gel, I feel bristles brushing against my fingers and, opening my eyes, my toothbrush is perched against the shower gel bottle. *What. The. Fuck?* I never brush my teeth in the shower.

Rolling my eyes at Cam's new idea of a hilarious joke, I make a mental note to tell him to grow up. This is the third time my shit has turned up in weird places. At first, I shook it off, thinking I misplaced my backpack, but now it's clear Cam has been messing with me. I guess this is his way of handling his rejection from Hadley. I knew that girl was fucking trouble; knew she would mess him up like this.

"Ugh," West groans, lifting up the couch cushions, searching for something, when I enter the living room half an hour later.

"What's up?"

"I can't find my glasses," he growls, still digging around down the back of the sofa. I have a sneaking suspicion I know who might have taken them, but I decide to give Cam another day or two of being an idiot, then I'll tell him to wise up.

Once he's finally found them, hidden in the coffee canister, and Mason has managed to drag Cam out of bed—you'd think the idiot would want to be around to witness the havoc he's causing—we head down for breakfast, striding into the hall with our heads up as we look down at our peers.

My lips pinch as I find Hadley's seat at our table empty. Why can't that girl be on fucking time? I shake it off though as I sit down, Cindy immediately attaching her mouth to mine. Mmm, if she directs her lips further south, I definitely won't say no to a breakfast blowie. God knows, with all the tension I've been carrying around, I need an outlet for it.

Hadley eventually storms in with her typical angry scowl, not looking at any of us as she takes her usual seat, stabbing her fork into her grapefruit. I've gotten way too much joy out of watching her grumble and glower at the measly piece of fruit, slyly eyeing up Cam's loaded plate of food every morning. Any other girl here would probably think I was being sweet by setting that in front of them, but I knew Hadley would fucking hate it. Not just the shortage of food, but the lack of control as well. She's just like me in that respect, she needs that control over her life. I saw it when I told her she belonged to Cam for the month. The hate in her eyes at my words, the spark of fear at her loss of control.

It's the same with the dresses and forcing her to come to our parties every Friday night. It's all about tearing her down. Although, I have to admit, I thought she would put up more resistance. She's taken it all like a champ, despite the pissy look on her face. The problem is I don't know her well enough to know how to get to her.

That's why I take the master key from the admin office and let myself into her room while she's in class. I need to know more about this girl in order to know how to get rid of her.

With the exception of a few stacks of books on her desk, a bunch of suspiciously new and expensive looking dresses, and a few uniforms in her wardrobe, you'd hardly know anyone even lives here. Her bed is perfectly made with the standard white sheets provided by the school. She hasn't brought her own covers or put posters on the walls. There're no photos or anything personal in the room.

Rifling through her drawers, there are a few measly articles of clothing, but otherwise it's empty. There's nothing under her bed either or hidden in books on her bookshelf. Nothing here gives me any indication as to who she is or what makes her tick.

Frustrated, I slam my fist into the backboard of her bookcase, but instead of the solid knock, there's an echo.

I stare at the spot in confusion before scanning my eyes over the bookcase. It's a freestanding bookcase with a few books on one of the shelves, but otherwise it's empty.

Yanking on one side, it easily pulls away from the wall and, peering behind it, my eyes widen in surprise. *Sneaky bitch.* There's a hole in the drywall. Wedging myself between the bookcase and the wall, I slip in behind it until I can look in, finding a black duffel bag.

Lifting it out, I set it on the floor, bending down as I unzip it. The thing is basically empty, nothing but a couple of old clothes. In an inner pocket I find a cheap, plastic ring, like one you'd get out of a gumball machine. Chucking it back inside, I push aside her clothing, pausing when I find a notebook buried amongst them.

She's always writing in her stupid notebooks instead of using the tablet, but why would she hide her schoolwork in the wall? I dig it out of her bag, opening it up. Flicking through the pages, my eyes narrow, and I only become more confused the more I read. *What the fuck is this?*

Snapping it shut, I set it aside, zipping the bag up and shoving it back where I found it. I push the bookcase back in place and with a final glance around the room to make sure nothing is out of place, I grab the notebook and get out of there.

***

Some faceless blonde is giving me the best blowjob of my life as I fuck her face. Nutting in her mouth, she swallows every last drop of my cum before leaning back on her heels, smiling up at me.

Her mouth opens as she goes to say something.

"AHHHHH," she screams, the loud, high pitched shriek making me jump.

What the ever loving fuck?

"AHHHHH!" she screams again. I turn to look behind me, but I'm frozen, unable to move. I bring my hand up to cut off her screams, but again, my arm won't move.

What the fucking hell is going on?

I jolt awake, flying upright in bed, the screaming noise still pounding in my ears.

No, wait. That's not in my head. Someone is honest to God screaming.

My door bangs open, Mason storming in.

"What the actual fuck are you doing in here?" I can barely hear him over the continued screams of some girl, my brain too fogged with sleep to wrap my head around what is happening. Who the fuck is screaming?

Glancing around my room, Mason's eyes narrow on my desk, stomping over to it and whipping open the drawer. The action has the screaming getting even louder. *Holy fuck, my ears.*

He throws my phone on my bed—aggressively. I snatch it up, glancing at the screen. It's my alarm. My alarm is going off? I silence it, my head still fuzzy and swirling with confusion.

"What the fuck, man?" Mason grumbles. "Why is your alarm set for the crack ass of dawn? Turn the damn thing off when it rings. Some of us are trying to sleep."

He fires a final glare my way, not waiting around for a response, grumbling something about how even he shouldn't be awake yet.

Completely confused, I look back down at my phone. It's barely four a.m. Opening up the alarm app, I notice it's set to go off every day at the same time, and the tone has changed from the usual soft wake-up one I use.

What the fuck? Seriously, Cam? I'm going to fucking murder you—in the morning, when I've had more sleep.

I've forgotten all about it by the time I wake up again, trudging into the kitchen in nothing but gray sweats. Pouring myself a bowl of cereal, I open the cutlery drawer, staring into it for far too long before it registers with me, and I slam it shut.

"Cam," I snarl, glaring daggers at him as he stumbles into the room, still half asleep, his hair sticking up in all directions as he lazily throws himself onto the sofa.

His head snaps up to look at me, his eyes pulled together in confusion. "What?"

"Where the fuck are the spoons?"

The expression on his face would be comical if I wasn't so fucking furious right now.

"Dude, what the fuck are you talking about? They're in the drawer."

"No, they're not," I hiss through gritted teeth. "You've gotta stop this. It was funny the first few times, but it's getting annoying."

"Man, I seriously have no idea what you're talking about."

I stomp across the floor toward him, and he gets to his feet, facing off against me, that same stupid look of confusion on his face.

"No? So you didn't set my alarm to go off in the middle of the night? Or hide my backpack behind the sofa? What about putting West's glasses in the coffee tin? And all the rest of it. The amount of crap you've pulled the last couple of weeks is ridiculous."

His eyes widen, his mouth dropping open. "That's been happening to you too?" He runs his hand through his hair, turning away from me as he barks out a relieved chuckle. "Fuck, man, I was beginning to think I was losing it."

I scrutinize him, taking in the relief written clearly on his face, my mind running a mile a minute.

"It's not you?" I clarify, but I'm pretty certain it isn't.

"No, man." Realization dawns on him, the smile slipping off his face and I can see the wheels turning behind his eyes. "Who is it then?"

I shake my head, trying to figure that out.

"There's no way it would be West or Mason."

I agree. Cam is the only one of us who would do something so childish. Outside of the four of us, there's only one person I know who would dare to sneak into our private space and mess with us.

"Hadley," I growl, watching as Cam's eyes grow even bigger.

"No way," he gasps in disbelief, but I can see he believes it too.

"That bitch," I snarl, unable to stand still, stomping back toward the kitchen.

"Hey, man. Now that's a bit extreme," he argues. His defense of her has me spinning around, storming back toward him.

"That's not all she's done."

He once again looks confused, but I push past him, not answering the questions in his eyes. He needs to see it for himself. Grabbing the notebook from my bag in the bedroom, I stomp back into the living room and slam it down on the table.

"Read that," I sneer, pointing at the book.

His gaze darts between me and the book before he hesitantly reaches out, lifting the book and opening it up to the first page.

I observe him closely as his brows draw together, his eyes scanning down the page before he flips over to the next one, doing the same. Page after page, his expression darkens, his eyes turning hard and his nostrils flaring.

"I don't...what the fuck is this? Where did you find it?"

"I don't know. She was hiding it in her room."

He focuses back on the notebook and we stand in silence for several long moments as he flips back and forth through the pages. I've already read it several times over, trying to understand why.

When he's finally sick of looking at it, he lifts his head, his icy stare meeting mine.

"What are we going to do about it?"

It's about time we were on the same page. I just had to prove it to him, make him see for himself that she was no good.

A cruel smirk lifts my lip. "I have an idea."

Hadley

Chapter 19

You know that feeling when everyone is talking about you, but you have no idea why or what they're saying?

Yeah, that's exactly how I'm feeling right now.

I cast my eyes around the room, taking in the students gawking at me. Others are flicking their eyes back and forth between me and their tablets, while some girls lean across the aisle, whispering to the student beside them. I don't know what the fuck is going on, but I can only guess it's not good. It never is.

My tablet is in my bag, but something tells me I shouldn't look at it here, with eyes on me. By now the whole room is watching me intently, some students blatantly staring, waiting for me to react, to do something. I'm sure as fuck not about to give them anything. Whatever fresh torment Hawk has unleashed, I'm not about to make it fodder for these pathetic saps. Today is the last day of the month. On Monday morning, a new girl is chosen, and I'm supposed to be done with this shit. I should have guessed Hawk wouldn't let the occasion go without a special send off.

Blocking them out, I pretend to focus on my schoolwork for the rest of class, impatiently counting down the minutes until the bell rings so I can escape and find out what's going on.

The last ten minutes of class feel like they last a lifetime. Every minute filled with hushed whispers and quiet chuckles under breaths. Not one person bothers to fill me in on what the fuck everyone is finding so funny, not even one of my old scholarship friends. I didn't really expect them to involve themselves, and I can't blame them—they're just trying to get through this school and start the future they've been working for the last four years.

When the bell finally rings, I stay seated in my chair, glaring down every single student that looks my way as they pack up their stuff and leave the room. Only when the last person leaves, closing the door behind them do I drop the tough girl act, bending down to dig my tablet out of my bag. Typing in my pin, I see a notification informing me I have received a new email.

With clumsy fingers and sweaty palms, I eventually manage to open up the email. It appears to be a mass email that has, by the looks of things, been sent to every student in the school. *Excellent.*

There doesn't appear to be any text, but there's a video file attached.

My breath comes out in quick, shallow pants, nausea churning in my stomach as my finger hesitates over the file.

Whatever this is, I can handle it. I have dealt with worse. I have fucking survived *worse.*

I slam my finger down on the screen harder than necessary, holding my breath as the video begins to play. The screen is black for the first few seconds until a light is turned on, illuminating a bedroom. *My* bedroom.

What the fuck?

I watch as I walk into my room, dropping my bag on the floor and closing the door behind me. From the looks of it, the camera was hidden in the bookcase by the desk, angled so that it pretty much catches the entire room.

I grab some clothes out of my dresser, dumping them on the bed before stripping off my uniform, in full fucking view of the camera. A tingling sensation starts up under my skin as I watch myself strip off my clothes, unknowingly revealing the tattoo snaking up my side, along with every single scar I've carefully hidden for the last couple of months. I feel every second of it as this new world I've precariously built around me comes crashing down. There's a reason I've kept those scars covered, and it's not because I'm embarrassed of them.

Now every superficial jackass in this fucking shithole masquerading as a prep school knows part of my deepest, darkest secret. They've seen the marks of my lowest moments. The times when I wanted to give up, when death felt like the only way out.

The video finishes then, with me dressed in a bra and fucking granny pants, a static image for every single student to roam their eyes over and do whatever the fuck they want with.

That tingling beneath my skin becomes a roar as shock is quickly replaced with insurmountable fury; that craving to punch something, to smash a particular someone's fucking face in.

Jumping to my feet, I grab my bag and storm across the room, throwing open the door, ready to do just that.

My steps falter, though, as I find what must be every student in the senior class gathered in the hall, lining the banks of lockers like they're expecting some sort of show. Behind them, I can see pictures pasted all over the walls. Someone has strung the same static image I just saw on the tablet over every available surface.

With every poster I glance over, my fury heightens, until it's an untamable storm. Eyes brimming with fire, I glower at every student, satisfaction coursing through me when some of them take a step back from me, their laughs faltering. The only faces I don't see are those of the other scholarship students. Well, at least they aren't here to witness whatever fresh hell this is.

Lifting my chin, I glare at every single fucker as I walk past them. Students talk to one another, no longer bothering to keep their voices low, so as I walk past, I pick up on some of their words.

Abuse. Self-harm. A traumatic accident.

All of them speculating what the fuck happened to me. Like it's any of their goddamn business.

"Yo, Hadley! Nice panties," Deke, the fucker, yells, his buddies whistling and chortling, slapping him on the back. *Yeah, fucking hilarious, douchebag. You're clearly winning in life.*

I've only made it halfway down the corridor when the crowd at the end of the hall parts, revealing none other than the

Pricks themselves. I wondered where they were. There was no way they would miss this little showdown of their own creation.

My eyes don't stray from Hawk as I storm toward them, ignoring every other asshole around us as I take in his stupid fucking smirk and the glimmer of satisfaction in his eyes. Gritting my teeth, I throw him my coldest, hardest glare, dropping my bag as I close in on him.

"What the fuck is wrong with you?!" I snarl, shoving him in the chest with every ounce of strength I have. He has to take a step back to steady himself, but it's nowhere near enough. I want to see him flat on his ass, staring up at me, wondering how the fuck I bested him.

The smirk drops off his face, his eyes narrowing as he scowls at me, mirroring my own dark look.

It takes everything in me not to go apeshit on his ass, but just enough common sense gets through to me, reminding me *he's* the Prince and I'm a nobody. I'll be out of here so quickly I won't have time to process what the fuck happened before I'm dumped on the sidewalk, with no education, nowhere to live, and no prospects for the future.

"You fucking proud of yourself?" I sneer, finally turning away from Hawk to glare at the other three fucktards, making sure they know I'm talking to them too. They are each as responsible as he is.

Mason wears his usual look of indifference. He could be watching paint dry right now, that's how unbothered he looks by this whole thing. Flicking my gaze to West, he at least has the decency to look uncomfortable. His lips are pinched and I can see what might be regret in his eyes. Too fucking late, buddy, regret does me fuck all good now. Where was your conscience when you were recording me? When you were clicking send on that email?

Shaking my head in disappointment, I finally look at Cam, my lips parting with a quick intake of breath at the molten hatred in his eyes. His posture is tense, his back ramrod straight, his hands clenched in tight fists. Everything about him says he's a raging inferno ready to explode, the intensity of his fury suffocating. The extent of his animosity seems out of place, but I can't work out what I could have done to warrant such loathing.

Did he know? Did he tell them? My shirt was on when we had sex, but he might have seen something. His fingers could have grazed over a scar.

Confused, I move my hardened gaze back to Hawk.

"You didn't think I'd let you get away with walking around these halls defying me," he simply states, like somehow this is all my fault because I didn't listen to them before now. "Making fools out of us."

Stepping in so I'm inches from him, I snarl, "I didn't do anything to you, but you can bet I'm going to do something now." Glancing at the other three again, I add, "I'm going to burn your pathetic little lives to the ground."

Snatching up my bag, I keep my head held high as I storm out of the school, making a beeline to the only place that brings me peace in this hellhole.

I pummel the heavy bag over and over, not giving a shit that I'm in my uniform and my bare knuckles are turning red. Throwing everything I have into each hit, I pretend it's Hawk. West. Mason. Cam. Every single one of them deserves my wrath. What the fuck is their problem? Hawk has had it out for me since that first day, when I ran into him in the corridor; and he's only gotten madder since then, as I got closer to Cam.

Maybe he's got a hard-on for Cam? I snort at that thought. Damn, that would be pretty fucking funny. Cam is most definitely a vagina lover, though. What other reason could he have? No normal person gives that much of a shit about who their friend is in to. Maybe it's because of who I am? My past. The whole 'you, us, and them' crap Bianca spouted on the first day. Cam has definitely deviated out of his lane by pursuing me.

Based on the look in his eye today, Cam fucking hates me. I set that friendship on fire and destroyed everything we might have been. I didn't mean to, but since when did that matter? Regardless, you'd think Cam's newfound hatred would have appeased Hawk. Fuck, I don't know. Who the hell understands the inner workings of teenage boys' minds?

I have no idea how long I pound on the bag, but based on the ache in my hands and the sweat making the back of my shirt stick to me, it's quite a while. The rage is still pouring off of me when that crackle of electricity alerts me to his presence. *Great, what the fuck is he doing here?*

"Go away," I growl, only getting more frustrated when I hear him move further into the room.

"You need to do something more than beat on a bag," Mason says, somehow knowing exactly what I need.

I continue to ignore him, instead pounding even harder on the bag. He's fucking right, though. Sure, this is working to drain some of my energy, but it's doing absolutely nothing for my rage.

"Come on," he taunts, "show me what you've got."

I bark out a caustic laugh. "So you can tattle on me and get me kicked out? Yeah, I don't think so."

"I won't."

I don't move, though. I can't trust him, and as much as I want to beat his face into a bloody pulp, I want to remain enrolled in this school more.

"Everyone in the school just saw you at your most vulnerable." His words only fuel my anger. "Guys are going to jerk off to your image for the rest of the year." I try to zone him out, knowing he's baiting me, but every single one of his words worms its way into my brain. "I was surprised to see the scars, after all, I've seen you in just your sports bra; but then I realized, you always keep most of the lights off when you're in here."

Another beat of silence as I continue to fight against my desperate need to throat punch him.

"You know, they're all out there right now, speculating about what happened to you," he continues. "Some people have invented an entire sob story for you. A tragic car accident that killed your parents and left you with all those scars." I can't help it; a snort of laughter leaves me at that notion. *If only.*

"Others think you're a self-harmer. That your life is just so damn pathetic you need to cut yourself open in order to feel normal."

I roll my eyes at that emotionally dense and equally wrong theory, the continued slap as I hit the bag my only response.

"I think they're wrong." I can't deny I'm curious as to what his theory is. None of the pretentious twats in this place could even wrap their judgmental little minds around the truth of how I got these scars. They have no fucking clue of the life I've endured. They all sit up there in their ivory towers, perched on their thrones of money, judging the fucking world around them, but the truth is they wouldn't have survived in the world I grew up in. So they can whisper and speculate and judge, but at the end of the day it all means nothing, because I've already been to hell and back, and I'm still fucking standing.

"I think someone did that to you. I think you *let* someone do that to you," he clarifies. "Or maybe you were a weak, pathetic, helpless, little girl, and someone saw that you weren't made to survive this world, so they did what they had to do to toughen you up."

His words penetrate through my tough exterior, embedding themselves under my skin, sucking me into their dark depths. I'm not in the gym anymore. I'm not eighteen. I'm not a fighter. I'm exactly as he just said. I'm a weak, helpless little girl, crying and begging for *them* to stop. Promising I'll do better as blood drips onto the floor.

I don't know when I stopped punching the bag, nor do I remember closing the distance to Mason, but the next thing I know, my fist is flying into his face, finally shutting him the fuck up.

It's too late, though. I'm too far gone. I can take the shit that's been thrown my way since I stepped into Pacific Prep. I can deal with the whispers and taunts. I can even handle the speculation about my scars. What I can't fucking cope with is being thrown back to that little girl who couldn't fight for herself. I might not be her anymore, but she's still very much a part of me.

I watch as I rain down punch after punch on him, barely grasping what I'm doing. I feel like a spectator in my own body.

Rage, fear, hurt, and hopelessness, the feelings of both my past and present, melding together, creating one hell of a firestorm inside of me and using my body as a vessel to let it all out.

Mason doesn't even try to fight back as my fist collides with his jaw, sending his head snapping to the side. Another blow to his kidney has him grimacing, while a well-placed right hook has a cut opening up at the edge of his brow.

The whole time, he just stands there, taking every blow like the fighter he is. I have no idea how long I attack him like he's my own personal punching bag, but I don't stop until I've exorcised myself of every painful emotion, and I'm so exhausted I can no longer stand upright.

He catches me in his arms as I sag forward, barely able to keep my eyes open as exhaustion slams into me, my adrenaline finally burning off. He wraps his arms around me, slowly lowering me until we're on our knees, his body propping me up.

He feels so warm, the regular rhythm of his heart steadying as I come close to giving into this bone-deep weariness. I don't have the brainpower or emotional bandwidth to understand what we are doing right now. I should not be letting him hold me like this, but I just can't bring myself to give a shit.

It's like my body was a bath. The plug was in and the tap was on, and I was overflowing with emotions, unable to contain them. At some point, when I was beating the crap out of Mason, the tap was turned off and the plug pulled out, allowing everything I was feeling to drain away. What's left is a large, empty tub, a voidless expanse within me.

The next thing I know, we're lying on the floor, my body draped over his. I feel him stroking his hand over my hair, but my eyes refuse to open, a small groan escaping me.

"Shhh, you're okay. Sleep. I'll look out for you."

As though he's just said the magic words, my body gives up the fight and I succumb to sleep, letting it suck me into its dark depths.

When I next wake up, I'm back in my room, tucked into bed with wet bandages wrapped around my knuckles. I don't remember how I got back here, but there's only one person who could have done it.

Mason.

But why?

Mason

Chapter 20

It starts out slow, one or two kids whispering. I barely even notice, but when a low hum of activity settles over the library, I can no longer ignore it. Glancing over at the other tables, students are staring wide-eyed at their tablets, some of them laughing.

"Eww, no wonder she's been trying to hide *that* all year," I hear a girl at a nearby table say to her friend.

A couple of jocks are sitting at the table beside me, staring eagerly at whatever is on the tablet.

"Damn, even with all those marks, she's fucking hot."

"Right? I'd totally fuck her."

"Hell yeah, I'd have tried it on with her sooner if I knew she looked like that under those crappy clothes she wears."

What the hell are they talking about?

Setting the tablet in front of me, I open up my email, finding a video file attached to a recent, unopened email. That must be what everyone is whispering about.

Pressing play, I stare transfixed at the video, unable to believe what I'm seeing. There's only one person who would do this, but to go this far? My hand clenches tightly around the device, a notification popping up, showing a new message in our group chat.

Hawk: *Meet outside the east wing at the end of class.*

Not willing to wait that long, I stuff my things in my backpack and storm out, arriving at the east wing just as the bell goes. West is already there, his face pinched as he glares at the passing students. The entire way here I heard them all whispering about her, about the video. Are their lives so goddamn empty that they have to talk about a girl they don't even know, speculating about the damage that's been done to her? What the fuck is wrong with them?

"Did you know?" I snap at him as I arrive.

He grits his teeth, glaring at me. "No. Of course not."

"He's gone too far this time," I growl, my body practically vibrating with rage.

His eyes run over me, taking in my clenched fists and wide stance. "You can't do anything here. Let's just get through whatever he has planned and then we can talk to him."

I fucking hate that idea. What the hell else does he plan on doing to her? He's right, though. I can't say a goddamn word until we can get back to the dorms, and I can ream him out in private.

So instead I grit my teeth, donning my usual mask of apathy and watch as Hadley fights fire with fire, showing us just how resilient she is as she tears us a new one before storming off.

"Show's over, get the fuck out of here," I roar at the lingering students after Hadley's departure. Everyone quickly jumps into action, scurrying away from us, until we're the only ones left in the hall.

"I don't know what the hell you were thinking," I snarl, rounding on Hawk. "But we're going to fucking discuss this later."

Before I can give into the urge to punch him, I storm out of there, ignoring him calling after me.

I know where she would have gone to, and while I'm probably one of the last people she wants to see, I also know exactly what she needs right now.

***

For the last few months, I've watched Hadley beat on the heavy bag harder than some trained professionals, ridding herself of whatever she was feeling; but standing watching her today, she was completely different.

Sure, the rage coming off of her was a palpable thing sitting heavy in the air, but it was more than that. She seemed almost haunted, as though her demons were pressing in around her. I know that feeling. I understand it.

When I wrapped my arms around her, I was only trying to catch her before she collapsed, but holy fuck. Holding her against me—she fit perfectly in my arms. I've never held anyone like that, nevermind someone so vulnerable. Whether it was because some part of herself trusted me, or she was just so lost to her pain—pain that we caused—whatever the reason, holding her like that hit me in a way I never expected.

Tucking her in, I brush a stray strand of hair from her face. Even in sleep, it's scrunched up. *What the hell happened to you?* Brushing my thumb lightly across her cheek, the lines on her face flatten out and she leans into my touch. Grudgingly, I turn away from her, ignoring the pit in my stomach, the part of me that wants to go back and stay with her as I silently close her door behind me. With anger coursing through me, I storm back to our dorm. Hawk and I need to have some fucking words after that shit he pulled today. What he did was fucked up. And not to tell us? Dick move.

Throwing open the door to the apartment, I storm in, finding Hawk sitting in the living room. West is standing over him, with his arms crossed and a similar scowl to my own on his face.

"What the hell was that about?" I bark out, slamming the door shut behind me, glaring at him as I close the distance between us, coming to stand beside West.

Hawk's eyes widen as he takes in my appearance. Yeah, I imagine I look like shit. I can't say I thought I'd ever be beat up by a girl. Not only do I deserve it, but I'm so fucking turned-on by her ability to beat the shit out of me, I don't even care that everything hurts.

“What the fuck—” West starts, before Hawk cuts across him.

“I did what was necessary,” he says with a nonchalant shrug.

“Necessary? What the fuck does that mean? You completely violated her privacy.”

“What the fuck do you care?”

Unable to answer that, I purse my lips.

“You saw her scars. You *know* what leaves marks like that,” I spit the words out between gritted teeth, the ink-black tone of my voice giving away the roiling emotions within me as I fight to block out the traumatic memories of my past.

Maybe that’s what differentiates me from Hawk. Where he saw scars and pain and an opportunity to strike; I see a five-year-old boy struggling to hold himself together as blood flows down the shower drain, crying out in pain as water hits the open lashes on his back.

The guys all know what I’ve been through, but there’s a difference between hearing about that shit, and actually living it. I’ve let him go around, putting her in her place all semester, all in the name of presenting a united front to the rest of the idiots at this school; but today crossed a fat fucking line. What he did is *not* okay. The second he saw that video, he fucking *knew*, yet he *still* sent it out to everyone.

“How has Cam not already torn you a new one?” I snarl.

Looking completely unfazed by my aggression, he snorts, shaking his head, a cocky grin lifting his lips.

“He knew what I had planned.”

I gape at him, his words playing on repeat in my head.

"He what?" West barks at the same time I blurt, "Cam knew?"

The man himself comes strutting into the room, looking far too fucking nonplussed given all the shit that's gone down today.

"I knew what?"

"You fucking knew what he was going to do?" I growl, turning my glare on him.

What the actual fuck is going on here? I know he's butt hurt over her rejection, but he needs to get the fuck over it. After what I saw today, her insistence that she belongs to no one makes even more sense. How can he not fucking see that?

His features shutter as he locks down whatever emotions he's feeling, making it impossible for me to read him.

"I found this in her room," Hawk informs us, dropping a notebook on the coffee table. It looks just like every other one Hadley owns. She's one of the only students that insists on writing everything instead of using her tablet.

"Her workbook?" I ask, frowning at it in confusion. Picking it up, I flick through the pages, hesitating when, instead of school notes, I find clip outs. The first few pages are all of Cam's dad, followed by a handful of news articles on the rest of our parents and their company, each one with handwritten scrawls beside it.

"What the fuck? What is this?" I can't tear my eyes away from the damning pages in front of me. Insights into our parents, into our lives. Information she could only have gained from us.

"I don't understand."

What the fuck is this? Why does she have it?

West tears the notebook out of my hands, his eyes narrowing as he slowly scans each page, that computer brain of his analyzing every word.

"She was clearly using us," Cam snarls, venom thick in his tone. His hands are clenched, his lip curled in hatred. *Fuck, he's pissed.* It takes a hell of a lot to enrage him, but he is fucking furious right now.

"For what?" I can't make sense of it all. What does she want with our parents?

"How the fuck do I know. She's street trash, she probably wants what every other girl wants—money, security, and a better social status."

"I told you she couldn't be trusted." I round on Hawk so quickly, the room spins, glowering at him. That shit isn't fucking helpful right now. Ignoring him, I turn to look at West who is still flicking through the notebook.

"What do you think?" I ask him, needing someone with a sensible head to have some sort of input into this asinine conversation.

"It doesn't fucking matter," Cam barks, waving his hand toward the notebook. "Why she has all this...information, or what she's doing doesn't matter. Hawk's right, she's been using us this whole time. Everything she said, every move she made, was some preconceived plan designed to bring us closer to her." My eyes narrow on him, trying to read between the lines. He's never said anything, but he's way too annoyed about all of this for Hadley to have simply been another girl he was chasing after. Something more must have happened between them for him to be this pissed off. "She's been using us, manipulating us all year. What she got today was the least she deserved."

After listening to him waxing fucking poetic about her all year, it's a shock to hear the bitterness in his tone as he spits out each word. Sure, he was hurt after her rejection, but he's hardly said anything about her since then. Not a bad word against her, but the rage coming off him is a palpable thing reverberating in the air around us. Underneath it all, though, he's concealing a hell of a lot of pain over her betrayal. It burns out some of the fire I came storming in here with, taking the edge off the anger I had at Hawk.

I still don't agree with what they did, but this notebook certainly complicates things. What the hell is she up to? What interest does she have with our parents?

"By forcing her to be Cam's girl, we gave her exactly what she wanted," Hawk snarls.

"But she turned him down," I argue, still not totally in agreement with his assessment of her. He hasn't been thinking straight when it comes to her. She was the first person of the year to cross him, and he's decided to make her life miserable, but there's no real reason for his dislike of her.

"What do we do now?" Cam asks, still looking furious over the whole thing.

"Let the rest of the school deal with her. After today, they'll hopefully tear her to shreds," Hawk states. "*We* have nothing more to do with her. We can't give her any more information than she already has."

"Don't you want to know what she's up to?" I ask, surprised.

"No. I don't give a shit. You all just need to stay the fuck away from her, okay?"

***

"Do you always sneak into other people's rooms in the middle of the night?"

Flicking on the lamp, she spins toward me, her eyes wide when she finds me sitting in a chair in the living room, watching her.

I've been waiting for her all night. I knew she would show up at some point. She's spent all semester putting together this notebook on us all, there's no way she would just let it go. Besides, she's shown she's capable of getting in and out of our rooms undetected. Even after we changed the locks, she still managed to get in and mess with us. Last week she took all the cables for the TV and game consoles and hid them amongst towels in the airing cupboard. It took us a full day to find them.

"Holy shit, you nearly gave me a heart attack," she whisper yells. "And I don't think you can really say anything about sneaking into others' rooms."

I ignore her dig, refusing to be sidetracked from my task of getting some answers out of her.

"What are you doing here, Hadley?"

The lines around her eyes tighten as she glowers at me. "I need my notebook back."

"Why?"

Come on, just tell me something, give me some reason as to what this is all about.

"I just do."

"You've gotta give me something." I sigh. "Hawk and Cam are convinced you're using us—well, Cam—to get to our parents...is that the case?"

She pauses, her eyes burning with defiance. Before she even opens her mouth, I know she's not going to give me the answers I need.

"Is that why you sent everyone that video? Because you found my notebook? Or are you just so bored with your privileged lives that you need to destroy someone else's just for shits and giggles?"

Her head tilts slightly as she scrutinizes me, trying to get a read on me, to understand the motives behind today.

"No," I snarl, annoyed that she thinks any of this is just fun and games to us. "We—"

"Did you think that would break me?" she snaps, cutting me off before I can say anything further. Not that I had any clue what I was going to say. "A video? I guess someone like you couldn't possibly understand what I've had to endure."

Unable to bare the distance between us, I cut across the space until I'm standing right in front of her, her chest brushing against mine. I'm angry at Hawk and Cam, at her. I'm confused, and I need answers, but despite all that, I still can't ignore this connection I feel with her. And after this afternoon, it's only gotten more intense. I need to feel her small body pressed up against mine, wrapped around me once more.

Towering over her, I drop my head so our faces are inches apart. "You assume you're the only one with a fucked-up past, little warrior?" I murmur, staring deep into her stormy eyes, swirling with so many emotions I can't identify any of them. "Do you really think that just because we have big houses and fancy cars we don't have our own traumas we're working through?"

She returns my intense gaze, trying to read my carefully concealed thoughts. "Yes," she murmurs honestly, the word barely more than a whisper against my lips.

"I wish that were true." I give her a small, sad smile. "But you should know better than anyone, everyone wants to keep the scars of their past a secret, and just because they might not be visible, doesn't mean they're any less real."

A tense moment of silence stretches between us, until she speaks up again.

"So, Mason, if we're sharing war stories, what are your scars?"

"What are yours?" I rebut, not willing to share anymore of myself with her. She already sees too much, knows too much.

Her eyes bore into mine, showing me all of her, every painful crack and open wound she always keeps so carefully covered. At the same time, I can feel her probing inside me, peering in hidden boxes, delving into my dark secrets, each of us letting down our walls, however briefly.

"Why do I feel like our pain is the same?" Her words are a barely heard breath, but with our lips basically touching and my every sense honed in on her, it would be impossible to miss her slightest movement.

"Because, baby, it is."

She doesn't say anything for a long time, and I expect she's not going to respond. Our lips hover dangerously close and all I can think about is kissing her, but loyalty to my brothers holds me back.

Eventually her lips part, her tongue flicking out to wet her lower lip. I trace the movement with a keen eye until her words distract me from wondering what she tastes like. "It was, at first…about finding information on your parents." She pointedly directs the conversation back to somewhat safer territory and something about the way she says it comes across as vulnerable, honest, and, god help me, but I'm inclined to believe her.

"Why?"

She shakes her head. "I can't tell you that."

I grind my teeth together. I need fucking answers. "What *can* you tell me?"

Again, she pauses. "Your parents aren't who you think they are."

My hands come up, squeezing her shoulders firmly. "What do you know about our parents?" There's no way she can know. Hell, we only just found out. How the fuck could *she* know?

"I can't tell you," she reiterates, her refusal to tell me what I need to know pissing me off as a growl of frustration rumbles through my chest. How can I go from wanting to kiss her to wanting to throttle her in mere seconds?

Taking a deep breath, I ask a different question, "What about now?"

"What?"

"You said you were using us at first…what about now?"

"Things have changed."

"With Cam?"

She gives a small, sharp nod of her head. "And with West…and you."

Me? Does she feel whatever the fuck this is between us? What does she mean 'things changed with West'? I didn't know they were close. Every word out of her mouth is only raising more fucking questions.

"And Hawk?"

"Hawk can choke on a bag of dicks for all I care."

I have to hold back a laugh at that, silence falling between us once again as I think through everything she's said. She hasn't really given me anything to go on. No reason why she's got that stupid notebook, no understanding of what she's up to. Yet something in my gut wants to trust her.

Staring into her eyes, her gaze roams over my face and she grimaces as she takes in the myriad of bruises starting to appear. She doesn't apologize, nor do I expect her to.

I don't understand this connection between us both, but I feel like she gets me better than anyone ever has.

"I'll get you your book. Give me a few days."

Her eyes widen in surprise before her brows pull down. "Why are you helping me?"

That's an excellent fucking question.

"I have no fucking clue."

Hadley

Chapter 21

The days after the video are a dark blur. The headmaster calls me into a meeting, demanding answers I can't give him; wanting to know who did this to me and why. Not once does he actually mention the video or the posters. He doesn't ask who I think is responsible; the word 'bullying' doesn't even pass his lips. It's a complete farce. Everyone knows who did it, but because they're the fucking Princes, they get away with it.

But that's okay. I don't need the school to dole out punishment. I'm more than capable of taking revenge into my own hands. In fact, I prefer it that way. I want to see their faces as I ruin them and tear their perfect fucking world apart.

Except Mason's words come back to me.

Do you really think that just because we have big houses and fancy cars we don't have our own traumas we're working through?

There was no faking the pain I saw in his eyes. I got a good look at his inner torment, and he made it sound like the others have experienced their own suffering too.

It doesn't make any sense. What could have happened to him that was so bad? But I *felt* it. I felt how similar our pain was, like he'd survived the same fucked up shit I had.

A knock on the door pulls me out of my circling thoughts. Ever since the video, I've spent every spare moment I'm not in class hiding out in my room. It's pathetic, I know, but I can't fucking take the looks and whispers from the other students, and if I have to see the stupid, smug smirk on Hawk's face one more time, I'm going to do something I regret.

I haven't even gone to the gym, too afraid of running into Mason. I don't know what the fuck to make of him after our chat the other night. Things got heavy and far too...real. All this time, I've firmly believed they are just like their parents. I've thought of them as these rich, controlling, pampered dicks with nothing better to do with themselves, but now Mason has me thinking I have them all wrong.

When I mentioned their parents, he was angry and surprised, but there was also a hint of fear in his voice, a spark of worry in his eyes. But why? Was that concern for me? Or because I might've found out something I shouldn't have, and he's worried about the repercussions to his family and business? But he took care of me that day, going so far as to tuck me into bed; and he was true to his word. I found an envelope with my notebook in it, shoved under my door two days later. Not to mention the strange connection between us, the steady strength I feel around him.

No, I can't afford to think like that. I can't let a couple of nice gestures and some stupid feelings soften my hatred. I need to hold on to this anger and use it to fight back against them, to show them they haven't beat me down.

Opening the door, I stare speechlessly at my visitor. I don't know who I thought it would be, it's not like many people want to hang out with me these days, but I definitely wasn't expecting Emilia. She was already not talking to me after Halloween; I expected this latest incident to be the final nail in the coffin of our friendship.

She's fidgeting nervously with her hands, glancing everywhere but at me. "Uh, hey." She gives me a weak smile, still not meeting my eyes.

"Hey," My voice lacks any of its usual warmth when I'm talking to her as I look past her, checking to see if she's alone. There's no one else about and my posture relaxes a bit.

"I, uh...I wanted to see how you were doing, after, you know...everything."

Huh, I wasn't expecting that.

"I'm fine."

What else can I say? We haven't spoken in over a month.

She nods her head, probably having expected that answer. She knows me well enough to know I'm not a 'pour my heart out' kind of person.

"Right. Well, I just wanted to check that you were okay."

She turns around to walk away, but I call out her name, halting her mid-step.

"Why?"

I'm not even sure what I'm asking. Why did she come here? Why now?

When she turns around, regret flashes across her eyes as she chews her bottom lip, taking a step back toward me.

"I thought about knocking on your door every day. I wanted to, but I was scared. It probably sounds stupid to you, but I like the quiet life I have here. I don't think I could handle the Princes messing it up for me, or having the whole school...well, you know."

Yeah, I do. The last week, since the video, the students have been relentless. If it's not some meathead jock asking if he can see my fucking panties, it's the girls scowling at me like I'm disgusting, ensuring they don't accidentally bump into me, like I'm fucking diseased or some shit.

And of course, there's also Bianca and the other Princesses. They didn't waste any time cornering me so they could make fun of my humiliation, and remind me just how much I'll never be one of them. It doesn't help that Cam chose Bianca *again* for a second month, a fact she likes to rub in my face every time I see her. As if the twisting in my gut at seeing Cam superglued to her side all the fucking time isn't bad enough.

"But I couldn't go another day without at least checking on you." She licks her lips nervously. "You maybe want nothing to do with me, and I wouldn't blame you...but if you ever wanna talk, I won't push you away again."

I don't know what to say to her, instead staring at her like a wide-eyed idiot while she glances awkwardly around the hall before giving a sharp nod of her head and slipping into her room.

That afternoon, I wander over to the admin building. It's a two-story structure on the far side of campus, as old as every other building, where the school reception is, along with offices for the headmaster and teachers. It's also where the school nurse is based, and the school counselor, which is who I've been mandated to see—even if I think it's a complete waste of both our times.

I rap my knuckles sharply on the door before I can talk myself out of it. It's not like I have any fucking say in the matter, so I may as well get this shitshow over with as quickly as possible.

"Come in," a gravelly voice calls out from inside the room. With one final deep breath, I wrap my hand around the handle and push the door open, stepping into the small office.

"Hadley?" the counselor questions when I walk in. I have to say, he is not at all what I pictured when I was told I'd have to see a fucking shrink. He must be newly qualified. There's no way he's older than twenty-two or twenty-three.

He's got neatly styled dark brown hair, moss green eyes, and just a hint of dark stubble dotted along his sharp jaw, all of which gives him a classically handsome look.

Paired with his black shirt and cute black waistcoat, he has that whole 'hot for teacher' thing going on. Although, I guess it's more 'hot for therapist'?

"It's nice to meet you," he greets, getting up from behind his desk and moving around it to stand in front of me. "I'm Mr. Jacobs." He holds out his hand, giving me a friendly smile, showing off his perfectly straight, white teeth.

"Yeah, hi." My greeting is much less enthusiastic than his as I ignore his outstretched hand.

His smile doesn't falter and I could swear his eyes flare at my attitude, but it's gone before I can be sure.

Lowering his hand, he gestures for me to have a seat on the couch. *Talk about cliché.* Ignoring the sofa in the corner, I instead stride over and plonk my ass in one of the chairs in front of his desk.

Thinking I hear him huff out a chuckle, I turn around to look at him, but I only find him watching me closely. Too closely; his expression unreadable. After a moment's hesitation, he saunters over to the desk himself, sitting down in the spare chair beside me, not seeming phased by my unwillingness to bend to his will.

Neither of us says anything for a moment, each of us scrutinizing the other. He's definitely not what I expected, but that doesn't mean I'm about to just spill all my dark secrets to him.

"I understand you just started at Pacific Prep this year," he begins. It's not a question, so I don't bother to answer him. Something he must realize after a beat of silence as he continues on, "How have you been settling in?"

I take in his overpriced haircut and expensive outfit, ignoring how his fancy aftershave has annoyingly permeated the air in the room, suffocating me with his cedarwood and eucalyptus scent. It's strangely comforting, but I remind myself it's a false sense of security, designed to lure in fucked-up people like me and get us to bare our souls.

Not. Fucking. Happening.

Pinching my lips, I sigh. "Why don't we just get down to why I'm here," I say, ready to get this stupid session over with.

"Alright," he agrees easily, giving me a nod of his head. "Why are you here?"

I narrow my eyes at him. He knows damn well why I'm here.

I don't say anything to his stupid-ass question, and he eventually tries a different tactic.

"Why don't you tell me what happened the other day?"

"There's nothing to tell," I grind out between gritted teeth. I sure as fuck am not about to rehash that fiasco.

When I don't elaborate, he leans forward in his chair, resting his elbows on his knees and looking me straight in the eye. "Look," he begins, a serious expression on his face, "I know you don't want to be here, telling your problems to some stranger."

"Does anyone want to be here?" I snark, gaining a small smile from him, and damn, it's cute as all fucking hell.

"You'd be surprised." He leans in even closer, as though we're sharing a secret. "These rich kids don't give a damn, they just want an engaging audience while they listen to themselves speak."

Cocking my head, I roam my eyes once again over his outfit. Yup, definitely designer. "Aren't you one of those rich kids?"

He doesn't answer my question, quirking his lips up in a sly smile.

"The school has raised some concerns. Given your less than ideal upbringing, they felt it would be in your best interests to come and talk to me."

Less than ideal upbringing? That's putting it mildly. I don't think he could have found a more diplomatic way to say 'the fucked up shit you've been through'.

"Of course they have." I snort, shaking my head at their audacity. "They're worried about how I got some old scars, but they don't seem to give a flying fuck about the threats, the dirty looks or anything else that's happened since I rocked up to this hellhole."

"You're being bullied?" He phrases it as a question, but he doesn't sound surprised. And why would he? I'm sure, just like everyone else, he's already heard about the video and the posters.

"Well, I didn't post that video or put those pictures up all over the school myself now, did I?" I reply sarcastically, feeling my body heat with anger once again over the whole goddamn situation.

Overlooking my attitude, he continues to stare intently at me. It's as though he's worried if he blinks or looks away for a second he will miss some important tell. I'm better than that, though. I'm not that easy to read and he's soon going to realize that. "How bad has it been?"

I glance away, not wanting him to see how affected I am by everything.

"Look." I sigh, so done with this whole stupid meeting. I knew it was going to be a waste of time. "I'm not here because of that. It's nothing I can't handle. The school referred me to you because they were obligated to do so, but there's nothing for them to be concerned about."

He stares at me intently for a long moment and I can feel him trying to dig under my skin, trying to work me out. *Fat fucking chance of that.*

"Hadley, I'm going to be honest with you," he says, his lips pinching as though he doesn't want to say the next words, but knows he has to. But words like that are never followed by anything good. Before he even says it, I know what he's going to say.

"I saw the pictures of you."

Before I can cuss him out—I mean that's gotta be all sorts of inappropriate, right?—he holds up his hand, silencing my unspoken words

"It was purely so I would know what the school was talking about. They were worried you were self-harming."

"And you don't think that?" I ask curiously, guessing from his tone that he hasn't drawn the same conclusion.

He looks at me for a long moment, the silence building between us until he gives a small shake of his head. "I don't."

I swallow around a lump in my throat, not entirely sure why I'm suddenly feeling emotional.

Coughing to clear my throat, I lick my unexpectedly dry lips. "Then what am I doing here? You know I'm not self-harming and I'm sure you're aware that any 'issues' with my home life before I came here are redundant now that I'm eighteen and no longer legally a child of the state."

"Because, regardless of whether or not you're still in a dangerous environment, someone did that to you. That kind of abuse leaves more than just physical scars."

I have no words. I literally have no idea what to say to that. He's more right than he could possibly know, but I'm still not telling him shit.

He seemed to realize he wasn't going to get anything out of me, not today at least, and, instead of the probing questions I was expecting, he let me go.

As I reach for the door handle, his words stop me.

"I think we should meet for the rest of the semester. Same time next week?"

It's not really a question, not one I can refuse anyway, so with gritted teeth, I give him a tight nod, not saying anything else as I pull open the door and storm out.

I have no idea what the hell he thinks he's going to achieve by having me come to his office every week. Does he think he'll wear me down? That if he forces me to sit and talk to him, I'll eventually spill all my dark, dirty secrets? *Ha. If that's the case, he's got another thing coming.*

***

It's late on Sunday when I pull open the dining hall door, not really paying attention to the few other students milling around as I make a beeline for the freezer, my head already debating which flavor of ice cream I should go for today.

Deciding on strawberry shortcake, I turn to head back to my room when I spot Emilia sitting at the scholarship table. I haven't spoken to her since she knocked on my door. I have no idea what to say to her, but I miss her. I miss the easy friendship we had.

Hesitantly, I take a step toward her, gnawing on my bottom lip as I approach.

"Hi." I stand awkwardly on the opposite side of the table, smiling—although it feels more like a grimace—as Emilia looks up from the book she was engrossed in, her eyes widening when she sees me standing there.

"Hey." A small, hopeful smile touches her lips. "How have you been?"

"Fine. I'm fine. You?"

"I'm good." She nods, the two of us staring awkwardly at one another.

"How are things with, uh, Andrew?"

A light brightens in her eyes, a genuine, happy smile taking over her face.

"Things are going really well."

I can't help but smile at the happiness radiating from her as I sit down, digging into my ice cream as she catches me up on everything that's been going on with her recently, the two of us falling easily back into our old chatter.

Beck

Chapter 22

This job is boring as hell, but when you're fresh out of college, neck deep in debt and you get offered a ridiculously overpaid job to listen to the pathetic problems of over-privileged rich kids all day? Yeah, you'd have to be brain damaged not to take it. Still, it's a total fucking bore. Who cares if Daddy won't buy you a new car, or Mommy spent most of her summer vacation fucking the pool boy?

Well, I guess I'm supposed to give a shit, but growing up in a tiny apartment in a rough neighborhood, learning to fend for myself at a young age because my mom was too busy working three jobs to make ends meet, makes it seriously fucking difficult to have any sympathy for these spoiled brats.

I'd just been going through the motions, barely paying attention to the kids that walked through my door, until *she* walked in. I know there are a handful of scholarship students here, but ironically, none of them ever need to come see me. I reckon, like myself, life has taught them how to suck it up and get on with it, even when shit is hitting the fan. So when my first scholarship student walks through the door, I'm intrigued, especially given the reason she's here. The bullying doesn't surprise me, what does surprise me though, are the images.

I've gone over case studies of children of abuse. I've read files, studied psychological theories, and learned about therapeutic treatments; but I've never had to actually deal with one. It was the last thing I expected to have thrown at me in this pretentious school of pampered princes and princesses.

I was taken with her the second I saw her picture. It had nothing to do with her scars, and it sure as fuck wasn't because she was mostly naked. I could barely tear my eyes away from her face to look at anything else. It was the same when she stepped into my office. She was the embodiment of everything I've read, yet she was a complete contradiction to what I expected.

With her hostile demeanor, prickly attitude, and wary manner, everything about her screamed distrust; her dry wit and evasive answers, those defensive measures designed to keep people at arm's length. All of it a protective defense, no one can hurt you if you don't let them in. No one can catch you unaware if you're constantly on alert.

Despite the ugly reason for why she ended up in my office, I couldn't help but be excited that she was here. She's exactly the distraction I need right now. A challenge I didn't know I was looking for.

Unlike the other kids that come storming in here, immediately blurting out their problems and expecting me to fix them, I'm going to have to actually work to get Hadley to talk to me. It's going to take patience and careful prodding, well placed questions and tactful sharing of information.

I get the impression if I can get her to trust me, to open up to me, to let me see the real Hadley she hides underneath all that sass and snark, she's going to make me question everything I've ever known.

The knock on the door alerts me to her arrival and I immediately sit up straighter in my chair, running my hand through my hair, smoothing it out. *Jesus, I feel like a tween about to go on his first date.* I'm a riot of nervous energy. Clearing my throat, I call out, "Come in."

The door swings open, and Hadley storms in, her face shuttered and back straight. Does she walk around the school with that attitude or is it just for me?

"Have a seat." I gesture to the chair in front of the desk, assuming that's where she'll sit since it's where she chose last time, but with a raised eyebrow in my direction, she strides over to the couch, dropping her bag on the floor and making herself comfortable, sinking into the couch cushions.

I have to force my lips not to hitch up as I swallow my laugh at her defiance. She never does or says what I expect.

In all the literature I've read, it explains how children of abuse grow up to be closed off, independent individuals. Hadley is certainly all of those things. But where the textbooks say they are also broken, nervous, anxious people, Hadley is all strength and defiance.

"I have some work to finish up. I figured you probably have homework you could start on, or there are books on the shelf, feel free to look through them."

Her eyes narrow slightly, the only indicator of what she's thinking. If I had to guess, I'd say I've taken her by surprise. She was expecting prying questions into her childhood, into whatever is going on at school, but I've already ascertained that that won't work on her.

I need her to trust me. I *want* her to trust me; and that starts with getting her comfortable in my presence. Saying nothing, she bends down, pulling out a tablet and notebook before getting to work.

Neither of us says anything for the next hour, both of us working away in silence. Only once the hour is up do I stop focusing on the pages on my desk, looking up at her. She's lost in her work, scribbling away in her workbook, transcribing notes from the tablet. Her face is softer than I've seen it before, making her look younger, more her own age. Just seeing her relaxed and focused like that feels like a victory already.

As though sensing my eyes on her, she snaps her head up, her face hardening as she glares at me. "Sorry," I apologize, looking at her for a second longer before breaking eye contact. "That took longer than I expected. Our time is up."

"No worries." She shrugs, shoving her belongings back in her bag and throwing it over her shoulder.

Just before she can head out the door, I call out, "Same time next week." Her steps falter and she hesitates, not once looking my way before giving a sharp nod, pulling open the door and leaving.

After she's gone, I sit back in my chair, replaying our, albeit very limited, interaction. She didn't give me much, but she said more than she realized. The fact she turned up is telling in itself. It's not like anyone would track her down and force her to come here if she didn't show. Equally, when I told her I was busy, she didn't try to worm her way out of the session by suggesting we reschedule. So without even saying a word, she's told me a lot. She showed me she's used to following orders, doing as she's told, even if she doesn't agree or internally rebels against it. My guess is the scars have something to do with that—pain and torture are excellent methods of compliance. The fact she was comfortable enough to focus on her schoolwork tells me that, while she may not want to be here, she feels safe enough in this room, in my presence, that she doesn't need to be constantly on alert. I have no doubt she's still finely tuned in to her surroundings, but she doesn't perceive me as an immediate threat—something I'll take as a win.

Our next few appointments go the same way. Me finding excuses not to conduct our session so I can silently observe her and give her time to get comfortable in my space. Each week I see her getting more and more relaxed, becoming used to the routine, but today I can tell I'm not going to be able to continue with this tactic for much longer. She's fidgety, unable to focus on her work, constantly casting glances my way. She knows it's only a matter of time before this silent truce between us comes to an end and the hard questions begin.

Before she can ask whatever questions are rattling around in her head, I speak up. Like I said, this only works if we trust one another. To do that, I'm going to have to share with her a part of myself.

"I grew up in a run-down one bedroom apartment in Black Creek. You've probably never heard of it—"

"I've heard of it." Her eyes are narrowed, skepticism written all over her face as she takes in my fancy-as-fuck suit and styled hair. Yeah, I'm a far cry from the Black Creek kid I used to be. I may not be that scrawny street rat any longer, but this suit isn't me, either. It's the persona I donned when I agreed to this job. The person I had to become to fit in with the uppity staff and pretentious kids.

If I'd shown up in my worn jeans and faded t-shirts, they all would have taken one look at me and sent me packing. It's been made very clear to me that appearances matter here. Everything ultimately boils down to how you look, how you come across to others. It's got absolutely nothing to do with who you are, how good of a person you are. It's all superficial bullshit. But the other students that I see would be straight on the phone to their parents, demanding a 'real therapist' if they knew I wasn't one of them. So every morning, I put on my unfamiliar, pretentious clothes, don my fake smile and pretend I actually enjoy this platitudinous job.

The only problem is, every step I've taken to fit in with the people here has created a wall between Hadley and I. One I now have to carefully deconstruct, forcing me to put my trust in her that she will keep anything I share to herself.

"You don't look like anyone I've ever met from Black Creek."

The fact she knows *anyone* there surprises me. The only people in Black Creek are mobsters and gangbangers. Not exactly your everyday folk; and according to her file, she's been bounced about from home to home all over California, but she's never lived in Oregon.

Rolling up the arm of my shirt, I show her the crude tattoo on my forearm. It's jagged and uneven, looking like a botched job. In fairness, it was. That's what happens when a bunch of thirteen-year-olds with nothing better to do attempt to tattoo themselves. I've added other professional ink around it over the years until the entire length of my arm is covered in various tribal designs, but this one still stands out.

Looking at the ink, I have to swallow around the emotion in my throat, shrugging away the painful tug in my chest; each harrowing memory hitting me like a punch to the gut. Despite its prominent position, making it impossible for me to overlook every day, I never let myself reminisce on the past and everything the tattoo once represented.

Setting aside her workbook, she stands up from what has become her usual position on the sofa, cautiously approaching me, as though I might be trying to lure her into a trap.

When she's in front of the desk, she leans down, getting a better look at the symbol on my arm. It's a crude shape of the number four, with the words 'Reaper Rejects' encircled around it in barely legible writing.

"Reaper Rejects? I've never heard of them."

"They aren't anyone." I sigh. "A bunch of kids who thought they were all that, wanting to grow up way too fast, but when their world crashed down around them, they didn't know how to handle it."

Her eyes flick up to mine for a moment, as if wanting to test the truth of my words, before she looks back down at the ink. "What happened to them?" Her voice is a low whisper, like she's afraid if she talks any louder it will break this moment of truthfulness between us.

"We all went our separate ways. I don't know what happened to the others."

The way Hadley is looking at me; for the first time since I laid eyes on her, her walls are lowered. It's still impossible to get a read on her, but understanding sits heavy in the air between us. The sense of shared trauma and unresolved pain, memories we would both rather leave buried in the past.

Clearing my throat, I glance down at my watch. "Our time is up." I had planned all along to tell her who I am, who I was, but I never intended to bring up *that*. That part of my past is not something I talk about. It's not something I *think* about. I spend a huge part of my day pretending it never happened, so to bring it up so easily, to share it with her, has left me raw and unsure of my next move. I can't think straight when my head's a mess like this, and her close proximity is playing havoc with my brain. I can't afford to do or say something that might undo the little bit of progress we've made today.

She stares at me for a moment longer. Her eyes are softer than they were before, like she's finally seeing past the privileged, rich, white guy facade I'm wearing, and glimpsing the real me.

Giving a small nod, she murmurs, "Okay," before moving back to the sofa and hastily shoving her things into her bag, pausing as she passes the desk on her way to the door.

"Same time next week?"

Unable to look at her, I give a quick jerk of my head. "I'll see you then."

It's only when the door clicks shut behind her that I let out a shaky breath, loosening the tie around my neck and bending down to lift out the bottle of bourbon and a coffee mug I keep hidden in my bottom drawer.

Pouring a small measure, I knock it back in one go, leaning my head against the headrest, closing my eyes and letting the memories flash behind my eyelids.

Despite the impoverished way we grew up, we were always laughing and smiling. We never complained about being hungry or not having the latest technology. Black Creek was our playground, where we made games out of dumpster diving and constructed toys from the trash littering the streets. Together, we were happy. We had each other, and we were naive enough to believe that was enough.

I'll never forget that day; the gunshots, the screams. Everything changed and before I could come to terms with it, my mom pulled us out of there, carted me off to a brand new town and made me promise I'd never step foot in Black Creek again, or reach out to my old friends.

It's been nearly ten years since that fateful day. Nearly as long since I last thought about them all, shrugging off any notions with false pretenses that they are probably okay, out in the world living their lives. In actual fact, they're most likely dead, or in prison at best.

Fuck it, I decide, pouring myself another glass of bourbon. It's not like I have any more students today and I'm already in a piss-poor mood. May as well drink my pain away until I'm too far gone to think about them, until I can numb the gnawing guilt inside of me for never going back for them, for never getting them out of there.

Hadley

Chapter 23

I hesitate with my fist in front of the door. Goddammit. Why did he have to go and mess with our usual routine of silence? Does he expect me to open up to him now after our little powwow last week?

Whatever happened in his past must have sucked, and he's clearly not the typical rich asshole I first thought he was. I was too quick to judge him, but just because he decided to share some deep dark part of himself doesn't mean I'm obligated to do the same. Trust me, despite how fucked up his history might be, mine is worse.

Straightening my back, I take a final deep breath and rap on the door, opening it when he calls out.

“I’m swamped with work today; do you mind just working on your own stuff?”

I let out a silent breath of relief at his words. I know he’s bullshitting me. Why would he insist on me coming here every week if he’s just going to do paperwork? It’s a tactic. Yet, each week I show up and not once have I said I could skip the week's session if he’s busy.

If I’m being honest with myself, I’ve come to enjoy the undisturbed hour in this room, away from the prying eyes and hushed whispers of the other students. I enjoy the companionable silence; often finding myself letting down my guard and getting comfortable. That’s not something I ever thought I’d do around other people. Life has taught me not to trust anyone, yet I trust him enough to be relaxed in his presence.

I have no idea what that means. Every time I think about it, it freaks me out and I tell myself I’m not going to show up to our next session. Yet every week, here I am, standing in his office like I just can’t help myself.

“Yeah, that’s fine,” I respond, heading over to my usual spot on the sofa and pulling out my tablet and books and getting to work.

I’m too distracted this week, though. Just like last time, I constantly find my attention drifting, my eyes repeatedly flicking up to drink him in. Maybe it’s because I know this quiet peacefulness we have going has to come to an end soon, but I also can’t deny I’m just insanely curious about him, especially after what he revealed last week. He’s more like me than I thought, than anyone else here at Pac could ever be. If there was one person who might ever understand what I've been through, it would most likely be him.

Despite the fact this is all a ruse, he appears to be actually working. His brow is furrowed in concentration as he taps away on his laptop, and he doesn't seem to be aware of me watching him. It gives me the opportunity to look him over with fresh eyes. He's wearing yet another one of his ridiculously expensive-looking waistcoats and shirts. Today's waistcoat is light gray, paired with a pale blue shirt; the combination making him look professional and straight laced in a *'I just stepped out of a hot male model photoshoot'* kind of way.

Unlike in our first appointment, where I saw the extravagant suit and ritzy hairstyle, I look beneath all of that, taking in the haggard lines on his face and the knowing look in his eyes that only comes from being forced to grow up too quickly; when you realize at far too young an age that the world fucking sucks. It's filled with horrible people willing to do whatever they want for their own gain and there isn't a fucking thing you can do to stop it.

Taking in his hands as they fly across the keyboard, typing at a speed I could never hope to replicate unless I wanted to write gibberish, I notice the toughened skin and calluses that come from manual labor. Those are not the hands of an upper-class kid raised with servants at their beck and call and taught to delegate work instead of doing it themselves.

"What made you want to be a school counselor?" I ask, surprising myself. I had no intention of engaging him in conversation, although now that I've asked it, I'm genuinely curious.

His hands pause on the keyboard as he looks over at me, a mixture of surprise and something else I can't place before it disappears. "I wanted to help kids like me, help them realize there is more to life than violence and gang wars. Give them more options than I had growing up."

All of that makes sense, and yet...

"I wouldn't think too many kids at Pac end up involved with gangs and drug lords."

A surprised burst of laughter erupts from him, like he wasn't expecting my sarcastic response, a slow smile growing across his face. Holy shit, does he look fucking magnificent when he smiles. His whole face lights up, his eyes sparkling. It's almost like smiling is a rarity for him, but when he does, he puts everything he has into it.

It leaves me a little breathless, and I have to subtly swipe my finger along my lip, making sure no drool slipped out; all the while ignoring the weird fluttering sensation in my lower abdomen. I've felt something similar on the odd occasion; when Cam gives me a heated look, or when West was pressed against me in the library, but it's never felt this tumultuous before.

"No, I'm sure they don't." He chuckles. "But college isn't exactly cheap, and I'm working toward my masters, so I couldn't afford to turn down such a well-paid job."

I simply nod my head, not sure what to say to that.

"Do you know what you want to do with your life?"

The question takes me by surprise and I let out an inelegant snort. "Not a clue. It's not like I had any prospects before I came here, and I keep expecting this all to blow up in my face and I'll end up back where I was."

He nods in understanding. "Life has taught you that when things are going well, it's too good to be true. It's ingrained in you not to trust the happy periods of your life, because they won't last."

"I don't know if having the Pricks hate me and the school whispering about me is necessarily my life 'going well'," I retort with a snark.

His brows pull together at something I've said. "The Pricks?"

"Oh." *Crap*. I hadn't meant to refer to them out loud like that. It's one thing to call them that in my head, or to Emilia, but the fewer people who know about my less than pleasant pet name for the assholes, the better for me. "The Princes," I clarify, figuring he's probably already deduced who I'm talking about, and even if he hasn't, what we discuss here is confidential, and I don't believe he would run off and tell them. He doesn't strike me as someone who would let themselves get stuck under the Princes' thumbs. He's probably one of the few adults in this place that might actually stand up to them, or would at least resist them.

Once again, his face brightens with that brain melting, panty-soaking smile of his, another deep, rumbling laugh escaping him as he shakes his head. "Very fitting."

A small smile lifts the corner of my lip, and I have to mentally tap that shit down. This isn't a friendly bonding session. In fairness, I don't know what this is, but it's definitely not that.

He must be able to see me erect my walls again as, without even looking at his watch, he says, "Our time is up."

I begin shoving my workbooks back in my bag. "Same time next week, Mr. Jacobs?"

"Yeah," he agrees. "And Hadley, you can call me Beck when we're in this room."

I glance over at him, finding him watching me closely. "Okay...Beck." The word tastes like dark chocolate and cherry, and I can suddenly picture myself crying out his name as he does very unprofessional things to my body.

With my cheeks stained crimson, I duck my head and run out of his office, desperately trying to forget the way my name rolled off his tongue, in his rich, husky voice.

***

It's pitch black out as I slowly make my way through the forest. I saw the others sneaking out earlier, so I know tonight is fight night. Tonight is *my* night. I don't know how often they run these things, but I've been patiently waiting for this opportunity.

After the first time, I promised myself I wouldn't come here again, that I wouldn't insert myself into the fights, but Hawk has driven me to this. Punching a bag isn't enough. I need blood. I need pain. I need to watch these idiots beat the shit out of each other for no other reason than because they want to.

Each step I take is silent as I traverse the forest floor, approaching the clearing; the howls and cheers of bored, over-privileged teenage boys guiding my way.

Reaching the same clearing as last time, I hide in the shadow of the trees, ensuring I stay out of the beam of the flashlights while I peer through the crowd, into the makeshift ring. Just like last time, the boys form a wide circle around the fighters—two juniors who can't punch for shit. The Pricks stand out like a sore thumb at the far end of the ring, the other students keeping a respectful distance, unwilling to get too close and accidentally jostle them.

I focus back on the piss-poor fighters right as one of them lands a lucky shot, knocking the other guy to the ground. Lying in a heap, he slaps his hand against the compact dirt, tapping out.

A couple of his friends rush into the ring, lifting him up and dragging him out of there while the other fighter does a victory lap, people in the crowd clapping him on the back as he passes by.

The sounds of victory quickly die down as Hawk steps forward into the ring, the previous winner scurrying to the sidelines before he can get pulled into another fight. Everyone here knows he wouldn't stand a chance against Hawk.

With his usual arrogant look and a slight curl to his lip promising pain, Hawk surveys the crowd, shrewdly selecting his victim.

This is my moment.

I stride out from between the trees, cutting silently across the clearing toward them until I'm standing unseeingly at the back of the crowd. Thanks to my smaller stature, the boys in front of me prevent any risk of me being seen by Hawk or the other Pricks.

"Who will it be tonight?" Hawk calls out, slowly turning in a circle, eyeing down each and every boy, all of whom quickly glance away. The resonating silence is deafening as everyone looks at the person beside them, not one of them having the balls to take him on.

“Me,” I shout out from the back of the crowd. The guys in front of me turn around, their eyes widening when they see me standing there. As I step forward, they jump to the side, everyone parting to let me through.

I keep my focus on Hawk as I step into the ring, watching as his eyes widen and brows lift in surprise before he covers it with a sneer.

“You?” He snorts derisively. “Please, I'd wipe the floor with you.”

With an impassive expression, giving nothing away as per usual, Mason steps forward into the ring, coming to stand beside him as he whispers something in his ear. He's probably trying to convince Hawk to back down. He's the only one who has seen me in the gym. Annoyingly, he's also probably telling Hawk he can't fight a girl—just because I have ovaries doesn't mean I should be underestimated.

I didn't come to Pac to get caught up in fist fights and brawls, but apparently that's exactly what I'm going to have to do. I'm sick of taking Hawk's shit. I'm not someone who can sit back and let people walk all over them. I was raised to be a fighter, taught how to give as good as I get. I've been letting him go around acting like the big man on campus because I didn't want to disrupt the hierarchy here. I've had more important things to focus on, but enough is enough. I'm fucking done. If this asshole won't leave me the fuck alone, then I'm more than happy to show him exactly who he's provoking.

Hawk swats Mason away, not heeding his warning.

“Then what are you so afraid of?” I taunt, smirking back at him.

"I'm not about to have everyone going around telling people I beat the shit out of a girl," he snarls in response.

I nod my head like I completely agree with what he just said.

"How about," I begin, tilting my head to one side, as though I'm thinking through what I'm about to say, but the truth is I know exactly how to play this to ensure I get what I want tonight—my fists crashing into his stupid, pompous face, "you pick one of these...boys," I gesture to the gathered crowd, watching our exchange with a mixture of excitement and apprehension. "And I'll fight them. If I win, then it's your turn. No excuses, no bullshitting."

He looks completely relaxed, his arms crossed over his chest as he snorts. "Sure," he agrees easily, not for one second believing I could beat any of these wimps. "Why not? It'll be your funeral."

I catch Mason shaking his head. I wish I knew what he was thinking right now. He's seen my moves, felt the power behind my hits, so he probably knows I can hold my own, but he's never seen me against an actual opponent.

West looks conflicted, as though he's torn between intervening and letting Hawk do whatever he wants. We all know he won't dare contradict Hawk in front of everyone, though. God forbid their subjects see them arguing. *Fucking pathetic.*

I deliberately avoid looking at Cam, a skill I've become quite adept at. Things between us have gotten so fucking complicated. Between his betrayal and my own deception, neither of us can trust each other, which has left us in this weird stalemate where we awkwardly pretend the other doesn't exist. It's fucking exhausting and I miss his easy, flirty banter.

“Marcus,” Hawk barks, pulling my attention his way as he points to a lean looking junior behind me. Turning around, I run my eyes over him as he steps forward without hesitating. Shrugging off his top, I can tell he’s packing some muscle—not much, but a bit. Flexing so he can show off for the crowd, I immediately know he’s all about the performance, not the actual talent and skill; and he already thinks he’s won—a fighter's worst mistake.

Mason seems to agree as I hear him snort behind me, likely knowing as well as I do, I’ll have this idiot tapping out in no time.

I pull my hoodie off over my head, leaving me in only my sports bra and lycra leggings as I flex my fingers, stretching the leather of my fingerless gloves over my knuckles.

“Fuck me,” I hear one of the Pricks behind me murmur, but I can’t tell who, and I’m not about to take my eyes off my opponent. Throwing my hoodie to the edge of the circle, I ignore the hushed whispers as, for the first time, every male in the school gets an up-close and personal view of the phoenix tattoo covering my ribs and the various scars I’m sure they’ve all seen from the video or pictures.

Widening my stance, I raise my fists, Marcus mimicking me, except he’s got a cocky ass grin on his face that I can’t wait to demolish.

The second someone shouts ‘go’, I pivot forward, sidestepping his extremely obvious right hook and grabbing a hold of his wrist as I swiftly move behind him, yanking his arm up behind his back. He cries out in pain as the move forces him to lean forward.

Honestly, this is probably enough of a demonstration, but I've been taught not to stop until someone isn't just down, but they're out. Besides, I saw that glint in his eyes. He was looking forward to having the upper hand and taking me to the ground, so why the fuck shouldn't I give him a taste of his own medicine.

Without hesitating, I step around him, maintaining my firm grip on his wrist, holding it in place as I bring my leg up, relishing in the satisfying snap of broken cartilage as his nose collides with my knee.

Letting go of my grip on his arm, he drops like a sack of shit, blood running down his face. "You broke my nose, you bitch!" His words come out slurred as he spits blood everywhere.

I should probably feel at least a little bad about that, but something inside of me is inherently broken. I can't feel the same remorse other people would. I get little sparks of it here and there; moments of humanity, usually when my emotions are running high or I'm under a lot of stress. I also find myself feeling more...human, more alive, when I'm around Mason, Cam and West...*and Beck*. Hell, even Hawk ignites more fire in me than I've felt in years. It's pure, unadulterated hatred, but still, it's something.

Ignoring the sniveling idiot on the ground, I lift my gaze to Hawk, finding him staring at Marcus with wide eyes. Glancing behind him to the other three, West and Cam are wearing similar expressions of shock and surprise, whereas Mason looks smug...almost proud?

Returning to Hawk, he catches me smiling smugly at him and scowls back.

"You owe me a fight, Davenport."

With a sharp nod of his head, he agrees, "A deal's a deal," stepping confidently into the ring as Marcus stumbles to his feet and into the gathered crowd, giving Hawk and I room to circle one another.

"You better not hold back just because I'm a girl, Davenport."

"I wouldn't dream of it, Parker."

Unlike the first fight, when someone shouts, "Go," Hawk and I continue to circle one another, each of us analyzing the other, getting a feel for the other's style, their movements, their strengths and weaknesses.

In those first few seconds, I learn that he's well trained. His footwork is impeccable and he never once lowers his fists, giving me an opening; but he's cocky, sure of himself, and *that's* his weakness.

We dance back and forth, each of us testing the other with a few practice strikes, but it doesn't take long before Hawk gets bored and makes his first real move; his first mistake.

With swift, sure movements, he lands a punch to my ribs and another to the side of my head, making my ears ring. I'm faintly aware of the crowd cheering around me, but I zone them out as I retaliate, landing a few punches of my own. Nothing with lasting impact, but enough to get him to back off.

His wide conceited grin pisses me the fuck off and he doesn't hesitate before coming at me again, this time trying to sweep my legs out from underneath me and take me to the ground.

Self-defense 101–never let them get you to the ground. As soon as they do, they have the advantage, especially if the asshole is easily double your size, like Hawk.

My smaller stature makes me lighter on my feet, faster, meaning it's easier for me to avoid his swipes, dancing out of his way every time he comes near me.

He quickly becomes frustrated, not expecting it to be this difficult or to take this long, and that's when he makes mistake number two. Instead of using his knowledge and insight, he comes at me with annoyance and indignation.

The combination of his arrogance and anger makes him sloppy and big-headed. We each share another few blows, neither of us doing much damage. He's got a split lip and I can feel the smarting of a bruise on my cheek and another one over my ribs, but nothing serious.

My punches get weaker, sloppier, as we continue back and forth, and it soon becomes obvious to everyone around us that Hawk is the better fighter, the one with more strength and stamina.

On my next hit, he grabs a hold of my wrist, yanking me toward him, giving me no option but to let him pull me in. Using his grip on my arm, he spins me around, wrapping his thick arms around me.

"Tap out," he growls in my ear, but I ignore him, wriggling helplessly in his arms. "You can't win this," he snarls, "it will only get worse for you."

His hold on me tightens to the point of pain, but he's already given me the in I need.

Slamming the heel of my boot down on the top of his foot, I throw my head back, feeling it connect with his nose. There's no satisfying crunch this time, but it's enough that he loosens his grip and I can bring my arms out, breaking free.

While he's still stunned, I spin around, landing a quick jab to his kidney, then his spleen, followed by several quick blows to his head.

Kicking out with my foot, it connects with the side of his knee, making it buckle. Between the instability and the disorientation, he drops to his knees.

"Tap out," I demand, not bothering to keep my voice low like he did. "You can't win this. It will only get worse for you."

While my words are defiant, when he looks up at me, I am secretly pleading him with my eyes to just tap the fuck out. *Don't make me do something more serious just to get you to stay down.*

Of course, the shithead knows how to push all of my buttons and his glare turns defiant. He's got no intention of giving up, of losing to a girl.

Before he can move an inch, my fist flies forward, connecting with the soft tissue surrounding his windpipe. As the impact from my hit forces his airway to close over, preventing oxygen from getting in and out of his lungs, his eyes bug out of his head, his hand coming up instinctively to grasp at his neck as he gasps for air.

"What the fuck? You throat punched him!" West panics, running over and bending down beside Hawk, frantically looking him over as Hawk gasps and wheezes. The crowd whispers around us, everyone shoving against one another to get a better look, but I ignore them all.

"He'll be fine," I assure him, waving off his concern. "He wasn't going to stay down. It was that or knock him out. I figured this was the better choice."

"You...what?" he stutters, frantically checking Hawk over. He's already starting to recover though, his pharynx opening back up as he gulps down lungfuls of air.

"See?" I wave toward a clearly alive and well Hawk. "He's fine."

Lifting my gaze, my eyes catch on Mason and Cam who haven't moved from their position just outside the circle. Cam is staring at me in shock, frozen in place with his mouth agape as he tries to compute what he just witnessed.

On the other hand, Mason looks like he's trying really hard not to laugh. His reaction takes me by surprise. I expected him to be as angry as West. I certainly didn't expect him to be holding back laughter. I don't think I've ever seen him laugh...or smile, for that matter. He doesn't exactly show his emotions much. Even when we're alone in the gym, he wears his usual stony expression.

The sound of Hawk coughing up a lung pulls all of our attention his way as he climbs unsteadily to his feet. I expect his typical glare to land on me, but when he glances over my shoulder instead, I remember that we aren't alone and that I've just shown up the reigning asshole of the school in front of them all.

As though realizing the same thing, West matches Hawk's glare, adjusting his glasses as his steely gaze roams over the crowd. "Get the fuck out of here," he barks. "Tonight didn't happen. You didn't see anything, and if we hear so much as a whisper, you'll regret it."

His threatening tone and icy expression once again remind me he has a darker side I know very little about, one he reserves for times like these—when there is a threat to their reign.

The crowd jumps into motion, everyone scattering back through the trees like the hounds of hell are on their ass. It takes no more than a minute before the clearing is empty and the sounds of people running through the forest become distant before tapering out, the stillness of the night air once again returning.

"You tricked me," Hawk wheezes, his voice coming out harsh against his bruised throat.

"You let your arrogance rule you," I retort. "You assumed you'd already won, so you got sloppy. You're only a winner when your opponent is on the floor. Remember that next time and you might not lose."

The glower he throws my way would have anyone else pissing themselves, but I simply roll my eyes as he storms off into the trees, heading back toward the dorms.

Cam doesn't spare me a glance before taking off after him, an action that has my chest tightening painfully. With a heavy sigh, West steps away to pick up the flashlights strategically placed around the clearing, turning them off as he lifts them until only one is left on, providing just enough light as he walks back toward me.

"You coming?" he asks Mason.

"Yeah, I'm right behind you."

As he passes by me, he pauses, looking at me for a long moment. We haven't spoken since before the video. I've made a point of sitting as far away from him in computer class, and he hasn't tried to talk to me—whether that's out of respect for my need to be alone, or because he's pissed over the notebook, I'm not sure. I can't say I'd blame him if he was angry with me, not that I can explain anything to him. I shouldn't even have told Mason what I did, but when he was looking at me with those eyes full of questions and doubt, it fucking bothered me.

It's impossible to read anything in his expression in the weak light of the flashlight, but after a moment he glances away, shoving a spare flashlight into my hand before following after Hawk and Cam, the yellow beam lighting a path through the forest as he leaves Mason and I behind in the darkness.

Neither of us move or make a sound, listening to the noise of twigs breaking and leaves rustling as the three of them head back toward the dorms.

Silence once again surrounds us when Mason speaks. He had been standing several feet away from me when West left us, and I didn't hear him move, but his voice comes from right in front of me, inches from my face. I can feel his warm breath on my lips. "I never thought a woman would bring any of us to our knees, but you're constantly surprising me, little warrior." His voice is like gravel; dark and sinful, thickly coated with lust. Every word oozes sex, not to mention his nickname for me that sends shivers up my spine.

There's something about the inky black of darkness; not being able to see your surroundings, make out faces or read emotions. It bolsters confidence and makes people act in ways they otherwise wouldn't. The dark is where depraved things happen and secrets come to hide. It can push people to carry out disturbing acts; commit crimes and inflict pain. Yet, it's also in the dark where we find the courage to take our first steps; to do something reckless, like, for example, kissing Mason Hayes.

It's only because we're concealed by shadows and I'm still riding the high of the fight that I reach out, wrapping my hand around the soft fabric of Mason's shirt and pull him in against me.

It's because no one is around to see us, that tomorrow we can both pretend this never happened, that he lets me.

Our lips collide in an explosion of fireworks, the magnetism an undeniable force spreading outward from where they touch, running through my nerves and setting fire to my skin.

My lips part, his tongue sweeping in, staking his claim as, for the first time in my life, I lose myself in something; in someone. He tastes exactly how I'd expect—all quiet contemplation and steady reliance. I get lost in him, in the feel of his strong arm wrapped around me, his hand tangled in the strands of my hair, pressed firmly against the back of my head, holding me captive.

We take our time, savoring the taste of one another, like we have all night. I have no idea how long we kiss, neither of us taking it any further; simply enjoying this moment, knowing as soon as it's over, we will go our separate ways and pretend it never happened.

Using his tight grip on the back of my head, he deepens the kiss, our tongues sweeping hungrily over one another. He kisses me like I'm a lifeline, like he's barely been surviving, but now he wants to live on the taste of me.

When we break apart, I feel like my whole world has been rejigged. I'm not the same girl from a few minutes ago. My world feels brighter and I don't feel so alone. Like, somehow, Mason has taken some of my burden off my shoulders, lightening my load. It's almost as if I'm no longer fighting this battle on my own.

Mason knows nothing of the secrets I carry or the darkness I bear, yet I get the impression he *knows* at least some of my burden; understands my pain.

I'm still lost in the taste of him, my lips still tingling as his arm slides from my waist. His hand untangles from my hair and he slips into the shadows, disappearing as if he was never here, like this was nothing more than my imagination.

I stand in the darkness for who knows how long, wrapping my mind around what just happened, before deciding there's no point in overthinking it and flicking on the flashlight, grabbing my hoodie and following after the four confusing as fuck men that have my head all screwed up.

Beck

Chapter 24

I always sneak out to watch the fights. It would be impossible not to know when they're happening. It's the worst kept secret. You can see it on the boys' faces—the antsy anticipation, the way they eye up others that have crossed them or done them wrong, ready to call them out in the ring.

Watching the fights is the only thing in this damn place that gets my blood pumping—well, until Hadley showed up at my door. I can't participate in them, nor would I be welcome, but I can hide in the trees and watch. Even from a distance, the violence and bloodshed sates that restless inner part of me. I should probably be reporting them, but who the fuck would I tell? Not a single teacher here, Mr. Phister included, would stand up to the *Princes*. It's a complete fucking joke.

I spotted Hadley before anyone else as she strode up to the back of the crowd, her back ramrod straight, focused determination written all over her face. Once again, she completely took me by surprise. I never expected to see her here, but of course she is. Where every other girl would scrunch their nose up in disgust and turn their backs on the whole thing, pretending it doesn't exist, she wants to dive right into the middle of it and bathe in the chaos.

Hiding among the shadows of the trees, I watch as she rises to Hawks' challenge, unlike every other wimp pretending to be tough. Not one of them knows what it's like to actually fight for your life, to fight for survival and not just for sport. But it's clear Hadley knows—not that I expected anything less.

Standing prepared for battle in a fighter's stance, with her glove-covered fists raised, the swirls of black ink dipping beneath the lining of her leggings and up over her ribs, she looks like a fierce warrior. Combined with the impassive mask on her face, she's all business, not someone to mess with or take lightly.

I'm captivated as she takes down the first kid without breaking a sweat, not that he was much opposition. But Hawk...she gave as good as she got, neither one of them holding back. I admit, at one point I nearly blew my cover and stormed over there to break them up, worried he was going to injure her. The contempt in his eyes was enough for me to know he would have no issues doing whatever it took to win, regardless of how much it could hurt her.

I should have known she had it all worked out. Every move she made had already been planned out before she even stepped into that ring. She likely already knew what sort of a fighter he was, and if she didn't, one look told her all she needed to know for her to use his weaknesses against him.

The whole fight had me rock fucking hard in my jeans. Who knew watching a girl beat the crap out of someone bigger than her could be such a turn-on? Although, I'm pretty sure it had more to do with the fact that the girl was Hadley.

I was already taken by her; her quiet, strong composure enough to have me intrigued, but seeing her mete out her own justice tonight has pushed me over the edge into obsession. I have to have her. I have to make her mine. I never thought I could find a girl that would understand my past and accept the part of me that is still very much a Black Creek kid at heart.

Regardless of the over-priced suits and expensive haircut, violence still thrums in my veins, anger still swirls in my core, only expanding every day I have to remain in this insipid school, pretending to give a shit about vapid, self-obsessed students. This is not what I went to college for, this is not the future I wanted for myself. Unfortunately, I'm not here for just myself. As much as I might hate it, this opportunity can help me do a lot of good in the future, I just need to get through the here and now.

I feel my phone vibrate in my pocket as West barks out for everyone to get lost, and I slip into the inky darkness of the forest, heading back toward the staff accommodation on the far side of campus before anyone can catch me lurking.

When I'm far enough away from the clearing, I pull out my phone. Two missed calls from a private number. The phone goes off again in my hand, the same unknown number calling.

With a low groan, I answer the call, knowing ignoring it any longer will only infuriate him more.

"What?"

"Watch your tone with me!" he shouts, already infuriated and we haven't even gotten to the reason he's calling. "Why didn't you answer the first time?"

"I was busy. I don't just sit around and wait for you to call. I have a job, you know."

"I'm hardly going to forget the job *I* got you now, am I?" he sneers, making me grit my teeth. I should have known such an opportunity would come with strings, but I was too blinded by the prospect of it all. I was too naive to this world to realize how fucking corrupt the people in it are.

"What do you want?" I spit the words out, wanting this conversation over with as soon as possible.

"Lunch at my house on Christmas day. Two o'clock. Don't be late."

"I can't, I'm going home." It's a lie. Mom is working all of Christmas—it's always easy to pick up extra shifts around the holidays and people are always more generous with tips at this time of year, so it just makes sense—not that he needs to know that.

"Cancel. You're coming here. I won't hear otherwise. We have things to discuss. I had to use favors to get you that cushy job of yours, it's about time you paid me back."

Before I can get a word out—not that I know what to say to any of that—he hangs up, the silence from the disconnected call reverberating in my ear.

I squeeze the phone tightly in my hand, fighting the urge to throw it against a tree. *The fucking infuriating bastard.* It's moments like these that I seriously contemplate just leaving. What the fuck am I even doing here? Then I think about the number of other graduates who are in retail or working minimum wage, dead-end jobs because no one is hiring school counselors in a recession. Despite having him hold shit over my head, I'm lucky to have the job I have. Not only that, but I'm getting my degree to become a professional. Something that will open doors for me and create better opportunities. Plus, I can send money home to Mom to help her out a bit. It's the least she deserves after all she's done for me. I can suck it up for one meal and deal with him. How bad can it be? At least I'll get to eat the best turkey dinner I've probably ever had.

Cam

Chapter 25

It's three a.m. It's three a.m., and I've got the biggest swim competition of my life tomorrow, not that it really matters. I may be quickly working my way up to qualifying for the Olympic team, but my family will never let me actually compete at that level, not when there's a business to run and responsibilities to uphold. My father just wants to brag that I made it. He'll push me all the way there, dangle the golden ticket in front of me, then tear it all away; and he'll get off on it too. *Sadistic bastard.*

Despite how painful it's going to be to turn down my dream, I want to win. I want to go all the way to the end, even if I have to say no. I want to live that dream for even a moment. God knows I'm going to need something to hold on to when I'm stuck behind a desk, bored out of my fucking mind. Yet, regardless of how much I want it, it's three fucking a.m. and I'm wide awake, thinking about *her*. I've done everything I can think of these past two months to get her out of my system. Despite Hawk insisting she be forced to hang around us like a fucking gnat, I ignored her, blocked her out, even went as far as to flirt and mess around with other girls right in front of her, ignoring the fact my dick was like a wet noodle the whole time, only coming to life when she was nearby. Breakfast was fucking torture, having her sit beside me...smelling her. It only infuriates me more that she can get to me like that, and I don't seem to affect her in the slightest.

Her turning me down, in front of the whole class no less, was a hit to my ego. There's no denying that. No one has ever said no to me before, but, of course, I should have fucking expected that to be her answer. She's always saying no to me. She's only ever given herself over to me twice, and I stupidly mistook that for her wanting more, for her feeling what I feel.

Finding that notebook has just pushed me over the edge. How could I have been so fucking stupid? Of course she didn't want me. She wants my father, or one of our fathers. We're just stepping stones she's happy to crush beneath her boots on her way to getting exactly what she wants—money. Hawk has been saying it since the beginning, and I should have fucking listened to him. Well, I'm listening to him now. I've been avoiding her ever since, just like he told us to do.

Bianca's been a somewhat decent distraction. With some imagination and her face shoved in a pillow, I can get myself off...eventually. But seeing her last night, the way she took down Hawk like a trained professional, holy fuck, my dick's been stuck in erect mode ever since, and Bianca's C grade pussy just isn't cutting it.

Anger pulses through me. How fucking dare she have this effect over me. She continues to walk around this school—*our* school—like nothing fucking happened, like she didn't try to pull one over on us, on me. But you know what? I'm fucking done with that. I'm fucking done with ignoring her. It isn't enough. That video wasn't enough. She needs to be taught a fucking lesson, to know she can't just mess with people like that, she can't mess with *us* like that.

Throwing back the covers, I jump out of bed, fired up and ready to aim my anger at the person who deserves it most. Not bothering to throw on any clothes, I storm out of the apartment in just my boxers, making it over to the girl's dorm in record time.

The scholarship girls all have the ground floor, and it doesn't take me long to find out which room is hers. It's the only one without any personalized crap on the door. Of course it is, because she never shows anyone anything about her true self. She keeps everything about herself locked down tight. I should have fucking realized. All those nights in the dining hall, chatting, I thought we were getting to know each other, but looking back on it now, I can see the probing questions from her, asking about my parents, my father, my childhood, yet she expertly dodged every question *I* asked *her*. Not once did she give me a scrap of info on her childhood, any idea of her inner thoughts. Her wants. Her desires. *How the fuck did I not notice that?* I was too busy thinking with the wrong head, that's what was wrong. Well, not anymore.

I bang on the door far too loudly for this time of night, but who gives a shit. Hopefully it will only make her life here harder if people hear of me coming to her room in the middle of the night. I raise my fist to bang again, but the turning of the key in the lock halts my movements as it swings open, a sleepy, disheveled Hadley standing in front of me in a pair of barely there sleep shorts and a tank top. The scars across her chest and the tops of her arms are fully on display now. I've noticed that recently, too. Ever since the video, she's stopped wearing her baggy, oversized t-shirts. She now wears these tight, revealing tank tops that make her tits look unbelievable as she walks around, not giving a shit that everyone is gaping at her damage.

I thought for sure that video would break her. She's been hiding those scars all semester, there's got to be a reason. If it's not because she's embarrassed, then why?

"Cam?" Sleep is thick in her voice, but one look into the fiery pits of rage in my eyes and her eyes widen, her back snapping straight. Barging into her room, I don't give her any choice but to move aside, inspecting her inner space as she closes the door behind me. Once again, there's nothing personal here. No knickknacks, no photos, nothing that tells you anything about the girl that's lived here the last few months. Whatever, I no longer care who she is.

"Cam, what are you doing here?" The sleep is gone from her voice, leaving her sounding both weary and on edge. What the fuck does she have to be weary about? I'm the one that's weary. I'm fucking exhausted, tired of all the lies and deception.

"Is that why you came here?" I ask, still refusing to look at her. "To get close to one of us? Did you really think you'd get to our parents through us? What would you have done then? West's dad is the only one who openly cheats on his wife, or were you happy enough to settle for the role of mistress so long as you were paid enough?"

I finally turn around to face her, seeing my own fury reflected in her face as she glowers at me, her teeth grinding as her eyes spit fire in my direction. *Yeah, give me that fire, baby. Burn me with it, because if I'm going to hell, I'll be bringing you down with me.*

Taking a step toward her, she doesn't falter. I've seen her in the ring, I know how tough she really is. Tougher than I ever realized, but her hostility and refusal to answer just pisses me the fuck off.

"You never back down, never give up," I snarl, taking another step toward her. "You didn't even flinch when I wrapped my hand around your pretty little neck."

She tilts her chin, staring me down. The angle accentuates her neck, drawing my attention. Her eyes scream defiance, but something about the move almost feels like she's daring me to try.

How can I hate her and want her all at the same time? My head and my dick have never been at odds like this before, and I'm getting pretty fucking sick of not knowing what to do.

I came here to hurt her, to quiet that rage that's been simmering inside of me for the last two months, but now that I'm here, my dick already hardening in my boxers, I don't know what to do. Do I hurt her or fuck her? The answer comes to me out of nowhere, hitting me like a zap of lightning. For the first time in too long, every part of me is in agreement—do both!

My hand snaps out, wrapping around her throat, feeling her steady pulse thrumming beneath my fingers. Is she really not afraid of me? Of the power I have right now? My dick, that's always sporting a semi around her, stands to full attention, like a soldier reporting for duty, more than ready to dive into battle so long as the fight ends in it being buried deep inside her.

Squeezing ever so slightly, she doesn't move an inch, doesn't speak up or fight back. Why? If anything, she's shown us how much of a warrior she is, so why isn't she fighting me now? Does she know something I don't? Does she think I won't really hurt her? *I'm* not even sure of that right now, so how could she be?

With my free hand, I push down her shorts, tearing at the thin straps of her top until I can push that down too, leaving her naked in front of me so I can see every perfectly flawed part of her. If anything, her scars only enhance her beauty.

My fingers flex around her neck as I take my time looking her over, drinking my fill. I can feel every struggled breath she takes, yet that power, that control, only makes my dick harder. For too long, I've been feeling weak. I think it's time I claimed back some of that power.

Using my tight grip on her neck, I push her backward until her back slams into the door. Still she says nothing, only glaring at me with defiance—*and is that a flare of lust?*—as I push my boxers down, wrapping my hand around my painfully hard dick. Unable to look her in the eye, I kick her legs apart and slam into her in one quick motion, surprised at how wet she is as I feel her spasm around me, adjusting to the intrusion. *Fuck me, is she enjoying this?*

A slight moan escapes her lips, but I tighten my grip on her neck, cutting it off as I pound into her at a ferocious pace, every thrust meant to rid myself of this helplessness I feel, of this rage I have toward her; meant to punish her for her betrayal, her lies.

My anger still isn't sated, but it has somewhat abated by the time the familiar tingling starts and my balls draw up, my eyelids drifting closed as I explode inside of her, not even giving a shit that I didn't wear a condom.

Her pussy spasms around me as though she's about to come. My eyes snap open, taking in her lidded eyes, blue-tinged lips and the crimson flush rising on her cheeks and cascading down over her heaving chest. The blush *could* be due to the lack of oxygen, but there's no denying she's about to cum all over my dick.

Before she can do just that, I pull out, not letting her see my surprise as I fix an impassive look on my face. Her eyes snap to mine, the lust from a moment ago quickly replaced with irritation as she glares at me. Smirking at her, I use my still tight grip on her throat to fling her body toward the bed where she lands in a heap, my cum smeared over her inner thighs as it leaks out of her. Ignoring the twisting in my stomach, I tuck myself away, not looking back as I open the door and leave her behind.

***

Feeling like my old self, I strut out of the changing rooms to cheers from the stands. I once again dominate in my race, beating the other kids by a mile, a huge, shit-eating grin on my face as I throw my arms in the air, facing the crowd.

As students line up for the next race, I spot my dad standing at the far side of the pool. Grabbing a towel and running it through my hair, I drape it over my shoulders as I head toward him, knowing he won't leave until he's once again reminded me Rutherford's are winners. Doesn't he know by now that every time he spouts that crap, it only encourages me to do the opposite? I'd deliberately lose at swimming to piss him off if I didn't actually give a damn about winning. I don't have the same reservations with my grades, though, so he's just going to have to accept the passes I'm barely scraping.

As I get closer, I notice he's avidly watching someone up in the stands. I'm standing right behind him, when I hear him murmur under his breath, "Elizabeth?" Glancing up, I scan my eyes over the crowd, but I don't see anyone I recognize with that name. The only person who stands out to me is Hadley. Her head is ducked as she scurries away, attempting to hide in the crowd, likely trying to get out of here before I or one of the guys spots her. I don't even know what she's doing here. She's made it clear she doesn't give a shit about me, so why even bother showing up? If she was hoping her presence would throw me off my game, then more fool her. Nothing could interrupt my focus when it comes to swimming.

"Who?" I ask, pulling my gaze from Hadley, once again searching for whoever my dad saw. He startles at the sound of my voice, not having heard me approach.

"Who was the student I just saw? The new girl."

I shrug my shoulders, really not wanting to talk about her with him. "Just some scholarship student that started this year."

"Huh," he puzzles, frowning. "I didn't realize the school was taking on any new scholarship students."

I shrug my shoulders again. *Whatever. What the fuck does it matter?*

"What's her name?"

I give him a weird look out of the corner of my eye, something about his tone is off. It's sharper than usual, his eyes more beady looking. Maybe he's on something?

Whatever, not my fucking problem.

Knowing if I don't just hand over the name, he'll make me, I say, "Hadley Parker."

He probably just wants to dig into her file. He's a control freak, always needing to know everything about everyone around him, so he probably thinks he's doing his due diligence by checking her out, making sure the school hasn't accidentally accepted an application from some sort of delinquent. I'm sure the school does their own thorough background checks on new students, but whatever.

"Why?" Despite the fact I tell myself I don't care, I ask the question anyway.

Waving me off, he simply says, "Just curious. You know I like to stay informed of who all attends Pacific Prep with you. Good job today, son. You did the Rutherford name proud. I can only hope you'll bring the same drive and determination to the company with you."

Right. Unable to think of anything constructive to say, I give him a tight smile.

"You'll be home for Christmas break in a few days. We'll talk more then. We have a lot we need to discuss with you boys."

Yeah, I bet you do. Like maybe the fact the company we've always been told we'll inherit one day is actually a front for a black market mercenaries-for-hire organization. Well, too late. We discovered that little nugget of information on our own, thanks to West and his next level genius skill with computers.

It blew our minds. Fucking obliterated them. Our parents have always been cold, detached...ruthless almost. But then what prominent businessmen aren't? I remember West telling us once that some of the most successful business leaders are actually psychopaths, or have similar traits to them. Something like that anyway. Sure, our parents are successful and they share some of the tendencies West mentioned. They're definitely egotistical and apathetic, and they certainly never gave a shit about us beyond how our successes or failures reflect on them. Even so, I never would have thought them capable of this.

We've discussed every scenario, but regardless of what we come up with, there is no denying they are involved. We haven't been able to find out anything regarding the inner workings of it all, only that all four families co-own and oversee the overall running of the organization. Maybe we'll get more answers when we're home over Christmas.

My father takes off to speak to the coach as I spot the guys leaving the stands. After a quick shower, I meet them outside the changing rooms, all three of them sporting huge grins as I pull the door open.

"Well done, man," Hawk congratulates, bumping my fist as West slaps me on the back.

"You were on fire out there," Mason enthuses.

Their praise lights me up. Why can't my father show such genuine happiness at my successes? These guys make it seem so easy. We always have each other's backs, we're always supporting one another. I can trust them to stand behind me in anything. That kind of loyalty is hard to come by, but what we have is forever. No girl will ever come between us, and definitely not someone like Hadley.

"Come on." Hawk jerks his head toward the exit. "We've got some celebrating to do."

Hadley

Chapter 26

I don't know why I went to that stupid swim meet, especially after what Cam did last night. I'm both disgusted with myself, shocked at his actions, and, most disturbingly, turned-on by the whole thing. I'm clearly sick in the head. I've spent my whole life around abusive, dominant men, and I know that exposure has seeped into my sex life. I like my sex rough—although, I never hand over control like that—but last night was on a whole other level. I was lightheaded and on the verge of passing out when he released his grip on my neck.

I've no idea why I let him treat me like that. I could feel the pain pouring off him and I guess I felt...guilty?

Yet, despite his hatred of me and the anger emanating from him, I went to that meet. I had to know he would win. I had to see him in action, because, regardless of what he might think, I do care about him. He made me fucking care. I was never supposed to fall, never supposed to give a damn. Except all those late nights I spent with him, trying to find out more about their parents and listening to him talk about his childhood, it made me see him as more than just the flirty guy I needed to get close to. Combine that with the way he used to look at me like no one else in the room mattered, not to mention the unbelievable sex...how could I not fall for Cam Rutherford?

Shaking him out of my thoughts, I walk through the campus gates. This is the first time I've been outside these walls since the day I arrived. I meant to do this ages ago, but, well, life kind of got in the way. Crossing the road, I head down the wooden steps to the beach. It's insane that the school is this close to the ocean, with this view, yet they stuck the dormitories all the way at the back of the campus.

Stepping onto the beach, the smell hits me first. The brine of seawater is so strong I can practically taste it. Looking around the uneven shoreline, strewn with rocks, shells and chunks of seaweed, I find myself alone, except for some man at the far end of the beach. My boots sink into the sand and I hastily kick them off, feeling the hot grains between my toes with every step I take toward the ocean. The crash of waves and seagulls crying are the only sounds I can hear.

Just before I reach the water's edge, I drop my boots and sit on the sand, my legs outstretched in front of me as I slide my hands through the rough grains, enjoying the feel of it beneath my fingers. My eyes soak in the sight in front of me, the steady push and pull of the tide, the waves rolling inland before they dissolve into foam on the beach. It's bliss. Here I can forget about Pac Prep, the Pricks, the Princesses. The reason I'm here.

Tilting my head back, I close my eyes, letting the sun hit my face, warming it; the cool breeze just enough to offset the heat of the day. For a long while, I pretend I'm just some woman on a beach, enjoying her day of relaxation, until I feel someone watching me. Snapping my eyes open, the guy I saw earlier has walked down the beach toward me. He's dressed casually in jeans and a t-shirt, with a tattoo covering one arm.

With the glare of the light, it's impossible to make out his face, but as he gets closer, recognition dawns. Beck. He must see me as he heads this way.

"Fancy seeing you here," he calls out as he approaches. "I thought you'd be busy packing for the end of term."

"Foster kid, remember? I'll be spending all my holidays here for the rest of the year."

"Ah, I wasn't sure. Do you mind if I sit?"

Shaking my head, he lowers his athletic body onto the sand beside me, keeping a respectful distance between us. God, I thought he looked good in his preppy waistcoats, but holy shit, he's fucking lickable right now. I hadn't realized his tattoo went all the way up his arm, and his t-shirt does nothing to hide the fact he clearly works out.

His eyes roam over my face, his lips thinning as he takes in the purple bruising on my cheek. Emilia lent me some of her makeup to cover up the worst of it from prying eyes and whispering students, but the swelling and discoloration is still obvious up close.

The two of us sit in silence for a while, comfortable enough in each other's presence now that neither of us feels the need to say anything. Only a few short weeks ago, I wouldn't have been able to sit beside him like this. Not without my every sense in overdrive, waiting to see what he would do, ready to react if he made one move I didn't like. Instead, my nerves are ablaze for a completely different reason.

"It's beautiful out here." His voice is filled with awe as he takes in the view in front of us, seeing the same beauty as I do.

"It is," I agree. "I've never had time to just sit and take it in before. I've caught glimpses of the ocean, watched other kids playing in the sand, but I've never just sat and enjoyed it."

He doesn't pry further, something that I appreciate. I think that's what has endeared me to him most. If anything, he's shared more with me than I've shared with him. He's entrusted me to keep his secret about who he really is, without asking anything of me.

Licking my lips, I pull my legs up in front of me, wrapping my hands around my knees before blurting out, "When I was thirteen, my only friend was murdered in front of me." He doesn't respond, but I can feel his eyes on me, and even though I don't look away from the rolling ocean, I know I have his full attention. "She was killed because she wouldn't do what some scumbag lowlifes wanted her to do."

I rarely let myself think about Meena, but it's thanks to her I'm finally free. If only she hadn't had to die for me to realize there must be more to life than what we'd been subjected to.

"She always talked about coming to the beach," I say in a flat, monotone voice. "We'd tell each other all the things we were going to do when we got here. I promised her we'd see it one day, together."

My chin trembles as tears prickle behind my eyes, my chest aching with the grief of her loss as I press my forehead against my knees, taking a few deep breaths to collect myself.

Beck keeps quiet, not saying anything as he gives me the time I need to gather myself together. Eventually I sit up, leaning back on my arms, pressing my hands flat against the sand. "She would have loved it here," I murmur as I look out over the sea-green frothy water, taking in the sun's glow on the horizon. It's so picturesque. Better than anything we could have dreamed up.

The feeling of a warm hand on mine pulls my attention back to Beck. His features are soft as he looks at me with empathetic eyes, a sad smile lifting his lips.

"I think she'd be proud of who you've become," he murmurs gently. "The depth of your strength is incredible."

We both sit in silence for the rest of the day, only making a move back toward campus when the sun starts to set, its yellow-red rays painting the sea a bright amber.

Despite not having done much with my day, I'm exhausted by the time I make it back to my room, and I'm really not in the mood when I find West leaning against the wall beside my door.

"What are you doing here, Wes?" I sigh, unlocking the door and pushing it open.

"I need to talk to you." His tone is pressing, his brows furrowed and his lips pinched, all of it making him look more serious than normal as he watches me closely. Unable to handle his overbearing gaze, I push through into my bedroom, not giving a crap if he follows me or not.

Dropping my bag on the desk, I turn around to face him, crossing my arms over my chest as I look him over.

"Okay..." I raise an eyebrow impatiently, wishing he would hurry up and get to the point; tell me whatever he has to say so he can leave me alone.

He steps hesitantly into the room, closing the door behind him and standing awkwardly in front of it, glancing around like he's never seen the inside of a girl's bedroom before, but I know he's been in this exact bedroom so I've no idea who he's trying to fool.

"I like what you've done with the place."

The room looks pretty much the same as it did the day I moved in. *Sarcastic asshole.*

"We don't all have money or time to waste on decorating," I snipe at him. If he's just come here to insult me, I'm going to be fucking pissed.

I notice his eyes lingering on the bookcase.

"I've found a new hiding spot, in case you were wondering."

"I wasn't."

His words have my eyes narrowing on him. Is this some sort of recon mission? Are they trying to get the notebook back?

Taking another step toward me, he holds out a file I hadn't even noticed he was carrying. Staring at it warily, like it's a bomb and not a collection of papers, I make no effort to take it from him.

"What the hell is that?"

"You said you were raised in foster care, right?"

I hesitate before confirming, my thoughts racing as I try to figure out what he's getting at, my eyes flicking up from the envelope to his watchful gaze. "Yeah."

Fuck, if he's been doing some digging, he'll have discovered my backstory is a complete lie. There's no way he can know the truth, though. Even if he did somehow stumble across it, there's no fucking way he would believe it. No one in their right minds would.

My heart races, every muscle tense. Everything inside of me is screaming that this is bad.

"Do you know who your real parents are?"

"What are you getting at, Wes?" I demand, snapping at him, not liking one bit where this line of questioning is going.

The fucker just raises his eyebrows, waiting for me to answer him.

"No," I snap, "I don't."

Realizing I'm not going to touch whatever the hell is in that folder, he inches toward the bed, dropping it on the covers. My stomach churns, this gut wrenching feeling that I know exactly what is in that folder making me feel physically sick.

"What did you do, Wes?" I glare at him. Who the fuck is he to stick his nose in my business. Why the fuck would he even go looking for my parents. Does he think he's doing me a favor? Just because he's got the perfect rich family, he thinks we all want to know where we come from?

Wrong!

We can't all have picture perfect families like him. Why the fuck would I want to know what teen mom or druggie parents decided they didn't want me?

"I don't want to know who they are," I blurt out, before he can tell me anything I *know* I don't want to hear, looking pointedly at the floor, not wanting to see the judgment on his face. This is my decision to make. If I don't want to know, then I *don't want to know.* That's my prerogative. I won't let him make me feel bad for that.

He nods his head. "I get that." There's something in his voice that makes me look back at him. I can't place it, but when my eyes connect with his, it's like he gets me, understands my need to not know.

His lips press together, a pained expression flashing across his face. "But, in this case, I think you need to know."

What the fuck does that even mean?

"Ever since you showed up, I've been noticing things. Small—"

"Nope," I snap, my sharp tone cutting him off as I shake my head vigorously. "No. Get out! I don't want to hear any of this." Striding toward him, I'm not even able to enjoy that usual calming energy between us as I slam my hands against his chest, failing miserably at shoving him toward the door. The fucker doesn't budge an inch, standing his ground as I continue to push against him.

His hands come up, his long fingers wrapping around my upper arms in a tight grip, holding me in place as he gives me a quick shake.

"Hadley." His voice is a firm bark and I slowly lift my eyes to meet his, my head shaking side to side as I silently beg him not to say anything more. I know. I just fucking *know* his next words are going to eviscerate me. I can already feel the cracks as my world explodes around me. Hasn't he done enough damage? Does he need to inflict more pain on me?

I can see he doesn't relish in being the bearer of this news, but, despite the regret in his eyes, he hardens his resolve, sticking to his guns. He doesn't give a shit how much this is going to fuck me up, he's going to tell me, anyway.

"I honestly thought I was imagining things. I didn't think anything would come of it," he murmurs, more to himself than to me. "It was a long shot, ruling out an impossibility, more than anything else."

I don't say anything. I'm incapable of saying anything, the lump in my throat blocking any words I might have. I feel completely numb, his words coming at me through a dense, incomprehensible fog.

"Hawk is your brother."

Silence reigns in the room, his words bouncing around in my head as I stare at him stupidly, my mouth agape as I struggle to comprehend his words.

"What?" I croak, frowning at him. There's no way I heard him right. "What did you say?"

That numb, earth-shattering feeling is quickly receding, the familiar fire of anger replacing it.

"Do you think I'm fucking stupid?" I snap, shoving him once again in the chest, shaking off his grip on my arms. "Do you *seriously* think I'd fall for that shit after everything you guys have done to me?"

I bark out a sharp, caustic laugh as I take a step back from him, shaking my head as I increase the distance between us. My heart reshapes and hardens with every inch of space I create.

"Playing the family card?" I growl, every muscle in my body quivering with uncontrollable rage. "That's so fucking low of you! I expect this shit from Hawk, even Cam, but you?" Sneering at him, I shake my head in disappointment.

"What? No!" he exclaims, but I'm not hearing any of it. I can't bear to listen to another fucking word that comes out of his mouth.

"I get that you all sit up there in your ivory tower, having a laugh at the rest of us plebs down here trying to survive one day to the next, but you have no idea how fucking difficult it is to go through life without knowing who your family are. Not knowing who *you* are, or where you come from, and the fact you'd do all this as some sick joke is just fucking disgusting." I'm yelling by the time I'm done, my chest heaving as I glare at him. I'm practically vibrating with anger, so fucking done with their shit and pissed off with myself for expecting anything more from any of them. They aren't capable of being decent human beings. Tonight just proves that.

"I thought you were better than that," I sneer, glowering at him with hate-filled eyes. "But I guess I was wrong."

"Hadley, no—"

"Get out!" I demand, cutting him off once again. When he still doesn't seem to be getting the message, I make it super fucking obvious for him.

"GET THE FUCK OUT!" I yell, my fingers wrapping around the first object they find, throwing it across the room. The fact that my aim misses only pisses me off further.

Seeing how close I am to going full psycho on his ass, he finally concedes, dropping his gaze from mine. With a final sigh and shake of his head, he turns on his heel, not looking back as he lets himself out of my room.

I storm after him, slamming the door shut and flicking the lock behind him, my legs giving out beneath me as I slide down the door, my hands shaking as I curl into a ball on the floor, an uncontrollable wave of emotion crashing over me. I've been holding myself at bay for so long. I think I just finally found my breaking point.

I don't know how long I lie there, curled up in the fetal position by the door, completely numb to everything around me. When the tears finally stop and I feel like I can get back to my feet, I make my way over to the bed, intent on crawling under the covers and blocking out the rest of the world, hoping the sweet oblivion of sleep will claim me quickly.

The crinkling of something underneath me as I drop onto the covers, has me rummaging around in the sheets, trying to find what I'm lying on. Pulling out the envelope from underneath me, I stare at it for a long moment, torn between seeing what's inside and chucking the whole thing in the trash.

I told West I don't want to know. But is that the truth? I spent my whole life wondering who my parents were, and the answers are right here in front of me, in some stupid non-descript envelope. It's not like knowing is really going to change anything. They're probably long dead by now. Even if they aren't, it's not like I have to go track them down.

I stare unseeingly at the envelope for a while, going back and forth before curiosity finally wins out and I tear open the sealed tab, pulling out the small pile of papers. Looking at the first page, it's headed with the name of some sort of lab. *Okay, not quite what I was expecting to find.* Scanning through it, most of it is a bunch of medical jargon I don't understand, however, one paragraph sticks out.

Find enclosed a detailed analysis of the provided DNA samples. We can confirm that the DNA provided by one Hadley

Parker and one Hawk Davenport share common markers, indicating the tested individuals are biologically related.

Shuffling through the other pages, they all say something along the same lines, all of them reports from different labs. Spreading the papers out on the bed, I sit and stare at them for a long time. What does this mean? Is this all an elaborate prank? What if it's not?

Noticing an address and phone number at the bottom of each of the reports, I do a quick google search. When nothing suspicious stands out, I grab my phone off the bedside table and dial the number for the first lab. When a receptionist answers, confirming it is in fact Synex Labs, I do the same with the second and third reports, getting the same corroborating response.

With my head spinning, my thoughts jumping all over the place, I gather the papers in my hand and storm toward the door, intent on getting some actual answers from the assholes themselves. There's no way I'll be able to focus on anything else until I get to the bottom of this.

Flinging open my bedroom door, I freeze when West falls backward into my room.

"What the—" I stare down at him in confusion. He must have been sitting on the floor, leaning against my door. How long has he been sitting there for? Has he been here since I kicked him out?

"What is this?" I demand as he climbs to his feet, shoving the papers against his chest.

"I tried to tell you," he snarks, glaring at me as he throws his hands up in the air. "I believe you didn't want to listen to me."

"Well, I'm all ears now," I throw back, crossing my arms and planting my feet, waiting impatiently for him to explain himself.

"I told you." He sighs, jerking his head toward the papers. "Hawk's your brother."

"You tested his DNA?"

"Yeah, against yours."

"How did you even get mine?" I demand before quickly changing my mind. "Actually, don't answer that. I'd rather not know. I don't understand what made you even *think* to do that."

"I'm perceptive." He shrugs, like that explains anything. "I pay attention."

"What the fuck does that mean?"

"I noticed things. You have Hawk's eyes. You both have fucking awful tempers."

"Are you serious? That's *all* you had?"

He sighs heavily, gritting his teeth. "It was more than that, but it's hard to explain. Like I said, I honestly thought it was all in my head, but Mason and Cam picked up on it too. They mentioned something off-hand about how similar you both were, and it got me thinking. I started paying more attention, and that's when I sent the samples off. It was an off chance that I *may* be on to something. I honestly didn't expect to be right."

I don't know how long we stand there; me lost in my own thoughts, openly staring at West with an unfocused gaze as his words echo in my head, nothing really resonating with me.

I have a brother? And not just any brother, but fucking *Hawk*, a fucking asshole who I hate. *Of course my luck is that shitty.*

"What does this mean?" I eventually murmur.

He gives me a small, sympathetic, half-smile, his hand reaching out as though he's going to, I don't know, comfort me? Whatever it was he was going to do, he decides against it, dropping his arm back to his side.

"I don't know," he answers softly, giving a small shake of his head as he shrugs his shoulder.

Licking my lips, I nervously ask, "Have you told Hawk?"

"No." His reply is instant. "I haven't talked to anyone about this. I figured you'd want to know first."

I'm surprised he put me above his friend like that. I don't understand why he would, but I appreciate his thoughtfulness. It gives me time to come to terms with this bomb drop and prepare for Hawk's backlash.

"I need to tell him, though. He has a right to know. I, uh...I wasn't sure if you would wanna be there when I talk to him?"

"No, definitely not." I adamantly shake my head. "It will be better for everyone if I'm not there." Hawk hated me when he had no good reason to. I can only imagine how well he will take this development.

"It's not like that," West tries to explain, clearly knowing where my thoughts have strayed. "It's not you. He hasn't had an easy life."

"An easy life?" I interject, barking out a sarcastic laugh, unable to believe his audacity. "Yeah, I'm sure the poor prince has had it rough," I snarl. "Spare me the pathetic *woe is me* bullshit. I don't wanna hear it."

With his lips pressed together, he gives me a tight nod, saying nothing else as he takes the DNA reports from my hand, leaving me alone with my tumultuous thoughts, the soft click of the door closing behind him resonating around the room.

West

Chapter 27

Fuck. I lift my glasses off, rubbing my eyes and pinching the bridge of my nose in frustration. Putting them back on, I run my hand through my hair, not caring I'm messing it up. That went about as horrendously as I expected—worse even. Seeing her shocked expression as I blew apart her world, and Jesus, listening to her faint cries through the door. I nearly kicked the damn thing in, the urge to comfort her riding me hard.

I've been humming and hawing for nearly a week now, over what to do with the results. They both needed to know, but I couldn't work out how to tell them. There's been a strange sort of stalemate between us for the last month, all four of us actively pretending we don't notice her when she's around, but Cam only pays attention to Bianca the second Hadley enters a room. Mason has completely ignored his girl all month, and I've caught him watching Hadley when we're in the same room. Of course, I've only noticed it because I've been watching her, too.

Seeing her and Hawk fighting the other night just made it all the more clear that they needed to know. Now. They need to get past this shit. They're fucking family. Whether or not Hawk likes it, or Hadley wants to be, she's one of us. I don't know what the fuck happened for her to end up with the life she's had, but all these years...she should have been with us. Should have grown up with us, been at the cabin with us in the summers, and attended Pac with us the last four years.

There's a lot going on with her that we don't know or understand, but all the issues between us and her need to be resolved. Hawk's too caught up in his need to control her, and Cam's too lost in his hurt. Both of them too proud to be the bigger person. I honestly don't know where Mason stands with her, so I guess that leaves me to try and create some peace between us all.

Pulling open the door to the boys' dorms, I release a heavy breath. As badly as that went with Hadley, I know it's going to be ten times worse with Hawk.

Letting myself into our apartment, I glance around the open living space, checking if he's around. He's slouched on the sofa, playing a video game as I make my way over to him.

"Hey, man." My steady voice doesn't give away any of the jittery nervousness I'm feeling.

"What's up?" His eyes never leave the TV as he races around a corner on a motorbike.

Taking a deep breath, I know I need to just rip off the Band-Aid. Sitting down on a chair opposite him, leaning forward, my elbows resting on my knees, I pierce him with the same serious expression I used on Hadley. "I need to talk to you."

He must sense the gravity in my tone, as he pauses his game, setting the controller down before turning to look at me. "Sure, what is it?"

"I found something out about Hadley," I start, unsure how to actually say the words to him. This is so much harder than it was when I broke the news to Hadley, and that was fucking difficult. Seeing that pain on her face. I've never seen her look so broken before. She puts on this impenetrable front, always acting like everything just bounces off her. It makes me forget sometimes that she's fucking human underneath it all. She's still got the same insecurities as the rest of us. Hell, I've a feeling she's got more issues than most.

Growing up the way she did, not knowing who her family was, I can only imagine what a bombshell it must be to suddenly find out you not only have a family, but that they're right under your nose, and they're stinking rich. And on top of that, to know your own brother has been your tormentor for the last few months? Yeah, that must sting.

"You did? What did you find?" His voice is threaded with excitement, a wide grin on his face. Fucking hell, he needs to get over his infatuation with her. Now more than ever. I know he's had a lot going on, we all have, and I know he was worried she was using Cam. I'm honestly not sure what the hell was going on there, and I can't explain the notebook we found in her room, but I get the feeling there's more going on here than he and Cam seem to think. I don't know how I know that; I just do.

"Man, I don't get it," I admit, needing answers before I share with him what I've found out. "What is your problem with her? And don't tell me it's about the notebook. You and I both know this started long before that."

I have to tell Hawk this news—he has a right to know. But after seeing Hadley, after hearing her sobbing her fucking heart out through the door, I can't let him do any more damage to her. I need him to explain this vendetta to me.

"I just don't like her." He scowls. "I don't trust her. She's up to something."

I sigh wearily, not understanding his cryptic answer. It's the same bullshit he's been saying all year, but there's never an actual fucking reason. "Are you sure you're not just worried 'cause Cam has feelings for her? It's the first time any of us has actually given a shit about a girl before."

His eyes narrow on me. "Don't bullshit me, I know you've taken an interest in her too."

I simply shrug my shoulders, unable to deny it. What can I say? The girl intrigues me. There's something about her. She's tough as nails and fiercely independent. She's got walls so thick I don't think she's ever let anyone in; then there are moments like today when I see a rare vulnerability in her. All of it speaks to one complicated woman. As if that wasn't enough to have me curious, there are odd things about her I just can't explain. I want to know about her inability to use technology, why she doesn't drink, and about the wariness in her eyes when she's around others. I can't understand any of it, which of course only fascinates me more. I can't help it, I'm a sucker for a puzzle, and Hadley is exactly that—a complex enigma that's just screaming at me to be solved. She draws me in. It's like she's begging me to figure her out, to understand her. I want to know everything about her, which is fucking weird, because I've never given a damn about a girl before. Never even been all that interested in them until Hadley showed up.

"Look." I sigh, preparing myself for the Hawk shit-storm that's about to rain down on me. "You're not going to like what I've gotta say, but you know me. I've done my research, I've checked everything out. I have the proof right here," I say, waving the same file I just showed Hadley. "What I'm about to tell you is the truth, and I need you to not lose your shit over it."

"Jesus, man." Hawk chuckles nervously, confusion apparent across his face. "Just spit it out already."

Fuck. Here we go.

"Hadley's your sister."

He looks at me for a moment before he bursts out laughing.

"Fuck, man. You totally had me! That's hilarious." He continues to laugh, shaking his head as he grabs his controller from the table and relaxes back onto the sofa again, getting back to his game.

He's still laughing when I drop the file of lab reports on the sofa beside him. "I'm being serious," I state, gesturing to the file when he glances my way.

He casts his eyes down to the brown envelope before flicking them back up to look at me, his brows pulled together in confusion as he takes in the tight press of my lips and critical look in my eye.

His game forgotten, he slowly sets down the controller, picking up the file and rifling through the pages.

"What the fuck is this?" he finally asks in disbelief, his words an echo of Hadley's as he continues to scan his eyes over the pages.

He's not really asking me, so I don't answer, waiting patiently for him to take in what I've just said, what's written in black and white on the pages in front of him.

"I don't understand," he finally murmurs, glancing up at me. "You tested our DNA? Why the fuck would you do that?"

I try again to explain to him what I tried to explain to Hadley, but it's difficult to find the words. It was a gut feeling, a hunch as much as anything else. Simply saying that they have the same unique shade of stormy blue-gray eyes and fiery tempers isn't enough justification.

It was every time one of the guys laughed off how similar they were. It was in the small mannerisms they share, the green skittles. It was the way her jaw clenches and her nostrils flare when she's pissed off, the slight tilt of her head when she's concentrating, how she absently plays with the hem of her skirt or a pen or the corner of a page when she's distracted. All things Hawk does, too. All things no one who doesn't know Hawk as well as I do, or pay as much attention to Hadley as I do, would ever piece together.

I'd sound insane if I said all that, or like a creepy fucking stalker.

"There must be a mistake," he insists after another long moment of him trying to internally process the news. "There's just no way this is true. For starters, I'd fucking know if I had a sister. My parents would have said something, or there would be some sort of proof somewhere, a photo or something at our house. Even if she was my sister, how the fuck did she end up in foster care?"

All excellent questions that I've been trying to figure out the last few days too.

"I dunno, man," I admit. "I don't have the answer to that. I just know the tests don't lie."

"Well, I don't fucking believe them," he snaps out, his anger finally making an appearance, like I knew it would. "They've made a mistake. There's an error."

"By five different labs?" I reason.

"I don't fucking know," he yells, jumping to his feet, his hand gripping the pages tightly, crumpling them. "But there is no fucking way this is true!"

He paces furiously back and forth across the apartment, grumbling to himself as he tries to come up with an alternative to what is right in front of him. Knowing there's no point in arguing with him when he's like this, I get comfortable in my chair, watching him as he wears a hole in the hardwood, stomping the length of the open space and back, his thoughts running a mile a minute.

I don't know how long we stay like that for, but eventually, the front door opens and Cam and Mason walk in. They stop just inside the door, immediately catching on to Hawk's angry state.

"What the hell's going on here?" Cam asks, eyeing Hawk warily as he moves over to claim the spot on the sofa Hawk vacated.

Mason doesn't move from the doorway, his eyes following Hawk as he continues his pacing, ignoring their arrival.

"Hadley and Hawk are related," I say, not beating around the bush.

Cam's head snaps toward me, his mouth dropping open. "They're what?" He gapes. "Like distant relatives? Second cousins twice removed or some shit like that, that doesn't even count?"

"More like siblings," I clarify.

Even Mason's eyebrows raise at that piece of information. "Wow," he exclaims.

Cam, clearly incapable of forming words, continues to gawk at me.

"What? When? How?" he finally splutters.

"In the same way as any other siblings," I retort sarcastically. "If no one's had the birds and the bees talk with you yet, I'm sure as fuck not explaining it."

He scowls at me, not impressed with my scathing tone. "Don't be such a dick. You know what I mean."

Mason, finally ungluing his feet from the floor, pulls his eyes away from a still pacing Hawk, coming to join me and Cam.

"How did we not know Hawk had a sister?"

I shake my head, not having an answer for him.

"Hawk, man, stop whatever the fuck you're doing. We need to sort this shit out," he barks. His words must get through to Hawk in some way as he stops pacing, spinning to glare at all of us.

"Sort what out?" he demands, storming over. "There's nothing to sort out. So what if she's my sister or whatever? That doesn't mean anything. No one even has to fucking know. We can just tear this shit up," he rants, waving the pages in the air, "and pretend none of this ever happened."

“Dude, what the fuck? You can’t do that!” Cam snaps, reaching out to tear the pages from his grasp, glancing quickly at them before handing them to Mason.

“Why the fuck not? Clearly my parents have decided she doesn’t exist. Why can’t I?”

“Because you’re not them,” I snap at him, unable to believe he’s even thinking of burying this shit. “You may be acting like an ass right now, but you’re not the same dicks your parents are.”

Hawk grinds his teeth, glaring at each of us, but he doesn’t argue the issue any further, knowing damn well we’re right.

“You haven’t told her, have you?” he demands, his pissed off expression drilling into me.

Cringing, I respond, “Yeah, actually. I have.”

“She knows?” Cam exclaims before Hawk can tear me a new one. “Not that I care,” he tacks on, mumbling under his breath.

Sharing a look with Mason, I roll my eyes at him. Between him and Hawk, I’m not sure who’s being the greater asshole right now. Cam needs to get the fuck over his hurt pride and see the bigger picture.

“She must be a mess right now,” Mason says softly, his forehead furrowed in concern. Huh, the fact his thoughts immediately went to Hadley is proof enough. I knew he was interested in her by the way he watches her, but he seems to actually care about her. How did that happen? When did it happen?

I mean, I get it. There’s something about her that draws you in, that makes you want to give a damn about her, even when alarm bells are going off in your head. Walking out of her room and leaving her there after I just dropped that life-altering bomb on her was so much harder than I thought it would be. Even now, my thoughts continually stray back to her, wondering what she's doing, how she's coping with it. Is she on a rampage like Hawk is? Unable to sit still, stomping around her room? Or has she withdrawn into herself, blocking out everything around her while she tries to process what all of this means?

"You told her?" Hawk barks, reminding me I have my own Davenport problem to deal with. He grinds his teeth as he glares at me, his hands repeatedly clenching into tight fists, like he's imagining ripping my head off right now. "Why the fuck would you do something stupid like that?!"

"She had a right to know," I respond calmly. "Just the same as you do."

"I'm supposed to be your best friend," he shouts. "You should have told me first. I should have been the one to decide if she should know or not."

"And that's exactly why I didn't tell you first," I snap, getting pissed off. "Because for some stupid reason, you're on a mission to destroy her, and it's blinding you. You can't fucking see that this affects her just as much, if not more so, than it affects you."

Hawk doesn't say anything, but I'm pretty sure he's picturing his hands wrapped around my throat. I'm not stupid enough to think his silence means I've gotten through to him or that he agrees with me. He's just so fucking furious right now he can't even talk.

Sighing, Mason interjects before tensions can escalate any further, "Regardless of whether or not she knows, this raises a lot of questions. Questions we need answers to."

"Yeah," Cam agrees, nodding his head in agreement. "Like, why the fuck your parents never told you about her."

"Or how she ended up in foster care," Mason adds.

"Do you think she knew?" Cam questions. "Is that why she had the notebook?"

All three of them turn to look at me. "No way," I insist, giving a vigorous shake of my head. "She didn't have a clue. She threw the same hissy fit you're having right now," I wave my hand toward Hawk who still looks like an angry bear with his arms crossed over his broad chest as he stands, towering over the rest of us.

Glowering, Hawk finally unclenches his jaw enough to suggest, "She could have been lying to you. Look how she manipulated Cam all year; she's clearly gotten inside your head, too."

My fingernails dig into my palm, my fists clenched tight as I try to reign in my anger. "She wasn't," I spit through gritted teeth, scowling at him before turning my frustration on Cam. "And I don't believe everything between you and her was a lie, either. Do you not see the way she looks at you? The two of you need to talk and sort out your shit. You can't keep going around blaming her for everything. I know there are a lot of unanswered questions," I say, holding my hands up to get him to keep quiet, "I know she hurt your pride, but man, you've gotta get over it."

He doesn't say anything, pressing his lips together, not pleased with the reality check I just hit him with.

"How the fuck are we supposed to get answers to any of these questions?" Hawk challenges. "Hadley's a closed fucking book, and it's not like I can just say to my parents 'hey, remember that other kid you had that you never told me about and apparently forgot ever existed? Well, she's enrolled at Pac now and knows all about the rich family that abandoned her.'"

"Well, you probably shouldn't say it quite like that," Mason retorts unhelpfully, making me scowl at him.

"You shouldn't say anything to them at all," I snap.

Hawk's eyebrows rise in surprise at my words.

"Your parents clearly kept it a secret for a reason," I explain. "Just do some snooping while you're home over Christmas break. We need more information before we confront them, or before anyone else finds out about this."

Before he can argue with me any further, a sharp knock on the door draws all of our attention, and I get up to go shoo away whatever idiot thought it was okay to just turn up at our apartment unannounced.

Hadley

Chapter 28

I pace back and forth for god knows how long before giving up and storming out the door. West can't seriously drop that bomb and just expect me to sit here and stew in it.

I have a family. A fucking family.

Except that family is Hawk.

I'm really not sure how I feel about that.

Why couldn't I have had a nice little cookie-cutter family with a white picket fence and a dog?

Oh yeah, because this is me we're talking about, and even when I get something I never thought I would have, life still has to go and fucking shit all over it.

I climb the steps to the fourth floor of the boys' dormitories, pulling open the stairwell door and stepping into a small hall. Unlike the other floors, there's no hallway with numerous doors along it. Instead there's just the one door right in front of me.

Pursing my lips, I bang my fist against the door and wait impatiently for someone to open it.

West doesn't seem surprised to see me, but he sure as hell doesn't look pleased about it as I stomp past him into their dorm, finding the other three assholes spread out around the open living space. They all look my way, but I can't tear my gaze away from Hawk, as I run my eyes over his face, trying to see whatever West saw. I'm not surprised when all I see is the arrogant dickwad I've seen every day since the first day of school. Sure, his eyes are maybe similar to mine, and his nose is straight like mine, but that's it.

His eyes narrow as he turns to face me, Cam jumping to his feet beside him, as the two of them stride toward me. Mason, at a slower pace, stands up, but he stays back by the couches, assessing the situation from a distance. "What are you doing here?" Hawk demands.

"I'm guessing West told you the good news, *brother.*" His icy glare promises all sorts of heinous acts as he practically snarls at me, but I shrug away his shitty attitude. West said we had similar tempers? There's no way I'm as infuriating as this asswipe.

"He shouldn't have fucking told you," Hawk growls, briefly flicking his glower from me to West.

"Are you for fucking real?" I snap, directing his ire back his way. "Of course he should have fucking told me. You think I wanted this to be my fucking reality? Wanted *you* to be my brother? I'd take pretty much anyone else."

"Please," he snorts. "You just landed yourself the answer to all your fucking problems."

When I simply look at him like he's got three heads, not understanding what he's going on about, he continues on, "That's assuming you didn't already know about any of this." Hawk's penetrating gaze stays firmly pinpointed on me, scrutinizing my every move. "Is that what that whole notebook was about? You were learning everything you could about us before coming clean about who you really were?"

"What?" I gape in shock; but of course, that's what he assumes the stupid fucking notebook is about. "No."

"She's telling the truth, man," West insists. "I saw the look on her face. She was as shocked as you."

"So you claim, but like I said, she's a good liar."

I glance at Cam, taking in his thinned lips and the distrustful look in his eyes, trying to forget the uncharacteristic softness I saw in them after our rendezvous in the locker room.

I'm looking right at him when I speak the god's honest truth. There is a lot they don't know about me—not that they've earned the fucking right to know any of it—but there is one thing I am certain of. "The feelings I had for you were real. The…time we spent together? All of it meant something to me."

I swear his eyes soften, just a little. But it's highly possible I'm only seeing what I want to see, because the rest of his face is still shut down, pinched tight in anger.

Mason coughs uncomfortably, drawing my attention his way as he rubs the back of his neck in awkward embarrassment. Noticing my attention on him, his gaze latches onto mine, a private moment passing between the two of us. I have no idea what it means, though. I don't know what that kiss meant in the clearing, or what any of this means, really. I'm beyond confused at this point. None of this is what I expected to find at Pac.

"I don't give a shit who you are, or what you are to me," Hawk snarls, his nose wrinkling in disgust as his gaze drops to take me in, no part of me meeting his standard. The sheer hatred in his eyes stalls the breath in my throat as I stand frozen, gaping at him. "As far as I'm concerned, you're unwanted trash. I don't care if we are related, I don't want anything to do with you. These idiots are letting their dicks make all the decisions for them right now, but pretty soon they'll see you for you who really are—a pathetic nobody, trying to fuck her way to a pampered future as some old guy's mistress."

Despite how fucking infuriating he is, his words cut deep. He might not be what I want in a family, but he *is* my family. Something I've wished for and dreamed about my entire life; and he's just shit all over it with his nasty, untrue words and disgusted look. I'm not sure what I expected when I came up here. I knew it wouldn't be all hugs and celebrations. It's Hawk, of course he's going to fight it tooth and nail, but the unrelenting hostility in his voice is painful to hear. I can feel my chest cracking open with every foul word he spits my way.

I try so goddamn fucking hard to hold it all together, but I feel it when the mask slips. It's only for a second, but it's enough. It's more vulnerability than I've shown anyone, ever. Before I can do something completely embarrassing, like cry, I duck my head, spinning on my heel and nearly running over West in my hurry to get out of there and away from Hawk's toxic malice.

Fleeing from their apartment, I don't stop until I'm slamming through the doors of the gym. I'm not really sure why I came here, of all places. I'm not dressed for the gym and I don't have my gear with me. I guess I knew it would be empty so late at night.

Skirting my way around the darkened room, I wander through into the swimming pool. Other than when I came to watch Cam's swim meets, I've never set foot in here. Since I'm a shitty swimmer, it seems like a smart choice to avoid coming anywhere near a deep body of water, especially with all the enemies surrounding me these days. All it would take is one little push. I can guarantee you none of those bitches would dive in to rescue me, and Hawk would happily stand idly by and watch me drown.

There's something oddly peaceful about this place, though. The gentle lap of water, the way the lights shine from the bottom of the pool. Even the stench of chlorine is strangely comforting.

Keeping a safe distance from the edge, I carefully walk around until I'm at the shallow end of the pool, on the far side of the room. Before I can think better of it, I strip out of my jeans and top, taking off my bra and panties too, setting them on a bench before dipping into the warm water. I'm probably insane for doing this, but the water calls to me. I can feel the tension draining from my body as it laps against me, soaking my skin. With my feet firmly planted on the bottom of the pool, I bend my knees, slowly lowering myself until the water hits my shoulders.

Spreading my arms out, I trail my fingers through the surface of the water, watching the ripple effects of my movements. Life's a lot like that, someone does or says something that causes a chain reaction. Their behavior influences everyone else around them, for better or worse. Most of the time, we don't even think about how our actions might affect those around us. Or people like Hawk just don't give a shit. But it's folks like me that have to live with the consequences of others' crappy choices.

A sudden noise from the gym next door has me snapping my head up. I quickly duck to the corner of the pool, hoping in the dim lighting I won't be noticed. I barely breathe as I listen for any signs of someone coming this way.

The door to the pool bangs open and Beck storms into the room, looking just as pissed off with the world as I imagine I did when I first arrived.

Reaching behind his back, his large bicep flexes as he grabs his shirt, pulling it over his head in a sexy-as-fuck move that has me drooling. My mouth is suddenly parched as his sculpted torso is revealed to me. I've spent weeks wondering what he's hiding underneath his fancy waistcoats. I thought he looked pretty damn fine earlier in his t-shirt, but, *hot damn*. Naked, he's a mouth-watering masterpiece of perfection. He's got a panty-melting swimmer's body—all lean with sharp edges. A firm chest, with a sprinkling of dark-colored chest hair, gives way to a prominent six pack just begging for a girl to run her tongue over. My eyes follow the faint outline of a treasure trail down to the lining of his swimming trunks, which sit snugly on narrow hips and wrap around his muscular thighs.

Throwing his shirt carelessly behind him, he plunges into the water in what I imagine is a perfect dive. There's barely a splash as his body is submerged, gliding smoothly through the water.

He doesn't come up for air until he's halfway across the Olympic-sized swimming pool, his arms moving in synchrony, rising out of the water, one at a time in a perfect arch, propelling him forward.

I watch in awe as he reaches the shallow end of the pool, doing some fancy flip under the water before kicking off the side with his feet and gliding effortlessly back to where he started. Back and forth he goes, never faltering or slowing as he swims from one end to the other. I can't do anything but hide there and gawk at him, mesmerized as he moves like an unstoppable machine through the water.

After several lengths, he must feel my gaze on him, as he stops mid-stride, his gaze jumping about the room until he finds me lurking in the corner of the pool like a common stalker.

"What the—" he breathes, squinting to see who would be creeping about in the pool this late at night.

Taking a small step forward so I'm not hidden in the shadows, I try to swallow around my suddenly dry throat.

"Hadley?"

"Sorry," I begin, "I, uh, needed to clear my head. I didn't think anyone would be here."

He doesn't say anything as he swims toward me, stopping when we're a few feet apart.

"Is everything okay?"

"Yeah," I breathe out, my automatic response to fob him off coming out before I've even thought about the question. "No...I don't know." I give a small chuckle. "It's been a crappy day. I..." I trail off, the words getting stuck at the back of my throat. I want to tell him about today, about Hawk, but I'm fucking shit at telling anybody anything. It doesn't come naturally to me, and apparently, it's harder than I thought to just blurt out stuff about yourself.

"I'm a mess," I eventually admit. Not what I want to say, but fuck if it's not the truth.

His eyes roam over my face, taking me in, likely seeing for himself how true those words are. My eyes still feel puffy from earlier, and despite trying to fix my mask back in place after running away from Hawk, it no longer fits quite right.

"You are far from a mess." His words take me by surprise. He listens to the whining, superficial problems of teenagers all day. I'm pretty sure I'm the most complex case he has. "You're the embodiment of strength...I don't know what you've been through," he murmurs, trailing a finger along an old scar on my collarbone, making me aware of how close we've drifted as he towers over me in the water. "But I can tell you're a survivor. Your scars? Your pain? They only make you more beautiful."

I swallow around the lump in my throat, my heaving chest only inches from his, my stomach a riot of butterflies as I watch rivulets of water trail over his pecs and down his abs. I've thought about this moment for months now, wondered what would happen if we were alone like this.

"I've wanted you from the moment you stepped into my office," he murmurs. His voice barely more than a whisper, the gravel tone scraping under my skin, igniting my nerves.

Tilting my head back, I look up into his eyes, seeing his usual bright moss green irises darkened with lust. "I don't do this. I don't seduce students, but I just can't seem to stop myself with you."

"So, don't," I whisper the words so quietly I'm not sure he even hears me. He gazes into my eyes for a moment longer before his hands slide around my neck, his fingers tangling in my hair as he angles me just perfectly. His lips hover over mine, both of us savoring this moment before everything changes.

Unable to hold back any longer, his lips descend; moving slowly, teasingly, against my own. My eyes drift shut as my body lights up, his kiss like a thousand volts of electricity, making me feel alive.

I open beneath him, moaning as he sweeps his tongue into my mouth, our tongues sliding over one another in the most delicious kiss. He unhurriedly explores my mouth, driving me wild as he takes his time getting to know every part of me, memorizing my reactions to his every touch.

We drift closer until our chests are pressed up against each other, my arms winding around his shoulders, my fingers running through the small hairs at the back of his neck.

Using the buoyancy of the water, I wrap my legs around his hips, seating myself in his lap, relishing the feel of his hard length pressing against my core.

His hands stroke their way down my body, roaming over my back and sides until he grabs a handful of my ass cheeks in each palm, groaning as he realizes I'm completely naked. Tugging me in closer to him, he grinds against me.

"Beck," I murmur, tearing my lips from his as my head falls back, granting him access to my neck. His lips feather across my skin as he licks and nibbles his way down my throat and across my collarbone. Every light touch has me panting harder, grinding against him, needy for more.

I want nothing more than to pull down his trunks, wrap my fingers around his cock and slide myself down his length, but he needs to be the one to take control here. He has to make that move. After all, he's the one risking everything right now.

His hand slips down between our bodies, his fingers deftly sweeping over my clit before sinking inside of me. I'm so wet, he meets no resistance. I don't need any working up at all—more than fucking ready for him.

"Fuck," he groans. "You feel so good. You taste so sweet. I need to be inside you." He hesitates before sheepishly adding, "I don't have, uh, a condom."

"I'm covered."

I've barely gotten the words out before he's pulling down his trunks, his pink, veiny, erect dick springing free. I reach down between us, wrap my hand around him, angling him at my entrance as I sink down on top of him, and gasp while I adjust to him. He's got a slight bend that rubs perfectly against my G-spot, eliciting a dirty moan from the back of my throat as he seats himself deep within me.

"Fuck," he hisses between gritted teeth, his hands tightening around my hips, leaving half-moon fingernail marks in my skin.

I can't do anything but wrap myself around him tighter as he begins to move. With every thrust, he hits that perfect spot, and I cry out, quickly rushing toward oblivion as I meet him move for move.

My fingernails dig into his back, leaving scratch marks as I lose myself in the feel of him pounding into me.

"Beck," I cry out, feeling that familiar, intense uncoiling in my lower abdomen. I can feel him swelling within me, close to coming himself as his thrusts turn erratic.

I fall over the edge as his cum hits my inner walls, both of us collapsing into one another, our chests rising in symphony together. He loosens his grip on my hip, wrapping his arms around me as he lazily kisses me, his tongue tangling with mine in slow, lavish strokes, both of us catching our breaths and coming back to reality, but still refusing to leave this little perfect bubble we've created for ourselves.

"You're incredible," he murmurs between kisses. "I want to see you again. I want to get to know you, to spend time with you."

"You mean an hour a week isn't enough?" I joke.

His voice is serious when he responds, "Not even close."

Eventually we pull ourselves apart, climbing out of the pool and re-dressing. He even gives me his towel to dry off with so I don't have to attempt to pull my jeans on over wet skin. With one final passionate kiss, he watches as I take off back toward the girls' dorms, replaying over in my mind the unexpected end to this bizarre day.

Hadley

Chapter 29

The next day, excitement is in the air as parents and drivers arrive and everyone gets ready to leave for two weeks. Everyone except me, apparently.

I thought even some of the scholarship students would stay behind—not that any of them talk to me—but nope. It's just going to be me and an empty campus. *That's not creepy at all.*

On the plus side, with no one around, I should have plenty of opportunity to sneak out to see Beck. My cheeks turn red just thinking about him and what we did in the pool last night. I swear, I'm not going to be able to keep a straight face at Cam's next swim meet.

The thought of him swimming through our juices, nearly has me bursting out in laughter. I hope he accidentally swallows some pool water. It would be exactly what he deserves.

Most of the students seem to be gone, the halls eerily quiet as I make my way through the school. Rounding a corner, I come to an abrupt halt when I find Beck and West at the far end of the corridor. That in itself isn't necessarily strange, but the dark scowl on West's face is surprising. He only ever looks like that when he's with the other Pricks, and they're making a stand in front of the entire school. Even then, I've never seen him look at anyone the way he's looking at Beck. It's similar to the way Hawk looked at me yesterday, disgust and vehement hate written all over his face. What issue could he possibly have with Beck to instill such violent emotions?

"Don't fucking bother. I don't want anything to do with you," West snarls before storming off. Beck watches him leave, running a hand through his usually perfectly in place hair. Sighing heavily, he shakes his head before following West, the two of them disappearing out of sight.

What the hell was that all about?

For the next three days, I focus on completing the mountain of homework they gave us to do over the break. It's strangely peaceful having the whole place to myself, eating alone in the dining hall, being the only one in the library; however, after several days of solitude, I'm officially bored. I tell myself the desire to talk to another human being is the reason I'm standing outside his door, but if I'm being honest with myself, I just want to see him again.

Despite how opposed I was to this whole counseling thing—and still am—I've found solitude in this room over the last few weeks, found comfort and safety in Beck's presence. Growing up always on alert, never knowing where the next danger will come from or when the next hit will strike, that's saying something.

Unsure if he will even be here—it is Christmas break after all, I'm sure he has better things to do—I rap my knuckles on the door, turning the handle, and actually surprised to find the door opens when I push on it.

"Hadley," Beck says with pleasant surprise, an easy smile on his face as his eyes drink me in. I'm wearing jeans and a tank top, but he obviously didn't get the memo that no one else is here, as he's dressed in his usual attire of preppy waistcoat and chinos—not that it matters. He clearly looks hot in anything.

"Hey." My reply is much more awkward and uncertain as I step into the room, closing the door quietly behind me. "I, uh, wasn't sure how to get in touch with you, so I figured I'd see if you were here."

"You hunted me down?" There are laugh lines around his eyes as his smile stretches wider.

Rolling my eyes, I retort, "I was bored," as I move to sit in the chair in front of his desk, bringing my knees up in front of me.

"Well, we can't have that now." He leans forward in his seat, his arms resting on the desk as he continues to watch me. "I'll give you my number, you can text or call me anytime."

Biting my lip, I nod my head. My heart is racing, smashing against my chest, and my palms are sweaty. I don't even understand why I'm so nervous. I've never been like this around him before.

"I can see your thoughts running a mile a minute. What are you thinking about?"

"I...What are we doing?"

His lazy smile is back as he gets up and circles around the table, coming to stand in front of me, perching on the edge of the desk.

"I believe they call it dating." He still looks like he's enjoying himself way too much at my expense, as I shake my head.

"I don't know how to do that. I've never..." I trail off, my unsaid words hanging between us. How pathetic is it that I've never gone out with anyone before, never been on a date with a guy?

"Hey," he soothes, crouching down in front of me. "We don't need to put a label on it. We'll just do us—go at whatever speed you want, do whatever you're comfortable with."

I stare into his deep green eyes that easily ensnare me, holding me captive, giving him the opportunity to really *see* me; see all the insecure, fucked-up parts of me I keep carefully locked away.

"What if I'm bad at it?" The words are barely more than a whisper and I don't think I've ever felt so exposed, so vulnerable, not even when that stupid video was going around.

He reaches out, tucking a stray bit of hair behind my ear, running his fingers through the messy strands.

"I don't, for one second, believe you will be. I was captivated from the minute you stormed in here, full of fire and quick wit. It had nothing to do with what you've been through. It was just *you*, your inner strength, your tenacious ability to thrive when anyone else would crumble. The hour I spend with you is the highlight of my week."

"You must have a very boring life, if that's the case," I grumble, deflecting him away from the heat in my cheeks and the fluttering feeling in my chest that I can't place.

A slow smile makes its way across his face. "I'm pretty sure I could spend my free time skydiving and base jumping, and I'd still say you were the best part of my week."

Fucking hell, he's trying to kill me with sweet sentiments.

Leaning forward, I lower my legs, planting my feet on either side of him as I bend down and kiss him. Not wasting a second, his hand slides around to the back of my head, holding me to him as our tongues dance together, affirming every sweet word he just said to me.

He untangles his hand from my hair, slipping his hands beneath my thighs and lifting me up, making me wrap my legs around his waist. I feel him growing hard as I am pressed against him, neither one of us breaking the kiss as he carries me over to the sofa, dropping down onto it so I'm straddling him.

Before we can get too carried away, he pulls back. "We've gone about this all backward," he breathes. "I want us to do it right."

"Are you saying no to sex?" I tease, nipping on his earlobe before kissing down his neck, loving the feel of his fingers digging into the flesh on my hips.

"I'm definitely not saying that," he growls. "God, all the dirty things I want to do to you right now." I can hear the strain in his voice as he holds himself back, and, as much as I want him to do exactly that, I want him to be comfortable in this thing between us, too. He's already assured me we can go at my pace, but I want him to enjoy this, and if he wants to do it 'the right way', then who am I to stop him?

Pulling back, creating a bit of distance between us so I can actually work through my hormone-addled thoughts, I look him in the eye. "How do we go about doing that?"

"We start by getting to know each other." He must feel me tense in his lap because his hands start rubbing soothing circles up and down my back. "Nothing big, nothing you don't want to share. We'll start with the small, simple stuff." He's got no idea that nothing about me is simple, and what he's asking is much harder than he thinks it is. Yet, I find myself giving him a hesitant nod.

The pride in his eyes at that one small concession almost makes it worthwhile, but it doesn't calm the thudding in my chest or the nervous flutter in my stomach.

Pulling me in closer, he lies back on the sofa, taking me with him so I'm lying on top of him, my head resting on his chest. When he doesn't immediately start firing off questions, I slowly relax, kicking off my boots and entangling my legs with his as I get comfy. His fingers dip beneath my top, drawing lazy circles on my hip, while his other arm is bent at the elbow, with his hand resting underneath his head.

Holy hell, why have I never done this before? There's something to be said for just lying with a guy, feeling the steady thrumming of his heart beneath your palm, feeling his body pressed up against yours. It's calming, stabilizing, reassuring. I never knew I could feel this way with another person. Any time I tried to picture doing crap like this with a guy, it always looked awkward and uncomfortable. I could easily fall asleep on him, and I'm pretty sure it would be the best damn nap I've ever had.

I'm lying half-asleep on top of him, when I feel him move, his lips kissing the top of my head in a strangely sweet gesture that has every girly part of me squealing in delight. I have to bury my head in his shirt to hide the stupid grin on my face.

"What's your favorite color?" he murmurs, the question taking me by surprise. *Okay, that I can easily answer.*

"Umm, blue, I guess, but like a deep, rich blue-green color, like teal."

I can feel the rumble in his chest as he chuckles. "I should have known you wouldn't just come out with a standard, generic color. That you'd actually have given it some thought…I like that."

I glance up at him through my eyelashes. His eyes are closed, and he's got a small, peaceful smile on his face.

"What about you?"

"I've always been a fan of bluish gray shades, kind of like the color of your eyes." I lift my head to catch him already watching me, enraptured, as I look down at him. "There's something so…energetic but calming about it. The outward appearance of composure and determination, yet you get the impression there's so much more going on beneath the surface."

I simply gape at him, unsure of how to respond. Probably sensing my internal panic, he leans up, giving me a quick, reassuring kiss.

"What about your favorite ice cream?" he asks, moving the conversation along.

With a grin, I settle back into my position on his chest. "Well, I'm slowly making my way through every flavor in the dining hall, but so far, my favorite is lemon and lime."

"What?!" he gasps. "Tell me it isn't so! Lemon and lime? That has got to be one of the worst flavors. You could only top that by saying vanilla."

I chuckle at his dramatics, enjoying the easy banter.

"Alright, Oh Wise Knower of Ice cream Flavors. What is your favorite?"

"Chocolate fudge brownie, obviously," he states, like there could be no other option.

"I haven't tried that one yet."

"You haven't—?!" he sputters, shaking his head. "Well, we'll have to rectify that as soon as possible."

The fact he doesn't ask me why I'm working my way through the flavors in the dining hall, or how I've never had such a common flavor as chocolate fudge brownie, means more to me than he can ever realize. We spend the rest of the day just lying there, talking. There's no awkwardness like I thought there would be, and any time he hits a sore spot, he quickly waves away the question and asks something different, never prying or asking for more than I'm willing to give.

I've never felt so at ease around another person, so accepting of sharing a part of myself with them—even if what I'm sharing is light and superficial. It's still more than I've shared with any one person before.

Before I leave, we swap numbers and he pulls me into him, planting a heated, passionate kiss on my lips.

"Just because I didn't fuck you, doesn't mean I didn't spend all day thinking about bending you over that desk," he murmurs against my lips, the deep gravel in his voice only making me wish he'd done exactly that.

"Next time," I whisper, sealing the promise with a kiss.

I can't fight the smile from my lips as I make my way back to my room. Maybe being the only ones left on campus isn't so bad after all.

The rest of Christmas break goes by uneventfully. Beck and I text back and forth, and I even get a few messages from Mason and West. I don't hear anything from Cam or Hawk, not that I'm surprised. Anything Hawk would have to say to me would only be more hateful words I don't need right now; but it bothers me more than I'd like, not to hear anything from Cam. I even went so far as to pull up his details on the tablet and stare at the screen, re-reading the last few messages we sent to each other, not knowing what to say and eventually closing out of the app altogether. We've done too much damage to one another. We've both destroyed any trust there could have been between us—me with my deceit and him with his betrayal, assuming he was the one that told Hawk about my scars. If he didn't, well, I guess it's all my fault. I broke us. But how was I to know he would come to mean something more to me? That I'd actually give a damn about him. Hell, I came here to kill him, not develop a fucking crush on him. But standing over him that night, I couldn't fucking do it. He might have been nothing more than a flirtatious idiot back then, but he wasn't at all what I expected. He didn't deserve what I had planned for him, so I came up with an alternative plan to exact my revenge. Of course, that kind of blew up in my face, too. God, I was never this sloppy or off my game before I got here. All these guys are messing with my head, preventing me from thinking straight and distracting me from my goals.

On Christmas day, the kitchen staff put out a feast, even though it's just me here, and I spend most of the day going back and forth, sampling a bit of everything. It's all delicious, and I'm annoyed every time my stomach threatens to blow the button on my jeans, and I have to begrudgingly stop eating.

All too quickly, the end of the holidays approaches and the day before classes commence again, with students starting to return to campus.

A sharp rap on my door pulls me out of the book I was reading, and I swear I'm going to fucking murder whoever is disturbing me. Not only was I at a particularly juicy scene, but the book was doing wonders at making me forget about tomorrow.

Unfolding myself from the bed, I don't even care that I look like a hot mess in a baggy t-shirt and tight boxing shorts, with my hair scraped back in a messy bun, as I answer the door. I've barely gotten it open when someone shoves their way through it, storming past me.

"What the hell?" I shriek, spinning around to glare at my intruder.

Hawk.

Of course, it's fucking Hawk.

My fucking brother, a fact I still can't wrap my head around. I've gone back and forth all break, between fixating on the matter, and pretending West never stormed in here and turned my world upside-down.

I wasn't sure if he would be hell-bent on making my life even more miserable now that he knew exactly who I was, or if he was intent on forgetting the whole thing ever happened. I guess he's decided he's still pissed, based on the sneer he's sporting and the still burning pits of hatred in his eyes. Clearly, two weeks wasn't enough time for him to simmer down.

Glaring back at him, he's impossible to ignore in the confines of my room. He's got such a demanding presence, his larger frame seemingly taking up all the space in my small room.

"I don't see it." His head is tilted to one side as he scrutinizes me in much the same way I imagine I'm looking at him.

"Yeah, well, neither do I," I agree, standing taller and snapping my head up to glare at him.

He continues to trail his eyes over me, taking his sweet fucking time, while I stand there awkwardly. Curiosity swirls with the ever-present hatred in his eyes, his brows drawn together in confusion.

"What do you want?" I snap out when I can't stand his eyes on me anymore.

He holds out a shoebox-sized box he was holding, not bothering to answer my question with actual words.

"What is that?" I ask hesitantly, once again sensing I don't want to know what's in that box. While it might give me answers, I get the impression it's only going to further solidify this whole 'brother' thing. I've been living quite a nice life of denial the last two weeks, and I'm not sure I'm ready to burst that bubble just yet.

"Stuff I found at the house," he grunts out, stretching his arm out further in another bid to get me to take the box. I still don't move though, frozen in place as I stare at the unassuming item. How can something so small and innocent looking hold all the answers to the questions I'd given up on asking?

When it becomes clear I'm not going to take it, he closes the space between us, shoving the box against my chest until I have no other choice but to grasp it or risk the contents spilling out all over the floor.

Once it's in my hands, I can't resist the curiosity brimming within me. Moving over to set the box on the desk, I hesitantly reach out, lifting off the lid and absently setting it on the table as my eyes settle on the first thing I see. A picture of a girl, a toddler. She's got white blonde hair and chubby cheeks, a mischievous grin on her face. Her clothes are covered in dirt, soil smudged on her face. Standing beside her, clean as a whistle, is another white-haired toddler. This one's a boy. His eyes are narrowed as he scowls at her, but there's a slight curl at the corner of his lip, like he's trying hard not to laugh.

"This is...us?" I whisper, the words barely audible. It's a redundant question though, of course that's us. I'd recognize Hawk's glower anywhere. I can't tear my eyes away from the photo. We're so young. I look so happy. *I don't ever remember being that happy before.*

Despite not needing to, he answers me anyway, "Yeah." The word is barely a grunt, but the closeness of his voice catches me off guard, and I pull my gaze from the picture, looking up to find him standing right behind me, staring into the box. *When did he move so close?*

Pulling out the photo, I carefully place it to one side. There are a couple of other photos of a baby that I'm guessing are of me as well. Not lingering on them, I move on to the page underneath them. Tugging it out, I'm still processing what I'm looking at, when Hawk states the obvious, "That's your birth certificate. It's got your real name on it, and the day you were born."

My eyes hover over the name on the page, the words feeling both foreign and familiar at the same time.

Elizabeth Jane Davenport.

Elizabeth? I don't feel like an Elizabeth. Hadley is a much more suitable name for me. Elizabeth sounds like it belongs to a pampered princess, someone who's lived a life of luxury, who's never had to fight every day of her life, who hasn't had to endure the pain and torture I've had to live through.

Maybe I was an Elizabeth once, but I'm not that girl anymore.

Not feeling comfortable with this new identity I'm trying to reconcile myself with, I swiftly move on, glancing further down the page until I find a date of birth.

"I was born on January eighth?"

"*We* were," Hawk says over my shoulder.

We? We're twins? I guess that makes sense. I probably should have thought of that before.

"That's only a few days away," I murmur absently, staring obliviously at the birth certificate until Hawk pulls out a brown envelope from his pocket, setting it down in front of me.

"What is this?" I ask, wariness creeping through me.

"Why don't you open it and see." His haughty tone immediately has my back straightening, and it's with shaky hands that I reach out and break the seal, lifting out the folded pages inside.

The first page is a photocopy of yet another birth certificate, however the name and date of birth are different.

"I don't..." My words trail off as I move on to the next page. This one is a photocopy of a passport, with the same name and date of birth as the certificate.

Hadley Parker. Born August twenty-third.

Except, the image on the passport isn't of me. It's a girl with long dark hair. She's got a wide smile on her face which shows braces on her teeth. This Hadley looks nothing like me. She's carefree and full of life.

Looking at the next page, my heart thumps rapidly in my chest as I scan my eyes over the photocopy of a newspaper article.

'Teenage girl dies in a tragic car accident'.

Quickly skipping over the article to the next page, I can taste bile at the back of my throat as I once again see my name on another page. This one is a death certificate.

Apparently, I died three years ago last month.

"What is this?" I choke out. But it's a futile question. I *know* what this is. I didn't know this girl, I've never seen her picture. I didn't know how she died, but I knew she was dead.

"This was the *real* Hadley Parker," Hawk growls from behind me, his voice regaining its harsh quality that he seems to reserve only for me.

He reaches up, spinning me around and grabbing on tightly to my shoulders, his fingers digging painfully into the bones. He towers over me, standing so close there's nowhere else for me to look, but into his menacing eyes that are overflowing with distrust and malice.

"So the question is," he sneers, "who the fuck are you?"

Epilogue

"I found her."

I finally fucking found her.

"What do you want to do?"

"I want her back," I snarl down the phone. "She's mine."

She thinks she can escape me? I've waited *years* to have her, and right when she was about to become mine, she disappears. Well, I won't let that happen again. I searched fucking everywhere for her. I never thought I'd find her at a fucking prep school, of all places.

Not that it matters, she'll soon be back where she belongs, and I'll do what I should have done years ago. I'll make her mine—in every possible way. She won't *ever* get away from me again. I'll chain her to my fucking bed if that's what it takes.

"I'll put in a call."

His blunt, professional tone settles some of the anger that's been coursing through me recently, and I disconnect the call knowing he'll get the job done. He doesn't have a fucking choice.

I won't throw away years of hard work, years of plans in the making. I've been patiently playing the long game, but I'm fucking done. She might not realize it yet, but we belong together.

I hope you've enjoyed your freedom, dove, because I'm coming for you.

Acknowledgements

There are so many people, without whom, this book wouldn't be half as good. The biggest thanks goes to my PA, Nikki. Not only does she keep me in line, but she alpha'd the book, and made all the gorgeous teasers and the beautiful cover. She was there every step of the way, helping and supporting me and for putting up with me, she's an absolute superstar!

I also owe a huge thank you to my beta readers – Nikki, Shawna and Artemis. Thank you so much guys for making this book as good as it is. I'm so lucky with the top-notch team I have around me!!

A thanks to my street team and those who signed up with affinity to read and review Broken Trust. I appreciate all your hard work promoting every week and I've absolutely loved reading your reviews and seeing your edits.

I should probably also thank my husband who is starting to realize I might actually be able to make a go out of this whole author thing (lol).

Lastly, a huge thank you to all of you for picking up this book and reading it. Without you none of this would be possible!! If you loved this book, please help me spread the word by leaving a quick review.

Also by R.A. Smyth

Crescentwood Series

#1 Three Divisions

#2 Two Forces

#3 One Family

***

Pacific Prep

#1 Broken Trust

#2 Brutal Lies

#3 Beyond Vengeance

#4 Break Free

***

Black Creek Series

#1 Rebels & Rejects (coming early 2022)

About the Author

R.A. Smyth is an author of dark romance. She lives in the UK with her husband, although they frequently talk about moving to live abroad (so who knows).

She has always been an avid reader, starting from the Harry Potter books as a kid. It's an interest that has grown into an obsession over the years and becoming an author has been a secret lifelong dream of hers.

When she's not writing, Rachel enjoys spending time with her family, drinking cups of tea (or glasses of wine or gin) with a good book and exploring the small island of Ireland with her family.

Printed in Great Britain
by Amazon

19007249R00223